Readers are raving about *Dreaming Maples*!!!
Here's what a few are saying:

"Dreaming Maples is an intuitive novel, reaching deeply into the heart and soul of the daughter, mother, and grandmother whose story is told. Claudia Ricci's descriptive style allows the reader to identify with each character experiencing the angst and beauty, trauma and love, of mothering. The novel's rural setting in a Vermont sugarbush provides a balance that only nature has to offer. One you start reading Dreaming Maples, you will find it hard to stop."

—JoEllen Kirsch, Editor-in-Chief,
The Cracker Barrel, Wilmington, VT

"Dreaming Maples is a visceral story about women whose characters are as beautiful, misfortunate, and unbreakable as the rural New England hill towns where they live. This is a story which is both tragic and comic, as lovely as spring one minute and as harsh, agonizing, and bloody as giving birth on the floor the next. Claudia Ricci's writing beats with the pulse of life."

—Dr. Eugene Mirabelli, author of
The Language Nobody Speaks

"A fast-paced story where I could hardly turn the pages fast enough. The characters, relationships, and writing kept making me go back through the pages for a second and third read. Seldom do I get a book that makes me want to read faster, and slower, both at the same time, and then, again and again. Dreaming Maples captured my whole being, and then fulfilled all my hopes for a novel. If you have ever enjoyed a book so much that you keep checking to see that you have enough pages left, so that you can read it for a long, long time, then Dreaming Maples is your kind of book. When I sit down with it the next time, I will make sure it lasts."

—Dr. Gregory Topakian,
Upton, MA

"Dreaming Maples will lead you into the forest that is called 'family' with an earnestness that bares the souls of the characters as it bares your own. The novel draws you in and holds you there, mesmerized, the way the leaves of a maple tree burning red in autumn can hypnotize. If you have ever been a - parent standing on a precipice between your own childhood and your own parenting; if you have ever wondered about the ironies of birth, and the imprints of the others who make up family, then read this book. Let yourself dip into the curves of the road from the back of a motorcycle, right alongside Candace Burdett, whose mission is as beautiful and twisted as her mother's was years before. The author's unique, layered prose uncovers the grist of intention in the parallel journeys of Candace and her mother, and in the life that Candace's grandmother Audrey has created in a tiny village among the maples. You will be swept away by unconventional characters who dare again and again — characters whose daring creates harrowing consequences for each of the others, and yet still manages to elicit love and other dreaming. I could not put this book down!"

—Liza Frenette, Author of
Soft Shoulders* and *Dangerous Falls Ahead

"Mud season in Vermont is sugaring season, and it's then that the women — Audrey, her granddaughter Candace, Pit, Martha, Francine, and more — work their hardest. This year, they're facing endings and beginnings of the most profound kind, as past and present weave together while the sap is running. Claudia Ricci writes of these women and this time with lyricism and love, her poetic style creating an extended song of their tragedies and joys, and the complexities of their hearts and lives. Sit back, relax, read, and enjoy."

—Barbara Chepaitis, Author of
Feeding Christine* and *These Dreams

"...[I] very much enjoyed it! The characters were wonderful! It was a great blend of places that I've been, and it was cool to read about Brown! It was a great read."

—Dr. Elizabeth Hane, Research Scientist,
Proctor Maple Research Center,
Underhill Center, VT

"Once I started to read Dreaming Maples, I couldn't put it down. I was captivated by the depth and humanity of the characters. The way their stories were interwoven, through time, was masterful. Personally, I didn't want the book to end. I am still wondering what the future might hold for them all. Maybe there will be a sequel?"

—Shelley Rolf, Social Worker,
Bennington School, Bennington, VT

"Dreaming Maples *makes three generations of women come alive. Candace and Eileen and Audrey remain part of my literary landscape. Claudia Ricci has a rare ability to make her language alternately soar and take root: sometimes a fevered dream; sometimes a clear, cold breeze. Echoes of this book have come to me at odd moments when I walk in the woods, when I look into the face of my own daughter.*"

— Ron MacLean, Author of *Blue Winnetka Skies*, and Publisher, Swank Books, Boston, MA

"*Claudia Ricci writes with intensity and insight about the love-hate relationships — the roadblocks and the miracles — of four generations of mothers and the daughters they bear — and who bear them, sometimes more and sometimes less.*"

—Ruth Bass, Columnist, *The Berkshire Eagle*, Pittsfield, MA

"Dreaming Maples *is a story of mothers. From the first page, I was completely captivated by the world of this Vermont sugarbush. I was compelled to enter this world multiple times and with each reading, I was able to fully absorb and experience the beautiful imagery. As we read and see how each women's story differs and is intertwined, we are compelled to examine and redefine our own assumptions of motherhood.*"

—Dr. Peggy Woods, Assistant Director, University of Massachusetts Writing Program, Amherst, MA

"Dreaming Maples *is a novel filled with complex relationships and raw emotion between a grandmother, mother, and daughter. Claudia Ricci's characters are so lifelike that you slip into their lives and feel the depth of their kinship. One senses the beauty of Claudia's descriptive powers and comes to feel Vermont's sugarbush as she does. This is an artistic, literary page turner.*"

—Abigail Kirsch, Author of *The Bride & Groom's First Cookbook*, *Invitation to Dinner*, and *The Bride & Groom's Menu Cookbook*

"*Mother Maple's branches embrace a world of women sharing history, birth cycles, and life journeys over several generations. The characters come to life in the old Vermont homestead and through the snow-covered woods to the sugar shack. These characters stayed alive for me long after the last page. Claudia Ricci's sensuous language and tactile descriptions ushered her book into my heart and lodged in my mind.*"

**—Leslie Gabosh,
Spencertown, NY**

"*Human life cycles and complexities are expertly woven throughout this book and mirrored in the seasonal awakening of maple trees. I loved it!*"

**—Pat Rotondo,
Boston, MA**

"*I just love the character development in this novel. I felt like I was vicariously experiencing the lives of these women well after the book came to an end. A sequel certainly would be greatly appreciated by this reader!*"

**—Ginny Rifenberick, Associate Dean,
Academic Support Services,
University at Albany, SUNY**

"*The author's creative use of language and the lyrical quality of her writing make this novel a truly enjoyable treat. The characters became real living women and I could identify with certain aspects of each one. This is a book to be read more than once.*"

**—Dr. Helga Straif-Taylor,
University at Albany, SUNY**

"*I just couldn't put it down!*"

—C. Dena Ricci, Pittsfield, MA

"**Dreaming Maples** *is a wonderful story and first novel. Claudia Ricci's characters are so intriguing...*"

—Carole Beauchamp, Bisbee, AZ

"With Dreaming Maples, Claudia Ricci takes us through the pain and tribulations in families and reminds us that in spite of everything, we will survive. This is a story of heartbreak and hope and when everything in life seems wrong, family remains constant."

—Diane Eberts, Kalamazoo, MI

"Dreaming Maples is a poignant novel about three generations caught in the tangle of culture and religion, anger and cruelty, shame and remorse, but ultimately, love and healing. Claudia Ricci has a unique talent for creating intense feelings and vivid images in the reader's mind. A must read for anyone who has struggled with the tug of emotions that so frequently tears families apart."

—Karen Ricci, RN, MPH, Santa Clarita, CA

"Dreaming Maples is a beautiful and moving story of the challenges three generations of women face and the choices they make to wrestle with those challenges. Superbly written, the novel transports us with beautiful imagery and poetic language that resonates long after we have finished the book."

—Renee Geel, Delmar, NY

"In drawing her characters, Claudia Ricci blends their inner and outer lives with skill and intense insight. They seem as real as my next door neighbors. She brings forth a level of intensity that keeps the reader turning the pages."

—Steve Bentley, Littleton, Colorado

dreaming maples

a novel by

claudia ricci

Star Root Press
Post Office Box 112
Austerlitz, NY 12017

Cover image, "Dreaming Maples," and cover design, by Pat Rotondo, Boston, MA
Inside pages set in type by Bonny Curless, Albany, NY
Printed in the United States of America by Digital Page, Albany, NY

Library of Congress Control Number: 2001119774

ISBN 0—9717180-1-6

Dedicated to my incredible husband and my family:
I am able to do what I do,
far better,
thanks to the love you give me.

PROLOGUE

In the dream, it is early evening. Fall. All the shadows have melted into the ground and the sky is a sweet milky blue. Candace is lying in the grass, too tired to move, staring into the giant maple in Audrey's front yard. A single star appears. The star is a dazzling pearl, a distant pinprick of fire in the clear night. And then the marvel happens. The star comes cascading out of the zenith, hurling itself toward earth with the speed that only light can have. It touches a leaf on the tree and the leaf catches fire and burns brilliant yellow. Miraculously, though, like Moses' burning bush, the Mother Maple is not consumed in flame. Soon another star shows itself in the sky and it too is a grain. And again, it flies down from the heavens and a second leaf explodes into red flame. The same thing happens, over and over again, stars falling like fireworks from the heavens, stars bursting into leaf, the light coming to life in orange, crimson, and a host of glowing fall colors. Every star is a match to a leaf. As the tree billows up, Candace stands, because the scene is a miracle and it takes her breath away, the Mother Maple, incandescent in the yard, filling the night sky.

Later, when she is older, and the dream comes true, she wonders. Do dreams set fire to our worst fears? Or do they lead us like searing biblical visions into lands that we can only bear to see first with our eyes closed?

PART ONE

PART ONE

AUDREY X

Start here, at the cusp of spring, as the snow is poised to begin melting in the forest. The March fog is lifting through the dark maples like a million delicate spirits. It is here, where on some winter nights, the moonlight throws the snow and the maple bark into blue and purple shadows, that Candace will bring her baby. It is here where the trees are already whispering, *please don't let the baby die, please don't let the baby die.*

Audrey hears something as she stops just a few yards short of the sugar house, beside the old tree, the one she and the other women call Frieda. She has fog all around her, and snow awkwardly cropping up beneath her grey coat, so that with each step she sinks deeper. The powder crusts her coat in ice and reaches up her thighs until in some places, it is almost at her crotch. She is breathing hard from fighting up the hill. A sound curls and presses inside her and at first she thinks it is her own heart beating in her ears. But as her breathing quiets, and the wind stills, she turns her gaze into the stark grey branches around her. Somewhere out there is a hum, a soft but persistent rhythm, almost like the thrumming made by fingers gently striking a drum.

What she hears in the absence of wind makes her uneasy.

The great granddaughter of a Yorkshire woman who healed with herbs, Audrey believes fervently in rooted angels, sanctified trees of mercy, and fabulous fairies in enchanted gardens. She knows the protective powers yielded by burning Juniper and dried holly. She knows the myths of every flower living in the fields. She has memorized the recipe for oaten cakes that, at moonrise on Midsummer's Eve, will work a fairy spell: take vervain and yarrow, mistletoe and rue, thyme and bay, and sweeten the mixture with honey and the oil from a rose. She knows every ancient ritual and pagan tale linked to aspen and alder, silver birch and bramble, rowan, apple and ash.

She knows, too, since childhood, the wild Tree Dance. Charmed by jugs of wine and tight white rolls of marijuana, she has taught the whirling to the women who live with her, all of them still braless, all still faithful to their art and equally, to the maple sugaring.

Audrey knows too that if trees can heal, then certainly trees can warn. And so she is fearful of the sound. Soon, though, Candace will arrive to help with the sugaring and she will deliver her news, and Audrey will be relieved to hear it. She will take her granddaughter in her arms, and kiss the top of Candace's orange hair. Tucking her fears aside, Audrey will decide that it wasn't a warning she heard in the forest, but rather, a promise, an awakening of life and breath. She will tell Marjory, her partner of nearly twenty years, that the tree spirits once again were showing off, yearning to be the first to herald Candace's announcement about the baby.

Much later, though, after the disaster, Audrey will recall this day, and that thrush of sound. And all that dark pressure pooled like grey fog inside her chest. Looking back, she will understand that she dismissed her fears too quickly. She was so happy to hear Candace's news that she failed to listen closely enough to the winds whispering through the trees. Instead, Audrey turned away, refusing to hear, closing herself off to the undulating black gloom that was already circulating in the forest, already set in motion that day.

She reaches up to one of Frieda's lower branches now, brings it closer to her eyes (no eyeglasses, as much a miracle as anything at Audrey's age) and she inspects the swelling red bud. Frieda, whose name derives from Freya, goddess of wisdom and fecundity, has been around since Audrey's great grandmother's time. Local lore has it that Clara O'Malley came from Yorkshire and settled in Vermont in 1833 and planted this maple tree. Eventually, Clara began the sugaring that Audrey continues to this day.

Frieda should have long ago dropped over, as she is more rotten than not. But her sap was said to make the purest, sweetest maple syrup ever tasted on the mountain. And as history counts many miracles, here is just one other: that Frieda is believed to be approaching her third century of life.

Audrey's frosty blue eyes lock onto the red bud, its tip tight and cold and as sharp as the point of a pen. Within the fragile tissues of that bud, wrapped and overlapping, is all kinds of potential. The lips of cherry-colored tissue, like all of those in the sugar bush, promise to swell, to open, to bloom into a lush of shady green leaves come May. But first, the trees will pause for sugaring, yielding sap to the women the way they, as mothers, yielded milk to their young.

Satisfied with the condition of the bud, Audrey lets the branch snap back into place. She bends to pick up a rusted pail and plows forward toward the sugar house. Tree shadows fall in grey and blue lines, quartering the snow. The light is spring light — bright and strong. But the weather isn't right. Not quite yet. Winter still has her bony grasp on the trees, choking each maple's throat. Just before she reaches the door of the shack, a cloud of fine snow blows up. Ice powders Audrey's face and she inhales the fine crystals and coughs. She smacks the red mitten over her mouth. Feels the wheeze left by last year's pneumonia. *If you move south with me*, she hears Big Martha whispering, *life will be so easy, you'll live a century.*

Ignoring the voice, she slides the skeleton key easily into the lock. She stops. She always dreads this moment, unlocking the sugar house door after a winter season's long absence. She hates facing the dust, the cobwebs, the musty cold air. The door itself is a disgrace. Splintering, squawking on rusty hinges that are pulling out of rotted wood, the sugar house door is disintegrating just like the whole sugar farm around it. If that local boy, Jimmy Dryer, were still 14 years old, like he was when the women moved in, and not a grown man with a family as he's been for ten years, things like this door would be rebuilt. Painted.

Damn him.

Audrey sighs. *I need this like a hole in the head. I need this like a hole in the tree.* She smiles. She leans into the sugar house door. It squeals its familiar rusty protest and she proceeds inside.

CANDACE

Now consider Candace. Consider the glory of her sunny red hair, eclipsed by fluorescent orange dye. Note her mud puddle eyes, and the gold ring at her eyebrow, and the Pippy Longstocking freckles that splatter her face. Place her, that night before she leaves for Vermont, in soft grey sweat pants, loosely drawn and resting low on her narrow hips. See her short blue T-shirt, which exposes her soft belly. At her bikini line, tattoo a tiny red rose with green petals.

Candace stands in the kitchen, barefoot, about to murder her mother. Or so it appears.

Certainly anyone watching the fiery-haired young woman bellowing and swiping out at Eileen, chopping wildly through the air with the rusty butcher blade that Noni Lucy once used to decapitate chickens, would call Candace Burdett dangerous and perhaps, mentally unbalanced. One could safely conclude that Candace hates her mother and, at the very least, is hell-bent on hurting Eileen. Perhaps, in rage, she even contemplates murder.

Candace would disagree. Yes, she is angry, furious even, driven to a new canyon of despair by Eileen's mean words, by the spitfire look in her mother's coal-colored eyes, but mostly by the abominable suggestion that Eileen has just made about the baby. But in the tender core of Candace's heart, the part she always keeps safely walled off from her mother, she is certain she has no intention of hurting Eileen. At most, she means to scare her.

Only she ends up scaring herself more.

When the fight is over, a tearful Candace will flee upstairs to her bedroom, where she will cry her muddy brown eyes into a wide peaceful stream. As she drifts off, she will swath her face in the frayed remains of her yellow and white kitten blanket, the beloved afghan she has slept with as long as she can remember. Noni Lucy, Candace's other grandmother, assembled the blanket for Candace out of the same feathery angora wool she used to make the doll that came to be known as Dollcake Number Two — a doll with a rubber face and a wide crocheted skirt that also served as the doll's blanket. Lucy delivered Dollcake Number Two to Eileen in the hospital shortly after Eileen delivered Candace.

The truth be told, Noni made the afghan — and the doll — as much for herself as she did for her granddaughter. Lucy crocheted the doll in secret celebration, and she brought it to the hospital unbeknownst to Eileen's father, as a peace offering to her daughter. Lucy made the blanket in a total state of despair a few weeks later, after Eileen ran away to California, taking with her the yellow crocheted doll, but abandoning baby Candace to her parents. Overnight, Lucy and Frank Rosetti became responsible for raising Eileen's two-month old infant, a squalling bundle of blueberry eyes and wisps of strawberry pink hair.

In the few moments Lucy had between changing Candace's diapers, feeding her formula, and rocking her to sleep, Lucy sank her heartache over Eileen into every stitch of that soft blanket, knit all her regret, her anger, her endless hurting into the wool. Her daughter's face in mind, Lucy kept pulling up the soft yarn, looping it securely with the expert flicker of her hook, tying the ends on the squares tight, adding white between, the whole time consoled by the sight of the growing blanket and by the hopeful colors of the yarn. There in the blanket was the pure promise of white, and the healing of yellow, yellow as bright as an egg yolk, as reassuring as the sunflowers she and Frank planted every summer at one edge of their tomato garden.

Ten years later, when the prodigal Eileen phoned from California and for the very first time asked to speak to Candace, Frank grabbed the phone from Lucy, swore into the receiver, and hung up on his daughter. Lucy, meanwhile, mounted the stairs, swept Candace away from her Barbie dolls on the rug and with no explanation, led the child to her canopy bed, where she wrapped her tightly in the kitten blanket. There on the bed, Lucy locked her granddaughter in her arms, rocking her, not saying a word in reply to Candace's repeated questions. Later that week, a one-line note addressed to Lucy arrived. "Ma, get Candace ready, I'm coming home."

❦

Perhaps the fight between Candace and Eileen gets as mean as it does that night in the kitchen because it has been a whole decade in the making.

It begins about 9:30 p.m. on a cold March evening with Candace on the phone in the kitchen, making plans with Audrey. Candace's bare feet straddle the black wrought iron grate in the kitchen, so that air blowing from the furnace warms her ankles and billows out her short blue T-shirt, exposing her soft belly. Her once coppery red hair, now as orange as a plastic Halloween pumpkin, is caught up in a sloppy ponytail.

She is telling her grandmother that she will leave at seven the next morning, will drive up to Vermont in her own car. She will arrive at the farm in time for pancakes and crisp sausage patties, the breakfast that the women always hold to launch the sugaring season. Candace will help Audrey and the others hang pails the first day, and stay on, as always, a week or two, lugging full pails of cold sloppy sap to the evaporator, taking her turn in the sugar house, helping with the endless boiling. She won't leave Audrey's place until the sugaring is complete.

When Candace hangs up the phone, she is whistling the new single by Dave Matthews that Mark loves so much. She goes to the hall closet for her duffel, singing now, totally off key. She pulls the duffel from the high shelf and is carrying it through the living room, preparing to take it upstairs to pack, when Eileen casually looks up from the HBO movie she's watching.

"Something puzzles me," Eileen says as Candace cuts in front of her mother's feet, resting comfortably in slippers on the hassock.

"What?" Candace has the duffel on her head, her arms raised to hold it there. The soft landscape of bare flesh around her middle lengthens, revealing the tiny rose tattoo planted just southwest of her belly button.

Eileen speaks while keeping her eyes on the TV. "You're supposed to be taking it easy. And now I hear you're going up to

Vermont to break your back lifting pails. Please tell me, how does that translate into taking it easy?"

"Ma, you know how important it is to me to be there. To help Audrey."

"More important than your baby?" Coal meets mud, as Eileen's eyes shift, locking onto Candace's.

Candace stands frozen. She knows exactly where this is headed and she doesn't want to go one step closer because she has been there before. She lets the duffel drop to the floor.

"You stood here a week ago, Candace, and swore you were turning a corner."

"And I am. I'm taking care of myself. I go to bed every night before eleven."

"Yes, but that's after you sneak out and dye your hair that miserable frisbee color. The dye, my dear, is full of chemicals. And you continue to smoke half a pack a day and drink beer and who knows what else. Oh, and half the time you skip dinner and hit Burger King where I'm guessing you eat nuggets and fries and chocolate shakes."

Candace considers pointing out that there is protein in chicken, and milk in the shake. But she knows if she does, Eileen will take the opportunity to deliver another of her lectures on fat. Always the goddamn dangers of fat. "Ma, look, I'm trying. I read part of that nutrition book you left on my bed. At least I eat breakfast now and I have something healthy for lunch." She grins. "An apple anyway. You know what they say about an apple a …"

Eileen mutes the remote. Faces Candace with a trembling lower lip. "I can tell when you're making fun of me Candace."

Candace drops her head like a bull. She fingers the ring in her eyebrow.

"I told you last week, Candace, that you had a choice. And you still do. You can keep this baby and maybe, as you say, it'll be the best thing that ever happened to you. But frankly, I don't see it that way. I don't see you living the clean life you promised to, Candace. Which makes me wonder. Maybe, just maybe, you aren't as ready as you think you are to be a mother."

"Maybe JUST maybe I don't want to listen to you right now, OK?" Candace scoops up the duffel and stomps off.

A week before, after the car accident, they had covered more or less the same territory. In that dispute, Candace declared that absolutely nothing, not even Mark's disapproval, could possibly dissuade her from going through with this pregnancy. And so, she assumed the matter was settled. She certainly didn't expect to be getting the third degree about it again from Eileen. And certainly not so soon.

"Come back here," Eileen demands, jumping up. Candace stops, but doesn't turn around. "I'm not finished, Candace."

"Oh yes you are," Candace calls back hotly. "I told you to stay out of my business, and it's about time you got it through your thick head, Ma."

Eileen jumps over the hassock and in two seconds she is there, in Candace's face once again.

"You better listen to me, and listen good. You don't have a clue what it means to be pregnant, or to have a kid. If you did..."

"Cut it out Ma, will you please!" Candace drops the duffel so she can cover her ears with her hands. But even with the sound muffled, Eileen's low voice booms through.

"...and here you are now, trotting off in your car that's just been taped together, not even repaired. You're traipsing up there, pregnant, for what? Damned if I know. Or if you do either. I know one thing, though. You're going off to do this silly sugaring thing when what you should be doing is studying. Here you are barely half-way through the semester, a semester *I'm* paying for, and you're already skipping class."

Candace wants to respond, wants desperately to counter her mother's tirade, to say something cool and sharp and right to the point. But Eileen is serving up words so fast and thick that it makes Candace dizzy. This is how it has always gone between them. Ivy League Eileen talks and talks, and community college Candace gets tongue-tied and withdraws. Or she attempts to talk back, to defend her point of view, but ends up quaking, or saying the first thing off the top of her head, making a fool of herself, or worse.

Candace is trembling, frantically searching for some scathing insult to hurl back at her mother, one that will shut Eileen up for good, hitting her so hard that she will drop the attack, at least for tonight. But Candace's head goes blank and what comes out of her, red-faced, is simply this: "I'm an artist, just like Audrey. And I'd rather be with her than anyone else, including *you*. You see, Ma, *she's* always been there for me. She and the other women at the farm. They cared. Unlike you. *You* were never there for me. You had a baby but got scared and ran away the second you had the chance."

Eileen's face is pinched, and for a brief moment Candace is satisfied that at last, one of her arrows has struck its mark. Candace goes into the kitchen. She needs something to drink. Eileen follows. When Candace turns around to the kitchen table to pour milk, there is Eileen, leaning back on the refrigerator, ready to enter the ring for round two.

"Candace, you are just so young. You think you know everything. You think you know what it means to be a mother. You think taking care of a baby is all sweet powder and pink rattles and musical mobiles and teddy bears. But there's another side to it, one you can't begin to understand. You don't have a clue what happens when you have a baby. How hard it can be." Eileen eyes Candace with a steady, unrelenting look and then calmly goes for the jugular. "I honestly believe that if you really knew what you were in for, you would rethink your decision. I bet you'd have the abortion."

A wave of milk catches in Candace's throat and threatens to choke her. Trembling, she sets the glass down on the table and sputters. "So then I can get rid of my baby, the way you got rid of me?"

Eileen's eyes swell, and then a slap goes stinging across Candace's face. Candace feels it at the same time she hears it ringing through both ears. Her mouth falls open and she sets both hands to her red cheek. Then, tears spring up, and soon she is crying and screaming at the same time.

"BITCH! You are such a stupid bitch, I hate you!" She dives toward the kitchen drawer, the one where Noni Lucy always stored the ravioli cutter and the spaghetti tongs and the blocky cleaver she used to pound bracciole meat. She scrambles through the drawer, and her hand lands on the rusty butcher knife, squared and dulled from doing in so many chickens. Waving the knife overhead like a sail, she sweeps through the air at her mother all the while screaming, "BITCH! BITCH!"

Eileen ducks and throws her arms overhead. Screeching, she flees the kitchen.

As soon as Eileen disappears, Candace lets go of the knife and it drops point first, stabbing the kitchen floor. The knife stands upright like a spear.

Cradling her bare middle, Candace sobs. Fear spins up around her like a sticky brown web. "Oh God I hate you," she moans over and over. "I hate you so much. I wish you would drop dead so I would never have to think about you, ever again."

AUDREY X

She is sitting on the edge of the bed in khaki pants and a red flannel shirt. Bending, Audrey ties the laces of her sneakers, greyed by age. Every year she wears them to do the sugaring, and every year the women laugh and say she's mad to dress that way. They say she should be wearing heavy rubber boots. Which, of course, she should be. But then she should be doing many things she's not. She should still be living in North Adams. She should still be carrying the name Mrs. Jack Burdett. She should still be wearing her silver hair knotted in a bun. It made sense, considering that she wore that tidy hairstyle for so many years, so long ago, when she was young, when she only knew Marjory the other way. When her whole world was Jack Jack Jack.

Instead, in 1973, she renamed herself, shedding not only her husband and married identity, but also her maiden name, Andrews. That name too, she believed, had come as an inheritance from a man. Thus, she changed it, and came to be, legally, Audrey X.

Had she never lost the second baby, had she never discovered sculpture, or carved the Hannah rock, or resurrected her great grandmother's leather book on herbs and natural healing, nothing might have changed. Despite Marjory, she might have grit her teeth and, as bad as it was, kept the life she had, as Jack's devoted wife. Indeed, she might still be making a home for him. No matter that in 1979, Jack died, his nose red, his eyes threaded in a roadmap of lines. No matter. Audrey might still be folding socks and ironing sheets and handkerchiefs and shirts. She might still be sleeping in the same mahogany bed that she and Jack got as a wedding present. She might still be filling her time scouring crusty stove rings with rusty Brillo pads. She might still be madly filling dinner plates with chops and ribs, mashed potatoes and ham.

Instead, she goes for spiced tofu now, for kale and tempeh, quinoa and brown rice. She walks in sneakers in the snow. She lives in Vermont, meditates daily, and sleeps naked every night, legs and arms tangled around Marjory, her unofficial wife. She wakes with peppermint tea and makes herself sleepy with passion flower and cowslip. She swears by feverfew for headaches, primrose for rheumatism and arthritis, echinacea and red poppy for head colds, coughs, and flu.

Mostly what keeps her healthy, though, is that she is no longer doing for a man: she sews no one else's buttons and vows never to iron again for the rest of her life. She sweeps, but only when the sawdust in her studio gets too deep. She sleeps late on Sunday mornings, except today, because she knows this weather — the first run of sap is coming.

She glances down at Marjory, curled, a tight knot underneath the wedding quilt. Marjory's head, a brillo of iron grey hair, is buried. Audrey leans, lifts the quilt, presses her nose and lips into the warm hollow below Marjory's ear. "I'm going," she whispers. Marjory groans, receives the kiss, then rolls, and tents the quilt overhead.

Downstairs, Audrey stokes and loads the stove. She warms her hands over the crackling fire, then drops the lid. Moving through the frigid kitchen, she catches her vest and jacket off a peg and pulls from the shelf her red wool mittens and her "mad" hat, the one in a kaleidoscope of colors that Marjory knit for her three years ago. Marjory has knit her many hats, but none so nice as this.

Unlatching the mud room door, she stands before a sky that is blotchy, blue and white. Right away, there is honking overhead. She tips her eyes up to see the familiar stretch of necks, the Northern geese like slender black hairpins arranged in partial Vs. A crow calls, and a dove, and now she is off the porch, sinking, thinking, *ah, well, at least the breeze is gentle.* Yesterday, after she left the sugar house, she faced an icy slap of wind for nearly three hours as she trailed Shag the workhorse, breaking trails through crusted snow.

Shag leading, Audrey slowly gained the hill, guiding the horse along the gathering road. At the top of the ridge, she goaded the animal to a spot about ten paces from the place where the trees yield

and the field opens up. Tying the horse to a tree there, she bent first
to one and then to both knees, as if to pray. Instead, though, her
mittened hands went into the snow like claws, pawing it quickly,
trusting from memory that she was in the spot she should be. Soon
enough she got there, where she wanted to be, had the first glimpse
of mottled marble, cranberry red and white. She dug more, uncov-
ering a stiff curl of Hannah's hair, the top edge of a face. Pulling off
her mittens, her fingers groped for a smooth space, and it appeared:
the forehead, and below was the nose, turned up and rounded.
Soon her fingers found the eyes, came to rest there. Like Audrey's,
Hannah's eyes were blue, were streaked black and flecked in white.
But now the eyes are just a double absence, a permanent stare
caught in ice cold marble, a gaze into nothingness across a Vermont
field blanketed in drifts of snow.

This morning, Audrey passes Hannah with only a nod, and a
quick blessing for her daughter. She is headed instead for the upper
level of the bush. It is slow going in canvas sneakers. In places, the
snow has drifted thigh deep, and despite the trail carved by Shag the
day before, Audrey's legs move slow. Snow is creeping into her socks,
freezing her snow-caked toes. In this painful pinching, though, she
is reminded of her queer purpose for wearing the summer shoes.
Each year, they are her sign of faith that the weather will cooperate,
that temperatures will rise above freezing by day and fall again by
night. Audrey allows herself the sneakers as a small bit of superstition,
maybe because the sap rising remains a fundamental mystery, and the
sugaring is much too fragile an enterprise, dependent as it is on the
vagaries of nature, on the fleeting and altogether unreliable interval
between winter and spring. No chance with maple syruping that the
women will ever prosper. Their goal always has been simply to survive —
this year, to pay out of pails the $4,672.39 needed for taxes on the land.

She reaches that section of the sugar bush where last fall she and
Candace and Marjory planted 30 new maple saplings. The crooked
twigs claw at the sky, reach toward a cloud cover like cheesecloth
knotted over blue cotton. Hazy sun patches through. Halfway up the
hill, she is flushed, breathing hard, wishing she had never touched
a cigarette or the occasional thin brown cigar she still relishes and
Marjory holds her nose to.

At the ridge, she stops between two towering maples. Extending
her arms to either side, she twists at the torso, letting the ample

weight of arms pull her gently around. Every March, as soon as the first
trails are cut, Audrey moves her morning exercise outdoors, all except
the floor stretches, exercises which require her to lay on the floor
and tug her knees toward her nose, then lift each log of a leg in turn.
That, and the sit ups, she continues to do inside, beside the wood stove.

Now she bends at the waist, begins reaching her fingers toward
her sneakered toes, not touching, or even hoping to, but only moving toward. She has never been able to stretch the whole distance to her
feet. Even dropping halfway, the hamstrings protest. Shifting, gratefully, she does 10 Jumping Jills (she had her fill of Jack), and for five
minutes, her jacket tossed in the snow, she thuds in place. Her toes lift
only an inch or so, her flesh shifts and bounces against its lower surface.
The payoff comes beneath the green and puffy vest, the flannel
shirt, the waffled thermal underwear, when moisture beads across
her back and pools at the center of her chest. She walks the rest of
the way to the sugar house, to get the drill and spouts, warmed by a
mild buzz of energy.

Soon she is beside a tree, testing the drill's metal point against
her fingertip, feeling it sharply against her flesh. Satisfied, she fits
the bit securely into this, the breast drill, called that because its
metal shaft extends and ends in a plate that is curved and wooden
and fits tight against the chest for bracing. Leaning against the plate,
she fixes her left hand on the handle, places the auger point into a
furrow of bark. She turns the drill, eggbeater style, and the auger
bit curls in, a metal barber pole piercing, spitting back first grey, the
outer bark, then quickly the chocolate layer underneath, then finally
the wood itself, a color quite like that of cooked white chicken flesh.
Audrey's right arm is winding fiercely: her elbow hurts, and her
hands. She uses everything: back and hips and thighs and buttocks,
to drill these tap holes slanting into wood.

She can't predict the next sensation: her breast is pressing against
the plate, and simultaneously, the sap begins bleeding from the tap
hole, the clear liquid leaking in a wet and widening stream, turning
the tree bark a darker grey. She stops, stares, and then, suddenly,
her body remembers — clear as day, as sap — being full of milk, and
how it was to feed a baby: her breasts hot, hard, brimming over the
infant's hidden face. Nothing will erase that from her mind. The
breasts were always ready, letting down, that familiar pinch and tingle;
just the baby's crying enough to bring on a hard ringing up for milk.

Any baby crying anywhere brought out two dark patches on her
blouse. Now, instead of milk welling up inside her, she has a flood
of memories, the hungry mouths of two children, the one who lived,
the one who didn't. When Hannah died in infancy, the milk kept building, pressing against her breasts. She cried and held the older child,
Rusty, against her chest, tempted to let him, at three, start nursing
her again.

She got so far that day as to lift her blouse. She was alone in the
house with the older child, "Daddy's boy," as Jack had started calling
him once Audrey got pregnant a second time. Audrey begged Jack
not to go, not to leave her alone just yet, but he said he had to, he
had things to do. Booze, she said. She knew he was going out to drink.
As he was leaving, he stood with his back to the bedroom door and
told her that she was going on too long, that her grieving for the
dead child wouldn't help, that crying would never bring the baby
back. He left and she lay on the bed and pulled Rusty against her.
Nestling his head of auburn curls beneath her chin, mother and son
fell into a quiet sleep.

When she woke, her breast was hard, the milk trickling, and without thinking, she began to inch her blouse up, was about to bare her
breast, when Jack appeared. She had miscalculated. Usually he
stayed at the bar longer. But there he was, swearing, calling her
shameful. He yanked Rusty, scared, crying, from the bed. She buried
her head in the pillow then, hid there, where Marjory came and
found her, three days later, dehydrated, staring into space.

Now, she lifts the hammer and blows the memory out. She
drives the spout deep inside the tap hole, hammering harder than
she needs to. And when the spout is secure, she hangs the pail and
sets the metal roof, and it looks to be a tiny house. It rests against
the tree, which is waiting and almost ready.

CANDACE

It is the morning after the fight. Candace holds tight to the last fragment of her yellow and white kitten blanket. It is a scant pillow, but it still brings some measure of comfort as she lies cocooned upstairs on the cold hard tile of the bathroom floor. She didn't sleep well last night. She moved here just about an hour ago, right before sunrise when she came in to pee, and then caught sight of herself in the mirror. The sorry-me face staring back set her tears going again. She sank to the floor, feeling hateful and then guilty about her own hate. The longer she lay there, the longer she waited to get up, until finally, she fell asleep again.

Now awake, she is staring numbly up at the yellow water stain in the ceiling, and at the peeling paint in the corner. The stain has been looking more and more lately like the head-on view of a sheep or a cow. But now, she is horrified to see that the cow has mutated into another shape — that of a plump female uterus. A pained Candace looks away.

Eyes closed, she begins reviewing her behavior of last night, and grows more and more troubled by what she did. She is trying to figure out what she would do differently if she were given a second chance. Alternately, she weeps and swears and whispers Hail Marys, telling herself that there is no way she is a murderer. She wouldn't kill her mother. Nor could she, under any circumstances, consider killing her unborn baby.

After all, she reasons, I can't even bring myself to kill a ladybug. Up at the farm, Audrey always wants to vacuum up the orange bugs when they swarm the windows in spring. But Candace and Pit are always opposed, so much so that the two of them spend Saturday afternoons knocking the helmeted little bugs into empty Mason jars — the same kind used to store the maple syrup. Standing on the front porch of the farmhouse, beneath the mother maple, Candace and Pit make a ceremony out of setting the insects free, while Audrey laughs at their enterprise, insisting that the spotted bugs simply circle around to the back of the farmhouse and reenter the windows once more.

That image of herself, saving ladybugs, puts Candace at ease. But then, when that picture disappears and is replaced by the one of her wielding the butcher knife, she cringes. Nothing awful happened. Still, something easily could have, and Candace never would have forgiven herself if it had. Now Candace keeps remembering the way Eileen jumped back, and especially the way horror played awkwardly across her mother's face, played like a shadow in her eyes. Something in that face terrified Candace, made her see that Eileen was perhaps more familiar with savagery than she ever let on before.

"I don't care," Candace seethes now, sitting up against the white cabinet of the vanity. She rubs the nubby fragment of yellow blanket over her cheek and tries to rid the image of the knife from her mind for good. "I wish sometimes she never came back."

In the same breath she says those words, though, Candace recalls that bright day in June ten years ago when her mother returned from San Francisco. Despite Frank's warnings to Candace, as the two of them sat beside the purple irises, never to trust her mother, Candace was ecstatic that Eileen was coming. So many times she had prayed for the day when, as she kept telling Becky Bucknell that Friday afternoon, she would finally meet the woman she could call Mom.

Eileen came on a Saturday. That morning, Candace jumped rope for two hours straight trying to contain her excitement while she waited. Then, just before noon, when Candace didn't think she could wait one more minute, the white rental car finally pulled into the driveway, spraying gravel. She dropped the handles of her jump rope, gave out a small shrill scream and practically leaped across the lawn. Standing beside the driveway, Candace stared at her mother through the car window, seeing only the dark aviator sunglasses that shrouded Eileen's eyes and the cloud of black hair that billowed over her mother's shoulders. Suddenly Candace was scared — would

Eileen like her? think she's pretty? Candace was so excited that she
began twisting her hair with the middle fingers of both hands.

Finally, she had to cross her legs, because she thought she actually
might pee her pants. That's when her mother opened the door and,
sunlight glinting off the car window glass, she emerged from the car,
wearing tight stone washed blue jeans and pointed black boots and a
starched white blouse with the sleeves rolled up. Candace held her
breath and closed her eyes and whispered, "Hi, I'm Candace. Are you
Eileen?" Eileen took off her sunglasses and slipped them into a hard-
shelled case. The case snapped shut and Eileen nodded and replied,
"Yes, Candace, I am Eileen. And I am awfully glad to meet you, sweetie."

Candace was in love with her mother all that day. Undaunted by
Papa Frank's dark looks and Lucy's nervous pacing, Candace spent
the afternoon and evening parked right beside Eileen, making a
place next to her mother everywhere she sat down, tracing the play
of smiles on her mother's lips, the lay of frowns on her forehead,
the dive of her long straight nose. Eileen's nose sank at a steep slant,
just like Papa Frank's did, but then Eileen's curved up again, ever so
slightly, at the tip. Eyes closed, Candace hung on the deep purr of
her mother's voice and inhaled her mother's sweet fragrance: a mixture of soap and cologne that Candace could later only describe to
Becky Bucknell as oranges stirred into roses. Not once that day did
it occur to Candace that Eileen spoke hardly at all to Noni Lucy and
Papa Frank.

Toward the end of that first day, that blessed first Saturday, Eileen
leaned over Candace and whispered, "Can I put French braids in
your hair?" Candace practically started to cry. The two of them sat on
the canopy bed, Candace staring into the mirror at Eileen, who
stared at the back of Candace's salmon-colored head. As her mother
took a comb from her purse and started tracing a part in Candace's
scalp, separating her hair into two portions, goosebumps shimmered up and down Candace's arms and she thought her heart
might just burst because she had never been more happy in her
whole life. But then, unbelievably, she became even happier when
Eileen's comb reached the base of Candace's neck and Eileen
released a breathless *ahhh* at her discovery there.

"My heavens, Candace, your hair is two different colors back
here," Eileen marveled. "The part on top is strawberry and this
secret layer is glowing blonde."

Candace shook her head up and down, thoroughly delighted. "I know," she said. "Noni doesn't know who I got that secret part from, but Papa Frank says it doesn't really matter. He says what it means is that someday I might turn out to be a princess."

At that moment, Candace's and Eileen's eyes met in the mirror and held there. Eileen smiled and bent over, and Candace thought for a moment that her mother was about to kiss her on the cheek. Instead, she felt Eileen's warm breath against her neck, and heard Eileen whispering into her ear. "I think you might be a princess, too, because why else would your hair be so full of the colors of starlight?" Eileen looked up then and winked at Candace in the mirror. Candace winked back, or tried, and felt that moment like she really *might be* a princess.

Candace gazes into another mirror now, the bathroom mirror. She is standing up and all she can see is a reflection of the almond-colored shower curtain. Her bare feet are parked on the black iron register that pours out hot air. In her hands is a tiny heart-shaped candle, squat and red, the one Audrey bought her last September at the Common Ground Fair in Jackson. The candle cracked as she lit it this morning and now warm wax smelling like cinnamon is spilling over her fingers like blood.

She is just beginning another Hail Mary and thinking maybe she should add an Our Father, too, when down the hall, Eileen's door opens. Scuffing slippers approach the bathroom door and stop. Silence.

"Candace, I'm sorry but I really have to go." Eileen's voice is tired and gravelly, probably from all the screaming last night. More silence. "Look, Candace, if I didn't have to, I wouldn't think of asking you to come out. But under the circumstances I have no choice. Unless you'd like me to pee in the backyard."

Candace pictures it. Pictures her mother in the old green terry bathrobe. Pictures her pulling the robe and nightgown up, poking her bare backside out into the forsythia that will soon come into bud.

She smirks. She could do it. She could actually force her mother to pee outdoors. Candace, meanwhile, would remain safely inside, holed up in the warm bathroom all day, and tomorrow, too, and who knows how long after that.

But for one reason, she won't. *This* is the morning she promised Grandma Audrey she would go to Vermont to help with the sugaring.

Blowing the candle out, she smells smoke and it brings her back, to Saint Anthony's church, to Stations of the Cross, and to Sunday High Mass with Noni Lucy.

Keeping her eyes closed, she gets up off the floor and opens the door. Stone-faced, she pushes by Eileen, keeping an ample space of air between them. As she passes her mother, she clamps her teeth and holds her breath.

CANDACE

Candace has wished her mother dead more times than she can count, but the time she remembers best was the first time, the summer Eileen returned from California. For two weeks, Candace and her mother could not have been more happy; nor could they be separated. Every morning, Eileen rose early to make the special breakfast that Candace had selected the night before: blueberry pancakes with crisp bacon one day, sausages and French toast with powdered sugar the next. After breakfast, the two of them would retreat to the same large easy chair, where they read aloud a new chapter of *Anne of Green Gables*, the book they had selected from the library together. When they didn't read, Candace worked with her water color pencils, sketching, while Eileen watched, praising her daughter's talents. One day, Eileen said she thought that Candace could be another Picasso. Candace looked up from the starry sky she was drawing and said simply, "I don't know him, so I'd rather grow up to be my grandmother's friend, Marjory."

Often, after Candace finished sketching, the two of them would go shopping. In those first two weeks, Eileen bought Candace fuzzy new bedroom slippers, a set of yellow baby doll pajamas, a cheap opal ring, a purple backpack, and one day, in a fit of generosity, Eileen splurged, buying Candace a silver hair clip made in the shape of a star. After lunch, they often baked cookies and once, Eileen showed Candace how to make *real* California granola from scratch. Some days they took hikes at Mount Greylock, with Candace counting Monarch butterflies and Eileen yelling every time she saw a woodpecker. At night, mother and daughter ate together, separated from Lucy and Frank. Twice, the two of them roasted hot dogs and marshmallows. Otherwise, they feasted on pasta and garlic bread or Eileen brought in pizza and they ate it together, side by side, watching television.

One morning shortly after the Fourth of July, however, the fantasy began to unravel. Instead of having their lazy morning together, the two of them stood watching while a long Atlas moving van backed up to the front door, and two beefy-armed men in T-shirts and tatooes carried Eileen's belongings down a sloped plane and up the front steps of the house. (Candace's grandparents left the house early that morning and stayed away all day.) Standing in the second floor hallway, Candace watched while Eileen showed the movers where to put her water bed, her bentwood rocker, her desk, her bookshelf, an antique oak bureau and oval mirror. Standing outside Eileen's bedroom, she watched while the movers piled box after box on the floor. Sitting on Eileen's unmade bed, Candace watched her mother pull blankets and sheets and towels and a black gooseneck lamp out of one box. She watched her pull dozens of paperbacks and oversized textbooks out of another box and set them on shelves. And then, just when Candace thought she would die of boredom, she saw Eileen pull out of a box with rolled posters and framed photos and a brightly colored Indian blanket, six plain black sketchbooks, books exactly like the ones Candace used to do her own drawing. Eileen set the books on the floor and at once, Candace sat up, interested.

"What are these, Mom?" she asked, kneeling and reaching for the book on top. She opened the book in her lap, was marveling over it, over the fact that it contained no type at all, just a person's scribbled handwriting, a puffy-looking scrawl, when suddenly Eileen jumped out of nowhere, scaring the pants off Candace. Eileen tore the book right out of Candace's hands.

"Those *aren't* for you," Eileen barked, in a harsh and reprimanding tone Candace had not heard from her mother before. Wounded, Candace lifted herself off the floor, and slowly circled Eileen's bedroom one more time while Eileen set the black books on the top shelf of her closet. Her face drawn into a pout, Candace slipped out of her mother's room and went into her own bedroom and quietly pulled apart the French braids her mother had plaited that morning in her hair. Then she proceeded downstairs and called Becky

Bucknell to tell her that yes, well, maybe Becky was right all along, maybe in the end all mothers really are the same, all mothers can turn into witches or evil stepmothers in the blink of an eye.

Candace surmised right away that the person to whom the handwriting in the black books belonged was her mother. And so the next morning, fueled in equal parts by anger and curiosity, Candace decided to investigate the books further. When Eileen left on her morning run, wearing pink iridescent shorts and a tank top, Candace slipped back into Eileen's room and pushed the bentwood rocker into the closet. Climbing on the seat, Candace tipped back and forth, bent-kneed. Reaching for the uppermost shelf where the black books lay, she almost had her hand there, had her fingertips grazing the fake leather spine of one book, when suddenly Eileen's voice scissored through the air.

"What do you think you're doing in there?" Instantly the rocking chair shuddered back and forth and then tilted into the closet, spilling Candace into her mother's blouses and skirts, her dresses and blazers. For an instant, Candace was conscious of her mother's perfume, that wonderful fragrance of lemon and oranges and roses, and then it was the next moment and horror descended. Candace grabbed helplessly for the cross pole to break her fall, but as she caught hold of it, the pole snapped in half, bringing down Candace and the hanging clothes and all of Eileen's fiery Italian temper.

With Eileen bellowing behind her, Candace ran screaming into Noni Lucy's bedroom, where she sobbed and begged her grandmother to send Eileen and all of her stupid clothes and books back to California. Lucy took Candace in her lap and asked what had happened and then patiently explained that Eileen was there to stay. And on that day, a broken-hearted Candace decided that maybe the only solution was to start praying right away for her mother to drop dead.

Eileen didn't die that day, though. Later, after lunch, she knocked on Candace's door. Candace opened it, but then immediately ran back to her bed and buried her face in her kitten blanket. Eileen followed, carrying a large grocery bag in her arms.

"May I sit down?" Eileen asked, in a very small voice.

Candace shrugged and hugged her blanket and didn't say anything. Eileen sat down anyway, and placed the bag on the bed. "I have something for you, Candace."

"What?" she said, her hopes rising. It must be an ankle bracelet, she decided, one with her name on it, the kind she had seen with Eileen in a store just the week before.

"Well, it's something I took to California with me a long time ago, when you were a baby and...and I want you to have it now because it's really always been yours."

Her hopes for the bracelet dashed, Candace frowned, reached for her pillow.

"Go ahead. Look in the bag," Eileen said, pushing it closer.

Scowling, Candace sank her hand in the bag and pulled out a funny-looking doll, a doll made, oddly enough, out of the very same yellow and white yarn as the kitten blanket. Only Candace's blanket had lost its fluff, while the doll was still feathery.

"So where did you get this from?" she asked her mother.

Eileen didn't answer. She simply sat there, frowning intently, staring as Candace nuzzled the doll against her face. Finally, Eileen cleared her throat. "You see, honey, grandma Lucy made that doll and brought it to me in the hospital, when you were born. I had the same kind of doll when I was little and her name was Dollcake and then Grandma made this one and I named her Dollcake Number Two."

"Oh, so she's *your* doll, not mine," Candace pouted, setting it aside. The doll was peculiar-looking after all, with its big wide ruffled skirt and its rubber face. If Candace was going to get a present today from her mother, she had decided she would hold out for the ankle bracelet.

"No, Candace, honey, I told you...Dollcake has really always been yours, *your* doll, honey." Candace looked up then because her mother's voice had begun to sound kind of...wobbly. Eileen was holding the doll close to her chest and her mouth was wrinkled, and the rest of her face looked like it was about to crumple up too, like she was about to cry. "Oh God, Candace I missed you so much...you have no idea, baby, I used to sleep with Dollcake every night and... and pretend she was you."

Eileen reached out for Candace then and Candace, seeing her mother sobbing and holding the pathetic little doll, felt sad, and not mad at all anymore. Actually, she felt very sorry for having done that stupid thing in the closet, because until then, life had been so wonderful with her mother. Candace let herself be hugged by Eileen, and after a few moments, she returned the embrace.

"It's OK, Mom," Candace declared after a while, breaking the hug, "Maybe we could...you know, *share* Dollcake." Without thinking, Candace reached for a tissue on her bedside table and began wiping away her mother's tears, just like Noni had always wiped Candace's tears.

And so they shared Dollcake, passing her back and forth countless times over the next few years, making the yellow crocheted doll into something of a good will ambassador, a little messenger who might go forth when both of them were frightened or reluctant, someone small and unassuming who could make amends, repair bad feelings and help to end fights. Typically, the yellow doll resided in Candace's room until, for one reason or another, Candace and Eileen argued, and Candace screamed at her mother, "I WISH YOU WERE DEAD," or, "I WISH YOU'D NEVER COME BACK," and then, generally, within a day or so, Eileen found the little yellow peace offering in her room once more.

Dollcake did her peacemaking duty until she was almost as worn and frayed as the kitten blanket. In the last four or five years, though, the doll has hardly moved across the hall at all. Eileen last recalls giving DC-2 (the nickname that grew up with the doll) back to Candace one morning shortly after she and Candace locked horns, when Candace was 15 and intent on dating Ben Schaffer, known to everyone as Mr. Tattoo. Candace claimed Ben was nineteen when Eileen was certain he was at least twenty-three.

❧

Today, the morning after Candace and Eileen battled over the baby, peace offerings are nowhere in sight. Instead, Eileen finishes in the bathroom and afterwards, she approaches Candace's bedroom door and knocks. The door is locked. Candace has no intention of answering it. She's half dressed, and as soon as she pulls her boots on she will take the duffel and go to Vermont.

"Candace, I want to talk."

Right, Ma. Dream on.

"Candace?"

There is one problem, though. How will she get out the door and down the stairs without facing her mother? She considers the window.

"Look, Candace, I'm not going to lecture you anymore. Or scream. I promise. There's nothing more I can say. But I've got something I want to give you though. Today. Before you leave."

Candace's ears perk up. *At least she recognizes the fact that I'm leaving. That I'm going out that door and up to Vermont and maybe, just maybe, I won't be coming home anymore.* Candace stands, uncertain what to do. She is feeling altogether new today, maybe because she penetrated unchartered territory last night, when she threatened her mother with the knife.

"Candace, please. I am all out of ideas. I have nothing left. But I am trying. I really am. I want you to open this door. I promise you I will not deliver one more lecture. But there is something here you are going to want."

"Want?" Candace asks. "What could I possibly want from *you?*" In her head comes a vision of the bentwood rocking chair, which she once asked her mother for.

Eileen waits before answering. "My journals," she says matter-of-factly. "I've decided I want to give you my journals."

Candace turns. Her forehead furrows. She crosses the bedroom, the heels of her cowboy boots digging soundlessly into the plush carpet. She gets to the door, hesitates. "If this is some kind of perverted joke, I swear I'll…"

"No. This is NOT a joke. I swear on Lucy's Sunday missalette. I've got the journals right here."

More slowly than she ever has before, Candace opens the door. And then, on the floor, she eyes them. The stack of black books she hasn't seen in ten years. Ever since that day Eileen scolded her and took the books and hid them. "I've decided it's time," Eileen is saying, her voice sorrowful and so weak it sounds like it might be drowning in her throat. "I knew someday that I would have to let you see. I knew you'd have to read it all for yourself…"

Eileen sighs. She is still in her terry bathrobe and her black hair, in disarray and heavily seeded by gray strands, looks like a nest. Bending, she picks up the top book and holds it open, holds it out to Candace in two hands, like a platter of warm food. She sniffles and leans into the doorframe and Candace thinks, *don't, please don't cry. Because I just can't take any more of your crying. It's making me sick.*

"You knew I'd have to read what all for myself?" Candace whispers, swallowing hard and taking the open book gingerly into her hands.

Eileen inhales and exhales, then speaks. "I started these journals when I was pregnant with you. When I...when I first knew I was going to have a baby." The last few words are not even a whisper. They are delivered in a voice so delicate, so humble, that Candace looks up. She sees a fatigue in her mother that she has never seen before. And something else, too. Something in her mother's owled eyes takes her by surprise. Eileen looks reduced. Shriveled. Like there is less of her today than there was yesterday.

"Are you sure you want me to read these?" Candace asks in a hush. She is absolutely awestruck by this book, absolutely amazed that she is actually standing here, holding it. For the last 20 years, there has been this record, a detailed map of the terrain she was born into. And until this instant, she hadn't a clue it existed.

Eileen, her brow knotted, keeps shaking her head. Doesn't speak for a moment or two. And when she does, her shoulders seem to collapse in on themselves. "Yes. I'm sure. I'm giving them to you because I don't know what else to do. I don't know any other way than to let you read them for yourself. Because I keep trying to say the right thing, and I can't. I want to say the thing that will convince you that this idea of yours, to have a baby, maybe to make up for what I did wrong with you, it's..." Eileen's voice drops to a whisper again. "I guess I just want to let you see how hard it was for me." And then she clips one hand over her lips and twists them shut.

Candace flips slowly through the book, the same kind of artist's sketchbook that she uses for drawing. Only this book smells like must and mildew. And it has no sketches at all. Instead, there is just page after page of handwriting, that puffy handwriting Candace knows so well to be her mother's own rounded scrawl, each capital letter swollen larger than it need be. The pages that most intrigue Candace, though, are those few in thick red magic marker. Those pages look absolutely tortured. There are stars and squiggles and exclamation points and splotches, where something must have spilled on the paper. On those pages, the red magic marker has left a trail not unlike tears or diluted blood.

Eileen clears her throat. And when she speaks this time her voice is stronger, but it's fluttering. "I couldn't sleep last night. I was lying there going nuts. Finally I got up and started reading these old books of mine." Eileen's teeth dig into her lower lip, and dig deep. "As I read, I kept thinking about..." Eileen sniffles, raises a clenched fist beneath her chin. "About how hard it was to have you and then…" She shakes her head again. "How hard it was…when finally I had to leave you."

Candace looks at her mother curiously. Never before has Eileen said that she "had" to leave, as in, she was forced. Always before Candace has assumed that Eileen made the choice, completely on her own. As Candace's gaze drops to the stack of black diaries, she is wondering what unknown history lies buried in this pile of books.

Eileen, meanwhile, has wandered into Candace's bedroom. Her eyes are ringed and gloomy and her gaze is riveted to the floor. "You have no idea how strange it is for me sometimes, to be here, because this is the same house, the same house I grew up in, the same house I brought you home to…your grandfather, my father, stood right here, argued with me right here. And then, when things got so bad…it was right there, right in that spot…"

Now Eileen is pointing to the bedroom floor and crying openly, and Candace sees it. And somehow she isn't hating her mother, not anymore. Maybe because Eileen is talking about Papa Frank, which she does so rarely, and when she does, she always has sorrow in her voice, sorrow and anger.

"Look, Ma, I'll read the journals," Candace says, touching her mother's arm. "I'm happy to. I'm happy you decided to give them to me. I'll take them with me up to Vermont. Really. And then, hey, maybe we can…talk about them when I'm done. It might be…" Candace shrugs. She is about to say "fun," but thinks twice. "It might be…OK."

Eileen looks up. Doesn't smile, but squeezes Candace's hand. Hard. "Thank you, honey," she says. "I know my going away was…I know it wasn't easy for you. But you have to know that I always always loved you. I never ever meant to…" Eileen's voice breaks off. She lets go of Candace's hand and takes hold of the throat of her bathrobe. Twisting the terrycloth closed, she leaves the room and hurries to her own room.

Hours later, after Eileen has gone back to bed, and slept, and gotten up, and is feeling a bit more refreshed, she opens her bedroom door only to catch her breath. There on the floor, she finds the old peace offering. Candace has left DC2, her skirt more ragged than ever, perched on the kitten blanket, sitting right outside her mother's door.

AUDREY X

She steps onto the back porch and immediately realizes she doesn't need the hat. She pulls it off and silver hair spills in waves to her shoulders. Scratching at her papery scalp, she considers the new kaleidoscope-colored cap that Marjory handed her, wrapped up in tissue paper, last night. After all these years, after all these hats, how could Marjory, a knitter who has no match, make such a mistaken hat? One that's so tight, so goddamn scratchy?

Audrey sighs. A small army of Chickadees is resting on the wooden porch rail. She lifts the bag of black oil sunflower seed from a decrepit bench and spills it into the tray of the feeder. A redwing blackbird lights on the lawn. That means, in all likelihood, the sugar season is staring her in the face.

Some years it starts with a bolt, it goes so fast that the women trade down jackets for T shirts in the course of an afternoon, and the wood stove, even tamped down as low as it will go, still cooks the living room. Green cracks snake across the ice of the pond, widen within a few hours, fracturing the neat circle the women have shoveled all winter for skating. The sap flows with urgency then. Often fog will hover above the snow and feather the bare branches like white cotton candy sheathing ragged sticks. But when the sap starts that fast it can also turn out to be a false alarm. A day or two later, the weather may snap back to being winter.

After the snow, mud is guaranteed, mud that is slick and slippery or some mornings crystal stiff, its thin surface of ice patterned like beaded ferns. Mud makes its way everywhere, cannot be kept outside where it belongs. It follows in on the bottom of boots and shoes, clinging foul and triumphant in its mighty season of reign. And yes, rain, too. It falls, churning the mud, the runoff pooling in mammoth puddles, bringing everything down to one common denominator of soft sucking earth.

The mud reaches out in the shape of feet, tracks pile up each on each just inside the small mud room that Audrey's great grandfather built so many years ago precisely for this purpose. But mud rooms do not contain mud, not perfectly, not with a throng of women crossing out to in, toting arm-splitting loads of wood quickly to the stove, dragging clumps of mud and slush and bits of bark in on their thick black soles. The kitchen is always first to fall, the dirt from shoes grinding the gloss off the wide pine planks, the wood in places worn down almost to white. The oak floors in the hallway are helpless to follow.

Finally, the fine pink and green flowered sofa in the living room succumbs, the sheen on the polished cotton surface soils, no doubt from mud on someone's pants. It can't be helped. It can be cleaned of course, the sofa, and it is, usually just before Easter, most years, as part of a concerted effort to keep the outside out, to preserve the inside in, because the women don't want to be reminded of what's outside patiently waiting.

When the sap runs, the boiling goes around the clock and the women hardly sleep or eat for days and they swear to each other, all except Audrey, that is, that they won't — no, they absolutely can't — do the sugaring one more year. They won't break trails through crotch-deep snow, they won't drill holes or carry pails or stand for hours by the boiling pan. They can't possibly do all that again, not one more year, and certainly they can't do it when they're old and feeling ill. "So what will you do?" Audrey asks one or the other of them. "Who will take you in? Who will feed you and give you time for your work?"

Usually it's toward the end of the run, when the sap pooled in the bottom of pails is tinged faintly green or yellow and has begun to taste of buds. The women are huddled wearily in the sugar house, coated in sticky sweet steam. All of them are cross and tired. Someone sighs and says her back is sore, or that she just can't take any more walking or standing or bending over. Someone else might start to cry, not Marjory or Francine, but maybe Pit if she is feeling sicker than usual, or Big Martha, because she cries — and laughs — so easily.

Audrey is passing the skimmer through the last of the froth, and Francine is sinking a teabag into the bubbling sap to make one more cup of maple tea. Audrey is hidden in maple steam, a cloud of it is rising up so thick around her that she almost disappears on her side of the boiling pan. But her voice comes through clear nonetheless. She asks her questions and they hang in the air for a few moments, roiling in the maple mist until finally Francine says, "Oh Lord, who knows what we'll do, who even cares what we'll do when we get old." Silence descends a moment, and then Big Martha chuckles and adds, "You mean old-er." Her black cowboy hat is tipped back, away from her forehead, the red feather ragged and pointing downward. And then for effect Big Martha sets her hand to the small of her back, and twists side to side. Some part of her backbone cracks.

Everyone falls quiet again and Audrey's questions without answers rise, mixing with the white mist from the pan. All of it travels upward through the rusted stack at the top of the sugarhouse. There, the words, the steam, all pass out together and disappear, mixing with the cool fog of the early morning sky.

Audrey, sitting on the old bench now, reaches into a bag of cracked corn. She scatters a handful over the rail of the porch and watches the hard little yellow kernels sink into the soft snow on the ground. A mourning dove is there, two chickadees and a bossy jay. In the distance, she hears the sound of an approaching car. A car and then a pick up truck.

Candace and Rusty. Grinding up the muddy road, one following close behind the other.

CANDACE

The road's surface is a slick pudding, pocked with holes and gleaming puddles, all of them shining up at Candace like white eyes in the silvery morning light. This time of year, Undermountain Road is always one long twist of ruts and ridges, a muddy chocolate ribbon pressed everywhere with zigzag lines and chunky imprints left by rubber tires. Today the mud is having its way with Candace's cherry red Toyota, forcing the car into the road's deepest ruts. No matter how she holds the wheel, or tries to turn it, the car goes just where it wants to, pulling left and right, bouncing in and out of puddles, tipping into ridges, bumping hard up and down against her will.

Candace has driven mud before, has driven this road before, so many times she cannot count, in seasons much worse than this one. But maybe because of the accident, or because of last night, Candace is edgy this morning and the mud is just making things worse, making her grip the steering wheel that much tighter.

In her mind, the car keeps careering across a black glaze of ice, as slick as a wet window pane, and she's frantically pumping the brakes, the way her father told her to should she ever go into a skid. She did exactly what she was supposed to the night of the accident, but it didn't help, nothing did. In the end, the car whipped around in a complete circle, and the headlights flashed across the dead winter trees in the dark, splashing the branches with a wild blur of light. The car's rear fender hit with a heavy thunk against the stone piling of the railroad bridge and even now, almost three weeks later,

Candace cringes at the way her neck jerked forward and then hard to the right. The shoulder belt snapped tight across her chest, taking her breath away, and leaving a purple and yellow bruise running diagonally between her breasts.

This is different from the accident, Candace keeps telling herself. The car was flying that time, couldn't be controlled on the ice, didn't respond no matter how she pulled at the wheel or pressed on the brakes. Here, though, the mud is an anchor. *Yes*, she thinks, *mud is so much better than ice, it sucks you in, glues you. All I have to do is keep the car on the road.* Thinking that, she relaxes, loosens her grip on the wheel, ever so slightly, just enough so that she becomes conscious of her sweaty palms.

At once, as if the Toyota senses somehow that she has eased her control, it swerves hard left and then sharply to the right. She grips the wheel tighter, but now the car is plunging through a series of huge puddles, first up, then deep down, bumping along the road as though riding over chunks of lumber. Suddenly, one front wheel sinks completely, hits the biggest puddle yet, and muddy water swamps the windshield. Candace fumbles for the windshield wipers, but before she can switch them on, the car hesitates, the red generator light flashes on and off, and then the car just dies. Candace has both hands on the steering wheel, like she's praying over it. She inhales, lets the air out slowly, ruffling her lips. The tears that have been building up for God knows how long start to leak out, and then, peering into the rear view mirror, realizing how foolish she must look sitting in a little car stuck in the mud, crying, she sets her forehead on the steering wheel. She leaves it there a moment and then looks up.

Swiping her sleeve across her eyes, she peers out at the sky through the top of the windshield. Blurry grey is giving way to milky blue, which means the women will soon be tramping through the snow hanging buckets. Candace reaches into the back seat for her down jacket, opens the door, steps out into the cold. Night gloom still encloses the dense pine forest. Snow is banked high on both sides of the road and small puffs of cool fog swirl between the trees. The sun won't be visible for at least an hour.

Unlatching the hood of the Toyota, she stands the slim metal support pole in place so the hood will stay open. She hasn't a hope of diagnosing the problem, but still, she gazes under the hood at the unfamiliar sea of black rubber hoses and brightly colored wires and dark, grease-glazed metal surfaces. Steam — or is it smoke — rises up from several points, and Candace wonders if that's normal, or if the car stopped running because it was overheated. *At least it's warm under here*, she thinks, rubbing her hands and holding them out over what she assumes, because it has a series of thin fins, is the radiator. After a few minutes, Candace concludes that nothing, absolutely nothing, looks out of order under the hood. If she could, she would call Mark, relay the symptoms, get him to figure out the problem. But as it is, she simply lets the hood fall shut.

The night of the accident, Candace got out of the car before the ambulance arrived, even before the first car pulled over. When the sheriff appeared, she was telling everybody she was OK, that the car had just gone into a weird slide. *I'm so incredibly lucky*, she kept saying, the car did a 360 and only hit on the right back fender. Secretly, though, she wondered if she was OK. Lightheaded and shaky, she was feeling terribly chilled. And fearful, too, because she knew that soon she would have to explain and make her excuses.

She had just come from Jill's party, and she had had three, OK, maybe four beers; but that was hours before. And then she had the one short line of coke, but that wasn't the reason she'd gone into the slide. It was black ice on the road and everybody knows how scary black ice can be. Still, her stomach tensed at the thought that the cops would demand a breath test, or whatever they demanded — walking a straight line? What did they ask for when they suspected somebody of doing drugs? The trembling really kicked in then, and that's when she crossed her arms on her chest, held herself tightly, felt the down of her jacket start to collapse. Still she shook. Finally one of the cops, the younger one with the blond mustache — she didn't know cops were permitted to have such bushy mustaches — began to question her.

"Are you sure you're OK?" he asked. What she noticed was his hat, the tall part, behind which the bright blue lights on top of his car sparkled, so that it looked like his hat had a wild blinking halo. Then the blue lights, still dancing, began to elongate, turn wavy, until the hat disappeared and Candace was stumbling, reaching backward, realizing she was falling, hoping she would land in soft snow. The next thing she knew, the siren was roaring in her mouth, it was that close, it was covering her mouth, some piece of rubber or plastic blanketed her lips, and she smelled something cool and clear like the outdoors. She looked up and there were dim lights on either side, and she was under a blanket. The cop with the mustache wasn't there, but a young woman with short dark hair and a navy blue jacket with a red and white emblem was bending over her, holding a clear plastic contraption over Candace's nose and mouth saying "we'll be there in a flash don't you worry you leave it to me you will be just fine."

The woman's face evaporates as Candace slips back into the car behind the wheel and turns the key, peppering the accelerator. Once, twice, three times she steps the pedal to the floor, and three times, nothing happens. Nothing, that is, except that heat rises up around her neck, and her face flushes, and she has a rush of something Eileen said two nights ago. "Well I personally think you're foolish not to bring the car in and have it repaired, the tail-light and bumper fixed, *before* you leave, just to make sure." Eileen's words keep ringing in her head, loud and clear enough to bring on the tears again.

Flinging the car door open, she bolts out onto the road, her slim cowboy boots sinking into the ooze. She covers her ears, because now she is hearing something else Eileen always says in winter: "Candace, wear your other boots, the Sorrels, because you know you'll end up wrecking the leather boots in the snow and mud and..." The voice floods her, pushes her on, even though the walking couldn't be worse. The mud is creeping ankle deep. Over and over, she keeps recalculating the distance to the farmhouse. Driving, she had passed the sharp curve, but she hadn't quite reached the old foundation, the squarish pile of crumbling fieldstones where a small barn once stood. So she figures she has at least a mile to go to Audrey's place. She is beginning to feel how long the trip will be, how her boots will be ruined, swallowed up by the road, just like her car tires. Thinking about the tires, she looks down, notices the zigzag impressions on the road, the precision of the tread patterns, how interesting they look, how nice they would be to draw, just tread patterns in mud, in black on white. Simply that. At that thought she stops short and turns back. She has forgotten her backpack. Inside are her art supplies, but more important, Eileen's black journals.

Unlocking the Toyota's trunk, Candace considers the backpack. Simultaneously, she eyes the muddy road. Walking is a stupid thing to do, she concludes. The boots will be totally ruined. And how far can she possibly get? Squashing her way back through the soft road to the driver's side door, she opens it, and settles inside. After wiping the top layer of mud off her boots with a wad of Burger King napkins, she reaches into her backpack and carefully removes the book labeled "Diary One." She holds it with both hands and stares, and suddenly, a thrill chills her. Here is her mother's life, or the most important part of it, about to unfold. Here is her mother, who has always kept big chunks of her past a secret, now pressed between two hard covers of a book, a book just begging to be read.

Sliding the front seat as far back as it will go, she slumps down behind the wheel, so that just the bright knit cap Marjory made, is visible. She raises her knees against the wheel and cradles the book in her lap. As she flips open to the first page, it hits her: *this diary, which is my mother, is propped squarely over my belly. And only a few inches below, safely embedded in me, inside my flesh and blood and placental fluid, is my baby.*

If Candace's calculations are correct, the fetus is two to three months along, which means, according to the chart in the pamphlet she picked up at the clinic, that the heart is pumping madly. It means the limbs are more than buds but less than arms and legs. It means the forehead looks like a clear bulging sac. It means the baby's tiny ears are forming out of flaps of skin on the side of the head. Candace turns back to the book. She begins reading, and as she does, she feels her own heart pumping. It's doing the work of two. And it is shooting what feels like warm fluid into her arms, through to the tips of her fingers.

EILEEN

February 21, 1972

My legs are two wet mountains rising out of soap-suds, my knees are glistening flesh peaks, and I'm staring between the mountains the length of the tub, through the valley of snow. Holding this book on a towel over my chest feels a little absurd and it's hard writing like this but what the heck. The bubbles are making that sizzling sound, disintegrating around my ears. When I blow on the bubbles they separate to either side in big soapy drifts and I get a glimpse of my two tits sticking up like cherry red tree stumps and the dark hair below. Every time I hit my swollen breasts they hurt, and at the far end of the tub is a metal plate with a handle and to me, lying here, the handle hangs down like a nose and the two screws holding it to the tub on either side are the eyes and they are staring at me, accusing me of something that definitely is not my fault, or at least not completely.

I called Corinne last week at her parents' house in Berkeley the night after I got home for winter break, and told her I was half nuts after only one day home and she said why don't you write about it, keep a journal, which I've never done before. I probably wouldn't have started except that three days later what arrived in the mail but a big padded envelope and inside was this black book, an artist's sketchbook, plain white pages, no lines. Corinne sent it with no note, but she filled the first two pages with pieces of poems and inspirational messages, one from *The Rubaiyat of Omar Khayam* and another from Henry David Thoreau, and another from *The Prophet* by Kahlil Gibran, which she and I take turns reading out loud every night before we fall asleep in the dorm at Brown, and one also from *The Little Prince*: "It is the time you have wasted for your rose that makes your rose so important."

So now I am determined to try to make sense of my rose, or should I say, my life on paper. But that will be hard because it doesn't make sense off paper. Ma keeps begging me to eat, last night she made me cacciatore, carrots, and even the Italian egg cookies I always loved as a kid (big core of chocolate in the middle.) And I forced myself to pick at the food and kept telling her my stomach wasn't right. So after supper she brought me up a shot glass full of Fernet, that black ink from Italy, and I tried a drop on my tongue and couldn't swallow it. "Lucy, let her be," my father said. So I took Maalox instead, and ate three bowls of Rice Krispies, some toast, and drank ginger ale. Ma keeps wanting to know what's wrong, and I keep telling her I must have a virus, it'll clear, but at this point I'm pretty sure it won't. God, I've missed two now, two, TWO, and I've got to make some decisions, some kind of decisions, FAST, but first I'd better find out for sure. Funny how I don't feel that writing in this book is private, AT ALL, well it is and it isn't, I can say whatever the HELL DAMN SHIT I want, but then, there's no lock, and even if there were, no lock could possibly make me feel secure. So I have to write as if this isn't for my eyes only, because I don't trust it not to fall into the wrong hands, Lucy's to be exact, or worse yet, my father's. God forbid the book were to end up with Frank, resting on those yellow callused palms. He would certainly have me then, totally exposed, as vulnerable as one of those naked little birds I used to find in the lawn, broken too soon from a pale blue shell. I would see no end of hell for what I've done.

Lucy is forever looking under the bed, cleaning out the closets, lifting the mattress, dusting, dusting, dusting, flipping over the mattress once a week whenever she changes sheets, which is once a week. (At the dorm I change maybe once every other month, but I wouldn't tell her that.) She's nuts on cleaning, and so I don't think I can be too careful about what I say here and I don't dare hide this book the same place every night. (I think tonight I'll squeeze it behind the books on my shelf or in between my mattress and springs.)

Anyway, Corinne said right away when I missed number one that I could go to California. Her father, Dr. Rivers, practices there. She said he would "take care of things," he'd do it for free, he's done it before and even for a few famous people she couldn't name and it's probably true he would take care of me and maybe it's no big deal, but I would be too too scared of something happening. All I can picture is the rusty coat hanger covered in blood clots, of course he wouldn't use one but it's just this idea I have in my head that is real and terrifying. Mostly I'm scared of somebody finding out and of me burning in hell forever. But what is the alternative? I can tell Rusty, tell him everything — he called tonight, calm, friendly — I could tell him and he'd know damn well it's his fault, he brought the drugs, he dared me to take them. He'd probably say something stupid like fine, let's get married, my god he just might too. I still can't believe this is happening to me. One goddamned time I don't use the goddamned thing and that is definitely his fault and what happens? Bang.

If only I could go back eight weeks and relive it all and call John and tell him the things I was too afraid to say — "John I want to be with you," go sailing, hiking, skiing, looking at art galleries in Boston. I want to eat muffins at The Pewter Pot in Cambridge Square, I swear wherever he wants to take me I'll go, I'll tell him (and mean it this time) that I'm completely finished with Rusty, he's past and I'm definitely ready for the future.

The bubbles are practically gone now, I see myself clear as day in the bath water and maybe it's the way the water rolls around in this tub or maybe my stomach really is getting worse but I feel like I'm riding the waves, my stomach is flip flopping and so I'm going to end and write more tomorrow or tonight and pray that things will by some miracle turn out right.

Speaking of praying, I am SO glad I didn't go to church yesterday even though it was Lucy's birthday, even though I know she won't forgive me anytime soon, but I couldn't bring myself to trot down the aisle at St. Anthony's, to cross myself with holy water, to genuflect at the pew, in full view of the true blue Virgin, all the while smelling that incense Father Crucele shakes at the front of the church. It's hard to believe that once upon a time I wanted to be a nun, and then, an altar boy, I was dying to help with mass. Now I'd sooner die as step into that church. Ash Wednesday comes the day after tomorrow, and I know Lucy will tie her scarf under her chin and head off to church by 8:00 and come home to make breakfast with the black smudge on her creased forehead and she'll try to make me go at noon and I will absolutely refuse. Ashes to ashes, dust to dust, that's what they say, hey maybe that's why Lucy is so fanatic about cleaning...

February 23
Ash Wednesday, ha, wouldn't you know it would start this way this morning, the throwing up, all day it's been going on, the gagging feeling won't stop, maybe I'm being punished for the things I wrote down the last time, all that stuff about the church, the Virgin, but I won't change a word of it, only I wish this feeling would go away, my stomach burns and bubbles and rolls all at once. I'm supposed to go back to school on Sunday and if this keeps up how can I possibly go oh my God I can hardly pick my head off the pillow. I feel like I'm in a boat in a big storm, or on a roller coaster without even the car, and I've got the brown basin by my bed, and I'm praying over it, and my mother is hovering over me, she keeps putting wet washcloths on my head and I don't have the heart to tell her to stop.

"You got something," she keeps saying, shaking her head, feeling sorry for me. Once in the middle of the morning after I woke up from a nap I let her take my temperature and it was up just a little. I wish she wouldn't watch me with the evil eye. Every time I throw up she mutters "madonna" and she brings me pastina and soup and jello and they don't help and now I think it's coming up again or maybe not and I know in a day or so she's gonna want to take me to the doctor — and then what? What am I gonna do or say oh hell it is coming, the water in my mouth, and I surely can't write and puke at the...

February 28 (It's hard to tell one day from the next...)
There is nothing to describe this. Just how horrible I feel now. I am lying in a sea of white sheets staring at a white ceiling and outside the window there is still a foot or two of snow and the branches are lined in white but everything else is black, especially Lucy's moods, she is scowling continually, or crying or both. I had to tell her. I've thrown up four or five times a day for the last week and I was supposed to leave for school yesterday but what a joke. And today, this morning, she was determined to drag me to the doctor or the hospital, I heard her on the phone making an appointment, I heard the words, "college," and "sick stomach," and "no fever" and then I knew what I had to do.

She came up the stairs, the way she always comes up, slowly, the wood squeaking, leaning on the railing, stopping every two or three steps so she won't tax her heart.

Breathing hard, coming over to the bed, she said, "We're going at three to see the doctor," and me crying then, for the first time the tears sliding. I shook my head back and forth, and she said, "What's wrong now? It's just the doctor, you sick, you gotta go see a doctor."

I pulled myself up and ran my hands through my hair, I haven't washed it in almost a week, and I said, "Call him back." Just that. "Call him back." She looked at me, and for that minute, I felt bad, that I had to do this to her, but there was no other choice, because the doctor, I knew he'd figure it out and then she would find out too.

"Ma, I don't think I'm sick," I said as she turned to leave the room.

"Ah, you crehzee," she said, and she even laughed, sort of. "Since you been to college, you been goin' crehzee." She's been saying that lately, more and more. And then as she was almost at the door, her hand on the handle, I said, "No, Ma, I'm not crazy. But maybe I'm going to have a baby."

She stopped, facing the door, frozen with her hand on the knob and her shoulders sort of shriveled, slumped, or am I imagining that part? I held my breath and shifted the basin on my lap, and let my head go back into my pillow. I didn't have to tell her, I didn't have to, but I did, she's got to appreciate the fact I was honest. But in the next instant I wasn't sure what possessed me to think she could hear this. I wasn't sure at all, because when she turned, her black eyes were full of terror, wide and round, like an animal trapped in headlights, and the creases in her forehead were deeper than ever, and her mouth was open just a little, and her lips made a strange, crooked line.

"You...you...you," she said, that's all she said at first, over and over, all in one tortured breath, then she started shaking her head. I closed my eyes and she left, she left the goddamned room, the door slightly open, as if she could just pretend that I never said what I just said. So maybe I made a mistake telling her. I haven't heard a word from her all day — a bad sign — because that means she's either downstairs in the kitchen, crying with the door closed, or she's building up, she's building up to something bad. And of course, she is almost certainly going to tell my father, and that's not only bad, that's another whole matter altogether.

CANDACE

Candace glances up from the diary when she hears the low thunk of a truck engine. Her face is wretched. The diary has unlocked something. Something creepy. Something that makes her feel ill, like she ate something old for breakfast. Candace feels exposed, ashamed, and most of all, guilty, as if she is responsible for making her mother's life a mess. Throwing the diary aside, she clears a circle out of the fogged window with her elbow. The faded red truck pulls up alongside her car. Candace knows that truck, scabbed so badly with rust that the doors are lacy with holes.

She opens her own door. Her father leans over to the passenger side of the truck and rolls down the window. The Beatles, "When I'm Sixty-Four," floods out.

"Funny meeting you here," he says, running a thumb across his mustache. He grins, revealing a front tooth that has been chipped ever since he got knocked in the jaw with a two by four when Candace was little. "Getting in?"

Candace climbs into the truck. "I was beginning to wonder if I'd be stuck here all day." She splays her hands against the truck's heater.

"So," Rusty says, switching off the radio. "You OK?"

Candace nods. "Yup." The diary lingers, like raw garlic repeating on her breath.

"Kiss?"

Candace leans over, smooches his cheek. She goes months without seeing her father and then, during sugar season and summer, she sees him daily. Rusty lives ten miles away, in a hill town called Jackson, with his second wife, Suzy, a potter, and their two sons, 8 and 11.

"So what's up with the car?" He parks the truck ahead of the Toyota.

"I wish I knew. This road is so bad, I think it just threw something out of whack. All I know is, I splashed into one puddle and then, wham, the car stopped."

"Just like that, huh?" He chuckles. "My door is stuck, so we have to get out on your side." Candace slides out, and her father follows, lifting his stiff leg and then gently lowering it to the ground. Eight years ago, he fell off a third-story scaffolding installing a modern arched window in somebody's renovated attic. He shattered his leg and was out of work for a year.

Limping around the Toyota, he stops at the back fender. The splintered taillight is wrapped haphazardly in grey duct tape. Rusty whistles. "Hmmm. So I hear you and your car got mixed up with a bridge and some ice."

Candace stiffens, studies her muddy boots. "Yeah. Mom was pretty pissed."

Rusty makes his way back around to the front of the car, lifts the hood. His hair, a wavy mixture of grey and blonde and Candace's own strawberry red, is caught in a ponytail at the nape of his neck. Whistling the Beatles, he wiggles a couple of wires, pokes at a hose.

"Can you see what went wrong?" Candace leans under the hood beside him.

He just keeps whistling the song. But soon he's opening the driver's door and swinging himself inside behind the steering wheel. Wincing, he lifts the stiff leg into the car. He rolls the window down, turns the key, leans his head out. "Still no radio in your car?"

"No, Dad, no money for a radio." During the year he was laid up, Rusty listened to music night and day, and now he always has a radio playing. "Anyway, I'm trying to save up for a CD."

"Nice," Rusty says, peppering the accelerator. Nothing happens at first, then the car sputters and comes to life. He pumps more, and the car chokes, sputters again, then roars. Oily fumes shoot out the tailpipe.

"I tried that...sort of," Candace says, putting her face into the front window. Rusty smiles, smoothes his mustache against both sides of his upper lip.

"Get in," he says, nodding toward the other door. Candace circles the car and gets inside. Rusty floors the gas pedal, revving the engine a couple more times while he stares distractedly out of the windshield. Then he turns to her.

"What happened is you went through that puddle and shorted your electrical system."

"Oh. So, is that serious?"

He grins. "No. Not if your father happens to drive by to help you get the car started." He whistles something she can't identify. Stops. "So now I'm all ears. Tell me about the accident." They sit side by side in silence.

Candace studies her thumbnail, then bites at it. "What do you know?"

"Ha. Obviously, not enough. Come on Candy, spit it out."

"God, Dad, please not Candy. You know how much I hate that."

"Sorry. I forget. But stop stalling and tell me everything."

Candace twists her mouth to one side. "Alright. So I was at a party, at Jill's place. She had us over, no big deal, just a little get-together for the people in my life-drawing class."

"Sometime," he says, interrupting, "I'd like for you to show me a drawing of life."

"Dad, *please* don't. Please don't say dumb stuff. I'm not some ten-year old kid."

"OK, OK, I'm sorry. I didn't mean anything by it."

"So OK, we had a few beers, and we, well, we...we just..."

"Just what?"

"Well I just left. Mom said I had to be home by twelve, so I left at, maybe twenty of, and I dropped this guy off in town, and then, heading out to the highway, you know, where County 9 curves around real sharp and goes under that old railroad bridge?" Her father nods.

"Well, right there I just hit some incredible black ice and the car went flying. Spun right around. Really I did everything you ever told me about pumping the brakes, turning into a skid, all that, but nothing worked. I just flew into that bridge."

"You're lucky you didn't hit that damn thing head on. It's always been a menace." He lays his open palm on top of her knee, presses into her leg. "But anyway, you're OK. So how did you hit your head? Didn't Grandma tell me you passed out?"

Candace is busy crossing her thumbs back and forth.

"Hey?" She doesn't answer. "Candace please, just tell me. I'm not your mother. I'm not going to get angry like she did."

She looks up. Inhales. "I got dizzy."

"And?"

"Look, Dad. You know I'm not into drugs, right?"

"Hell, how do I know what you're into. It changes."

"Come on Dad. Be serious. It doesn't change. Not that much, anyway. Look, I've occasionally tried stuff, but nothing much, nothing really heavy." She looks at him, pleadingly. "But that night, somebody, this older guy from Pittsfield, he brought some coke."

Rusty nods. "Coke. And not the brown fizzy kind in a can."

"*D-a-a-d*. There you go again, being so ridiculous."

He shakes his head yes, as if agreeing with her. But he's got his eyes closed, and she can't read him at all, which isn't unusual. He opens his eyes, points out the window. "Look. The sun's up. You can see it flickering through those trees."

Candace's mouth drops. She's talking about cocaine and he's gawking at the scenery. Occasionally, like now, it seems totally incomprehensible that Rusty is her father. Or anybody's father. Then again, she'd rather him than anybody else.

"Dad?" Her voice is small and apologetic.

"Yeah?"

"I did only a really really small amount, I mean hardly anything at all. I just wanted to be able to say I tried it, you know. But maybe because I'm not used to it, or maybe because it was really strong stuff, or maybe because of the accident, well, I just got dizzy is all and fell back, and the cop on duty that night stuck me in an ambulance and flew me off to the hospital."

"Oh, Eileen must have *loved* that."

Candace pulls her wool cap off, and her hair falls over her shoulders. "Yeah, did she ever. By the time Mom got to the ER, they were testing me. And you know how she knows everybody in that stupid hospital, including every emergency room doctor and nurse and orderly. Even the cop, Robbie something, he's somebody you two went to high school with."

"Oh God, Robbie Cramer, it must have been. He once had a crush on your mother."

"Anyway, he told Mom he had to charge me, because the urine test came back positive, and then you know Mom, she's amazing, she managed to convince him not to, she just kept telling him I'm straight as an arrow, I've never even had a parking ticket and I'm in college and all that crap, my record is so completely clean it squeaks. And since nobody got hurt, they let me off with a warning. But now she's incredibly pissed at me."

Candace closes her eyes. She sees Eileen standing beside the ER doctor in hospital greens. She hears the doctor ask the "routine" question: "Before the X ray, is there any chance you might be pregnant?" Candace didn't answer right away. After she did, she glanced at Eileen's face. It's that look on Eileen's face that she would like to erase from memory now.

"Well, honey, I know it's rare for me to agree with your mother, but in this case, she's right to be pissed. It isn't funny to be fooling around with drugs. That's bad business."

"Yeah, well..." They sit in silence a few minutes, during which time Candace keeps glancing at the floor, at her mother's diary. What's in her head is that first entry in the journal, that part where Eileen said Rusty "brought the drugs" and dared her to try them.

Candace picks up the journal, turns to Rusty, has half a mind to say, "Hey, Dad, you're lecturing *me* about drugs?" when suddenly her father has leaned over to grab her.

"For chrissake Candace," he says, "you might have been killed that night." He pulls her quickly toward him and then backs away. "You..." he has his mouth open, looks ready to say something else, but then doesn't. He shakes his head instead. "Look, just stop messing around with stuff. You hear me?" He points at her nose. Candace wrinkles her mouth. Nods.

"Anyway, how's Mr. Mark these days?" Rusty starts opening the door.

Candace rolls her eyes. She and Mark have been together for nearly four years and for three and a half Rusty has insisted on calling him Mr. Mark. Why, she wonders, does he insist on being so foolish? What will he say when he finally gets the message that she's gone ahead and grown up?

"*MARK* is fine. He's been in Boston for a month recording."

"Oh. What did he say about your skating into the bridge?"

"Not much. I mean, I spared him the details." Yes, she thinks, including the information confirmed by the pregnancy test in the ER.

Rusty climbs out of the Toyota, swinging his bad leg after him. "Go on and drive ahead of me up to the house. And remember, this time, go *around* the puddles?"

CANDACE

The Toyota bumps along behind the pickup, the road
sinking deeper into trenches the steeper the hill gets. Undermountain
Road continues a half mile past Audrey's house, but nobody lives
beyond the farm. Like all the land circling the sugar bush, the road
dead ends at Snowstack, the big ski slope over in Prospect.

In the back of the truck, a padded grey blanket covers a hulking
load, a load tied but still tipping side to side as the truck swivels and
glides through the mud. "Whatever it is, it has shoulders," Candace
decides, studying the rounded blanket. If she had to guess, she
would say Rusty's cargo consisted of his now-famous rocking chair.
After crippling his leg, Rusty had to give up building his treasured
solar houses. He turned instead to making furniture, mostly cabinets, tables and chairs. Five years ago, he came up with a rocking
chair that had an unusually wide back tapered sharply at the seat.

"It looks like a scallop shell," Candace said when her father
presented the first chair to Audrey as a Christmas present. Rusty
made the next chair even more graceful, fanning the long thin
spokes out from a center point at the back of the rocker. "Much better,"
Candace said when she saw the second version at Easter. "This one
will sell."

And sell it did. Summer people from New York said they liked the
chair because it looked so fragile, but wasn't. Not long ago, Candace
put together a color brochure to display her father's furniture,
including the chair. As an afterthought, she designed an ad featuring
one of her own pen-and-ink drawings of the "Russell Shell" rocker.

Rusty ran the ad last fall in *The New Yorker*, and since then, orders for the chair have been pouring in from as far away as San Francisco.

Candace's car shimmies through the first of the sharp turns that precede Audrey's house. Mud spatters her window, and the back tires spin, and in the next second, the car stutters, and its undercarriage scours the road. "Oh my God, please, not again," she yells out, and then, as if somehow He hears and responds, the car is delivered out of the slime.

Freed from the ruts, Candace guns the car and reaches the top of the hill. With no warning, the big white farmhouse rises abruptly on the right side of the road. No matter how many times Candace visits, the farmhouse always takes her by surprise, appearing out of nowhere as it does like the mighty prow of a ship. Today, the house floats on billowing waves of snow, drenched yellow by the low morning sun. The silvery Mother Maple hovers over the front yard, its symmetrical boughs like gigantic arms protecting the porch. Slowing the car, Candace rolls down the window. There is no place she likes better than this house, and especially the porch that wraps it on three sides. On this porch, Candace has listened to more of Audrey's ghost stories, more of Big Martha's guitar music — and more of her poor renditions of Joni Mitchell and Carole King — than she cares to remember. Here, too, she has drunk glass after glass of Francine's hand-squeezed lemonade and her yeasty homemade root beer.

It is here, too, one summer night when she was only 15, that Candace enjoyed her first tokes from a joint, thanks to Francine. What Candace remembers, aside from the bitter taste of the smoke, is lying back on the grass, watching the stars start to twirl, glittering and blurry in the clear black sky. The next morning, Audrey didn't say a word about it to Candace. But that afternoon, a terrible scene erupted in the kitchen between Audrey and Francine. Candace, who was sketching up in the sugar bush, heard Audrey thunder: "I really think you have a screw loose, Francine. What in God's name made you do it?"

Candace pulls into the driveway just as Audrey emerges from the back door, followed by Marjory, who is still in her bathrobe. Rusty is standing in the bed of the truck.

"Greetings, girls," he yells, untying the grey blanket. In the old days, the women would give him hell when he called them girls. But that was 17 years ago, a time the women now refer to as their "purist" period. In those days, Audrey and the others refused to use anything but maple syrup as sweetener. They also attempted to live off the land. For the first seven or eight summers, their gardens grew increasingly large and more glorious, with each woman attending to different vegetables and flowers. Audrey was known for her rainbow assortment of gladiolas, for perfect lettuce, and the best basil and arugula. She raised the sweetest strawberries, too, plump and red and ideal for the luscious shortcakes that Francine made every Sunday afternoon in June. Pit, maybe because she was tallest of the women, always planted sunflowers and corn, which grew to nearly her height of five feet eleven. Pit also planted bee balm because she adored the hummingbirds it attracted, and beets and watermelon for their Christmas colors. Big Martha harvested cantaloupe and honeydew, pumpkins and sweet potatoes. Martha also grew spectaculor roses, particularly the sweet-smelling climbers. Her Constance Spry climber grew to 15 feet, winding bright pink, teacup-sized blossoms over three trellises. For Marjory, who made everyone a knit cap, the only flowers that existed were day lilies; she loved them in part because they grew in every shade of yarn. Marjory couldn't resist any new variety of lily and at one point had 22 different lilies growing around the yard. She also earned the name "The Lady of Large Greens," for her mustard, collard, kale, swiss chard, and escarole — as well as for her gigantic zucchini, some of them growing as large as fireplace logs.

All the women took part in growing tomatoes. For several years running, Maple Hill's beefsteaks were the pride of Wilmont County. Lush and juicy, and as red as carnations, the tomatoes grew to the size of lunch plates. Come August, the women filled bushel barrels and drove them down to Boston, the station wagon overwhelmed with the warm ripe smell of tomatoes. In Boston, the women sold the tomatoes at the farmer's market. People were known to make a whole meal out of a Maple Hill tomato, slicing and eating it with crisp garden lettuce on top of homemade molasses oatmeal bread and mild Vermont cheddar.

At the end of every summer, the women canned vats of plum tomatoes and made sweet pickles. They froze string beans and put up peach jam from the trees out back. For a short time, the women kept animals: at one point, they had chickens, three pigs, 13 sheep, two Belgian workhorses, a goat, and a Guernsey named Rita. All of the women, except Big Martha, who was squeamish and highly allergic, drank raw milk, sometimes warm, right from the pail.

Eventually, things changed. As the women grew more involved in their sculpture and painting, their photography and fiction writing, they began to fight over who would weed and who would water, and who would feed and milk the animals. Gradually, the gardens grew smaller. The sheep and pigs, chickens and goat were all sold. Rita the Guernsey died, and was never replaced.

Today, the garden is overgrown with weeds, except for a small patch where Audrey still grows lettuce, strawberries, and basil. Pit continued for many years to raise the beefsteaks, but once she became ill, there were no more Maple Hill tomatoes. Today, the women buy their vegetables at a tiny farm stand on Route 100, and in the middle of the picnic table in the kitchen, they keep a large bowl of refined sugar. When Rusty addresses the women as girls, nobody seems to notice.

"Oh, God, would you look at that chair," Audrey gushes, descending the steps of the porch sideways. She's wearing a T-shirt, and her red flannel shirt is knotted around her waist. "How are you, sweetie?" Audrey places a kiss in the center of Candace's forehead.

"Fine, Grandma, but your road definitely is not. It is *bad*. My car died in a puddle."

Candace leans down to hug Marjory, who only comes up to Candace's shoulder.

"Yes, that road's a disgrace, I know," Audrey says, frowning, "but so are a lot of things around here. Now let me see this magnificent chair." Rusty hoists the rocker off the truck and hands it down.

"She'll love it," Marjory says, helping Audrey carry the chair to the back steps.

"And if she doesn't, then I might take it," Francine calls out. Her head is wrapped in a red bandanna and she is standing at the back door, hollering through the glass.

"Francine, keep a lid on it, will you?" Audrey scowls. Francine disappears inside the house.

"I told you, it's best to ignore her," Marjory says. "She knows she can get to you, so she just keeps doing it. She's frustrated, that's all. Whenever her writing stalls..."

"Oh her writing is *always* stalled," Audrey says. "I don't see why it should make a difference to her that we are buying a chair for Pit. We didn't ask her for a blessed penny."

"So then the chair is for Pit?" Candace asks, running her hand along the bowed back.

"Yes it is." Audrey sighs.

"Oh?" Candace asks. "A special birthday present?"

Audrey's eyes cut quickly to Marjory. "Uh, you might say that," she says flatly, but something in her tone rings an alarm in Candace.

"Come on, Ma, try her out," Rusty says, guiding his mother into the blond rocker. Audrey drops into the seat, plants her hands on the rocker's beveled arms. The graceful arch of the chair frames her face. Her frown dissolves. "Nice, very nice," she says, settling back.

"Lovely," Marjory chimes.

"My little Shelly, she's making me rich." Rusty pats the back of the chair. "As of last week, I've raised the price on her fifty dollars and nobody's hollering. You like the light stain?"

"Love it," Audrey says.

"Good job, Dad," Candace says, glancing at her father. Studying the rocker, and its pencil-slim spindles, it occurs to Candace that two arches like that would form the ends of a baby cradle. But she would want another color. The blond stain of this chair reminds her too much of Eileen's bentwood rocker.

"Pit will flip when she sees this," Marjory says. "Maybe Rus should drive it up to the sugar house when he plows the gathering road, so when Pit gets there, it'll be waiting."

"Nah," says Audrey, pulling herself out of the chair. "I'd rather see her face fall as she walks in the kitchen for breakfast."

"Oooh, breakfast," Rusty says. "What's Francine got today? Do I smell bacon?"

"Ham and eggs," Audrey says. "And pancakes. By now, though, she may be lacing the food with rat poison."

"Oh Audrey," Marjory is saying, "go easy on Francine."

"Why?" Audrey snaps. "Because she might break down and cry? I think, actually, that would be the best thing in the world that could happen to her."

"I don't know," Marjory says, her voice dipping into a whisper. "Crying hasn't helped me one damn bit this week."

The same alarm goes off again in Candace. She follows closely behind Marjory into the house, confused and a little frightened. She is accustomed to Francine and Pit fighting. They've been at each other's throats for so long that nobody expects anything else. But something else is amiss now. She will have to ask Pit, her best friend among the women at the farm, to explain.

❦

Francine stands at the counter, pouring the last of the buckwheat batter onto the griddle. One giant amoeba-shaped pancake takes shape. The others are at the picnic table finishing breakfast.

"Francine, come sit down and eat something," Audrey says. "You've got enough there for an army."

"I'll eat later," she says. "With Martha."

"You waited for little ole me?" Martha sasses, sticking her head into the kitchen right on cue. She's wearing her black cowboy hat, even at this early hour. Beneath the brim, her face is chunky and cheerful. There is a noticeable gap between her two front teeth when she smiles, which she does, quite often. Martha has the pleasant earthy look of somebody who grew up on a Minnesota farm, a girl with sky blue eyes and short bobbed hair the color of corn. Only the hair is dyed and she grew up in California, in a smoggy gray suburb east of Los Angeles.

"We are indeed waiting for you," Audrey says. "We wondered how late you intended to sleep this first morning of hanging pails."

Martha squeezes her thick legs, tight in blue jeans, between the picnic table and bench. "Now don't go getting rude with me, Ms. Audrey. I'm the one who will be pulling the all-nighters, if you'll recall. And here it is only ten thirty in the morning." She squints at her watch. "Oh, no, sorry. Eleven thirty. Anyway, it's still early for me." During sugar season, Martha covers the boiling from midnight to four. For 25 years, she worked the graveyard shift at a newspaper near L.A., first as a reporter/photographer, then, as city editor. She is used to being alert in the dark.

Francine sets a plate of pancakes in front of Martha, then sets a plate down for herself. Martha turns to Candace. Speaks quietly.

"Hello there sweetie. I don't want you to think I forgot you. I hear you took a bad spin in your car. Doing OK now are you?" Candace flushes.

"Oh, I'm fine," she nods, pushing a small piece of pancake on her fork through a puddle of syrup. She wonders how many times she's going to have to recount her story, and how many times she will leave out the most important part.

"And how long are you staying?" Francine asks, sitting at the table now and pouring syrup over her own pancakes.

"As long as you need me." It occurs to Candace then that maybe she should stay for good. Maybe she should clear out of Eileen's house and never go back.

Candace's spirits soar at the idea. Which makes it all the more difficult when Pit appears in the kitchen. Candace's jaw drops. All winter, Audrey has been writing to Candace about Pit, about her worsening thyroid, about a new tumor on her parathyroid. But despite the letters, Candace didn't expect this. Pit's face has a waxy grey pallor, and her cheeks have sunk into two hollows, as if she has permanently sucked in the skin on both sides of her face. Nearly six feet tall, Pit has always been skinny. But today, in a man's white shirt with the sleeves rolled up, knobs protrude on both wrists. Her arms look as thin and hard as the cane she is leaning on to help her walk.

Pit has one fist pressed against her mouth, and she is staring at the rocking chair, shaking her head. Someone thought to adorn the chair with a white bow and a sign saying, "HAPPY BIRTHDAY TO PIT, PLEASE, NO ROCKING OVER 55 MPH!!!"

Audrey rises to greet Pit. The others clap. Martha does a two-fingered wolf whistle.

"You guys," Pit bellows. "You are all too good to me."

Pit lowers herself slowly into the chair, dabbing her eyes with the sleeve of her shirt. Candace comes up and kisses Pit, aiming for the older woman's cheekbone. As her lips graze Pit's skin, a horrible thought occurs to her: is this what it feels like to kiss a corpse?

"You came, you sweetheart you," Pit's voice is raspy, but her British accent is as crisp as ever. "You didn't miss my birthday."

"Of course not," Candace says. "You never miss mine."

Standing there, her hand on Pit's brush-like gray hair, Candace recalls being five or six, and seeing Pit for the first time. "You look just like that scarecrow we have in the garden," Candace announced the first night Pit came to the farm for dinner. Dead silence descended on the table. Kneeling on her chair and slurping lemonade through a straw, Candace smiled pleasantly at Pit, and Pit looked back at her and laughed.

"You sit down right now, Candace, and eat your dinner quietly," Audrey scolded, using a tone that made Candace go wide-eyed and then collapse into her chair. She proceeded to knock over her lemonade and immediately she started crying, then ran from the table. Pit followed and found Candace hiding on the third floor.

When they returned to the dinner table, the two of them were holding hands. Pit, the giant, was bent over Candace, whispering. Candace was sniffling and wearing an old rhinestone necklace and bracelet Pit had dug out of a jewelry box. Candace has worshipped Pit ever since.

The back door opens now and Rusty, scraping his boots, blusters through the door. A gust of cold fresh air follows him in, and Candace is grateful for it. Maybe it will keep her from breaking down. "Rus, this chair is..." Pit begins.

"Now don't go giving Rusty a swelled head," Audrey says, handing Pit a plate of pancakes. "He's getting too big for his britches as it is. Anyway, Pit, try these buckwheats. We tried setting a candle in, but it fell. So now we've got an excuse to bake a cake later on."

Pit accepts the plate, gratefully, but lets it sit untouched in her lap. Her eyes, which are the blue of a robin's egg, start to water. Candace hands Pit a kleenex. Pit's eyes, she decides, are the only thing that still look alive. Pit blows her nose. A tinge of blood stains the tissue.

"Oh Pit, now don't go getting sentimental on us," Martha says. "It'll spoil your appetite. And you do need to eat. I mean, take it from a true-blue eater like me."

Francine rises from the table and starts collecting plates. "Martha, I'm sure Pit knows that she needs to eat," Francine says in irritation. "If I could get her to eat, I certainly would."

"But YOU certainly won't," Pit shoots back, her quiet words travelling at the speed of light. She sets her plate on the table with a clatter.

Candace is horrified, and judging by the silence in the kitchen, the other women are, too. No one else speaks. Francine sets cups upside down in the dishwasher.

"Oh come on you two," Big Martha says, "isn't it time you kissed and made up?"

Silence hangs like a stubborn fog. Pit speaks finally. "All of you are so sweet to me," she says, her tone now decidedly pleasant. "Getting me this chair is...well, you know you don't have to buy me anything, because I don't need presents, I've got everything I ever..." Her voice trails off. No one seems to know what to say. Finally, Marjory gets up from the table and comes to Pit's chair. Kneeling there, she takes Pit's hand. She speaks quietly.

"We want you to come sit with us in the sugar house. In this chair. All you have to do is rock. Not a thing more. We boil, you rock.

If you feel like bringing some knitting, you can, or maybe some poetry. You can read to us out loud. How about it? Are you up to that?"

Pit smiles, and nods. Candace leans her head back against the wall. God, her throat is thick. The last time she saw Pit, just after Christmas, she wasn't nearly this thin and sickly.

"There is one thing I wanna know, Pit," Rus says, looking very serious. "Yes Rusty?"

"Do you think Shelly rocks too slow? If so, you know you can tell me."

Pit laughs. "Get over here you." Rusty does, and he too, bends to Pit's level. She wraps both arms around Rusty's neck, so that she covers up his ponytail. Lately, Pit has been too weak to do her steel sculptures, so she sketches her designs and Rusty does all the welding.

Rus whispers something to Pit that nobody else can hear. "Don't you dare," she says. Her face goes grave. "But I do have one thing more I want you to do for me." She whispers in his ear. Rus pulls back, his face drained.

"Of...of course Pit," he says meekly. "I...I'd be honored." He rises quickly from the floor. Candace tries to see her father's face, but he has turned his head the other way.

"I wanna know what you two co-conspirators are cooking up over there," Big Martha calls out. "Are you gonna let the rest of us in on the secret or not?"

Rus exchanges a long glance with Pit. "That's not my call." He shrugs, hugs his arms around his broad chest.

Pit shakes her head. "No, Martha, it's between him and me only. You see, honey, it's always been my greatest desire to make you jealous."

"And now you have," Martha booms. She resumes eating her pancakes.

"Ladies," Rus says, clearing his throat. "I want you to know you can now make it all the way up the gathering road in the style to which you are accustomed. That is, walking through mud and ice. I have plowed the road. So now the day, and those sweet trees, and those ice cold pails, and that hellishly hot sugar house, and your gathering coach, all await you." He bows.

"Thank you, Rus," Audrey says. "You have a way of making it sound so enticing."

"My pleasure. Anyway, did anybody say there were leftover pancakes?" He sits down and finishes off the last stack Francine has been keeping warm in the oven. And then, when Pit leaves the kitchen to go back to bed, he eats her plateful, too.

❦

By the time Rusty is finished eating, only he and Candace are left in the kitchen.

Candace is rocking in Pit's new chair. "I love this chair, Dad," she says. "And it was great you made it for Pit."

Rusty goes to the stove for more coffee.

"I tell you, it's a real thrill to be able to make a chair," he says, stirring sugar into his mug. He stares distractedly at the chair. "Especially when you do it for somebody who...appreciates it."

Candace studies her father. His tone, at least for him, is subdued. It occurs to her now that she wants to tell him about the baby, if only to share some good news. It also occurs to her to ask him to build a cradle. But she can't figure out how to begin.

"I had no idea about Pit," she says. "I know you said she was sick...but wow... "

"Yeah. It's bad." He adds milk to the mug and dips a spoon in again to stir.

"I guess I couldn't help wondering what she said to you. In private I mean."

"Oh, well, that." Rus drops to the bench. "I guess that's a secret between Pit and me."

"Oh, sure, Dad, that's fine, I mean, whatever."

A few moments of silence follow. Rus sips from the mug. Candace rocks, faster. "Except."

"Except what?" Her chair inches backward until it knocks against the kitchen wall.

Rus sits forward, balancing his elbows on his knees. "It won't be a secret for long." He levels a steady gaze at Candace. "She asked me to make her coffin." His tone is hollow. "She wants plain pine."

Candace sucks her breath in. Gets up. Takes a seat close by her father and puts both arms around his neck. He circles her shoulders and lays his head against hers. "Oh God, Dad. Oh God. I'm so so sorry."

"It's OK. Actually I'm more flattered than anything else."   .

"Yeah, but it's so sad. And...scary..."

Candace remains there on the bench beside her father, her insides wrenched, her face nestled against his arm. It occurs to her that she hasn't felt this close to her father in years.

An hour later, the two of them are walking the gathering road together. Candace can't make much traction on the hill in the old rubber boots she's wearing, as they are Audrey's and three sizes too big.

"Dad, I had an idea, sort of. Actually, more of a request."

"OK, shoot, partner." Candace stops. That expression always reminds her of the days when she was a little girl and Rusty would take her on construction jobs. Whenever he had trouble keeping her entertained, he would make up hokey stories about cops and robbers, cowboys and Indians. Many of his stories included those two words, "Shoot, partner."

"Well, what I wanted to ask you, actually, what I wanted to ask you and…tell you was…."

"What?" They keep walking.

"I just…it occurred to me to ask you if…I mean, would you mind making *me* a chair?"

"Oh. Sure." Rusty shrugs. "Of course I will. But I can't believe that is what's got you so tongue-tied."

Candace's front foot slides sideways, her boot skating across ice. She grabs the sleeve of Rusty's Carhartt jacket. "Well, no, it's not. No…I mean, it's not just the chair."

"So come on, Candace, out with it. What's the rest?"

"Well, I was wondering, maybe, if you possibly would be able to make me…a…a cradle?" The word cradle comes out in a high-pitched squeak.

"A cradle?" Rusty stops, turns, stares blankly up into the sky, which matches his eyes.

"Yeah, you know, a cradle." She shrugs. "I was thinking if you made two of the Shelly rocker backs and put them together, you know, one on each end, then the…"

"Wait a minute. Wait just a minute. Back up please." He scratches his chin. "I'm well aware of how I might go about building a cradle. That would be easy enough. But haven't we skipped over something. Like what or who we are going to put into this cradle?"

Instead of answering, Candace raises her eyebrows high into her forehead.

Rusty whistles, a low soft whistle of amazement. "You know, honey, I'm slow. I am. But I think now I'm getting it. You mean…"

Candace shakes her head slowly up and down. "Yeah, Dad. I mean...*that*."

Rusty grabs her around the waist, giving her the second embrace of the day. "Wow," he says, letting her go. "Candace, I'm so...shocked. I mean, I'm not sure what to say. I'm...just surprised. Actually, I'm flabbergasted. Shit, I'm gonna be a grandfather. Well, hell, this is very good news. No, this is *great* news. Especially today. Just what we need. Great great news."

"I'm really glad you think so Dad. I mean, I think so too."

"And your mother? Is she..." he lifts an eyebrow in question.

"Oh, you know. She's..." Candace shrugs.

"Upset?"

"Oh, you could say that. You know her. She's always got to look at everything from a million analytical perspectives. Instead of just for once, letting me decide with my heart."

They resume walking, not talking for several feet. Then he starts speaking again.

"Your heart, huh?" He slips his hands deep into his pockets. "Yeah, that's a good place to...to *start*." Rusty stops, turns to her. "But...you know, honey, it's a *huge* responsibility to have a kid. I mean...I didn't realize that until you came." Candace nods and he resumes walking. "Anyway, I'm thrilled for you, honey, and for Mark. How's he feel about all this? I mean, he *is* the father, right?"

"Of course. But, I uh...I haven't, you know, since he's been away, I haven't actually had a chance to tell him. But I will, soon, I mean, maybe, probably even today...or tonight."

"Oh," Rusty says, his face shading over with concern. "Yes, I'd say you sure as heck better tell Mark right away." He pauses. "So, when is this grandbaby coming?"

"September," Candace says "I think maybe like the beginning or the middle."

"Oh, so right around your own birthday." Candace looks up. Is it her imagination, or does her father's face look sadly crooked?

"Hey Dad?"

"Yeah?"

"I really am glad that you're glad. I mean, Mom got so shook up over this it was not fun. Not fun at all. It means a whole lot to me to see that you're happy about it. Really."

"Oh sure." He goes forward, but stops when they come to the path leading to the sugar house. He stares out to the pine forest surrounding the sugar bush. Before he speaks, he clears his throat. "I...I was just remembering right now how...how it was when your mother told me she was going to have you. It's..." He shrugs and shakes his head. Smiles weakly. "It's great, Candace, it's great to have a kid. It's great to have you. I will be just delighted to make you a chair. And a cradle."

He smiles again. But what Candace notices this time is not the smile so much as the muscles that produce it. She never thought about the muscles in his face before, or more correctly, she never saw them work so hard when he smiled. "Thanks, Pop."

"Pop? You stopped calling me Pop a long time ago."

"Yeah, well, whatever." Candace beams, but not for long. Because now Rusty is teary-eyed. He hurries off to the sugar house, and Candace makes her way back down the hill. After all that's happened today, she needs to take a nap. First, though, she'll read more of the diary. Suddenly, she wants to know more about her mother.

EILEEN

March 3, 1972

This morning as soon as the sun was over the window sill, and as soon as I threw up once, because that's the way I wake up these days, puking within the first five minutes after I open my eyes, I walked outside, carrying my saltine crackers. The ground in places still has a foot and a half of snow, and it was chilly and there was a breeze, too, but for the first time, I smelled raw earth and thought of spring and something in the smell gave me hope, for what I'm not sure. I heard birds, too, for the first time all winter, or maybe before this morning I just wasn't listening. I forced myself to walk the perimeter of the backyard, and the whole time I walked, I felt like an inmate confined to a prison yard. Only instead of a barbed wire fence there was a dense row of white pines and I kept sticking my face between the branches and inhaling and little bits of snow or ice would shake free from the branch and they would drop on my nose and lips and melt right away and the cold numbed me inside and out.

I wore an old tent-shaped grey wool overcoat of my father's that I just grabbed off the peg in the kitchen by the back door. I felt miserable when I walked outside and I still did after I came in but not quite so bad. (My face is pale and puffy. Hormones or whatever have turned my hair dull and limp. It used to shine almost blue black, I know it did!!) But being outdoors was definitely better than being inside this stuffy bedroom so from now on I will walk the perimeter of the backyard at least ten times every morning. The smell of evergreen and pine settles my stomach. I will inhale big gulps of tree air.

When I came in I had to confront Lucy and Frank, sitting there drinking their white bowls of coffee with milk and eating their cold toast with butter (who started that peculiar tradition, I'm not sure). My father always eats soft-boiled eggs with his toast, and naturally, I got a glimpse of those god-awful watery eggs in the bowl and my stomach bulged and I just covered my mouth and hurried through the kitchen. We don't talk much, which is probably just as well, my father still hasn't said a word to me about the baby and my mother hasn't said too much either.

That first day I told Ma last week, she didn't speak for the whole day and that night, right after supper (which I didn't eat) she came back to my bedroom, offered me a bowl of polenta, which I actually kept down. She insisted on sitting there on the end of the bed, her eyes all red, until I finished eating. She said nothing at all until the end and then only "You gotta do what's right," and I handed her the empty bowl and was lying back against the headboard, the brown basin still in my lap (I used it a half dozen times that afternoon) and I couldn't decide if I was going to have to use it again, or how soon, and I couldn't bring myself at that very low moment to ask her what "right" was. But I have a feeling I know. Right would be what my cousin Cathy did when she got pregnant in high school five years ago. Her parents gave her a small wedding on a cold Tuesday night in November, and as she walked up the darkened aisle of the church in New Bedford, the votive candles flickered at the front of the church and her street-length dress was bulging below the waist. It wasn't a floor-length dress of course, and it wasn't perfectly white, either, because only virgins deserve to wear long white wedding dresses. Poor thing, my cousin looked as pale as the moon in a foggy night sky. She carried five red roses, tied in a satin ribbon, because there were only about five people in the church besides our family.

Oh god save me from one of those weddings, I would rather die, rather fry in hell, yes, rather have a baby ripped out of me, even that, rather than do what's right. And yet I am frightened to death of having an abortion, I hate the idea and don't know even one person who's had one...

Rusty calls daily and we talk about nothing much, his work, mostly. He's on a construction crew up at the new shopping mall on Route 2, and he knows I'm sick but I haven't told him why, not yet. Once last week he came by, but I was sleeping, and afterward, my mother came upstairs and I was still sleepy and she told me he had been here and then she said "He's a good boy," and then she asked me point blank, "Does he know?" and I had to say no. "You want your father to..." she asked, gesturing with her head, and that woke me up fast.

"Ma, please don't butt in," I said, and that was definitely the wrong thing to say.

"You bet we're gonna butt in," she wheezed, and her voice was a tight little twist, because by then she was crying, yet again, and she was shaking her head and biting her lip, and all the while she just kept putting away clean underwear in my drawer.

I'm going outside again this afternoon, because it's sunny and because it's the only thing I have to look forward to. I have my calculus and my microbiology textbooks, and the histology book, too, and I've been trying to study. I'm still thinking I will go back to school if I can ever shake this, the booklet I have says the nausea does pass. God I hope so. I will do anything to find some relief...

March 4, 1972

I said the last time that I was desperate, and I guess today was proof. I finally agreed to go see my mother's gynecologist. I didn't want to go, but I've been throwing up five or six times a day and I foolishly thought Dr. Veltrani might be able to help. He did just the opposite. I'll die before I let him deliver this baby.

After a few formalities, he started poking his fingers into me. He reached so far inside my pelvis at one point that I thought his hand, and my breakfast, would both come shooting out my mouth. But it was his lecture after the exam that really turned my stomach. "You know," he said, taking my bare feet out of the cold metal stirrups and pulling me up to a sitting position on the examining table, "some people think nausea is a sign of a woman's ambivalence toward her pregnancy. Or it could just be nature's way of preparing your body for the immense changes that lie ahead." I stared at him, trying to hold that foolish paper gown across my enlarged breasts. He sounded so damn arrogant. Like a talking textbook.

He turned to wash his hands at the sink. He had a head of short, tight salt and pepper waves, and a slight sheen to his hair and face. His appearance annoyed me right from the start. Now I thought about asking him an obnoxious question. "Did you know your hair looks really greasy?" I wanted to say. "Did you know that Italians are supposed to keep their hair squeaky clean, for obvious reasons?" Instead, though, I just sat there, with my mouth open, and the goo he had used for my exam oozing from my vagina. I made another appointment, but leaving his office, I vowed not to go. I would rather a butcher deliver my baby than that blockhead of a doctor.

March 5
This is how my days go: if I can, I walk the yard twenty times first thing in the morning, in the old grey coat, like a prisoner, or a guard. Sometimes, smelling the trees, I feel like a tree myself, a tree slowly moving around the yard. I wear my mother's old black rubber boots. I watch T.V. constantly, too: the morning news shows, the game shows, old sappy Nelson Eddy movies, and in the afternoon, soaps. "As the World Turns" is my current favorite. When "The Newlywed Game" comes on at 4:30, I turn the T.V. off. Then, back on for the evening news.

Last week, I watched Nixon and Mrs. Pat trot for eight days straight, all through China. Every night they hit a new hot spot: the Great Hall, where the Nixons watched ballet, then the Great Wall. Good old Walter Cronkite stood there all solemn-looking in front of the firing slits of the wall, bellowing his "good evening" while the sun was high in the sky. Ha. Normally watching Nixon makes me ill. But I couldn't get my fill of him last week. I sat there riveted to the evening news, fascinated to see him shake Mao Tse Tung's hand. And I was even curious to see him and Pat arrive home. They got a kiss and hug from that drippy Julie Nixon. Only now she's Mrs. David Eisenhower. Sorry, Julie, you should've known that the moment you got married you would lose your real name, in addition to your freedom.

Saturdays, I watch bowling and golf tournaments all afternoon. I especially like golf because it's televised from places like Georgia where the sun is always shining and the players are all blond and tan and the grass is as green, well, as a golf course. There are so many beautiful flowers. And trees. Monstrous pines. And trees with big wide, shady leaves. I want to live in a place like that. In a Mediterranean climate, where it's summer in March.

Last week, my mother and I were sitting together in the living room. She was knitting a sweater for her younger sister, Marie, and I was lying on the couch and at one point I said I wanted to live in a Mediterranean climate. She just shook her head. "I don't know where you get all your big ideas," she said. What I didn't tell her is that I'm thinking a lot about a specific Mediterranean climate — San Francisco, where my second cousin lives. But more to the point, Corinne lives across the Bay, in Berkeley.

I think I'm going out again, to do thirty more turns around the yard...

Corinne called last night and asked if I was coming back and I said I'll go nuts if I don't. Every once in a while I flash back on my old life. I mean it wasn't but a few weeks ago I was spending my whole day in class or at my carrel in the library or at the chemistry lab. In the free moments, I would be at Mother Earth, the coffee house at Brown, listening to Steely Dan or Cat Stevens or Arlo Guthrie or Moody Blues. We drank tea and we ate thick slices of wheat bread with muenster or provolone, all the while ranting about that miserably misguided Nixon and what he's doing to Vietnam.

If nothing else I have to go back to Brown to see John again, explain what happened. I haven't allowed myself to think of him the last two weeks because I've been too sick but now he comes to mind, most every night I dream about him, or the car, or the bay, I keep thinking about being in the sailfish on the water, and tipping over, and laughing so hard I almost drowned, my mouth full of salt water, and losing my sneakers and my wool jacket getting so heavy in ice cold ocean water that I had to slip it off because it was pulling me down. It was so strange the night we stayed together, I just wish I could go back and make it right.

Rusty is beginning to get suspicious. "What the heck is it with you?" he wanted to know the other night and one of these days he will come over when I'm not sleeping and then we'll have to talk and I'll have to face up to it. All of it. But right now I just get through the days any way I can.

March 7
Something about walking outside this morning knocked me for a loop, I was in my tenth circuit, and I had just stopped to breathe in

the evergreen when all of a sudden it hit me: my life has stopped. I
mean my old life, my walking around campus, meeting people at the
Blue Room or the coffee house for lunch, going to concerts, going
ice skating at the rink, taking skating lessons, going to class, chemistry labs, lectures; all that is over. I think I've been in some kind of
a fog the last couple of weeks. I've been so focused on feeling sick I
haven't been focused on college. I was fooling myself thinking this
was just temporary, this being sick and all. I've been waiting to wake
up and feel better and today I see that I am stuck in this life at home,
I may not get better in time to go back to school this semester and
that thought froze me in a pine tree, I grabbed the branch and started
shaking it and let all the water and ice wash down on my bare head,
and I started crying, for the first time I bawled and bawled and it felt
nice, sort of, to cry.

But there is no getting away from it. I miss school desperately and
I hate being home with my parents. I'm suffocating, my brain is
dying, all we ever do is watch T.V. I want to be back in the dorm with
Corinne going to class and even to chemistry lab, I would even
resume that stupid rat project I did last fall, anything but lying here
dead inside. Maybe I just have to push myself, I decided that yesterday,
so I got dressed and tried to walk into town; it's not that far, maybe
twenty blocks, and I got four blocks and started smelling car fumes,
so I turned right around. Thank God I didn't throw up on the sidewalk.
I waited until I got home. I am going to call Corinne tonight. I need
to talk to somebody, somebody who knows me, the old me, somebody
who understands why the new me is going absolutely crazy.

CANDACE

She is supposed to be hanging pails, but an hour ago, she snuck out of the woods and came here to the shoulder of Maple Hill. Seated on her open parka, she is shading a color pastel of Hannah. Somebody, probably Audrey, cleared a gaping hole of snow away from the top of the massive rose-colored head, and this morning's slanting sun is bathing Hannah, dissolving the remaining white beard off the marble chin and jaw.

All her life, Candace has adored this little girl. Has skirted her in play, climbed her fist-sized curls, traced her blank eye spaces, placed her face against the sleek warm silk of the marble's cheek. Allowed to roam free from an early age, Candace wandered here almost every day in summer, climbing the sculpture like a rock, scattering stiff summer grass over the head, pretending that she and Hannah shared the same salmon-colored hair. Many a warm day Candace brought a picnic here, a chocolate bar for each, and when Hannah didn't mind, which was always the case, Candace would teach her a lesson by eating both Hershey's.

"You're such a bad girl, Hannah," Candace would cry, seizing the softened chocolate and easing a square into her mouth. As the big sister, Candace tried endlessly to get Hannah to mind. But Hannah never did. She was the kind of foxy little girl that Candace secretly longed to be, somebody who despite her stone exterior, ran free in the woods, wild and screaming, naked from head to toe. This very bad child led Candace frequently into the sugar forest, where together they played endlessly. The nice thing was, in Hannah's company, Candace never felt scared. She always had somebody there, somebody who knew the woods better than she did.

Early every spring, the girls became two robins, and together, they built an oversized nest. Sticks and twigs, grass and real feathers went in, and as time went on, old socks and strips of torn rag were added by Candace, who dutifully collected them from the farmhouse. With their ragged nest assembled, Candace and Hannah turned into baby robins and laid themselves down to rest. Cocooned together, arm in arm, they waited patiently to hatch. When fall came, the two of them abandoned the nest game and gathered all the rotting apples they could hold in Candace's apron. Then they toted the fruit back to their secret forest kitchen, where they baked pies.

Candace eyes the sculpture now. She has sketched Hannah no less than a hundred times, and, under Marjory's tutelage, she painted it first in acrylics and then in watercolors and oil. But try as she might, Candace has never gotten the sculpture quite right. Long ago, she decided that it had to be the sculpture's fault: the feisty little girl simply refused to be captured. Once again, she is foiling Candace's attempts this morning.

Examining the greasy craypas sketch, Candace yawns, then crumples up the paper. Turning, she leans into the marble and makes a survey of the ridge. The world from this vantage has always been just to Candace's liking. Maybe because on clear days she can see way over to Prospect Peak in one direction, and deep into the maples in the other. Or maybe because when her grandmother and the other women were younger, they would take their summer evenings here.

Typically, the evening began about five when, the best of their artistic visions played out for the day, the women would abandon their work — wood, canvas, metal, or half-empty typewriter pages — and begin filling large baskets with goodies. Marjory might fix a delicious chicken salad with walnuts and grapes, or assemble an array of soft cheeses. Audrey would pick lettuce, cucumbers, and arugula from the garden, or if it was August, she would collect a basket of fragrant basil and it would be eaten with slabs of mozzarella and the largest and lushest beefsteak tomatoes. Francine baked warm rounds of crusty bread and pans of chocolate brownies when she couldn't write. There were times when she baked nearly every night.

The women toted the food to the crest of the hill, and laid it out on blankets under Hannah's gaze. And then, while two women — usually

Pit and Marjory — built a bonfire, the others made a second trip down and back, for instruments and three jugs of chianti, Marjory's fiddle, Pit's slender wooden recorder, and Big Martha's harmonica and guitar. Audrey always played bongos, and there were shakers and tambourines for Candace and Francine. None of the women were musicians, but after a few cups of wine it didn't matter. The music sounded sweet to everyone, except maybe to Pit, who had studied violin back in Britain. Inevitably she whispered to Candace, "Pity the poor forest creatures trying to sleep."

To Candace, it was enough just to be outside on a divine summer night, the sunlight slipping away, the sky falling into its purplish evening glow. The smell of cool forest air, and the late day colors were all around them. Everyone agreed that it was a slice of heaven being on the mountain. And then it grew dark. As clear as she recalls the stars themselves, Candace remembers lying on a soft blanket between Audrey and Pit, looking up to the big dipper twinkling and tilting in the royal sky, and Pit speaking in her best British English, "I say, Candace, do you think maybe that huge cup is pouring some kind of magic star dust all over us?" Candace, naturally, would agree, and inch closer to Pit and declare that *she* had no intention of going to sleep. But it happened anyway. She always fell asleep and the next morning, she woke soaked in dew.

Years later, she learned what she missed while sleeping. The women partied late into the night. And then, when the magic dust had thoroughly doused the whole group, and there was sufficient wine sloshing in their bellies, the women would sit in something of a circle. A few joints would go into motion and soon one or another of the women would share a tale of woe: how some man had made life a total misery.

Candace grew up knowing Audrey's story, or at least the skeleton facts, more or less by heart. Audrey, she knew, started off happily enough, married to a man named Jack. But try as she might, her grandmother couldn't have a baby. To keep busy, Audrey began painting, and against her husband's wishes, she took an art class at a local college. As it happened, Marjory was her teacher, and soon enough, Audrey's best friend. Finally, at the age of 30, Audrey had some kind of surgery and got pregnant. Candace's father, Rusty, was born, and for a few years, things seemed "normal." Audrey painted, and took more art courses and raised her son; and Marjory, who was officially godmother, was always there. For tea at first. And later, for sherry or wine or a martini.

When Audrey got pregnant a second time, though, Jack started drinking more. He complained that Marjory's highfalutin' college ways were changing Audrey. He drank harder, going for days on binges. But even worse was what he did when he was sober. Once, sitting Rusty on his lap, he pointed to Audrey's swelling belly and whispered into the boy's carrot hair, "see there's another baby growing there, that baby is Mommy's. But you, Rusty, you belong to me."

Hannah was born the day before Christmas. A more perfect baby, Audrey decided there would never be: oversized blue eyes, frosty and streaked black like her own. A single tuft of wispy reddish hair, a creamy white complexion. Within hours of birth, though, Hannah's lips turned as blue as her eyes and the doctors discovered the defect: a hole in one valve of her heart the size of a quarter. Surgery temporarily fixed the hole, but the doctors advised Audrey that in two years, the child would require a second repair.

One morning when Hannah was six months old, Audrey woke humming the baby's name. She walked the short hallway thinking how the name balanced, how it sounded like breath itself rocking in an even singsong across her tongue, *Han-nah, Han-nah, Han-nah.* When she got to the nursery and peered into the crib, she found the baby lying face up, as purple as the violets growing in the kitchen.

What happened next Candace knows, but only in sketchy detail: Audrey collapsed, cried until she couldn't cry anymore. Or move out of bed. Finally, Marjory rescued her. A year later, the Hannah sculpture was born. Audrey shared the details of how her marble Hannah came to be more than once with the women as they sat on Maple Hill on summer nights, but Candace always fought and lost the battle to stay awake. Today, maybe because of her preoccupation with her own baby, she has decided she will ask Audrey more.

By the time the women were finished exchanging their stories beneath the stars, stories in which one or another woman inevitably triumphed, nobody was in much condition to speak. The women threw more wood on the bonfire. The flames grew, and grew gigantic. Then the wild songs and 'unladylike' dancing began. One or the other of the women would pull off a bra and send it flying into the air. Inevitably, it would land in the fire. That caught on, and soon everybody was bare breasted, burning bras or underpants. While

Candace slept, safely tucked beneath a blanket at Hannah's chin, the women reveled, hollering and dancing through the woods without any clothes.

Candace looks up. She should be helping with the pails. But now she's begun a second version of Hannah, using red craypas and white. And ice blue for those haunting eyes. After a few moments of sketching, she stops. "It needs something," she mumbles.

Her attention comes to rest on her growling stomach. She ate breakfast at eight thirty, but somehow she is already empty and now the queasy feeling is back. Slipping a short tower of saltines out of her jacket, Candace takes three of the square crackers and nibbles on them all in one stack. Immediately, Eileen's diary comes to mind. At least, she thinks, Eileen and I have this in common: our upset stomachs. She reaches into her backpack to get the diary, and more saltines, wondering if, like her mother, she might start throwing up. Opening the diary, Candace bites into the cracker and begins reading Eileen's first line — "I said the last time I was desperate, and today was proof," — when somebody shouts.

"Candace!" It's Audrey, standing between the maples. With her silver hair and the long grey coat caping her shoulders, she could be a tree. Candace studies her saltines.

"Hey, you promised, honey," Audrey calls. "We've got two hundred more pails to go. And the way the weather's looking, we'll see sap tomorrow."

Candace sighs and slaps the diary shut. Rips her sketch in half.

"OK, OK," she says wearily. She pulls herself up from the parka and just before she sets off through the snow, she glances at the sculpture again, at the familiar smile playing on Hannah's lips. For a moment, Candace is tempted. She can imagine running away. Just like those summers so long ago, she can imagine escaping to a place deep in the woods, a place that that only Hannah knows.

BOILING

For three days the sap has been running and now, Audrey is in a T-shirt, standing in the white witch's brew over the boiling pan, telling Candace to keep an eye on the bubbles. "First they'll be tiny," she explains, pinching her thumb and forefinger together, "but then, whammo, all of a sudden they swell, get huge, and bust like miniature volcanoes. Then you know the sap is turning."

Candace nods, but truthfully, she is having trouble listening. She is studying her grandmother's pink face, thinking she wants to tell her about the baby. But how to begin?

"There, now," Audrey says, pointing into the pan, "see how the sap looks like taffy? We're almost there." She lifts the spoon, and a sheet of thick liquid the color of ale drips off the edge. Audrey checks the thermometer bobbing in the pan. "Quick, get a pail." Candace sets a bucket beneath the boiling pan. A moment later, Audrey has the spigot open, and out comes a beautiful line of amber syrup. When the pail is something close to full, Audrey closes the spigot and hands Candace the skimmer. "I'll filter, if you, honey, will stir."

Candace takes the skimmer. "Grandma, I wanted to ask you about something..."

Audrey is carefully pouring steaming syrup into a pail lined in white felt. "Yes dear?"

"Well, when you had your kids, did you...were you, you know, ready?"

Audrey sets the pail down, pushes her Red Sox cap back from her glistening forehead. "Honestly, honey, at this point, I can hardly remember back that far. But if you're asking was I excited. Sure. Sure I was." She frowns. "But why do you ask?"

Candace sloshes the little shovel through the sap. "Oh when I was sitting up at the rock the other day, sketching Hannah, I started wondering things."

"What things?"

"Mostly how it was for you, after you had...after you lost Hannah." She lifts the skimmer out of the pan, and flicks one large gob of yellow foam, the color of chicken fat, into a pail.

"Honey, try not to let that sweet foam fly," Audrey says distractedly. "It makes such a sticky mess under the shoes when it sails all over the place."

Candace cringes. In the sugar house, hot gooey steam turns absolutely everything sticky. Hair and eyelashes form sweet crystals. Not only that, but sugar funnels its way into the nose and even seeps into the pores of the skin, so deep that anyone boiling for long loses her taste for sweet food and craves sauerkraut and dill pickles instead.

"I mean I don't remember exactly how it was you ended up doing the sculpture."

Audrey wipes her hands on a wet towel and bends to the firebox to see if it needs wood. It doesn't. She comes to stand beside Candace at the pan. "I think it was a kind of cosmic accident. But it's an accident that had everything to do with Marjory." Placing her hand over Candace's, Audrey forces the skimmer deeper into the sap. Candace stiffens. "Here, honey, let me stir. You see, if you don't go deep enough, the sap will burn, and we can't risk that." Candace frowns. Sometimes Audrey sounds just like a teacher, which in fact she was for a time, subbing in Wilmont's grade schools.

"Grandma, I can *do* this, really," Candace says, her voice somber and discouraged.

"I know you can. But for now, I'm fine here. I'm managing."

"So, OK, tell me how it was after Hannah." Candace tugs on a strand of strawberry hair. Audrey looks up. The world inside the sugar house is timeless, a greyish white bath.

"Let's see...where to begin." Audrey raises her eyes. Sighs. "So after Hannah died, your grandfather and I weren't sure where to bury her. I was in no condition to think, I mean I wasn't sure what my own name was. Finally, I called my father here in Vermont, and asked him for advice."

"Not your mother?"

"My mother, Constance, God bless her, had died the year before. Which didn't help my state of mind at all. Anyway, your great grandpa suggested we bury Hannah here at the farm. I thought right away, yes, of course, that's where she should be, surrounded by beautiful trees. Grudgingly, Jack agreed. So we arranged to bring Hannah here, to the top of the hill."

Candace studies the froth spilling over the skimmer. Suddenly, she can see it: the tiny casket. "God, Grandma, that must have been *sooo* hard," she whispers, goosebumps shimmying up her arms. "To lose a baby I mean."

"Yes it was…." Audrey's eyes glaze. "There's no way to explain it exactly, the hole it left. Thanks be to God Marjory was there for me, because Jack certainly wasn't."

Candace has a faint picture of her grandfather in mind, but the memory is so vague she isn't even sure it's real. "Were you and Marjory, you know, together then?"

Audrey shakes her head. "Oh heavens, no, not that way, not in those days. You have to remember, Candace, this was the 1950s. And I was supposedly a happily married woman. But she and I were close. Very close. She always knew what was on my mind before I did."

"So why did Grandpa dislike her so much?

"Well, because. Because deep down he knew. I never came out and said I had fallen in love with her, but he could see. He could see how happy she made me. All I wanted to do was be with her." Audrey laughs. "The funny thing was Jack kept saying he didn't like Marjory because she was too brainy, which of course she was. Both she and her father were brilliant. Marjory went to Smith. And her father taught economics at Williams College. Jack said he didn't trust people who went to college. Oh and he made all this fuss over her being Jewish. Marjory Leibowitz."

"So…then, what happened with the stone?"

Audrey takes the skimmer in two hands. "Marjory, in keeping with Jewish tradition, sat shiva here at the farm with me for a week after Hannah's funeral. I stopped eating, had no appetite at all, and she would bring me homemade chicken broth, with fresh parsley and rice. It was June, and everything was in that wonderful bloom of early summer, and I would take your father outside, and lie on the grass and stare at the sky. I don't know what happened to time.

Finally I went home to be with Jack, but...I wasn't myself. I could barely make a meal or get out of bed. All that time, Marjory kept coming to see me, kept bringing me books and food and tapes to listen to. And she kept me company whenever she could."

Neither of them speak, and then Audrey continues. "It was almost a year later, when in Jewish custom it's time to place the stone over the grave. We hadn't put anything there except for a few flowers. It was Marjory who asked me, no, she told me, 'You have to pick a headstone.' All I could think of was a cold dead block of white marble, the kind we had placed on my mother's grave. And I remember feeling I didn't want a horrible stone like that for Hannah. It never occurred to me that there could be anything else. But I agreed to let Marjory put me in the car and take me up to Proctor, where the old Vermont Marble company is. I had been taking a sculpting course, and so I enjoyed walking through the lot, thinking of all the possibilities. Meanwhile, though, there were all these flat headstones glazed to a high sheen."

Audrey checks the thermometer, then sets another pail beneath the pan. "Just as we were leaving the place, I remember I had hold of Rusty's hand, your dad was only four, and he was standing there asking me questions about the stones, why people wanted to own such big stones, and I was laughing, trying to answer him, and we were almost out of the marble yard when I glanced up and saw this buff-colored rock. Just one edge had been cut and polished smooth, and the color of that surface was absolutely remarkable, blood-red, mottled with large jagged patches of white. It took my breath away."

Candace has an image of the marble in her mind, can see the way the sun was slanting on the sculpture's red and white forehead the other day. "I bet it was amazing, Grandma."

"Yes. It might sound silly, but honestly, Candace, that rock called to me. First the color, but then, almost immediately, the shape. I saw a face in the rock. It was inside the rock but inside me too. And I knew I just had to carve what I saw."

Pausing, Audrey flails more foam into the pail with her expert hand and disappears momentarily out the door of the sugarhouse. She returns with the empty pail. As the door opens, it squeaks and lets in a shard of dazzling daylight. She resumes skimming. "I remember the guy working there, a young fellow, he told us the marble was what they call a potato block. Champlain red, quarried up at Swanton, a rare stone. Today, that quarry is closed, all the red marble's gone. I remember turning to Marjory, whispering to her what I was thinking, and she said, yes, yes, of course you could. It took some convincing, though, because the guy wouldn't sell the block at first. He was a sculptor and wanted to cut it himself. But eventually Marjory convinced him."

Candace stands. "I guess what amazes me is how the sculpture helped you...get over losing Hannah."

Audrey shakes her head. "Oh no, Candace, you don't *get over* losing a child. Ever. You simply learn to live with it, make a place for the agony." Audrey sets her hand flat on her chest. "Hannah's death left this gaping hole. This pain. I could feel a huge cavity around my heart. In order to resurrect myself, to start living again, I had to find a way to build around it."

"I guess what I meant was..." Candace begins, but Audrey isn't finished explaining.

"...because if I hadn't done that, built a kind of scaffolding, I would have been swallowed up in the hole, in my own grief. I tell you seeing that scarlet marble was the beginning. I needed help, though. Marjory got me the tools, the chisels, all the claws and rasps you use to carve marble. But mostly she made me see I wasn't crazy. She had the rock delivered to the farm, she even called a sculptor she'd heard about, a woman near Manchester. She begged her to help me get started. I had done sculpture before, but nothing this big."

Audrey sucks in her breath, holds it. "I will never ever forget the first time I put the hammer to that stone. I felt it resist beneath the point, so I gripped the hammer harder, and hit harder, and that marble met every blow, every single ounce of force I sent in. It literally absorbed my agony, the pain that was holed up inside me." She stops skimming.

Candace crosses over to the other side of the sugarhouse, to a small dirty window covered in cobwebs. She gazes out through the murky glass to the trees, the blue sky, the neat stack of wood. "I can just see you, Grandma, smashing at that stone."

Audrey nods and leans both elbows on the boiler. Candace looks out the window, then notices something above her head, floating mid-air, silvery, iridescent against the dark brown wood of the sugarhouse. It is an amazing spider's web, a flickering globe, the finest strands organized in perfect angles, symmetrical all around the center.

The light filtering through the dirty window reflects off the web, this natural scaffold, and Candace instinctively blows on it, gently. It sways and radiates like it's alive, and full of an ethereal light. In the center of the web is a small brown spider, its appendages curved symmetrically outward. Within the web is a fly, partly bound in the fine silk of the spider. Candace marvels at the structure of the web, its depth, the strands hinged together all the way through like the most intricate net.

"So there you go, that's Hannah," Audrey says. She dips the skimmer back into the sap. Candace is watching the spider web, the fly. That the fly is so thoroughly trapped, and yet, in its trap, so wrapped in perfection, so much a part of the pulsing beauty of the web, is remarkable to her. She is enraptured, about to call her grandmother over to see the masterpiece. She also wants to say something to Audrey, to tell her how inspiring her story is, how it gives her, in her own situation, so much hope, a sense of immense possibility. Even in the depths of her despair, Audrey didn't succumb. Candace is more excited than ever to share her news with Audrey, to say that she, too, is beginning a new life. She doesn't get a chance to though, she doesn't say a thing because suddenly Audrey's shrill voice is piercing her reverie.

"Oh dear God," Audrey yelps, jumping back from the boiler. Candace whips around, frightened, certain from the sound of her grandmother's voice that she's been scalded. Candace expects to see boiled flesh, scorched hands, or maybe a badly burned face.

But Audrey isn't injured at all. She is, though, grabbing madly for the scoop, fighting back a huge fury of froth, a mountain of soft yellow foam rising over the top of the pan.

"Butter, Grandma. Grab the butter." From somewhere deep in her memory, Candace recalls other tumultuous boils, the women frantically casting butter into the frothing sap. Audrey already has the butter, and she is throwing it into the pan, and now she's at the firebox, closing it down. Candace, meanwhile, has forgotten all about the spider, her baby, all about Hannah too. She is back at the boiler, holding the scoop in two hands, using it like an oar, desperately paddling, splashing through the wild mixture trying to contain the seething ocean of froth, trying to settle it, reign it safely back into the pan.

EILEEN

March 13, 1972

Saliva is pooling quickly beneath my tongue, a sure sign that there isn't much time. But I am trying hard to be patient with my mother, so I let her keep talking.

"Italo's gives you a choice," she is saying, and if I weren't so sick, I know I would laugh out loud. "Besides the parmesan chicken and roasted potatoes, you can get the plain spaghetti, you know, just with butter, or you can get zitis with meat sauce, or with meatballs on the side. Or they'll even give you that white clam sauce with the garlic that's so good. And the price on the buffet includes a big salad and rolls and butter and soda for every table."

The whites of my mother's eyes are threaded with fine red lines. I look down, wondering whether the lines have always been there, or whether she's just been crying again. I start running my thumbnail back and forth along the fake wood grain in the brown formica table. My face is moist with a fine layer of sweat. I keep thinking I should get up, leave the kitchen by the back door, walk around the yard, go smell the pine trees again. But I'm frozen in my seat and I'm not able to think straight. "Whatever, Ma," I say, drumming my fingers on the table. My mother continues to study the menu in silence. Occasionally, she heaves a deep sigh. My nails tick sharply on the formica.

I am eating a little more these days. Cream of Wheat, jello, canned peaches and pears, pastina, scrambled eggs. Now and then I eat an apple. Last night I tried to figure out how many times I've thrown up in the past three weeks. I figure at least 87 times. But in the past day or so, I have thrown up only twice. I take that as a good sign.

Now that the snow is melting, I'm back to walking outside, breathing in the late winter air. I've decided it smells a little like the inside of a greenhouse. A smell that promises spring. I've taken to reading a chapter a day in my microbiology textbook, too. Today I stared at the twisted ladder they call DNA. I was trying to absorb the chapter on base pairs. I am determined to go back to school, finish out the semester. Mostly, I want to find John. I have to set him straight on how exactly I got myself into this mess, and how I plan to get out.

My mother, on the other hand, is determined to plan a wedding I don't want to have. She wants me to marry somebody I'm not even sure I want to see again. Somebody who doesn't have a clue that he's going to be a father.

"How can you know how you feel when you're sick as a dog throwing up," she keeps saying. "Wait till you feel better. When the baby moves, you wait. You'll feel life, you'll feel altogether different."

I don't think so. But we're both waiting. I'm waiting to feel better so I can take off. She's waiting for me to help her plan the wedding.

Only this morning, she stopped waiting. She went to see Art Italo, who owns the big Italian restaurant, the brick place my father helped build twenty years ago on South Church Street. She asked him if he could do a reception with just a few weeks' notice. He said he could, and she came away convinced that Italo's is the best Italian restaurant in the state of Massachusetts. All I know about Italo's is the smell of grease and garlic. The smell hits you in the furthest reaches of the parking lot. After you eat there, you have to air out all your clothes on the line.

She is still studying the menu. Her thick forefinger moves slowly along the scrolled red lettering. Her fingernail is yellowed, like old plastic, and the skin around it is dry, with white cracks. My mother does too many dishes. She refuses to wear rubber gloves. I stare at her nail now, and wonder how to tell my mother what I am planning to do, as soon as I am well enough to do it. She looks up, and for a quick second, we lock eyes, and I wonder if she knows already, if she heard me on the phone the other night whispering to Corinne. Or if she heard me last night, practically yelling at Rusty, telling him not to call again, or to come over. I told him I might be going away. He snorted.

"Where to?"

"I'm not sure."

"Back to school?"

"Maybe...look, it doesn't matter where."

"Yes it does. We need to talk."

"No we don't. I'm not in the mood to talk. I'm too confused."

"About what?"

"About...life. About...my future."

"YOUR future." He paused. "Only yours. Not mine?"

"No, Rus. Not yours. Mine."

My mother is watching me. Her eyes are hazel, I notice that now, a weak, watery green, the color of ocean waves in a certain warm afternoon light. Suddenly her eyes send me sailfishing again. It's last September, six months ago, that extraordinary Indian summer day when John came up behind me at my study carrel at the Rock. First I smelled his cologne. Brut. Then, before I could turn, he reached around me with both arms, breathing warm air on my neck. Goose-bumps covered me from head to foot. My hands started to tremble. Then he closed my histology textbook, stuffed it in my backpack, and led me by the hand out of the library to the sidewalk, where his beat up MG was parked by the curb. We drove out of Providence with the top down, the sun warm, the air plastering my hair away from my face.

We spent the next six hours sailing in Rhode Island Sound. The choppy water was a blinding dazzle, shifting patches of bright light. John wore white duck pants. "The pants of a prep school man," I kept teasing him. "A man going to medical school." His pants were rolled up to the knees, and his legs, like his arms, were tan, a won-derful caramel color, the color that comes from spending a summer sailing in the sun. He wore sneakers with holes at both big toes, and no laces, white canvas turned grey with use, and at one point I teased him about that, too. "Only rich boys can get away with sneakers like that." He grinned back at me, his eyes narrowed and he just kept staring, tipping his beer into his mouth, sucking more golden liquid out of the bottle.

I never told Rusty that John and I went sailing. I never told Rusty about John at all. I figured I didn't have to, at least at first. At first, what would I have said? Rus, I thought you should know I met this guy at school last spring, in my calculus class. He's a senior and he likes me, likes to take me places. We go to Boston to see the galleries, or to Cambridge for foreign films. We go to Newport to see the mansions, or occasionally we bike to Point Judith or go to the Sound, sailing. Once, last October, we drove all the way to Maine in the middle of the night so he could show me his grandmother's "cottage." The "cottage" turned out to be the closest thing I've ever come to a mansion. A beautiful old grey shingled house, right on the rocky shore. I woke up on the glassed-in sleeping porch, lifted my head off the pillow and there was the ocean, shimmering in the sun a few feet away. We drove back later in the morning, just in time to make biochemistry class that afternoon.

But don't worry, Rus, we haven't slept together.

I could have truthfully said that, too, until January 10th, about 5:30 in the afternoon. Until then, John was just being a tease. He kept insisting he had to keep his hands off me, because I had a boyfriend back home, my hometown honey, that's what he called Rusty, and when he said that, he always laughed at me, that husky, deep laugh that makes my face and neck warm, a laugh that pulls me toward him without his ever touching me.

If I close my eyes now I can see him laughing, leaning back on the boat, holding onto the main crossbar, the white sail whipping in the wind, as if it might rip apart, the sun reflecting off his round wire-rim glasses. "Why do you keep laughing at me?" I asked him that day, and I think he could tell I was irritated, because he stopped, and said, quietly, "Because I like you, that's all, I like you a lot. Can't you tell?" I shook my head no. "People who like me don't usually spend so much time laughing at me." And then he just looked away, out across the water, the swelling green waves. I wanted him looking back at me again, and talking to me, and laughing at me, if that's what he wanted to do.

When I think about it now, I suppose I looked funny, no, ridiculous, on the sailboat that day. Probably pale-faced and frightened, sitting cross-legged and seasick in the middle of the boat, holding on for dear life to both sides of the sleek white hull. I had never been sailing before, was scared to death of John's tipping the boat, sick with fear that the sails would collapse, which of course they did, that same afternoon. We went over in the stiff autumn wind and I swallowed big salty gulps of water, and flailed around, and my sneakers swelled up and my legs got heavy and ice cold and I had to wriggle out of my grey wool jacket. I can still smell my jacket in the car, the odor of soaking wet wool, as we drove back to Providence that night, staring into the clear autumn blue sky, rimmed in pink and orange at the horizon behind the cluster of tall buildings downtown.

The cool evening air blew through my wet hair that night, sent a chill through my whole body, and I huddled deeper into the bucket seat, shivering. I wanted a warm blanket. I glanced over at John, steering with one hand, staring straight ahead at the darkening road. I started to imagine him stopping the car on some little side road and wrapping himself around me, breathing on me, covering me like a warm blanket. In that moment, I even considered asking him if he would, well, wrap me up. I wanted him that badly. And what I didn't know that night, what I wouldn't realize for almost five full months (until he finally told me, at which point it was already too late) was that all I had to do was ask. That night, though, just the thought of asking made my face red. I brought my feet into the bucket seat, hugged my knees, and and bent my head forward, folding myself into a little ball. I stayed huddled like that for the rest of the trip, until he pulled up close to my dorm and kept the motor running.

"Cold, huh?" he said when he'd stopped. He covered my shoulder with his hand. I raised my head, nodded quickly and thought of reaching for his cupped hand. But by then I knew I couldn't bring myself to do it. Instead, I got out of the car, holding my jacket against my chest like a wet animal. I hurried into the bright lights of the dorm and I didn't see John again for almost two weeks. That's how it's always gone with John. We go off on some amazing adventure, and then we have no contact for weeks. Now, of course, I haven't seen him since the first part of February, two weeks before winter break. I know the day he went off for a week of skiing in Vermont was the same day I came home on the bus, starting to feel sick. Once or twice, I've tried calling him at his dorm, I've left messages, but he hasn't returned my calls. Maybe because he knows. Maybe because a rumor reached him.

"Maybe you'd rather we don't have Italian at all," my mother is saying. She eyes me, waits for a reaction, and when there is none, she just lifts her chin defiantly and begins scanning the back of the menu. "I mean, they say here they have the all-American buffet. They'll slice a side of roast beef and a ham, and they'll make baked beans and chicken. Maybe we could ask them to bake the chicken with rosemary."

Something about the rosemary triggers the switch. I'm not sure why. But with that one word, I bolt from the table and run for the tiny bathroom right off the kitchen. My aim isn't great, though, and I coat one side of the toilet bowl, part of the floor and the white wallpaper with little pink flowers in back of the toilet. My mother follows me into the bathroom with a towel. She runs it under cold water, wrings it out with two hands, and holds it against my forehead. Now she's crying again, and shaking her head, the same way she did the night I told her I was pregnant. "Madonna," she says now, her voice rising as it always does when she invokes the Virgin Mary's help. Making the sign of the Cross, she lets her head fall to her chest. I get a quick vision of her kneeling before her bed, the way she does every night when she says her prayers, her big black rosary beads knocking together in her hands, the cross swinging in the air. I look at Ma now, her hair iron grey. I want to say something, but before I can, she pushes out of the bathroom, whispering hoarsely, "Go lay down. Go on. I'll take care of this mess."

CANDACE

Candace snaps the diary shut, sets it on the night table, switches off the light. Leering at her in the dark is a strange combination of images: Eileen on a sailboat gliding through water in blinding light. And the other image, her mother throwing up in front of Lucy.

"Oh how gross." She raises her head from the pillow to see the clock. Midnight. After the incident with the boiling pan, Candace went back to the farmhouse, where she climbed into bed. She started reading the diary, but almost immediately fell asleep. She woke up for dinner, ate, and got right back into bed. And now, because of the nap, she isn't tired, and because of the diary, she is fidgety. She is more angry than ever with her mother. "She couldn't stand Dad and if she'd had a choice, she never would have had me." Over and over, she thinks these thoughts, flopping back and forth from one side to the other.

"Ah, hell," she says finally, throwing off the covers. She rifles her backpack until she pulls out a small, tightly folded piece of notebook paper. Wrapping herself in an afghan, she tiptoes downstairs and creeps silently into the kitchen to the phone. She dials.

Candace has on only a long T-shirt and no slippers. The pine floor feels cold, so she keeps lifting each foot, placing one gritty sole against the opposite soft warm thigh. For almost a month now, Mark has been camped out night and day in a studio in L.A., trying to finish up his CD. As of last week, he had only three numbers left to record, all of them jazz pieces he composed in Vermont on electronic piano the previous summer. The whole time he was writing them, sitting in the shade of the Mother Maple, Candace was lying in the grass sketching him. One of her notebooks is filled almost entirely with pen and ink drawings of Mark, in a ponytail, sitting next to the big tree at the keyboard.

Every other time she's spoken to Mark this month, he's been the one to call her. Now, though, she knows she has to call him. The phone rings twice and someone answers.

"Yeah?" It's a woman who sounds as if she was expecting the call all along, and was certain she didn't want it. Candace hesitates.

"Uh. Is Mark there?"

"Mark?"

"Yeah. Mark Sarazian. He's doing a jazz recording with Billy Platt and Lou St..." The woman interrupts. "Yeah, I KNOW who he is. He's out back. I'll switch you in." But instead of switching the call, the woman cuts Candace off. The low buzz of the dial tone fills her ear. Frowning, she boosts herself onto the counter and arranges herself cross-legged. She pulls the afghan over her head, letting it fall like a tent over her bare legs and feet. She dials again. The call goes through just as Audrey enters the kitchen. Candace peaks out from her afghan tent and waves. She has on Marjory's bathrobe and it's way too short. "Whatever are you doing up at this..." Audrey begins, but before she finishes, Candace is speaking.

"Hi," Candace says into the phone. "I'm the one who wanted Mark Sarazian? You cut me off. Could you? Yeah, thanks." Candace covers the receiver, whispers to Audrey. "I had to, you know, call him." She shrugs. Audrey nods. Candace looks down at the phone, twirling the cord around her finger.

"Hello? Mark?" She smiles shyly, and her tone is soft, as though she were addressing a small child. "Of course it's me, silly. Who else would it be?" She bites down on the nail of her middle finger and sinks into her tent, burying the phone. Her elbows rest on her knees.

Audrey takes a gallon of milk out of the refrigerator and reaches inside a cupboard for a small pan. She sets it quietly on the counter and is about to pour milk into the pan, when, glancing at Candace, she stops, puts the pan away. She takes a glass off the shelf and fills it to the top with cold milk. Then, sipping, she leaves the kitchen with the glass.

"I miss you too," Candace is saying in the same quiet tone. She glances up to see Audrey disappear. Her voice changes. "I...oh, I'm

OK, everything's fine, it's just..." She squeezes her eyes shut, and as if in response, tears rise out of the corners.

"No, I'm...uh... fine, re..re..really," she says. But now she's crying, and when she tries to talk, her voice catches, her chest heaves, and her words trail off.

"I...I...don't even know why I'm...crying," she says all at once. "I mean, I'm so happy." She smiles but then her lips fold down. She wipes her eyes with the bottom edge of her T-shirt. Rocking back, she pulls the phone to its furthest extension, and then lies down on the counter, staring up at the ceiling. The conversation isn't going like it was supposed to. She wasn't supposed to cry. And she doesn't want to continue. But she does anyway.

"Look, I'm really OK. Everything is fine. It's just that I..." Her voice breaks again, and she's shaking her head now, and she's trying to dry her eyes with the back of her hand. The more she tries to stop crying, the harder she cries. "It's just, I'm really missing you, that's all, and I had to call and tell you." By this point, she is sobbing and gulping in one crescendo after another, wiping her nose with the back of her hand.

"I'll...I'll call you back," she manages to say, and she's about to hang up, but all of a sudden Mark is saying something to keep her on the line. Her sobbing subsides, and she holds her forehead and pushes damp hair back from her brow. Her face is blotchy pink and gleaming. "If you could come, that would be great," she says in a low, tired whisper. "Yeah, I'd love it. Sunday would be fine." She clears her throat, and for a moment it sounds as though she is in control. "No, I'm OK. Just tired. Really, I'm fine." She manages a laugh. "See? I'll be telling jokes in a minute. Dirty ones, of course. I love you, too." She gets one more word out, just "bye," before she hangs up and breaks down completely.

Her face is buried in her knees, her arms are crossed in front of her and she's bawling, without even trying to stop. But suddenly Audrey is there, surrounding her, kissing the top of her head. Candace lifts her crumpled wet face. "Oh Grandma, I'm g-g-oing to have a b-b-baby," Candace sobs.

A moment passes. "You...you what?" Audrey whispers, her face ghostly.

"Yes," Candace nods, "I am. And just now I tried to tell Mark but I...I couldn't."

"Oh my dear." Audrey collapses in the chair and takes Candace's hand. "Oh Candace. I never expected to hear this. Not so soon. Not...not tonight anyway. My God, I can still see you so clearly as a baby yourself."

"No, grandma," Candace wails. "Please don't say that. Don't do what my mother does. Please. I'm grown up. You more than anybody has to see that." Her sobbing has tapered off but now she keeps catching, hiccuping against her breath.

"Oh Candace, yes, of course I see that. You are grown. It's just...it happens so fast."

"Grandma, I want this baby. Desperately."

"Desperately?" Audrey frowns. "But why honey?"

"Because I do. I just do. I love the feeling of it growing inside me. It's mine, all mine, for me to love and to care for, forever, and nobody can ever ever take it away from me."

Audrey drops Candace's hand and then stares at her own hands, cradled in her lap. "I see," she says. She picks up her eyes. "Are you sure part of it isn't to show everybody? I mean, to show...Eileen maybe?"

"But so what Grandma? So what? Yeah, so I want to show her I can do it. I want to show her that I can be a better mother than she was..."

"I see."

Both remain silent. Candace leans back and her mop of orange hair sweeps the back of the chair. "I've told Mom over and over how much I want this baby, no matter what, but she...she just doesn't understand. I mean she even suggested I..." She is crying again and covering her face with her hands.

"Oh honey don't. Come here." Candace slides off the counter and kneels before Audrey; soon Candace is folded in Audrey's arms, and Audrey is holding Candace's head against her shoulder, the way she did when Candace was a baby. "Of course you want the child. Of course you do. It's right and natural and I'm glad. And really, I'm excited for you."

Candace pulls back. "You are? You're not just saying that because I'm upset?"

Audrey chuckles. "No," she says, caressing her granddaughter's hair. "I mean it." She sets her callused hands over Candace's head, as if she's blessing her, and then gently kisses Candace right where her hair divides into two salmon-colored halves.

"Thank you, Grandma," Candace squeaks. "Thank you so much." She reaches her arms around Audrey's neck, and holds on as if for dear life.

EILEEN

March 18, 1972

The drug comes back to me in a wild dream, like it always does. Snow is falling on my shoulders and my hands. I'm catching flakes, some of them as big as baseballs, and I am tossing them in the air, throwing them back and forth to Rusty, who's laughing. Suddenly, the vision goes bad, like it did that night in December when Rusty and I dropped the acid together. The snowflakes shrink, turn to salt, and then white sand. It starts flying at me from all directions, stinging my face, so I put up my arms. I look down. The sand is swirling fast, settling, piling in a cone around my feet, my knees, finally creeping up over my naked hips, my shoulders, and face.

I worry sometimes that the drug made permanent etchings in my brain. Maybe it ate away at small but vital neurons, did away with important synapses. I think of clear acid, hydrochloric or acetic, dripping into the convolutions of my brain from a glass beaker, like the ones that smell so bad in my chemistry lab.

Sometimes it's green rice falling from the sky, but that too always ends up collecting around me, like a cone, with me at the center. The mountain is always going to suffocate me, suck me in. Sometimes I see only Rusty's stomach. In that one, I'm at eye-level with his firm taut muscles, the smooth ripples going up and down, over and over, out away from me like small shifting sand dunes. Then gradually my lips sink down onto his skin, grazing his stomach. All the energy is swirling in my mouth, the world is totally contained within the "O" of my pulsing lips. Or it's his lips, and his lips are on me, sucking at my breasts, and then my breasts swell into mountains, with me inside. Then they sink back into my tingling flesh and we're back on the bed in my dorm, rolling together, a mound of mixed-up sweaty flesh, the glaze on our skin exaggerated to a mirror, and everything is pulsing, reflected: flesh, feet, Rusty's face, magnified, monstrous against the white sheets.

When I woke up from the dream today, the light filtering through the bedroom shades was chalky grey. It's been raining, because water is dripping from one of the gutters. There's a sour taste in my mouth. I fell asleep after throwing up and forgot to brush my teeth. Downstairs, the washing machine is groaning, swishing back and forth. Somebody is talking to somebody else. One voice is my mother's. The other person, male, occasionally laughs. Gently. Definitely not my father. He wouldn't be home at this hour. And if he were, he wouldn't be laughing or talking to my mother. He'd be in the living room, watching T.V.

Lately, the drug dreams have started to wake me up in the middle of the night. The streetlight is always shining and a tree shadow flickers on the shade. My nightgown is always soaking wet. I get up to change, and then I put on my robe and creep downstairs. I don't want to face my mother with all my wild thoughts. Certainly I wouldn't want to see my father's pasty grey face. Usually, I pour a bowl of cereal and go back upstairs, sit on my bed and watch my hamsters. The two of them look like overgrown grey mice. They are sitting across the room from me in their cage. They're nocturnal, so they are more alert than ever at midnight. They sit right up, pink noses twitching, and they drink from the water bottle or nibble at their cedar shavings or make their exercise wheel turn. It squeaks.

Right now, though, the hamster wheel is quiet. The washing machine is filling for the rinse. I raise my head from the pillow. The laugh is low, unhurried. Rusty, of course. No doubt, he's sitting in the kitchen chair closest to the stove. His lanky legs are crossed, and his orange work boots, toes scuffed, are sticking half way across the kitchen floor. If he's been here more than fifteen minutes, my mother will have a plate of Oreos and a glass of milk in front of him at the table. Pretty soon, she'll ask him if he wants a sandwich.

One Friday afternoon when we first got together in high school, Rusty drove me home from school. My mother was in the kitchen, making cream puffs for a church bake sale. She offered Rusty a cream puff, then a second. Finally, she offered to make him a sandwich.

"You like pepper and egg?" she said, sponging the table. I wanted to die.

"Oh, God, Ma," I groaned. "He doesn't want a sandwich like..."

"No, no. That's OK, Mrs. Rosetti, I'd love one." Rusty, almost six feet two, stood behind my mother, smiling. He has reddish blonde hair and dimples. He waved at me so that she couldn't see. I shook my head, picked up my books and left the kitchen. When I came back a few minutes later, my mother was setting a plate on the table. On it were two thick pieces of her homemade bread with a crusty splatter of yellow egg and green pepper in between. Rusty finished it in less than five minutes.

"Can I help it if your mother takes pity on a starving boy?" he said later. His own mother has been gone three or four years. Ever since Audrey moved out, Rusty and his father have been living on T.V. dinners, take-out Chinese, and endless quantities of pizza.

I pull myself out of bed. My T-shirt is damp. I tear it off, put on a clean flannel shirt, one of two I took from my father's closet. I try to zip up my jeans, but my waist is too thick. I don't want to go downstairs, so I take the top off the hamster cage and I try to wake up Nixon and Agnew. At Christmas, I brought the hamsters back with me from Brown. I wasn't supposed to have them in the dorm, but I had to buy them. I walked downtown to a pet store in Providence one Friday afternoon in a snowstorm last December, just before finals. I had been killing white rats all fall for my independent study in physiology. First I would inject each of the rats in the back of the leg with blue dye. Then, a few days later, I would operate on the rat, to see how well the dye traveled from the sciatic nerve up through the nervous system. Not too well, I found out.

I learned that semester that I'm not the world's best rat surgeon. Several of my chunky white patients never made it, especially after I held the little cotton balls with chloroform over their noses. Those rats are ugly, truly ugly, with red eyes and long, ringed tails. Still, I couldn't bear the thought of them dying at my hand. I was so glad when the semester ended. I told John I wouldn't dare think of being a surgeon after that. Maybe I'll go into family practice. Pediatrics or podiatry.

I descend the stairs. As I come through the living room, I can see the back of Rusty's head. In the last year, Rusty has started to let his hair grow. The curls cover the collar of his denim jacket. But compared to some of the guys at Brown, who have long pony tails, Rusty's hair is short.

He turns, pulls himself up straight in his chair. His smile fades, and he drops his elbows to his knees, stares right at me. He looks sad. Three Oreos are left on the plate. Half a glass of milk. Next to that is a long white box. I stop at the entrance to the kitchen, lean my head against the doorframe.

"I told him you were asleep," my mother says. She's at her post at the stove, stirring.

"I woke up."

"So how do you feel?" he asks, quietly. Politely. I shrug, avoid his look. He holds the white box out to me. I take it, slip the satin ribbon off. Inside are a dozen tea roses, pale pink. Each of the flowers tapers gently, and the tips of the petals curve back on themselves. The first time Rusty and I ever made love, he bought me the same bunch of roses. Suddenly the roses, the way they curve back, their color, make me think of tiny ears. And suddenly my throat swells up. I feel angry. I don't want to start crying, for God's sake, but here I am, crying nonetheless. Rusty is going to get the wrong idea.

I set the roses on the table.

"Look," I say, wiping my nose with my flannel shirtsleeve. "You should take these. Take them back." Rusty is shaking his head. "No," I say. "Really. I really want you to take them." I can't believe that I can't stop crying. I'm not feeling sad. I am NOT feeling sad. Mad, maybe. Confused. But not sad. But lately I can cry over just about anything. Even soap operas and sappy T.V. commercials.

"I thought you might want to go up the mountain. Just to walk." In high school, we used to climb Mount Greylock "to walk." That was code for "making out."

"No, I don't think so, I'm so...you know, my stomach is just..."

"Empty," my mother says, placing a bowl of steaming soup on the table. "Eat this." I hesitate for a moment, staring into the spinach and bread crumb soup that she calls stracciatella. I pull the chair out, sit down. Rusty moves his legs aside to make room for mine. The soup tastes good.

I eat, gazing out the window. The sky is blank, without color. It's been that way, it seems, all winter, since I came back.

"It's cold out, isn't it?"

"Not that bad," Rusty says. "Mostly windy." My mother adds a plate of bread, some cheese. "Thanks, Ma," I say softly, wishing she would go away. She must get the message, too, because she unties her apron, signaling that she's done in the kitchen. After she goes, Rusty stands up, sticks his hands in the front pockets of his jeans, leans against the counter. His long legs are crossed. Besides being tall, Rusty is well-built. Powerful shoulders. Lean torso and hips.

The first time I saw him with his shirt off, he was working for my father on a split-level house just outside of town. That was three summers ago, when Dad hired Rusty and a couple other guys from my high school to work on roofs. One day, I drove out to the site to bring my father his lunch. Rusty was standing on a steeply sloped roof, in denim cutoffs and boots. He had a dark tan, which ended right at the waistline of his cutoffs. He had that sly dimpled smile. I suppose that's part of the reason why I never told him to stop visiting me last fall at Brown. Even when I knew for sure I wasn't into the relationship anymore, I was still into sleeping with him. Because it felt good. It felt good to wake up with every part of me pasted against him. Just that. And it felt good, after a week of classes, and long hours at the library, to look forward to Friday night, late, when he would arrive, and pull me down on top of him on my bed. All that felt good.

I hear my mother's feet slowly scuff up the stairs. Rusty says nothing. Just stands there, jingling keys.

"Rus, I don't mean to be difficult. Or to hurt you." At that, he snorts. "No, really, I mean that."

"OK, so don't hurt me then."

"It's just that things seem so...so..."

"So what?"

"So...hopeless, I guess." I'm not sure that's the right word, so I say it softly.

"Hopeless?" He seems surprised. But annoyed too. "Hopeless." He gives me a dirty look.

"Yeah. I mean, to me anyway." He's silent and the lower part of his jaw is shifting side to side. Finally he talks.

"I wanted to show you something. Out in the truck."

I sit there. "What is it?"

He shakes his head. "You have to come out. Get a coat." He's standing by the table, lifting me by the hand. "Come on. Please." I don't want to. I even shake my head no. But he's pulling me up and forcing me to go with him.

❧

Even with a coat and sweater, it feels raw in the truck. There is a faint smell of oil. He turns the ignition, lets the truck run. Then he reaches underneath the seat, brings out a long white roll of paper, held by a skinny elastic. He hands it to me.

"Open it." I look at him, and shimmy the elastic down the roll of paper. The elastic snaps as it falls off the end of the roll. Three sheets of paper are rolled together. The top one curls inward, has a blue drawing. I can make out a roof, windows.

"What is it?"

"What do you mean, what is it?"

"OK," I say. "It's a blueprint."

"Right."

"Of what?"

"A house. Or maybe a whole series of houses."

So why should I care? I stare at him.

"Don't you want to know whose design it is?"

I shrug. "Sure. Whose design is it?"

"Mine. I did it myself." I look at the blueprints again. They look extremely professional. Even the sharp, angular handwriting looks like what an architect would do.

"I didn't know you...could do this." He smiles.

"I didn't tell you. But I'm taking architectural drawing over at the college."

"Rus, this is neat. Really. I'm impressed." He reaches over, removes one sheet.

"Wait. You haven't seen anything yet. This is the best." He points to the roof.

"What are those things?"

"Solar panels. The design is built around solar. Now look at this." He points to something on the second sheet. The papers curl up. "This is a fireplace, right in the middle of the living room. It's huge, ten feet across. Fieldstone. For solar storage. Passive energy."

"Where did you learn that?"

"There's a guy at the college who's trying to start a solar energy business. He's convinced we could team up, build solar-heated houses together. But it was my design."

A scene flashes before me. It's last fall, maybe late September. A Saturday morning. I had just come back to my dorm after taking a shower. Corinne was talking to Rusty, who was up for the weekend.

"You think you'll regret it?" Corinne was saying.

"Regret what?" I said, closing the door, interested. Neither of them answered right away.

"Not going to college," Rusty said finally. I looked at him. He could have gone. He was smart enough. And he had good grades, at least until sophomore year in high school. That was about the time everything happened with his mother and father. Having Audrey walk out threw Rus for a loop. But then, when he found out his mother had moved in with her girlfriend, that they were "queer," he almost flipped out. He said he couldn't leave his father, or North Adams. He was afraid his father might drink himself to death.

I took a towel to my wet hair, then started combing it. I could see Rusty's reflection in the mirror over my dresser. He was sitting on my bed, his back propped against the cinder block wall. His eyes were down, his lips were pressed together, protruding a little, the way they do when he's thinking. Or when something's troubling him.

"I don't think every person in America needs to go to college." That's all he said. And Corinne, thank God, knew enough not to say anymore.

But other people in my dorm didn't. People like Candace Patterson, that New York snob who plays the viola every afternoon just before we go to the dining hall for dinner. She has those haughty eyes, half-closed, and that glamorous dark hair, almost black, like mine, but styled, like the actresses in Charlie's Angels on TV. Anyway, she waltzed into my room the Sunday after Thanksgiving when Rusty had just brought me back to school. He and I were sitting on my bed. She asked how the weekend was, but didn't listen to the answer.

"Well, did you bring 'em or not?" she said, and Rusty, when he realized she meant the drugs he had been promising her, shook his head no. She turned to go, but before she did she made a vicious remark, about how maybe she'd "do better getting the stuff from a local towney," implying of course that Rusty was a towney, too, only he was from another town.

She cornered me the next day. "Why isn't Russell in school?"

"His name isn't Russell," I said. "It's really Paul, but because of his reddish hair, he's always been Rusty. Or just Rus. Not Russell." Candace rolled her eyes.

"Anyway," I continued, "he isn't in college because he doesn't want to be. And he doesn't have to worry. He's got a high draft number." That worked for a while. But then one Friday night she and I were in the first floor lounge at the dorm while I was waiting for Rus.

"Doesn't your friend get bored working a blue-collar job?" she asked. I squirmed in embarrassment. "I guess not," I mumbled, "or he'd do something else." After that, I tried to hide Rusty whenever he came to visit.

I'm thinking about this as I roll up his blueprint. I feel guilty now that I let other people's opinions of Rusty affect me. "These designs really are incredible," I say, quietly. The elastic breaks, so I just hold onto the roll.

He's smiling, and now he slips the truck in gear and starts driving.

"I asked your father whether he would consider putting some solar houses over near the mountain, in that Greylock Homes development he's building. Passive solar. There's no doubt, that's the wave of the future." I glance over at Rus. He is absolutely serious about all this. And he is happy, proud. I look back out the window. The sky is pewter-colored in the direction we're going. He's heading toward the mountain, I know. I don't have the heart to tell him that I don't want to go.

The snow is patchy on the muddy pastures. Corn stubble sticks up through the snow like broken matchsticks. Everything is black, white and brown. Rus and I are both quiet as Greylock's wide grey mass comes into view. Closing my eyes, I picture a golf course in Georgia, or California. I imagine mountains and cliffs, and palm trees, and ocean water changing from green to emerald to blue.

"I want to know what's bugging you." My eyes snap open. Rusty has the windshield wipers on. The sky has a menacing patch ahead and a fine mist is icing up the front window.

No, you don't, I want to say. *I'm thinking about California. I'm thinking about the fact that Corinne says I can live with her this summer in Berkeley. I'm thinking about John, about the fact he will be driving his convertible across country to San Francisco.*

The truck slows. Rusty looks over at me.

"For chrissake, Eileen, tell me what's going on." I look over at him. In a strange way, I like the fact he's finally getting mad. It's so much better to have him angry than to have him look sad, or hurt, like he did at the house. Almost pathetic, like a puppy.

"What do you want to know?"

Rusty is staring straight ahead. Out the front window, I notice a small dead animal, lying crushed on the side of the road. Dark brown fur, fringed in black. The bloody carcass is split wide open, flat, red and gooey and pasted to the road. Another car passes us, lays on the horn. We're going too slow.

"I told you, I want to know what's up with you, why you're not back in school."

I exhale. "You haven't figured it out."

The truck slows further. Rus shoots a look at me.

"No." He continues staring. I return the look. "What?" he says. "Tell me."

"OK, then," I say, "I will. Pull over." He drags on the steering wheel and the truck moves sharply over to the side of the road. Another car honks and swerves around us.

"I'm pregnant," I blurt out, before he even shuts the engine. He watches me, that's all. He just watches me, as though he's going to see something miraculous happen, like maybe the baby will be born right here, right now, on the front seat of the truck.

Finally, he speaks. In a deadly quiet whisper. "How long were you going to keep this a secret?"

I look out the window. "Oh, I don't know. But you don't have to worry about anything at all. I am taking care of it. Myself."

"You mean?"

"No, not that. I could never have an abortion. The idea terrifies me. I guess I know too much biology. Besides, I wouldn't be able to live with myself. The old Catholic guilt."

"Good."

I glare at him. "What do you mean, good?" My tone of voice is ice cold.

He shrugs, apologetically. "I'm sorry, I just meant, I'm just glad...look, I just wouldn't want you to have to go through an abortion. That's all."

Silence descends. I am thinking about my mother reading Italo's menu again. The rosemary. I look down at the roll of white paper in my lap.

"My mother wants us to get married. She's ridiculous. I mean she even has the wedding menu all planned out." I chuckle. Silence again.

"Well, it's...an idea. Getting married."

My head snaps up. "Oh Jesus, Rus. It's an idea all right. An idea that's really stupid and won't work."

"Why not? I have a job, or at least I will, soon enough, I mean if these houses work out the way I think they will, I bet they will take off and I'll be in a position to..."

I am shaking my head faster and faster. "No, Rus. No-o-o-o. Don't you see?"

"Don't I see? What? Don't I see what?"

"Don't you see I'm not..." My voice falls into a whisper. "I don't want to be married." What I don't say is: not to you, anyway. We sit there, each staring a different direction. I try not to think what his face looks like. I don't want to see the puppy again.

"So, then, what exactly do you intend to do?"

I laugh. I mean, it's not the least bit funny, nothing could be less funny in the whole world, but I laugh anyway, uncontrollably. And then, hearing myself, I cover my mouth. Rusty grabs the blueprints out of my hand. When I turn to him, my mouth still covered, he's watching me again, but this time with an expression of anger and fear. More fear.

"Eileen, I could see us getting married. I could. I really would do everything to make it work. But you know, when it comes down to it, I could care less about actually being married. I mean look at my parents. My mother. What the hell. Why get married? I really don't care if I ever get married. It's basically a stupid thing to do. It sucks, OK? Is that what you want me to say? Fine. But I still care about you. And this kid. This is my kid, too. Did you think about that, even for a minute? I know things are crazy for you. But I just don't get you. You think this isn't totally strange for me too? I mean, for chrissake, you're pregnant. What the hell are you going to do about it?"

I set my top teeth against my bottom lip. I wait. "I...I want to leave."

"Leave." He says the word as though he doesn't know what it means. "Sure. Leave. And go where exactly?" He's challenging me and I don't like it.

"Well, first I want to go back to school. Finish the semester."

"But you're sick, aren't you? You've been puking your..."

"No," I say cutting him off sharply. "I'm better. I'm not throwing up so much now."

He looks out the window. "OK, fine. So you're only puking once a day. So you go back to school that way. Fine. Then what?"

"I'm thinking about some things for the summer."

"Some things? What things?"

"Look. I don't want to talk about it now. I don't need to...I don't have to tell you about any of it." I see his eyes open slightly, and I think for a second he's really mad, maybe mad enough to hit me. He takes a breath, squeezes the blueprints tighter. Then he tosses them on the dashboard and they open up.

"Fine. Fine. What do I care? Hey, why should I worry if you're not? You think I'm going to lose sleep over this? He shoves the truck in gear, gets us back on the road, and now he starts driving, fast, much too fast. We drive that way, in silence, the rest of the way up to Greylock. When he finally stops the truck, next to one of the trails, he reaches under the front seat and takes out a small baggie, some rolling papers, and quickly puts together a joint. He licks the end. Lights it. I sit there, my legs crossed, waiting.

He inhales, his eyes squinting, and then looks over at me, holding in the smoke. He offers me the joint, but I shake my head no. The joint makes me think about the LSD. I hadn't wanted to try it. But he begged me. He had put the yellow capsules in a little box, actually wrapped the box and attached a red bow. "It's your Christmas present," he'd said. I told him I was too scared. I had smoked dope before, but I had heard too many weird things about acid. I didn't think I could handle it. He just laughed. "My own mother's taken it, for God's sake," he said.

And that, oddly enough, was what finally made up my mind for me. Thinking about Audrey. If his old lady could take LSD, then I should be able to handle it too. I swallowed the capsules right after supper. I was up the rest of the night, the whole next day, and the following night. All I remember are waves passing through the white walls of the dorm. I remember feeling cooped up in the dorm, but frightened of the gigantic snowflakes outside. I remember begging Rusty to hold onto me so I wouldn't disappear into one or another of the little holes in the cinder block walls, black holes that kept opening up into giant chasms.

For almost two days, I forgot who I was. And more important, for one night, I forgot my diaphragm. Well, not exactly. I got it out of the beige plastic case, and looked at it, and thought how much it resembled the round plastic swimming pool I had as a kid. I set it down on the night table near my bed, and thought about putting it in. I also thought about pouring water into it, to make it into a little swimming pool. And then I imagined myself diving into it, floating around on my stomach doing the frog kick. And then it seemed so amazing that I would be floating in something that was actually inside me. So part of me thought I had put it in. And the other part of me promptly forgot about it altogether. Until the next morning, when Rusty wanted to make love again. I couldn't remember if I had it in or not. Then I saw it sitting on top of a pile of wet Kleenex. We had had sex two or three times during the night.

Looking at Rusty now, inhaling again, I realize I am so angry with him I want to scratch his face. For bringing the acid to Brown. For getting me to take it. For wrecking my life.

"I...think...I really...want to go home," I say, slowly, quietly. It has started raining again and the raindrops sound like needles hitting the metal roof. Rusty doesn't respond. "Freezing rain," I say. "The roads will be bad." But it isn't the rain, or the roads. I want to leave because I'm afraid I may cry or scream or worse, I'll hit him.

My eyes are closed as the truck starts moving. I focus on my breathing, the deep "belly" inhalation the Yoga teacher at Brown was always talking about. I listen to the rhythm of the windshield wipers. I'm starting to feel calm when, with no warning, I'm jolted forward, then jerked toward the door, as the truck hits something, hard. I open my eyes to see a deer glancing off the front left fender. Then it's skidding across the road. The worst thing isn't the blood on the animal's brown coat, or the dazed look in the deer's dark eyes. The worst thing is the sound of the hooves scraping on the asphalt, and the legs, awkwardly splayed like broken toothpicks, sticking out at unnatural angles. The deer finally comes to a halt at the other side of the road, in a heap of legs. Then the animal raises its head, reaches forward, feebly. Blood drips from its mouth.

"Oh, God," I scream, my hands over my eyes. But Rusty is already out of the truck, crossing the deserted road. I slide over, am just about to get out.

"Stay there," he yells, crouching by the deer. "Pull the truck around." I slip into first, do a U-turn, park right next to Rusty and the deer. He reaches underneath the animal's backside, tries to lift it. The deer is too big and bloated around the middle. He can't get a good grasp on it. I jump out of the driver's side of the truck. The rain pinches my face.

"Is it..dead?" I ask.

"God, how should I know?" He changes his grip on the deer.

Grunting, he tries to lift it. But he only manages to move it a couple inches off the ground. The legs dangle. The belly is too swollen. Then I realize. Maybe the animal is...

"Damn, it's heavy." He exhales loudly. I bend over beside the deer. Its eyes are wide open, glassy, unfocused. There is no sign that the animal's chest is moving. The long ears, soft at the edges, are perfectly still. I slowly reach out, touch the deer's neck, wondering where the aorta might run. I remember how it felt to set the razor-sharp scalpel into the rat's white fur, piercing the skin. This close, you can see that the deer's thick fur is a mixture of grey, brown, and black hairs. The belly is pure white. My hamsters are almost exactly the same coloring. I stroke the deer's coat, then move toward the belly. It's definitely bloated, as if there might be another smaller body inside. The deer doesn't respond to my touch.

"He's gone," Rusty says, softly. I keep stroking. I run my hand over the white fur. I open my hand, press the flat of my palm on the biggest part of the belly.

"No," I say. "I don't think..."

"Oh come on Eileen, of course he's dead," Rusty says, now irritated.

"Rus, give me a chance to finish. What I was trying to say is I don't think the deer is a he. It's a doe." What I don't say is, she looks so bloated I think she's pregnant. Rusty stands.

"Well, whatever. It's dead. Come on. Let's get going." For a moment, I think we can't just leave her here. There must be something else to do. Cover her, at least. But that's absurd. I stare into the deer's eyes. They are looking straight ahead, up the road, but from where I stand, the eye closest to me reflects back nothing but the bleak white sky.

Audrey X

The rain begins as a gentle patter, but by the time Audrey wakes at four in the morning, it is rattling the roof like nails. The alarm is a swarm of bees at the back of her head. She is up, and has shut the clock off before Marjory stirs. In the bathroom, she turns to the mirror and touches the saggy grey pools of skin beneath her eyes. She looks awful, but that is no surprise. Yesterday, she stood by the boiler for almost eleven hours. Bending to the sink now, she joins her hands and cups ice cold water to her face. Then she holds it with a towel.

Back in the bedroom, she sits on the bed, ready to pull on her khakis. It is so dark she cannot see her legs. Audrey is careful to be quiet, but suddenly, Marjory is rolling over.

"Ooh, you're just coming in?" Her voice is husky.

Audrey laughs, a single short sound. "No. Actually, I was just going out." She drops to the pillow, then sidles up against Marjory. "Except maybe," she says, exhaling, "I should reconsider. I feel like I could sleep for a week."

Marjory yawns. "And so you should." She circles Audrey's shoulders, holds her there. Audrey rests her head over Marjory's heart, is listening to the steady beat, is enjoying it, when suddenly a vision of Big Martha, tending the boiler, floods her head.

She disengages from Marjory's grasp. "I can't let Martha down," she says. "It's not fair." Swinging her legs to the floor, she reaches to the night table, switches on the light. "I was up before. About midnight."

"My God, Audrey. Why?"

"Well, first I got up for milk, I couldn't sleep. And then I stayed up for Candace. She was…upset. She couldn't sleep either, so finally I convinced her to get dressed and go up to the sugar house to join Martha."

"Why was Candace upset?" Marjory yawns as she paws both eyes.

Audrey pulls on her khakis and then reaches into the oak dresser for her rag sweater.

"That information, my dear, you will have to get from her."

"Sounds serious."

Audrey sighs, puts her head into the sweater and then emerges. "Yeah. It is." She sits back down on the bed. "I'd better go."

"Audrey?"

"What?"

"You should see yourself, honey. You look dreadfully pale. "

"Gee, thanks, Marj. But I have already seen myself. Scary, I know."

"So then maybe I should go up, and you should go back to sleep."

Audrey shakes her head. "No."

"I could wake Francine. For a change, she can take a turn babysitting the pan."

"Oh, sure. And then what do we do when the sugar house burns down?"

"You know perfectly well Francine can handle boiling just fine. She whines is all."

"I'm going, and that's the end of it." Audrey bends and lays her lips gently on Marjory's forehead. Marjory reaches up and lifts a stray hair from Audrey's face.

"There is something you *can* do, though," Audrey says, rising from the bed. "Maybe you could come up around eight, and bring those Ball jars I washed. We could put away some syrup for the house. Then I'll come down for a nap. After breakfast."

"Fine." Marjory slithers down under the covers again. "Who's on pails today?"

"Well, Rus said he'd be here by seven to help." Audrey shakes her head. "But I'm telling you. Without Pit, we are seriously short-handed."

Marjory's eyes snap open. "Well, then, maybe it's time we hired somebody. You can't keep going at this pace, Audrey. And neither can anybody else."

"OK, so maybe we will hire someone. We'll talk about it later. Now go to sleep. And dream about me." Audrey smiles, squeezes Marjory's shoulder, and snaps off the light.

In the kitchen, she goes to pour herself coffee, but the pot is cold. Francine forgot to plug it in. "Dammit all." She fills the enamel teakettle with water and sets it to boil. Then she takes a jar of instant coffee from the refrigerator and heaps two spoonfuls into a mug.

Outside, the rain is falling in thick sheets. She snaps on the porch light and considers the backyard from the kitchen window, wondering if she should wait for the rain to ease up. She hates to be late. But then, unlike Francine, Big Martha doesn't count each minute on her shift. She plays the radio, or brings her headphones and tape player. She claims to lose track of time tending the pan, and listening to Bob Wills and the Texas Playboys.

Of all the women, Martha is by far the easiest to live with. When she moved in, she volunteered to take the smallest bedroom, the tiny one on the first floor, right next to the kitchen, which according to Audrey's great grandfather's journal, was originally a big pantry.

"Living in the pantry makes perfect sense for me," Martha had said. "I mean who else in this house thinks so much about her stomach?" In exchange for having the smallest bedroom, Big Martha took over a second floor walk-in closet and turned it into a dark room. Lately, she has started travelling to a few shows to exhibit her landscape photography.

Audrey takes her lidded coffee mug into the mudroom, peering out the back door. The slanting downpour is rapidly dissolving the whaled humps of snow. Setting her coffee cup on the floor, she turns to the line of pegs beside the door. Beneath several wool jackets and Pit's long down coat, she finds her plastic green poncho, stiff and wrinkled. She flaps it open and slips it over her head. With her coffee and a flashlight, she sets out, folding her face down to avoid the cold rain. It drums hard on her back and shoulders and the top of her head. A chill sets immediately into her skin. She descends the stairs, the rubber soles of her sneakers squeaking into the wood of the steps.

Moving swiftly across the backyard, her feet squash into mud and puddles. Icy water floods her toes. She glances up occasionally, following the trail she knows by heart. A small core of flickering light is thrown forward by the flashlight. At the ridge, she cuts left into the trees. The rain eases slightly, thanks to the white pine branches overhead. Huddling over, she places her feet carefully into the slick forest floor. She looks up just often enough to make sure she is keeping to the trail.

When she is almost half-way to the sugar house, she walks a little too far to the left. She has been thinking about the taxes, and Pit's emaciated face, and Candace's news about her baby. And then she is thinking, angrily, about the fact that it's always up to her to set up the schedule in the sugar house, to see that the boiler is covered around the clock. Suddenly, she looks up, flashing the light around her. The trees are too close. The darkness and rain and the swirling mist swallow the light. She retraces a few steps, then flashes the light again. The trees open up a bit, but she's still in the wrong place. She climbs over a small rock, and then, with her left foot, she steps onto a larger one. Her sneaker slides, and her arms fly up. Coffee sails in all directions and the flashlight falls into the darkness face down. And then she, too, falls backward, landing heavily on her tailbone. Pain sears through the small of her back, and she yells.

She is lying on her back, a large rock jutting into her buttocks. "Oh God," she cries, trying to steady her breathing. Her heart flutters. Her right knee hurts badly, and suddenly she realizes her right foot is stuck beneath her buttocks, lodged against the big rock. The rain is pelting, battering her fully exposed face. She tries pulling herself up, but the pain in her back and knee is too much.

I am caught here, she thinks. I am limp and helpless, a small mountain covered by green crackling plastic, a heap of flesh pinned to the forest floor. Taking a deep breath, she releases it slowly. Her heart seems to be going faster. Her right wrist is throbbing. It hurts, severely, and her shoulder blades are both tender. One thing, though. She isn't cold. That much she is thankful for. So she fills up her lungs again and tells herself to release the air even more slowly than before. She will remain calm, she tells herself, and she will remain calm some more, and sooner or later, she will be able to move. Hopefully. Or if not, she prays that before too long, someone, Marjory, Rusty, Candace, someone, will come looking for her in the forest.

CANDACE

The door on the sugar house faces east, so when the sky starts to lighten, when the black swell of darkness begins to give way to silvery grey, Candace is watching it happen. She stands in the open door, leaning against the doorframe, staring at cords of rain spilling a few inches from her face. Occasionally, she pokes her hand out, severing the falling strips of water. The rain splashes her skin, soaks into her shirt, coins dark spots on her blue jeans. Then, as if she's teasing the water, she skips back into the doorway to escape the downpour. Overhead, the drenching rain sounds like ropes beating against the roof.

Candace yawns. There is a comforting blaze of heat on her back from the boiler and a cool mist of outdoor air on her face. Her skin is slightly sticky, finely coated in sweet. Sugar is settling into her pores, Candace is sure. Because she is hungry again, thinking about breakfast, but what she wants is wheat toast, poached eggs with salt, and especially, something sour. Maybe home fries with vinegar, or salad, or...suddenly she knows exactly what she wants to eat. For God's sake, she is actually craving a dill pickle.

Swiveling around, she walks to the boiler, where Big Martha is scooping thin yellow froth from the surface. In a few minutes, it will be time to draw. Again. Candace enjoyed the boiling, sort of, the first day. But now, she would rather not do it any more. She's bored, and now she realizes it isn't just a pickle she's craving.

"You don't have any cigarettes, do you?"

Big Martha looks up, an exaggerated expression of shock taking over her wide face.

"Of course I don't," she says, in a scolding tone, and Candace feels a twinge of paranoia. Does Martha know? Does she think it's horrible for a pregnant woman to smoke?

"Audrey would have a fit if we smoked up here," Martha continues, bending to read the thermometer. Candace returns to the open door, stretches her arms up, fills the frame. The rain is easing. Sticking her hand out now, she feels a thin web of moisture, nothing more.

Candace is down to three or four cigarettes a day. She had intended to give them up altogether, and she probably would have except, ironically enough, for Eileen. Candace has been smoking more in the last couple of weeks since she found out about the baby, and since she started fighting night and day with Eileen. The two activities — smoking and battling Eileen — seem, in Candace's mind at least, to be directly linked.

Thinking about Eileen, Candace feels sad. Reading the journals, she has had a strange reaction: she keeps wanting to fix something, to make things right for her mother. But how? "Grandma ought to be here by now," she says, forcing herself into another train of thought.

"Yup, she's late alright." Candace can hear the weariness in Martha's voice. "But she worked so hard yesterday. And last night." Martha shakes her head. "Look, when you get down to the house, see if you can't get somebody else to come up here, maybe Marjory." She lifts her cowboy hat. The rim has pressed a ring of sweat in her hair.

"Yeah, sure. So I guess I'll go then. Are you sure you'll be alright?"

"Me? I'm fine. I've still got a sandwich and plenty of coffee." She grins. "And one and a half of those yummy cinnamon buns."

Candace heads toward the door.

"Before you go…" Martha holds her arm out. "Here, take these." She is smirking mischievously. Candace opens her hand, not at all sure what's being given. She looks down. On her palm, Martha has placed two cigarettes, and a book of matches.

"If you dare tell Audrey I brought cigarettes up here, I'll come after you." She winks.

Candace smiles and hurries out the sugar house door. The morning air is bitter but at least it isn't raining now. She walks for several minutes, then pauses on the trail just before it pitches downward. Ripping a match from the book, she strikes a squat flame, cups it and lights up, inhaling. Her eyes narrow, and there, without any warning, her mother's face roars to life again: they are having another argument, or more correctly, the same one, in still another form.

"So if you have the baby will you still finish school, I mean, at least would you want to try?" Candace happened to be looking out the kitchen window, seeing only darkness, then her own image reflected in the glass. Her head was spinning.

"I don't know, Ma," she said. "I just don't know." She left the kitchen then, went out to the garage and lit up. Standing in the dark, her arms wrapped tightly around her chest, she stamped her feet up and down to keep warm. Afterward, she walked around outdoors trying to take the odor out of her clothes. It didn't help. When she came in, Eileen looked up from the newspaper she was reading at the kitchen table. She trained her eyes on Candace crossing the kitchen.

"What did you have, one, or was it two cigarettes out there?" Eileen's stare was endless and dark and her hand was cupped against her forehead in the shape of a chalice, one like the priest always held aloft in St. Anthony's during communion.

"Ma, I don't want to talk about it," Candace said softly, sweeping across the kitchen, her hands deep in the front pockets of her jeans. "Sometimes I just don't wanna talk about it."

"Well, I do," Eileen said, snapping her newspaper and rising so quickly from the table that she tipped her chair backwards. For a moment, until Eileen caught it, the chair threatened to fall onto the floor. "Young lady, you had better come back here this instant." Candace stopped, swiveling only her head. She saw Eileen blush, and her lower lip start to tremble. Candace recognized that trembling lower lip: inherited directly from Papa Frank. He had the same shaky lip when he got mad. How odd, Candace thought, that a little thing like a quivering lip would get passed on from father to daughter. Eileen was pointing a finger at her now. Candace looked at the ceiling, then at the back door. Anyplace but at her mother.

"What?" Candace whined.

"What do you mean, 'what?' 'What' is the cigarette you just smoked. If you think you're going to live in this house, and if you think you're going to keep that baby, then you are damn well not going to touch another cigarette. One thing I get paid for, remember, is to make sure that kids like you don't do stupid things when they're pregnant. And one of the stupidest things is smoking cigarettes. You of all people ought to know better."

It was true. One of Eileen's main responsibilities working for the County Health Center was to run a program for "at-risk" pregnant women, mostly unmarried teens or young women like Candace. The back seat of Eileen's car always had a box filled with colored posters or tri-fold brochures, all of them warning pregnant women not to smoke.

As she stood there watching her mother and thinking about the posters, Candace lifted her tongue under her top lip so that her lip protruded. She used to do that as a child. She used to stick her tongue out at her mother all the time this way, only now she did it without thinking. And the thought of it, that she was doing it again, out of some deeply ingrained body memory, made her laugh. And then, because she knew all too well the danger of laughing at her mother, she pivoted on one foot and disappeared from the room.

Later that night, Eileen made Candace throw the rest of her cigarettes out. She made her promise, too, that she wouldn't buy another pack. Candace had kept the promise. Sort of. She hadn't bought another pack. But a few days ago, at school, she had been dying for a smoke, so she bummed a cigarette in her environmental issues class.

With the cigarette dangling delicately between two upturned fingers now, she steps sideways and bent-kneed into the steep trail. This section has lost all its snow, but it is narrow and there are slick wet stones and deep ruts. Occasionally, her boot heels slide forward. Once she grabs for a branch to steady her descent and finds it and once she grabs for a branch that isn't there and her legs separate on the gravel and she almost stumbles but catches herself.

A woodpecker is knocking close by. Candace looks up but can't locate the tree where the bird is perched. All of the trees are locked in mist. A smell is coming up from the forest floor, an earthy smell that is at once a mixture of rotting leaves and rapidly thawing soil returning to life. The smell always promises something; Candace wouldn't be able to put into words what that something is, but the feeling isn't unlike the expectation she has about the baby. It offers to fill her life with some clear purpose, to bring some satisfaction out of ordinary body experience.

Just as she thinks that, the cigarette smoke circulating through her mouth and nose twists down toward her stomach. She has, after all, eaten nothing for hours and now the taste of the cigarette is foul. She is just about to fling the smoldering butt aside when she hears something, some human sound, a mumble of words coming faintly through the mist, incomprehensible at first. She stops altogether, braces her foot against a patch of moss just off the trail. The first thing she thinks is that this might be a trick, her imagination. Maybe, she thinks, I'm hearing things, imagining my mother's own voice reprimanding me for puffing three damn times on a cigarette.

But soon the voice becomes clearer, and she is drawn down the trail toward it, the sound so familiar and yet so strange, the tone gentle, almost weak, and yet persistent, reciting a string of words, singsong, something like a prayer ringing through the air. She stops again, listens more closely. This time she hears the voice clearly, rising out of the mist. Could it be? It sounds to her like Audrey's voice, yet strangely altered, Audrey almost as if she were drunk, or, if not drunk, then very, very tired.

"The woods, lovely, so lovely. Dark and deep. And promises to keep. And miles and miles to go, miles and miles and miles to go before I sleep. And no I cannot sleep, mustn't, must keep, must keep awake." The voice trails off and then a moment later resumes again, "Some say fire, some say ice. Ice. Ice is nice. But from what I've tasted of ice, no, desire, I hold with those who favor fire. But if I had to perish twice, in ice, no, twice, no, two times."

"Grandma!" Candace screams, stepping off the trail. Stopping again, she listens.

"I think I know enough of hate, to say, to say, what, to say what... what...what fate..."

"Grandma, answer me. Where are you?" Candace can see no more than ten feet ahead of her, but the voice can't be much out of that range. The voice has stopped dead, and the only sound is Candace's boots crushing twigs and branches. Candace leans her head toward that place where she last heard the voice.

"Oh, here, over here. Right here," the voice beckons, weakly.

"Keep talking, Grandma, just keep talking," Candace says.

"Here, I'm right here, oh thank God, Candace, I thought no one would ever come."

And then Candace has the lump of grey and green in view, she sees Audrey collapsed into the forest floor, the green poncho a cloak camouflaging her body, the hood covering her head, only the silver braid protruding, like some unnatural weed or vine, a whorl of silver growing out of the dead matted leaves and snow.

"My God, Grandma, what happened to you?" Candace drops down beside Audrey, pulling the hood back, revealing her grandmother's face, white as mashed potatoes.

"Oh I fell, I lost the trail somehow...I've never done this, but it was so wet and dark, I fell, what a foolish thing, and here, now, my right foot is stuck, can you help, maybe move me so I can get..." Candace places her hands under her grandmother's armpits, tries to take hold of her, to slide her onto her side, to move her great weight off her behind, and her right leg. But just when Candace thinks she has enough grip, enough leverage to push, her grandmother lets out a shriek and Candace lets go. Audrey collapses back to almost the same position.

"It's...the ankle or the leg or, oh boy...it hurts...s-o-o- badly, it must be...broken or," and now Audrey is weeping. Candace has never seen her grandmother cry.

"Shh, shh, shh, Grandma," Candace whispers, "it'll be OK, I'll go get help. I will." Candace wipes Audrey's tears with her sleeve, and now Audrey clings to Candace, holds onto her shoulders as though she were drowning and Candace were a life ring. "Please don't cry Grandma. You'll be OK. But I better go, right now. OK?" She strokes Audrey's head, feeling she might cry herself. Audrey lets go and settles on one elbow.

"Go," is the only thing she says, nodding. Candace passes her hand gently across her grandmother's forehead. She rises. She doesn't get more than two steps, though, before she turns back and peels off her jacket. Dropping to one knee, she lifts Audrey's poncho and tucks the jacket around her grandmother's shoulders. "Here," she says, patting the poncho back in place. She kisses her grandmother's cold wet face, and then races off for help.

CANDACE

Candace wakes before dawn the next morning, before the alarm goes off. Yawning, she sits up, keeps seeing her dream: a man she knows well has escaped prison, is eluding authorities by disguising himself, getting away, all the while saying, "I'm not guilty, I'm not guilty." And it's true, he's not guilty, Candace knows this, and it seems others do too, it seems as though everybody knows he has been falsely accused of some unexplained crime. Even so, Candace keeps telling him, "Stay put, stop hiding, stop running away."

Just before waking, she gets a final glimpse of the man, in a mug shot on the front page of the newspaper. The photo shows a "wanted man" — young and scruffy and badly in need of a shave. In an interview, the man said he had only one goal in life: not to get caught, not to have to take responsibility for something he didn't do. Suddenly Candace claps both hands to her open mouth, her yawn caught in horror. Of course she knows the man in question. It's Mark. She has been having an awful dream about Mark, and she knows why, too. Because he will be here later today. When she phoned him yesterday and told him about Audrey's fall, he said he wouldn't wait until Sunday.

Candace pushes the covers aside, drops her feet out of bed. The floor is freezing, the temperature dropped all during the day before, dropped more at night. When she and her father pulled into the driveway last night, coming home from the hospital, the steps were icy, which reminded Candace about the sap turning to ice in the pails. She had promised Audrey as she stood by her narrow bed in the emergency room that she would be up early, that she would check every pail, that she would take Audrey's place at the sugar house.

"We'll do it, Gram, don't worry," she said, holding Audrey's hand in both of her own. "We'll get the run done without you. Promise." Audrey lay in a cloud of silver hair, spread around her on the pillow. Dazed by painkillers and muscle relaxants and by the trauma of lying wet and cold for hours on the forest floor — Audrey had nodded weakly.

"Of course we'll do the run, we'll all pitch in, we'll get neighbors if we need to," Marjory said, matter-of-factly stroking Audrey's temple with the backs of her fingers. Audrey turned slightly in Marjory's direction, and then she just lay there, blinking. Suddenly, a tear started down Audrey's cheek, and when it was half way to her chin, Marjory caught it in a kleenex. Audrey's lids dropped shut, and soon, her mouth open slightly, she began snoring.

The doctor set Audrey's ankle in a cast about 4:00 in the afternoon. The X-rays beforehand had taken forever, or so it seemed to Candace, waiting outside the emergency room. The magazines on the table in the waiting room were horrible, yellowed editions of *Yankee* and *Country Life*, many missing their covers. There were a few children's books, dog-eared and crayon-scribbled, a soda machine that had eaten four of her quarters, and there was no television. A nasal singsong voice kept coming through the loud speaker. "Dr. Bandow, six oh three, Dr. Bandow, six oh three." At one point, just after her father came back with club sandwiches, Candace put four chairs together, stretched out and fell asleep until the doctor called out "Mr. Burdett, Mr. Burdett please." Candace woke, her cheek pressed into an orange plastic chair. Jumping up, she heard the doctor talking to her father, discussing "the multiple fracture."

"It's a rather serious break," he was saying. "She'll have the ankle in a cast for six to ten weeks, depending." The doctor wore green scrubs, and a stethoscope and a mask dangled around his neck, but what Candace noticed most of all were his teeth — perfectly even — and his smile — dazzling. By contrast, her father's look was wild: his hair, free of its pony tail, was hanging long and grey and tangled. "We see nothing in the X-ray, but she's complaining of pain above her tail-bone, so we'll schedule her for a cat scan later today."

"So she has to stay then?" Rus asked.

"I'd say one day, for observation. As soon as we get her into her room, you can go up." Marjory, meanwhile, was with Audrey, had stayed by her side ever since the EMTs freed her from the mud and icy rocks, and moved her gingerly onto a stretcher in the woods.

Candace is in the bathroom now, brushing her teeth, wearing Audrey's sky blue bathrobe. After she got home from the hospital, Candace had taken an extra long shower, then wandered downstairs in her nightshirt. Martha was lying on the couch, the newspaper over her head and an empty sherry glass lying on her chest. "Hey, Martha, wake up," Candace said, shaking the older woman's arm. But after a couple of unsuccessful tries, Candace covered Martha with two afghans and let her sleep on the couch. Still not sleepy herself, Candace had gone back upstairs to Audrey's room, where she sat on the bed, feeling lost and vaguely afraid. That's when she spied the blue bathrobe on the back of the door, where it always hung on a silver hook shaped like a maple leaf. Candace slipped into the robe, then took it back to her bedroom and laid it on the end of her bed. Having it there, covering her feet, made it easier to fall asleep.

Candace tries to look out the bathroom window now, but it's frozen over. The ice has assumed a beautiful fringed pattern on the glass, as if a mass of frozen white ferns were caught clinging to the pane. The temperature is awfully low, Candace thinks, meaning the sap must be ice in the pails, and maybe by now the sap in the storage tank is frozen solid, too. Turning back to the sink, Candace splashes water on her face. Her eyes are swollen, as though they are closing on their own. And the dream about the prisoner is hovering, too, just behind her eyes, promising to return should Candace put her head on a pillow.

At the first pail, Candace wiggles off the small roof, tries to take hold of the handle above the spout. Her mitten sticks to the mound of ice rising above the top of the pail like a snow cone. She picks up a stick, jabs it into the frozen sap, but the stick snaps like a wooden match. Digging into the leaves, she finds a sharp rock, hits at the ice around the spout. The handle still won't budge. "My God, this is stupid," she mutters, throwing the rock down. Leaning one shoulder against the grey bark, she grabs the pail with two hands. She puts all her strength into pulling on the pail and soon it comes free, but so, too, does the spout come flying out of the tree. The pail falls, and Candace almost falls with it.

"God *damn* it!" She slams the rock against the ice until the spout comes loose.

She drops to the ground and then, hearing a sound, looks up. Rusty is driving the gathering road in the truck. He stops, rolls down the window. "Are you up to this?"

She squints. "No," she whispers. "I'm not. But I figure I've got to try anyway."

"Look, I promised I'd help Suzy fire the kiln, and then I gotta see a guy about cabinets for a sixty-thousand-dollar kitchen. But if I hurry, I should be back by early afternoon."

"Sure. Look, Dad, is there a screwdriver or something in the sugar house, something I could use to dig these spouts out of ice?"

"There should be one up there," he says. "But Candace. Please don't go putting a hole through your leg, or your hand."

With the screwdriver and hammer Big Martha finds for her, Candace sets to work freeing up the next spout. She taps a few times on the handle of the screwdriver, and the metal shank sinks easily. Ice crystals spit out. Removing the screwdriver, she sets it into the ice again a few inches away, makes another hole. With three or four holes on each side of the spout, and one in front, she wiggles the pail free. She sets the pail aside, goes to the next tree.

Three hours later, though, she has only succeeded in freeing up eleven pails. And each one is heavy as hell to carry. "Martha, there are eight more pails out there and I'm going to have to ask you to bring them in," she announces after her third trip back to the sugarhouse. "After my next trip, I'm finished carrying pails, at least for today."

"Sure thing," Martha says, putting wood into the firebox. "I'll be glad to come out."

At the next tree, Candace slams on the hammer, driving the screwdriver in securely. Pulling the screwdriver out, though, the shank snaps in half, leaving her with just the clear yellow handle. *Dammit,* she says, *dammit.* Yanking the shank out of the ice, she presses her back against the tree and sinks slowly to the ground, holding the broken screwdriver.

She closes her eyes, and Eileen comes to mind. Eileen calling the sugaring *silly, backbreaking work.* Eileen calling Audrey *crazy.* Eileen saying Audrey *is living in a time warp, thinking she can live off maple syrup.* Thoughts of Eileen give Candace a second wind. She won't let her mother's attitude toward the sugaring become her own.

Getting to her feet, Candace remembers she hasn't told Eileen about Audrey's fall. She should call her mother today, but then what? Candace would have to defend this ridiculous decision to stay, to collect and boil ice. Eileen will simply insist that Candace come home. No, she won't call. She won't say anything about Audrey's accident until she gets home. Standing, she pokes the broken metal screwdriver idly into the ice of the pail.

That's when the sound begins. A sound like a chainsaw. It is all around her, but it is not a chainsaw at all. It is a motorcycle. Mark is riding up the gathering road, swiveling side to side. Clouds of grey smoke are rising out of the rear wheel, so great is the resistance put up by the muddy road. From time to time, he sets a boot alongside the bike, steadying himself, trying to stay upright. Just a few feet short of her, he bounces to a stop, swings half way around so that he is almost facing downhill.

Candace crosses the distance to Mark in two long steps. Her hands touch briefly on his shoulders, thick in black leather, and then she claps either side of his helmet and sets her open lips on his warm mouth.

"Get on," he yells, motioning her to the seat behind him on the bike. The noise is too loud to hear, so she points to a pail top-heavy with ice.

"Bring it," he yells.

She laughs, the first time in days, weeks, maybe. Picking up the pail, she hoists her right leg over the leather seat, settles herself, then pulls the cold pail protectively to her chest. "This is ridiculous," she says, laughing again, leaning against the backrest of the bike, both arms tight around the pail. The cold of the metal sinks quickly through her sweater, into her skin. Mark turns, sticks a finger into the ice, tastes it, makes a funny face. Revving the engine, he turns to face her and kisses her forehead, then takes the bike in a wide bumpy circle. The rear wheel chews into the road, but soon it pops free and they are going ahead up the hill in a wildly unsteady ride, as the bike jerks forward, moving in fits and starts, Mark's feet grazing over the frozen ground.

CANDACE

Just before they reach the steepest section of the gathering road, Mark twists the front wheel of the motorcycle to the right and cuts the engine. "Last stop," he says, turning. He takes the pail from Candace and sets it down. "My God this is heavy."

"You got that right," Candace says, lowering herself off the bike. Mark grabs her waist. Laughing, she pulls away, then faces him and knocks on his helmet. "Take that foolish thing off so I can see you." He lifts the helmet over his head, and instantly, her mouth drops. His dark hair is shaved so short that his scalp looks grey.

"Wh...where'd all your curls go?" she says in mock horror, touching his brow.

His face widens into a smile. "I'm growing them here on my chin instead." He points to a ragged beard. Swinging off the bike, he takes hold of her shoulders and presses her to his jacket. Dropping his face to hers, he cups her jaw and kisses her softly on the mouth.

"You should never stay away so long," she whispers.

"Four weeks isn't exactly a lifetime," he says, and she steps back, looks into his eyes. Oh but it is, she wants to say, it is indeed a lifetime, or at least time enough to discover one life. She decides she will tell him everything right away, as soon as they reach the top of the hill. She will tell Big Martha that she has to take a break, that she hasn't seen Mark in almost a month, that they have some catching up to do.

"So anyway, I wrote you a song," he says, running the tip of his thumb across her lips.

"You did?" She whispers, smiling. "What's it called?"

"You'll see," he says mysteriously. "When I play it for you."

"On piano?"

"Maybe. Maybe not."

"I wanna hear it." She pulls on his arm. "When can I? This afternoon?"

"Sure." He juts the toe of his boot against the pail. "Anyway, what's with this ice?"

Candace shakes her head. "It's stupid, really stupid. I can't believe we're doing it."

"So why are you?"

She twists a strand of hair. "For Audrey. When she fell, we told her we'd sugar."

"Since when do you boil ice?"

"We don't. I mean not usually. This — the pails freezing — hardly ever happens. But the season has been strange this year, a disaster really. The women won't make a dime. And that's bad. Very bad." Candace picks up the pail. "Anyway, I'm glad you're here."

"So am I." He takes the pail and they start up to the sugar house. "How's Audrey?"

"OK, mostly. But her ankle is a wreck." They round the corner of the grey shack. A curl of grey smoke rises tentatively into the sky. "I'd feel like a jerk leaving now, like I was abandoning everybody in their hour of need. And yet..."

"Yeah?"

She inhales. "Part of me thinks I should get the hell out of here."

When they push open the sugar house door, Big Martha is down on her knees in front of the boiler, blowing into the firebox. Pit is asleep in the rocker.

"So Martha, you're still boiling, then?" Candace says.

"Oh well, trying." Martha's face is bright red. "But my fire keeps dying." She eyes Mark. "Well hello there, Mr. Sarazian. How nice to see you. Especially today. I hope Candace has persuaded you to stay and help us tote pails."

"Sure," Mark says, setting his helmet on a shelf. "Glad to."

Candace shoots Mark a dark glance, one he doesn't see. They both begin speaking at once. "Actually, Martha," Candace starts, "I had hoped that he and I could..."

"It's fine with me," Mark says calmly. "We just rode the bike up here carrying a pail."

"You rode up this hill on your motorcycle?" Pit asks from her chair, chuckling. She coughs and spits into a Kleenex.

"We did," Mark says. He grins. "It was great. Hey, Pit, long time no see."

"Yes," Pit replies. "And you can see what a long time has done to me."

Mark silently fingers his gold earring. Before he can speak, Martha changes the subject. "If I was 25 years younger, I'd like nothing more than to ride up and down the hill with you on that bike." She laughs. "But I think we have all the wheel power we need in Rus's truck. Assuming of course he comes back. His plan for today is to establish pick-up points for pails alongside the gathering road. What do you say?"

"Sounds fine to me." Mark unzips his jacket. "God's, it's a regular sauna in here."

"Yes it is," Martha says, jabbing at a block of ice in the pan. "I say it takes a real man to stand up to the heat in this place." She takes her hat off and wipes a rag over her face. "And just wait. You'll get a lot hotter pulling those ten-ton frozen pails. Right, Candace?"

"Right," Candace mutters. "Welcome to the Ice Age."

By noon, the sun is warming the air. The sky is powder blue. The dark trees stand at right angles to their shadows, splayed in stark relief on the forest floor. A brigade, made up of Big Martha, Candace, Francine, and Mark, has spread across the sugar bush, each person carrying two pails at a time, all pails headed in one direction, to the road, where Rusty drives them up the hill. He is parked now, about half-way up the road, the truck belching blue smoke out one end, and from the window blares "Lucy in the Sky with Diamonds."

"Oh hark, I think I hear old-timers' music," Mark calls out, a pail in each hand.

"If I could, I would step outside and make you eat that remark." Rusty has his elbow on the open window. "But you see, the brake on this clunker is so old, I don't trust her."

"Oh right," Mark says, snickering. He's holding the pails over the back end, about to set them down. "You sure it's the truck Rus? Maybe it's just you who's too old."

Rusty guns the truck. Mark is left holding two pails in mid-air.

"I'm glad you're having so much fun," Candace says glumly, appearing with a single pail that keeps knocking against her knees. She's flushed. Mark circles her shoulder.

"Hey, honey, what's wrong?" he asks quietly. "When you're in a bad mood, I can tell you know. I can almost smell it. Here, give me that." He takes Candace's pail.

"I want to hear the song you wrote me," she says, pulling a water bottle from her pack.

"You will, I told you. But not if you're in a cranky mood. Maybe you should tell me what's wrong." Eying him, she tips the water bottle, drinks, dries her mouth with her hand.

"Not until we're alone." Without another word, she heads back into the woods.

Late in the afternoon, Candace is lying on the ground, just outside the sugarhouse, contemplating the crown of a tree. The wind is strong, strong enough to set the tree gyrating. She wishes she had her sketch pad, her charcoal pencils, because she would love to capture this upside down angle on the branches, the view clear up to the top of the tree. She sighs. She has carried enough pails for one day, and now she is going to lie here and wait for Mark, wait to say what she needs to say.

She sits up. Twigs and leaves cling to her sweater, and the seat of her grey sweatpants is soiled dark and wet from sitting on the ground. Lunchtime was a long time ago, and her stomach has that hollow, burpy feeling back. If Mark doesn't come pretty soon, she's going to have to go back to the house and get something to eat. Pushing to her knees, her feet, she walks to the gathering road, and takes a seat on a large rock.

She has rehearsed so many ways of breaking the news to him, has tried out a dozen ways of telling him, and each one works, at least in her mind. But when he finally emerges from between the trees, when he's finally walking toward her, smiling his kind, understanding smile, she forgets all that she has rehearsed. She simply stands, approaches him, takes one of the pails he's holding and without any warning, spills the news out just as though she were pouring ice cold sap onto his shoes.

"Mark, what would you say if I told you I was pregnant?"

"I'd say you were crazy and you shouldn't joke about things that aren't funny." He lifts a speck of bark off her cheek. She looks at him, not smiling. His smile fades.

"Cand, you aren't serious."

Her head goes up and down. "Yes. I'm totally serious." He looks skyward, and she can see his eyes, as dark as crows. She can see the whites of his eyes and the strange smoky spots that discolor the whites. Once he told her that only Armenians have those spots, but she didn't believe him. She still doesn't.

"How long have you known this?" His voice is a hoarse whisper.

"Oh...a while." She looks at her boot, shuffles it in a wad of slimy brown leaves.

"A while? What's a while?"

"A while. I...uh...I found out for sure the night of the accident."

"*The night of the accident?* Shit, Candace. That's almost three fucking weeks ago. How could you know and not tell me?" He turns, presses a fist against his teeth.

"You were away, remember?"

He spins around, sticks a finger in her face. "Yeah, sure, but I was in reach of a phone, for chrissake. I could have come home."

She continues to shuffle in the decaying leaves, but now it's the other toe. She looks up at him, her eyes squinting. Her voice comes out softly. "Mark, why are you getting so mad?"

His mouth drops, and his head starts bobbing, as if attached to a spring. "Why am I getting *mad?* Because, Candace. I'm getting mad because you just made the most incredible statement possible. You're pregnant, and that means I'm pregnant too, and you've been keeping it from me for a month. I think I'm entitled to be mad. I'm totally blown away."

She has a lot of things to tell him, but now her throat aches and it feels like it is rapidly swelling, starting to close. Sucking on her bottom lip, she stares out into the blank trees.

"How many weeks?" he asks.

"How many weeks?"

"Yeah," he says impatiently. "How far along are you?"

"Oh, I guess about two months. Yeah, I'm just starting into my third month."

"Well, so, then at least we've got time." He relaxes a little. "But still, we need to talk. Are you...what are you thinking about doing?"

"Doing?" She repeats the word mechanically, then turns, fear gathering in her eyes.

"Well we need to figure out something, don't we? I mean, what are the choices and..." Candace suddenly wants to cover her ears tightly, because she is hearing Eileen. It may be Mark standing here with her, but he might as well be Eileen, because he is talking just like Eileen, referring to choices, and soon, he will be weighing the differences between those choices, just the way Eileen did, weighing options a few nights ago. Candace hated hearing the word "options" then, and she hates much, much more hearing the word "choices" now. She squeezes her eyes shut, wonders how she will possibly keep from crying.

"Candace, do you really want to...I mean, are you...are we really ready for this, Candace?" But she seems not to be there. She's staring off into the trees, her eyes locked open, glistening. He sets a hand gently on her shoulder, and speaks kindly, the way he normally does. "Honey, come on. Talk to me...I mean, what are you thinking? Tell me. This is complicated, but you know, I'm willing to listen. It's just, you see, don't you, that we really need to be ready? I mean you just can't suddenly be...parents." He shrugs helplessly.

She wants to say yes you *can* just suddenly be parents. People do it every day. She wants to say that even if he's not ready, she is, and if he's not, then he should be. She wants to say I hate you Mark and please go away and take that song you wrote me with you. She wants to say I feel great about this baby, whether you do or not, whether you care or not, and if you don't care, then screw you, Mark, I hate you all the way to hell. She wants to tell him she will never speak to him again, and she won't hear him talk about an abortion, because she won't consider having one, because she wants this baby more than anything else in the world. She wants to say all that, or some of it, but she can't get a single word out because the ache in her throat has swollen into a gigantic dam.

"Candace? Honey? Come on, talk to me." But she doesn't. Instead, she drops the pail, abruptly. It narrowly misses her right foot before it tips, and sap drains out into dank black leaves. She pauses next to the pail for a moment, then sets her toe against the bottom and sends it flying across the gathering road. The pail rolls to a stop, clanging against a tree. Almost immediately, the faded red truck climbs into view, its engine working too hard.

Candace turns, sees her father's pickup. Covering her mouth, she hurries off.

"Come back, Candace, we need to talk!" Mark takes two or three steps after her. But she turns and gestures for him to stop, and the look on her face is so awful, so menacing, that he does stop, he lets her continue down the gathering road alone.

As she runs, her feet coming down hard on small rocks, ruts, clots of ice and snow, she realizes that it never occurred to her that he would get mad. All along she was expecting him to be thrilled, she kept telling herself that he would greet her news by lifting her in the air, twirling her around by the waist, racing her so fast in a circle that her head would tip back, her hair would billow out in a single flat wing behind her. She would sail for at least a few moments, fly there in the space of his arms, suspended. He would end up covering her face in kisses, and telling her over and over again how much he loves her.

It hurts to run, it feels like a weight is attached, dangling from her bottom. She stops now and then, bends, even crosses her legs. Soon enough, though, she starts running again. Because if she's running it's harder to think, she's distracted, focusing on one hurt instead of another. Tears are flooding down her face. By the time she reaches the backyard she's bawling, and it doesn't matter because nobody is around to see or hear.

As she races around the front of the farmhouse, she eyes the Mother Maple. The tree jogs her memory, reminds her of the endless times she raced around the tree as a child. That always made her happy, deliriously happy. She especially loved it when she and Hannah were together doing rain dances or just prancing in frenzied circles around the tree. Stopping now, she sets her fingers into the deep rivulets of grey bark, then slips her arms around the maple. Even now, she can't circle the tree the way she always wanted to. She can barely get her arms halfway around. Her face comes to rest on the bark. It scrapes her chin, the skin of her cheek. It has always been important to have this tree, to pretend it was hers, well, hers and Hannah's. But now, all that seems foolish, long gone. A bit of bark chips off and falls onto her lower lip. Her face is slick with tears. She is crying so hard that even the inside of her ears are wet, dripping. How ridiculous, she thinks. How can I be standing here, hysterical, hugging a goddamned tree? She scrapes her forehead back and forth against the bark until the skin stings and starts to feel raw.

MARK

Mark is sitting on the floor cross-legged, like a yogi, his shaved head tall, his back perfectly flat and all but resting against the sugar house door. He inhales, smells more of winter than spring in the cold night air. His eyes are closed, and he keeps seeing Candace as she was this afternoon, almost crying, jogging awkwardly down the gathering road.

"You know, you really are free to go," Big Martha says, wiping a jar. Working together, she and Mark boiled for four hours, producing twenty-six jars of warm syrup now lined up on the shelves.

"Thanks," Mark says, his eyes snapping open. "But if it's OK, I think I'll just hang here a while."

"Suit yourself," Big Martha says, looking sly. "I just hope your honey doesn't think I'm the one detaining you."

"Oh, my honey trusts me," Mark says.

"Of course she does. But does she trust me?" Martha winks. "Anyway, I closed the arch down tight, but before you leave, you might check the fire once more. Do you want this light on?"

"No, thanks, I'd rather it be dark. Just leave the door open."

Martha snaps on a flashlight and pulls the chain dangling from the light bulb over the boiler. She steps past Mark out the door. "By the way," she says, turning. "You were great today, Mark. Thanks."

"Oh sure," he says. "Glad to help out."

"Candace is a lucky girl," Martha says. "But I guess she knows that already." She smiles, heads downhill. Mark watches the wobbling flashlight disappear between the trees. The only light now is the dim fallout from the crescent moon and the bright pinpoints that are the stars. He closes his eyes again, but this time he sees Candace up close, her face morose and crumpling just before she raced off.

Sighing, Mark pulls himself to his feet and reaches for a shelf. He gropes in the dark until his hands land on an empty pail. He seats himself again, cradles the pail upside down between his knees and gently drums the bottom with his fingertips. He begins with an easy rhythm, hits tentatively at first, producing just a light flutter against the tin. Soon, though, his wrists bend sharply, and his hands are coming down hard in rhythm, full palms slapping the pail. Leaning over the grey metal, he concentrates on a complex riff, then goes back, tries to repeat it from the beginning, extending the rhythm a new way.

A few minutes later, he moves outside, into the clearing behind the sugar house. The night sky floats like a sparkling veil overhead, a veil that is knotted in the pines half-way down the hill. If it were daytime, and clear, one would be able to see through this wedge of sky to the purplish blue mountains over in Prospect. But there is nothing to see tonight. Mark stares idly into the fathomless divide, and resumes drumming. Before long the pail is singing, the metal rings out a rhythm that puts him into a trance. For more than an hour he drums, his hands dancing on the pail, stinging, turning numb.

He might have continued drumming all night, except that at some point, with no warning, he slipped into a slower, steadier rhythm that felt completely familiar, comforting, and yet, at the same time, deeply disturbing. Soon he realized why: out of the drum, and his hands, came a persistent pulsing that mimicked exactly the beat of a human heart. As soon as he heard the beat for what it was, he jumped to his feet and threw the pail aside. The seat of his jeans was soaking wet from sitting on the ground. Dazed, he started quickly down the hill, the sky turning light. At the horizon, there was a rosy stripe setting the stage for sunrise. Only then does it occur to him that the stars have disappeared, that he can hear the throaty squeak of birds, and that he is staring squarely into the slate grey dusk of morning.

CANDACE

She is lying half-asleep on the bed imagining that she can hold her breath until she turns blue. She tries to do it, draws in a breath, holds it, wills herself to hold it, longer, longer, longer. But each time, she manages not to breathe for only a short while, maybe 45 seconds, a minute at most, after which she exhales in a small explosion, then ravenously fills her lungs again, desperate for air. Sitting up, she feels dizzy. Only at that moment does it occur to her that passing out is probably not such a good idea for the baby. Horrified, she imagines the baby turning blue, its face smudged the color of a dark bruise, its lips pinched white. She sees the fetus turning to marble inside her. Frightened, Candace lies back on the bed, crosses her arms tightly over her head. Tears inch down her cheeks.

She falls asleep that way. When she wakes, one of her arms tingles, her hand is creased and painfully numb, and the room is darker than it was. Staring in confusion at the blank wall, she tries to shake her sleeping arm awake. She thinks of Mark and immediately tries to make his face go away. What comes to her instead is a new view of the wall. All of a sudden it is a sea of pink flesh. And floating in the rosy ocean is a tiny egg, diaphanous and white. What this vision is, she isn't sure, and what it means, she cannot say, but at least now she no longer wants to hold her breath. She no longer wants to sleep. She finds the vision so marvelous and exciting that she wants to paint it right away, right there, right on the wall where she is staring and seeing it all so clearly in her mind. She sits up, rises slowly to her elbows, her knees. She pushes away the quilt.

Wearing only her underpants and a T-shirt, she crosses the oak floor, barefoot, crouches to her backpack, squashed in the corner of the bedroom next to her mud-caked boots. She gathers her paints, heaps them on the bed, turns to the wall. All she needs now is a chair, a pail, water, a big wet sponge. She remembers: a sponge in the bathroom beneath the sink.

She applies the color swiftly and almost right away, it reminds her of pink insulation, the thick fluffy stuff her father used to lay in the attics of old houses for customers. In a moment, she is back to being eight or nine years old, and she is sitting cross-legged in the attic of a narrow old Victorian on a hill in North Adams, and it must be Saturday afternoon, for otherwise she wouldn't be with her father, and it must be winter, because her back is warmed by the brick of the chimney rising through the attic. Her father is hunched over a roll of insulation, the pink contained between plain brown sheets of paper. Every so often Candace looks up from coloring a page of Cinderella, from a pink-tiered gown, or an orange pumpkin, or a blue and silver coach. She watches her father push the bulky roll across the wooden attic floor, exposing the fluff. She watches him slash his knife through the insulation, the blade flickering in the single bare bulb of the attic. Then, lying on his stomach, the backside of his jeans covered in dust, he grunts and swears and reaches into the eaves, using a broom handle to stuff insulation into the furthest reaches beneath the floorboards.

The rosy hue brings her back further, too, takes her to pinpointed memories of the cotton candy she used to love. When her father would drag his gleaming blade through the thick pink layer of fiber glass, Candace would think with longing of summer, of the little church fair that Grandma Lucy used to take her to each year at St. Anthony's, the fair where only glazed apples and soft cotton candy were sold. Both, Grandma Lucy said, were guaranteed to rot Candace's teeth. Both were ordinarily banned. But once a year, at the fair, Lucy broke her own rules, permitted Candace the cotton candy, a lesser evil apparently than the red-shellacked apples.

Maybe because it was normally forbidden, the fluffy candy held a certain fascination for Candace. The sweet pink cotton seemed to grow magically in the giant metal vat where it was spun. It emerged out of air, all of a sudden it was just there, whipped into a fairy-like froth that danced in a circle and clung to a slender white paper cone. Candace loved the feeling of the sponge on her tongue, loved the way it dissolved and stuck to her lips, loved the soft touch of it, too, as she nipped small shreds of it off with her fingertips.

She has completed painting the bottom half of the wall when someone knocks.

"Yeah?" Candace is standing on the dresser, considering where she will place the yellow cushion, the nest for the tiny white egg.

"Candace, are you gonna eat something tonight? It's after eight." The voice belongs to Martha. She thought it might be Mark.

"Yeah, just...save me a plate of something."

"Can I come in honey?"

"Mmm...no, not right now. I'm...kind of...tired. Busy too."

"Is everything OK?"

"Sure," Candace says.

"Is something up with you and Mark?"

"No." Candace points her bare toe on the dresser.

"Then why did I leave him in the dark up at the sugar house just now looking so depressed?" Silence. "Come on, Candace, why don't you just open the door?" Candace steps from the dresser onto the bed and then down to the floor. She crosses to the door, opens it slightly, revealing only one blue green eye.

"Martha, I'd rather be alone right now, if that's OK."

"Fine. Just tell me, what's going on with you two?"

Candace studies the floor. It occurs to her now that she has far more mothers than she needs. "Please, Martha, I don't want to talk about it with anybody. Not right now."

"OK, OK, but if you change your mind, honey, just say so. When Audrey's not around, you know, I'm the one in charge."

Candace tries to shut the door, but Martha is talking once more.

"Hey. I smell something. Paint? Are you...are you painting in there?"

Candace exhales. "Yes. I'm painting. And...I'd really like to get back to it."

"Fine, fine. I'll tell Francine to save you something." Candace closes the door.

The wall has dried. When Candace eyes the color, she is horrified. It looks more orange than pink and it certainly doesn't look a thing like the idea she had in mind. She drops onto the bed, pulls the quilt to her chin and stares in disgust at the wall. Tomorrow, she'll just have to take a roller and paint over this mess. Turn Audrey's bedroom wall back to white.

The thought of all that work for nothing makes her tired. So tired that her arms and legs suddenly feel laden with cement. She is hungry too, so hungry she's hollow. The fatigue and hunger combine into something new: the feeling that she's going to vomit. She throws off the quilt and grabs the pail, swimming with water that looks like diluted blood. Nothing comes. After several minutes, her stomach calms. She drops back into bed. Now she is dying for food. But she's so exhausted that the idea of actually getting up, walking downstairs, feels impossible. She wants dinner right here, right now, served to her without having to go anywhere. For a short while, she fights sleep, but soon she loses the battle.

Hours later, in the dank light of early morning, Candace is still lying in the same position when Mark knocks several times and calls her name softly through the door. Finally, he pushes the door open, and finds her in the same position she was in when she fell asleep. Her mouth is open, the lights in the room are shining brightly, and oddly enough, half the wall is painted a horrid, vomit-colored pink. He stares at the wall, confused, and then considers Candace, her mouth a small O, her gawdy orange hair splayed in disarray over her shoulders and the sheets. She looks gorgeous, he thinks, she has never looked so beautiful before, nor so vulnerable. He snaps off the overhead light, and in just the dim light of the night table, he unbuttons his shirt, and slides out of his jeans and socks. Gently lifting the quilt, he glides in between the sheets, setting his cold legs against Candace's warm, baby skin. Propped up on one elbow, he delves face first into her hair. Then he presses his open mouth behind her ear, and slowly goes to work with his tongue, following the contours of her face, her jaw, taking into his mouth the beauty he just saw, wishing he could make her part of himself by swallowing her whole.

EILEEN

March 22, 1972 Friday

I called Bonanza this morning for the bus schedule. A bus leaves North Adams for Boston every weekday at 11:37. From Boston, I can switch to Trailways to go to Providence. With the stops, I figure the whole trip will take six or seven hours.

I made my announcement at breakfast. "I'm leaving for school Monday."

My mother, who never sits down to eat a meal, was pouring coffee into my father's thick white mug. My father had his elbows on the table. His palms were face down on either side of his plate. He looked like he owned the table.

Neither of them said anything. Ma's mouth tightened, though, like the drawstring on my cloth laundry bag. Avoiding my eyes, she turned back to the stove. I stared at her grey hair, done up in a donut-sized bun. With a potholder, she picked up the frying pan, scooped scrambled eggs onto my father's plate. Then she held the pan perilously close to my head.

"You wanna eat this morning or not?" Her tone was sharp, and just a little shaky. Which meant that I knew she heard me.

"Yeah, sure, Ma, I'll eat."

"How're you getting there?" my father asked, poking his fork into the fluffy eggs. My mother laid two slices of grilled ham on the plate. Flat pink flesh, with spots of brown from the pan. Then she bent over to butter his toast.

"Bus."

"A bus?" My father's eye, the one I could see from where I was sitting, opened wide.

"Sure. There's one in the morning."

"What about Rusty?" Naturally, Ma would ask that. Ever since I started college, Rus has carted me back and forth to Providence. My private chauffeur. In a crummy red truck.

"He's working. I told him I didn't need a ride."

My father snorted. Stabbed his fork into a pink rectangle of ham on the white plate.

"So, I guess you're gonna throw up on the bus?" My mother was finally at the table, eating the last of the eggs, now lukewarm. She placed one hand politely in her lap.

"Ma...I'm better now. I haven't thrown up for..."

"Two days," she interrupted.

"No, three. But before it was every day, four, five times some days, remember?"

"Oh, yeah, I remember. I remember just fine."

My father got up from the table. As usual, he left his dirty dishes for either me or Ma. He looked straight at me, his complexion the color of the ham. "So. You go back to school."

"Yeah."

"For how long?"

I ran my tongue along the inside of my teeth. "I want to...to finish off the semester."

He lowered his head, and both hands rolled into fists. Grey curly hair started right above his wrists. He raised a finger and pointed it at me. "You finish the semester, OK. But then, you come back here. Right away. You hear me?" He was still pointing, but now his finger dropped to my abdomen. "Because you got something else to finish...junior, there." He gestured with his head. His eyebrows rose, and his voice trembled, and the look on his face was mean. "You hear me, lady? Your party's over."

Swiping up his grey metal lunch box off the counter, he paused next to my mother and cradled his hand briefly under her chin. Then he opened the back door and in a moment, I could hear his heavy boots descending heavily down the steps.

❧

After breakfast, I holed up in the hallway and called Providence to talk to Corinne. It costs a fortune to call during the day, but my mother was off to St. Anthony's for her rosary society meeting. From where I sat, I could see the sky out the window. It was perfectly white. The radio said something about a big storm, starting about noon, getting worse by nightfall.

"If all goes well, I'll be there Monday night," I told Corinne.

"Oh God. That's great...except."

"Except what?"

"Oh, well. Is there any way you can get here Sunday?"

"I don't know. I guess there must be buses on the weekend too. What's Sunday?"

"Well, it's Sunday night. Holly Near is in concert at Meehan Audi..."

"Oh God, Corinne, why didn't you tell me that before?" Holly Near. The night John stayed with me, I lit a candle and some incense and played her first album. I played it three more times that night. If Holly Near was playing in Providence, then it was almost certain that John would be there. And that meant I had to be there, too.

"I'm sorry, Eileen, but the way you were feeling, I didn't think you'd be back."

"Well, I'm better. Mostly. Mostly what's making me sick now is my parents."

"That bad, huh?"

"They think I should stick around here and get married."

"Did they say that?"

"Oh, didn't I tell you? My mother brought home the menu for the reception. Then I threw up, right in the mid..." There was noise downstairs. The front door, which sticks, opened with its familiar shudder.

"Wait, somebody's here." I put the phone against my chest. "HELLO?"

"It's just me," my mother said.

I cupped my hand over the mouthpiece. Whispered. "I've gotta go. My mother's home. I'll come Sunday. What time is the concert?"

"I think 7:30. Or eight. I can check."

"No, no, that's OK. I'll come by seven. Wait for me?"

"Sure, we'll probably go out first for..." My mother's shoes were scuffing up the stairs. I jumped to my feet, and placed the phone back in its cradle, hanging up on Corinne before I could ask her about John, about whether she had seen him on campus. Or, whether by some miracle, he had come by or called.

When my mother reached the top of the stairs, I was standing in front of the phone.

"You're home early, Ma."

"Yeh," she said, a little out of breath from climbing the stairs. She had the laundry basket in her arms, filled with neatly folded towels, T-shirts, socks and underwear. I thought about my big striped laundry bag at school, how I stuff all the clothes back in it before they're even dry. I never fold a thing. "The roads were bad."

"Snowy?"

"Oh, who knows, snow, sleet, rain. This time of year the weather stinks." She headed for her bedroom, but at the door, she turned, rested the laundry basket against her belly. "You know you got an appointment with Dr. Veltrani Tuesday."

I hadn't given it a thought. Maybe because I wanted so much to forget my first visit.

"Well I'll be gone by then so you can just call and cancel it."

"Oh, no, you can't just cancel like that." My mother was shaking her head.

"God, Ma, people do that all the time. What's the big deal?"

Her eyes narrowed. She turned into her bedroom and dropped the basket on the bed. It fell over and the clothes toppled out. She came back out into the hall and started shouting. "He took you right away. He didn't have to. He is a good man and...and who do you think you are anyway, you don't need a doctor? You don't need a husband. What, you going to deliver this baby yourself you're such a big shot?" My mother was spitting. Her face scared me.

"Ma, look, he isn't going to mind," I said quietly, hoping to calm her. "And anyway I told you the other day I was leaving Monday." After talking to Corinne I had moved my timetable up. I would leave Sunday if I could. I came toward her bed, reached toward the floor to help her pick up the clothes. But she pushed my arm away, and launched into a rapid-fire tirade in Italian. Most of what she says in Italian escapes me, except for the swear words. I heard the one word I knew so well. *Putana*. Whore.

I covered my ears and left the room. By the time she stopped swearing, I had slammed my bedroom door.

❧

5:00 All afternoon, I've been lying on my bed, watching the snow. It falls straight down sometimes, or other times, it comes down at a slant. Sometimes the wind catches it up and twirls it in eddies and swirls that look like they will never hit the ground. Downstairs, I hear the growl of the vacuum cleaner. My mother is forever cleaning, but Friday is her day to go nuts. She does the whole house, top to bottom. Maybe that's why I've always hated Fridays. I associate them with eating cardboard fish sticks for lunch at school and then, coming home and swishing ammonia and cleanser around in the toilet bowl. I hate to clean, and I've never come close to doing it the way Lucy wants me to. I can push the vacuum cleaner around my room all afternoon, and then she comes in and lifts my bedspread and plucks balls of dust and hair from under the bed. Or she complains that my closets look *shambratha*, the clothes falling off the hangers. Ma wants each blouse buttoned and facing the same direction.

I spent half an hour trying to read a page of my microbiology textbook. At this rate, I'll be 108 by the time I finish the damn book. I started watching the snow again, and then fell asleep. When I woke up, the vacuum cleaner was quiet. I crept downstairs, my stomach empty. My mother, her hair wrapped in a kerchief, was kneeling in front of the open refrigerator, sponging the white walls inside. An open bottle of Mr. Clean was on the floor. I could smell it. I circled the table, which had all the bottles and leftovers from the refrigerator. There was a chunk of cold meatloaf and a big bowl of zitis, and a bowl of kidney beans, all covered tightly with Saran. I found the peanut butter next to the ketchup bottle, then I realized that the celery was in the vegetable drawer, which my mother was blocking.

"Can you hand me the celery?" My mother ignored my request. She brought her short squat body to a standing position. She picked up the Mr. Clean and a small white bucket filled with dingy grey water. The refrigerator door was hanging open. "Ma?"

"What?"

"Do we have any celery?"

"I dunno. Look yourself." I went to the refrigerator, got a whiff of ammonia. The celery was in a plastic bag in the bottom drawer. I broke off one outside stalk, and then an inner one. But they needed washing, and my mother was in the way at the sink. As I waited my turn, I noticed the ceramic bowl, with the pink stripe around the top edge, sitting on the counter, covered with a towel, which meant my mother had mixed up some homemade bread.

By the time I washed the celery, and was spreading a gob of peanut butter on the wide bottom half, my mother had put all the leftovers back in the refrigerator and was working at the table on her bread. She scattered a couple handfuls of flour on her chewed up bread board and turned the puffy white dough, like soft flesh, onto the middle section, worn lighter than the rest of the board. I sat at the table, crunching on celery, watching her hands squeeze and pat the dough. I got a nice whiff of yeast. She shaped two big loaves, and placed them side by side on a cookie sheet greased and sprinkled with corn meal.

I could have gone back upstairs, could have eaten in my room, but something about the bread, the smell of it, the look of it as my mother pressed her rough fingers into the soft white dough, kept me in the kitchen. By Monday, I kept thinking, I'd be back in school. All this would be behind me. I was beginning to see how I might miss her, a little. A very little.

"You do that well," I said, as she set a sharp knife to the top of each loaf. The wet bread dough separated cleanly at each cut.

"I should, after all these years." Ma's eyebrows met in a small dark knot in her forehead. Without looking up, she reached for the remaining chunk of dough, and sliced it into several small pieces. Then she stretched the pieces into thin round shapes. In some spots, the dough was so thin you could see through it. This too is a Friday afternoon routine, especially in winter. Every week she makes fried pizza. When I was a kid, she would give me the fried dough sprinkled with powdered sugar. Now, though, I like them with sauce and Parmesan cheese.

She poured oil into the square electric frying pan on the counter. When it was hot, she dropped the first three pizzas in the pan. The oil seethed around the dough, crackling in a rush of splattering bubbles. She took a step back from the frying pan. I got up, took the breadboard to the sink and scraped the dried layer of dough off it for her. I filled the ceramic bowl at the sink with soapy water. Then I stood to the side of the pan and leaned on the counter. I used to wait like this as a kid, eager for the round pieces of dough to finish cooking. She would spear the fried dough with a fork, let the oil drip off, then set it for a few seconds on paper towels. Then she'd set the dough on a plate, and spoon some sugar on top.

I was thinking about this as I watched the oil crackle around the dough in the pan. I was thinking, gee, I must be feeling better, because the fried dough actually smells good to me again. I was just about to ask Ma if I could have a piece to eat.

"Rusty called," my mother said suddenly, pushing the dough around the pan. The pizzas were floating like rubber rafts bobbing in water.

"Oh?" It occurred to me that I ought to tell him I'm planning on leaving. I haven't talked to him since we saw the dead deer. A vision of the animal, its unfocused eye reflecting the white sky, flashed across my mind. "So what did he want?"

She didn't answer. She forked the stiff circle of dough, dripping oil, onto a pile of paper towels. "Did you tell him I'm leaving, Ma? Huh?"

She set three more chunks of dough into the sizzling oil. "I told him."

It made me vaguely uncomfortable to think about my mother telling Rusty this news. On the other hand, I thought, it saved me having to do it.

"I told him he should come for dinner, too."

I looked up in disbelief. "Ma, you can't do that." But of course, she could, and she had. "Ma you're incredible. I really can't believe you did this." I stomped around the kitchen, my voice getting higher and higher. "You just won't let up, will you? OK, fine. Fine. You invited him to dinner, you eat with him. But don't expect me to. I'm....going out."

"Oh yeah? Where you think you're going in this storm?"

"I don't know. I'll figure it out though." I felt my face turning hot. And then, just as I was about to leave the kitchen, I glanced at my mother. Maybe it was my imagination, but I thought I saw a small, triumphant smile on her mouth. The sight of that sent me into a rage. The first thing I saw were the two loaves of bread sitting peacefully on the counter. I picked up the cookie sheet with the bread, and turning to face my mother, I started shaking the pan in my hand. She turned, alarm on her face. "Don't!" she cried, reaching out for the pan, but it was too late. I had turned the cookie sheet on its side. The bread took a second to come unstuck from the buttered pan, and then both loaves just dropped to the floor, slopping onto the linoleum with a solid wet sound.

My mother rushed at me with the fork still in her hand. "Matta!" she screamed, lifting her arm to hit me. I ran from the kitchen still holding onto the cookie sheet and when I was halfway through the living room, I threw it butter side down onto the rug.

❦

6:15 Rusty is coming for dinner any minute...I don't care...I'll be in my room....

7:00 Nobody has asked me to come down. I hear low voices, calm, controlled. Occasionally, Rusty or my father laughs. My mother must have salvaged the bread, because I smell it. She cooked some kind of meat, too. Probably braciola, rolled up with parsley. It smells divine. Now that I'm not throwing up, my appetite is getting enormous. But I'd rather die than go downstairs. I will listen to records: Cat Stevens or Simon and Garfunkel. Or maybe Joanie Mitchell. I keep expecting Rusty to come upstairs. I have planned to tell him about John. Maybe then he'll get the message.

10:15 About seven thirty, I got my pajamas on and climbed into bed. I was so hungry I could hardly stand it. I picked up the journal, but ended up writing a corny poem and tearing it out. I was too hungry to write. I heard the clink of dishes and silverware downstairs. And then, feet coming up the steps. I sat up. There was a soft knock at the door.

"Yeah, who is it?"

"Room service."

I got out of bed, walked to the door, opened it a crack. Rusty. Smiling, balancing a plate in one hand and in his other hand, a glass of milk. "Are you gonna let me in or not?"

On the plate were three juicy bracciola, covered in tomato sauce. Spaghetti on the side, and string beans. My mouth started to water. There were two slabs of bread, smeared in butter. I opened the door. He smiled, came in and set the plate on my desk. "Compliments of the chef."

He handed me a fork and knife, wrapped up in a napkin.

"Thanks."

"You're welcome. Actually, you're not welcome." His smile got bigger, more exaggerated, more triumphant, then he flopped down on my bed, crossed his legs. Folded his hands behind his head. "Why didn't you come down for dinner, anyway?"

I didn't say anything. I pulled my desk chair up, and sat down to the plate of food. I cut a piece of the meat.

"Well?"

"I didn't feel like it."

"Nice. That's real nice, Eileen." He stared at me while I ate. I started reconsidering whether I would tell him about John. If I do, I thought, we'll have to talk. I just wanted him to leave.

"So you're leaving Monday?"

I nodded, chewed on a mushroom, together with a string bean. I didn't want to have that conversation either. I didn't want to tell him I was actually leaving Sunday. He chuckled.

"What's so funny?"

"Oh, nothing. Except if they're right about the weather, you'll be lucky to get out of the driveway Monday. They're saying it's gonna snow all weekend. A blizzard." He grinned.

"It's March 22nd. Spring is here. How can there be a blizzard in the spring?"

"Easy. Just look outside." He sat up, looked at the records scattered at the bottom of my bed. I got up, raised the shade. Snow was falling in a steady curtain beneath the cone of light cast by the streetlight. Several inches were piled on the sidewalk and on Rusty's truck.

It can't snow all weekend. It can't snow on Sunday. I was thinking that as I looked at Rusty. I hated the cocky way he was smiling at me. "So if it's snowing this hard," I said, "shouldn't you be getting home?" I bit into the crusty warm bread.

"I've got four-wheel drive." He flopped back down on the bed. "Besides, I think your mother would just as soon I stay. Maybe even move in."

God forbid, I thought. But then it occurred to me, my mother might be desperate enough, stupid enough, to say something like that to Rusty. No, I thought, No. Never. Suddenly, I wanted to blow him right out of the water with one little sentence. "Hey, Rus, guess what?" I would smile while I said it. "I slept with this incredible guy named John." I ran the sentence around in my head. But something held me back. Maybe because if I actually said it, I also would have had to admit that I hadn't heard from John in six weeks.

"Rus?" I pushed my plate away, took up the glass of milk.

"Yeah?"

"I really want you to go home." I said it calmly, quietly, while I wiped my mouth with a napkin. I stared him straight in the eye.

His smile disappeared. He studied me a minute, then, slowly he got up from the bed. As he walked past me, he stuck his hands in the front pockets of his jeans. He left the room without another word. Downstairs, the front door squeaked open. I'm not even sure he said good bye to my parents. All I heard was him roaring away in the truck.

March 23, 1972 Saturday

The snow has been falling all day, so fast my father hasn't been able to keep the driveway or the front path clean. Occasionally, a plow scrapes along in front of the house, its orange lights blinking. I have stayed in my room, listening to the radio. Every hour, I turn it up to get the weather report. The message stays the same: "Heavy snow Saturday, with two feet or more of accumulation expected, especially in higher elevations. Snow tapering to flurries Sunday." What they don't say is what time Sunday the tapering will begin.

Looking out the window, I think the snow is going to suffocate me. The white blur covers every surface, rounding things, erasing sound. The world has become a white dead place. And it is erasing me. There is nowhere to go, nothing to do but sit and stare and write in this book. Only the writing, this string of words, saves me, maybe because it is me telling me who I am, and more important, who I am trying to be. I never figured when I started that it would be so easy to write. Writing before was always a chore. But now, I am doing it for me. I can't imagine living without this diary. It would be like living without the ability to speak or to think. Funny to think that letters from the alphabet can combine in words, sentences, and give a person sanity. By putting words, one after another on a clean white page, in a line, I am able to inch along. In the inching, I feel released from this dead white space all around me.

Shortly after noontime.

A few minutes ago, I opened the big blue suitcase I got as a gift when I went away to college. Inside, I laid a stack of underpants in one satin-lined corner. I left most of my stuff at Brown, so it didn't take me long to pack. I have one pair of bell-bottom jeans that still fits. Barely, and only because they are hip-huggers, and my belly hangs out above. I will wear those on the bus. I packed two pairs of sweat pants, too, and a couple of long flannel shirts I took from my father. I am putting off buying pants with a stretchy pouch as long as I can.

On top of my clothes, I laid three textbooks — microbiology, calculus and histology. I've hardly looked at them the last few weeks. But as I set them in the suitcase, I opened the calculus book. "Marginal and average rates of change...using the first derivative...logarithmic and exponential functions." My stomach fluttered. I've missed almost six weeks of classes. Six weeks of notes. And finals are in a little more than a month.

I slammed the book shut and dropped the lid of the suitcase. Just as I did, my desk light and the radio went off. It took me a couple of seconds to realize that the power was out. I opened the bedroom door. The light filtering into the hallway from outdoors was a silvery green. When I got downstairs, my mother was slicing a loaf of bread. She always slices by holding the loaves against her chest, then dragging the serrated knife close to her breast. I have never understood why she slices bread this way. And why she doesn't get cut.

A pan sat on the stove. But there were no lights in the kitchen.

"The electricity's out," I said.

Ma wasn't talking. She laid the thick slices of crusty bread on a plate, arranged a layer of provolone cheese, some roasted peppers and some paper thin slices of salami and prosciutto on another plate, then set both on the table. Even with no power, my mother will fix my father's lunch. My father must have telepathy, because just as she set the plate on the table, he appeared at the backdoor. When he opened it, snow drifted inside. He pulled his boots off. His socks were wet, and there were chunks of snow clinging to the cuffs of his green pants.

"It won't let up out there," he said, unzipping his grey jacket. My mother took it from him and shook the snow off the sleeves into the wastebasket. Then she hung it by the door.

"Quick, go change," she said. "Then you can eat. I got lunch all ready." My father was peeling off the wet socks. She took those too, and followed him out of the kitchen. Neither of them said a word to me.

I was left standing at the kitchen table. I have become invisible. And yet I haven't disappeared. It became clear at that moment that I have to get out of this house right away. Snow or no snow, I will take the bus this afternoon.

4:30 p.m. Stuck at Grey's Drugs...

I'm sitting here tired and cold and bored and wondering where to go. A few minutes ago I found out that there is no bus. Now what?

I snuck out of the house about 3:30. I lugged my suitcase through the living room on tiptoe because my father was napping on the couch, the newspaper resting on his chest. The least sound can wake him. In the kitchen, dirty lunch dishes were still neatly stacked on the counter by the sink. Only a power outage could make my mother leave dishes unwashed. I put the rest of the homemade bread in a plastic bag. I wrapped a chunk of cheese together with some salami. I took half a package of Stella D'Oro cookies from the lazy Susan under the counter. I grabbed two oranges and a speckled banana from the fruit-bowl. All of this I put into a big brown lunch bag. At the last minute, I threw in the last two bananas. I put the lunch bag into my backpack.

Then I heard the toilet flush upstairs. That meant I had about four minutes before my mother would be down to putter around the kitchen. I pulled my fleece-lined boots on and threw my running shoes into the pack on top of my lunch. I heard my mother's foot-steps squeaking upstairs as I took my down parka off the peg and zipped it up. I pulled gloves on, and slipped into the straps of my pack. I tried to open the backdoor, but it wouldn't budge. I pulled hard until the door gave way, shuddering as it did. As I stepped onto the back porch, cold air pierced my scalp and neck and cheeks. The fine snow stung my face. I pulled the zipper of my jacket as high as it would go and hurried down the freshly shoveled steps.

Buses leave town from Grey's drugstore, here at the corner of Main and Eagle. It's a twenty-minute walk to town in good weather. Today, though, with the snow and the suitcase, it seemed to take forever. None of the sidewalks were clear, including of course ours up on Pleasant Street. For a few minutes, I stepped through drifts that were up to my crotch. Finally, with snow crushed deep into my boots, I took to the middle of the street. Both of my big toes were frozen. I was breathing hard and the suitcase felt like a bag of cinder blocks hanging from my shoulder as I made my way down the hill.

Soon, both my big toes were numb. I tried to wiggle them as I walked, but it didn't help a bit. My jeans were icy and wet against my legs. I also felt something I have never felt before. Pressure between my legs; the sensation that something was pulling down on the bottom of my pelvis. The muscles across my groin were tender and slightly crampy. It never occurred to me how much being pregnant would slow me down.

Just as I came to the corner where Pleasant meets Church Street, a Volkswagen approached, its license plate bright green and white. Vermont. The driver hunched over the wheel, trying to see through a small icy arc on the windshield. Suddenly I had a vision of myself, trudging along this snow-covered road. The Volkswagen slowed because of a high drift, then pulled over and stopped. The driver got out of the bug and began scraping the windshield. He was tall and wearing a bulky ski sweater, and over that a bright red down vest. He had a rugged, athletic-looking face. A skier, perhaps. As I got closer to the car, I saw him take the scraper and start chipping the ice off the windshield. He looked up.

"Bad day to be out," he said, reaching across the windshield to lift the wiper. He had floppy black gloves with brown and white rabbit fur peaking out at the wrists. His face was tanned, except for a goggle-shaped mask of paler skin around his eyes. The skin across his high cheekbones, the arc of his nose, was taut.

A ski instructor, on his way back to Vermont, I decided. I was almost past the car when I stopped, set down the suitcase.

"Are you by any chance going up East Main?" As I spoke, I began, wondering if I actually was hearing my own voice. My weary body was speaking for itself.

The man paused, the long plastic handle of the windshield scraper poised on the window. The snow was quickly accumulating in the cleared spaces of the glass. He smiled.

"I'm going out Route 2 and then up route 8." He moved around to the other side of the car, quickly finishing up the windshield. He popped open the front door. It made a loud wrenching squeak. "We have no heat inside, but you are welcome to a ride."

"I'd really appreciate that." I picked up the suitcase and he helped me throw it into the backseat. I slid in front. The guy got in, and brought with him the smell of his wet wool sweater. And something else. A sweet fragrance that lifted my spirits.

Of course. Brut. John's cologne.

The man shifted into first, and the bug spurted ahead, sliding as it did.

"So where are you off to?" His breath came out in a white cloud. I detected an accent in his voice. German? Austrian? Swiss? I envisioned him taking someone out on a date. Formal. With a tux, a red cummerbund, a black bow tie.

"I'm going back to school."

"Oh? Where would that be?"

"Providence." He eyed me, and one brow popped up. He seemed more curious about me now. "Brown?"

"Well, Pembroke, actually. You know, the women's part of Brown."

"Right. Let's see, you'd have to be, what, a...junior?" I shook my head no.

"Sophomore."

"I graduated Dartmouth in '57." I calculated. He'd be in his thirties.
I said nothing. "So you can let me off right there at the corner.
I'll cross." A plow was behind us now. Its blinking light cast an eery
orange glow over everything.

"You have a ride from here?"

"Bus."

"To Providence?"

"Well, first to Boston. Then I switch." By now we were at the corner.
The bug fishtailed as he braked, then skidded up against a snow
bank at the curb.

"Well. Good luck." The wide smile. White teeth. Crest. He could
do a Crest commercial. I grabbed the thin metal handle and
opened the door. He pulled the suitcase over the seat and pushed
it toward me.

"Thanks. Thanks a lot." I stepped through an ocean of snow into
what should have been the curb. The light was against me, but there
wasn't a car in sight. On the other side, the driver held up his hand
and moved off through what looked like a soft white tunnel of snow.

The front door of Grey's pharmacy is angled to the corner. I pushed
the door open. The warm dry air felt wonderful on my face. I shook
my head, and big droplets of icy water flew in all directions.

An old-fashioned soda counter occupies one side of Grey's, faced
by stools covered in red plastic. God knows how many ice cream sundaes
and sodas I've eaten on those stools. I've eaten more of them than I
care to remember with Rusty.

Today, though, Grey's was nearly empty, except for somebody at
the pharmacy, opposite the soda counter. Mr. Gregorio, a small, bald
man with a dark mustache has owned Grey's ever since I can remember.
He always wears that white jacket with the high collar.

"Hello." He looked at me over the high counter.

"Hi. I wanted to get a ticket."

"A ticket?"

"Yeah. For the bus? I'm going to Boston."

Mr. Gregorio was shaking his head. "Oh, no, honey. Not today
you aren't."

I found the "honey" irritating. "Doesn't Bonanza leave from
here? I got information that said I could switch when...." He cut me
off, shaking his head rapidly.

"Sure, sure. Most days. But not today honey. There's no bus. They cancelled the whole route because of the storm. They even closed the Mass Pike." I stared at him in disbelief. It never occurred to me that they could cancel a bus route. Close an interstate. I dropped my suitcase to the squared maroon and white linoleum.

"You have a ride home?" He asked, squinting at me. His eyebrows looked bushy and black, just like his mustache. Staring at him, it dawned on me that he knows my mother and father. For years they have bought every prescription here.

"Oh. Sure. Right. Outside." I scooped my hand through the suitcase handle and turned quickly to open the door. I stood there, snow prickling my face. Then I came back inside.

Mr. G. stared at me. "Do you mind if I wait in here?" I said. "They'll be a while."

So here I sit, at Grey's, in the booth. In my wet clothes. Eating saltines out of plastic wrappers. And drinking a cup of greasy fake cocoa Mr. G. just fixed me. I'm writing all this down, so I can keep myself going. I'm hoping the words will point me somewhere, help me figure out what to do next. There is only one person, of course, I can call. But when I think about calling him, I think, God help me, I don't want to do that. Not at all.

March 24, 1972 Late Saturday night

I stayed at Grey's, writing, shivering, as long as I could. Finally, it was getting to be dusk. Mr. G. came over to me. "So...I'm closing up. Who's coming for you?"

I shrugged. Outside, the snow was falling harder than it had all day. "Give me a second. I'm going to call...a friend." I did. The phone, on the wall beside the pharmacy counter, rang and rang.

Finally, Rusty picked up. "Hello."

"Hi." I paused. "It's me."

"Yeah. So what do you want?"

"A ride." I turned away from Mr. Gregorio, who was standing behind the counter. I spoke quietly into the phone. "I'm...stuck."

"Where are you?"

"I'm at Grey's. I was going to get the bus...but it was...cancelled."

"Serves you right."

"Look, Rus, if you'd rather not come I'll call up my..."

"Stay where you are," he said, interrupting. Instantly the phone went dead.

I was standing outside Grey's, stamping my feet, when Rusty pulled up. The roof of his truck was capped by nearly a foot of snow. The truck itself was practically invisible between the white dunes on either side of the street. It was strangely quiet outside, as if the snow had absorbed all sound.

He made a U-turn and pulled up in front of Grey's. "I guess you're going my way," he said, sneering as I opened the door. He didn't offer to take the suitcase, so I lifted it into the cab and then hoisted myself up to the seat. My jeans and my jacket were wet, and snow caked my hair. My eyelashes were embedded in ice.

"I really want to go to Providence," I said.

Rusty laughed. "Hell, don't let me stop you." He shook his head. "You know, I truly think you're out of your mind."

I gnawed on my top lip. "Would you be willing to drive me tomorrow?"

"In this mess?" He shook his head. "Hell no."

"I mean if it stops. It *will stop*, you know."

He inhaled, stared out the windshield, the wipers passing back and forth across ice.

"I'll make you a deal. You stay at my place tonight and I'll take you wherever you want to go tomorrow."

I shook my head. "I can't believe you'd sink so low. A bribe. You're bribing me to sleep with you."

"Who said anything about sleeping with you?" A sly grin spread across his face. "Of course, if you insist, I might have to..."

I closed my eyes. "Rus. I'm wet. I'm cold. I'm hungry. And tired. All I want is a hot shower and a warm bed."

"Coming right up," he said, shifting the truck into first. Slowly, we inched ahead.

I slept for a few hours on the living room couch and when I woke up, Rus was staring down at me. Even before I was fully awake, he was offering to make me dinner. I pulled the blanket over my nose.

"Since when can you make anything but canned soup?"

He folded his arms over his chest. "Look, are you hungry or not? There are a few things I've learned to cook. Just ask Dad." Rus's father, Jack, was lying in the leather LazyBoy in front of the T.V. The living room of the Burdett's two-story house is in pretty sorry shape.

Rus and his father have two cats and a feisty young weimaraner named Roxy living in the house. The floors are gouged and scratched. One arm of Jack's leather chair has been chewed up. The rug is deep in cat hair. But Roxy is as pleasant a pup as can be. She loves it when I pet her sleek bony head. I began to stroke her ear.

"Rus makes a mean spaghetti sauce," Jack said from his chair. He burped. "I mean how can he go wrong...he opens up a jar." Jack laughed at his own joke. His chin, covered in grey stubble, was resting on his chest. He was on his third or fourth beer. Rus says his father many nights puts away a six pack, and he drinks even more on Saturday night. He usually ends up falling asleep in front of the T.V. No wonder Audrey wanted out. She's been gone now for almost six years.

"How about lasagna?" Rus asks, bending down to pet Roxy. The dog lifted her head, and Rus scratched her behind the ears. She whined appreciatively.

"You've got stuff to make lasagna with?" I asked. It's hard to imagine Rus going to a grocery store at all, let alone shopping in a snowstorm.

"Sure." He smiled, and Jack, on the other couch, let out a loud "Ha!"

"O.K.," I said. "What is it, a T.V. dinner?"

"You won't believe how good it tastes," Rus said. I laughed. I got a vision suddenly of my mother, spending all afternoon on a pan of lasagna. First she cooks the homemade sauce, then she mixes the filling, and boils and strains the noodles. Her face always ends up as hot and steamy as the macaroni when she's finished.

"I could eat anything right now," I said. Rus smiled. He seemed to appreciate that remark as much as Roxy appreciated having her head scratched. He headed for the kitchen.

"Rus?"

"Yeah?" he said, turning.

"Can we make some garlic bread? I've got this craving all of a sudden." My nausea, clearly, was a thing of the past.

"Sure. But all we've got is you know, the sliced white stuff."

"I don't care." I jumped off the couch. "I could eat a bag of Wonder bread myself."

Jack ended up falling asleep before dinner, so it was just Rus and me sharing the lasagna. He brought out a dusty bottle of red wine and a couple of mismatched candles. He set them in the middle of the kitchen table.

"What's this?" I said, pointing to the candles. "A holiday?"

"In a way." He stared at me while he pulled the cork out of the bottle. "Actually, I just want to be prepared in case the electricity goes out again." He poured two glasses.

I took a piece of garlic bread out of the tin foil. It was hot and soggy with butter. Suddenly the wine started to take effect. Or it must have, because I looked at Rus and had a peculiar feeling: like we had done this exact scene before: we had been here in this warm kitchen in a snow storm, eating lasagna and garlic bread. It made me nervous to look at him.

After dinner, Rus put the dishes in the dishwasher. He covered his sleeping father with a blanket. Then we went up to his room to listen to music. He had a new Moody Blues album and something by the Dead. His room is papered with Dead posters, mostly Garcia in concert. I sat on the floor, but there was no rug, so I moved onto the bed. I stayed at the foot of the bed, though, telling myself, be careful. Be careful.

He lit up a joint and passed it to me. I shook my head. "You're being good," he said.

"Shouldn't I?"

He held the smoke in for a moment. Then he shrugged, let out his smoky breath. "I don't think a toke or two would hurt the kid. Hey, I think my Ma even did some weed when she was pregnant with me." His eyes gleamed and his smile got dreamier.

"She would have." I watched him inhale again, hold his breath. "And you...you were, after all, the one who thought I'd love the acid." I got up from the bed and walked to the window. Lifting the shade, I could see the snow falling under the streetlight.

"I can't believe this," I said, watching the wind come up and blow a sheet of snow up and across the front yard. "It's almost April for God's sake, not January." I was thinking about the roads, how long it would take the plows to clear them in the morning, when suddenly Rus was kissing my neck, pressing up against my backside with his legs, his whole body. He slipped his arms under my sweater and around my chest and then gently fluttered his fingers across my swollen breasts. My body responded on its own, before my mind had a chance to register what was going on. I turned to face him. His body tight against me, he pressed me down to the bed.

"Rus, I...I can't," I said, but by then he had my blouse half off.

"Sure you can," he said, breathing on me. "Why not?" He started kissing my breasts. My mind kept saying no, but my body was saying yes, and not one word came out of my mouth.

Now I'm sitting here, in the middle of the night, staring into the dark at Rusty's naked back, writing by candlelight. I should get up, tiptoe out, sleep downstairs on the couch. I glance over at the clock. 2:40. Rus is face down, buried in the pillow we've been sharing. But his head is turned toward the wall, and he seems so deep in sleep that if I moved, chances are he'd never know the difference.

I have now moved here to the couch, and I'm shivering, and the realization is hitting me: I've done a really dumb thing, letting tonight happen. I should have stayed downstairs. I should have locked myself in a closet, or done whatever I had to do, to keep my distance from Rus. Suddenly I remember something I read in one of the books I have on pregnancy. It said that pregnant women have "a heightened appetite for sex," mainly because there is more blood circulating through the genital organs. I guess I can blame my biology, then. Still, I can't believe I let it happen. And I can't let it change my plans. I have to believe I can make the future happen the way I want it to. If I write it down, if I keep saying it on paper, if I keep the words "I am going, I am going, I am going," in sight, then maybe I really will get away. So maybe what I do here, writing things down, is like what my mother does all day: she prays. Morning and night, she says her words, her Hail Marys and Our Fathers, the whole rosary, all in the hopes things will go OK.

Jack is still in the leather chair, dead to the world. Only Roxy and I are awake. She whines, comes over to me as I sit here on the couch. There's only an afghan to use as a cover. I lay it across my shoulders, pull it up around my ears. There's nothing to cover me from my knees down. I'm tempted to go looking for another blanket, when suddenly, Roxy jumps up on the couch and settles next to my legs. Her body is warm, and her head presses reassuringly on my top knee. I rearrange the afghan so it doesn't cover her nose. I am happy to let her keep me warm and maybe now I will get sleepy.

March 25, early Sunday morning
I have been dreaming about John. It is summer, a blazing heat, and he and I are driving on the interstate to San Francisco. I look over at him in the front seat, and he smiles, and I tell him I want to pull over and stop and cool off at a lake. We're hauling his sailboat

behind the car and the sail is up and the car sways back and forth across the interstate. "I want to swim," I tell him, and I feel the light, buoyant sensation that floating in the water brings. "I want to swim," I say again, but the truth is, I want him, I want him to stop, I'm dying to make love with him right there on the side of the road. He drives on, though, his smile cool and detached.

Suddenly I'm awake, the afghan is on the floor. Roxy is up, hovering over me, then hopping down from the couch onto the floor. The sun is shining straight into my face. I glance over at Jack's chair. Empty. I sit up, rub my eyes, disoriented. I wonder what time it is, and whether Rusty is awake.

Later.

He was awake. Just as I was about to get off the couch, Rus emerged from the kitchen with a tray. On it was a tall glass of orange juice, a cup of coffee, with lots of milk, just the way I like it, and an English muffin with peanut butter and grape jelly, my favorite.

"I was going to make you breakfast in bed," he said, placing the tray on my lap. "But you didn't stay in bed. So this is coffee on the couch instead."

I looked up at him. He looked happy. Already showered. His reddish blonde curls were wet, slicked down dark on his head. He was wearing some kind of African dashiki, a shirt I'd never seen, and beads. Never before had I seen Rusty in beads. God, I thought, is he starting to go hippy on me?

"This is sweet, Rus, but..." I ran a hand through my hair.

"But what?"

"You...shouldn't...you shouldn't do this." I stood up, handed him back the tray.

A shadow moved across his face, settled there like a rain cloud. He stared at the tray. "For chrissake, it's just breakfast."

"I know. And it's really sweet of you, but..."

"But what? You're not eating breakfast today? You're nauseous again? You're not drinking coffee? You think I'm a total piece of shit? What? What is it this morning, huh?"

Jack came out of the kitchen, a mug in one hand, a cigarette in the other. He stood at the doorway until I caught his eye. He moved back into the kitchen.

"What it is is this. I'm leaving this morning, and I don't want you...waiting on me."

"What you're really saying is you don't want me waiting for you. That's really what it is, right? You don't want me waiting *for* you to come back."

"Yeah," I said, quietly. "I don't."

"Well don't flatter yourself," he said, turning, taking the tray back to the kitchen.

The window in the bathroom was steamy after I took my shower. I wiped a clear spot and looked out. The snow was three feet high, and higher where the plow piled it in drifts. The road was clear, though. As I toweled my hair, I decided I couldn't have Rusty take me back to school. Considering how miffed he was about breakfast, he probably wasn't going to.

When I got downstairs, Rus was nowhere to be seen. "He's shoveling us out," Jack said, squinting in a haze of his own cigarette smoke when I came into the kitchen. I set my suitcase down next to the table.

"So you're off," he said, standing up. He was doing a crossword puzzle. It occurred to me to ask Jack why he wasn't outside helping his son shovel.

"Yup, I'm off," I said, extending my hand. That seemed to throw Jack off. He hesitated, then took my hand, weakly, and held it briefly. His hand was moist.

"Well, good luck," he said. "And uh..." he pressed his lips together, and for a minute, it almost looked like he was going to cry. "Come and visit us sometime. I know Rus is going to miss you like crazy." He gestured outside toward where Rus was shoveling in back. Jack hardly ever says anything of consequence, so his saying that made me wince. What a mess I've got myself into. Amazing that it should be Jack who would remind me of it again, who would me make feel guilty. Jack of all people. I can still see him there, looking like an old man, his morning can of beer on the kitchen table.

I picked up the suitcase and headed out into the bright sunlight. Rusty came around the side of the house. His cheeks were deep rosy patches. He stood the shovel in front of him, upside down, and the sun glanced off the aluminum. For a second, it looked as though Rus had himself a shield. He stood there without saying a word.

"I'm off," I said, squinting into the light.

"You want a ride?"

"No. You've done enough. And anyway, it's too long a drive. In the snow and all, it'll be five hours to Providence. Maybe more."

"Eileen, I'm only talking about giving you a ride to Grey's." He sounded tired, or disgusted, or resigned, or mature, or maybe all of those things. He was not making any kind of fuss. "I'll get the keys." As he passed by me, stone-faced, carrying the shovel upright like a spear, I felt the second pang of guilt of the morning. Rusty was behaving so decently and here I was acting like a shit. When I let myself think about how I've been treating Rus lately, it bothers me. A lot. So I'm not going to let myself think about it.

And now, once again, I am sitting in the booth at Grey's, waiting for the second day in a row for a bus to Boston. Mr. G. says it's bound to be late...

March 25, 1972

There isn't a speck of snow in Providence. That happens. A lot of times, I call my parents in the winter and they'll be having a blizzard in the Berkshires and here on the coast we just get rain or fog or cold drizzle or maybe nothing falls at all. Today, when the bus pulled in, it was almost sunset and the dome of the state capital was a blaze of red and orange. The sky was a milky blue. The smell of bus fumes was overwhelming while I waited for my suitcase. I stepped out to the sidewalk, inhaled, and a hint of spring was hanging in the wind. I wanted to walk the distance to the dorm, but when the driver slid my suitcase toward me, and I tried to pick it up, I got a piercing sharp pull through my shoulder. I took a taxi up the hill.

The dorm was empty. I figured Corinne was at dinner...unless, of course, she had already left for the Holly Near concert. There was no note. I flopped face down on my bed. It seemed a year since I had left. My Indian bedspread was a mess, wrinkled, with a big stain — chocolate, maybe — right in the middle. Corinne knows I hate people lying on my bed. I rolled over and stared at the ceiling. When I closed my eyes, I still saw snow, piled on two sides of the street. I saw Rusty sitting on his side of the front seat, against the door, the engine of the truck running. Rusty looking away and refusing to say goodbye.

Suddenly a key jangled in the lock...the dorm door pushed open. "You came!" Corinne was screaming, and running toward me, arms wide, and then she crashed next to me on the bed. She hugged me, a hard tight squeeze, and I smelled her shampoo, and the familiarity of it was reassuring. I'm really back, I kept thinking. I'm back.

"How are you?"

"Well. I'm here." I shrugged. "Just don't ask how I did it."

"That bad, huh?" Corinne crossed her legs on the floor. Dustballs flew up from the black and white linoleum. Her sneakers squeaked on the floor. "They wanted you to stay?"

"Of course. They have the wedding planned."

Corinne just shook her head. "What are you going to do?"

I pulled myself to a sitting position on the bed, my back against the lime green cinder block wall. "Well, we need to talk about that." Corinne's mouth opened.

"You mean you'll come? You really will?"

"I don't know. Will you really have me? I mean, are you sure you want to hang out all summer with some sweaty pregnant woman who has back pain and varicose veins?"

"Oh that's incredible," Corinne said, laughing, standing up. "I never really thought you'd do it." She was wearing bell bottom jeans, which circled low around her narrow hips. What caught my eye was how flat her stomach was, and will be, indefinitely. I had my hand on my own thickening abdomen. I'll be in stretchy maternity jeans before the summer comes.

I slumped back down on the pillow. Suddenly I was so hungry I couldn't see straight. "You know what I need?" I said.

"What?"

"A hamburger. No, a cheeseburger. With bacon and fries. Ketchup, mustard, maybe mushrooms too. Do we have time?"

Corinne was standing at her dresser, pulling her hairbrush through her silky blonde hair. "Sure," she said, leaning into the mirror. "The concert's at eight. But wait, you hate meat."

"Not lately."

We walked down Thayer Street, me, Corinne and this girl, Candace Patterson, who lives down our hall. Corinne has gotten close to Candace in the weeks I've been home. Candace went to a fancy prep school named Dalton in New York City and her father is some kind of diplomat. She rides horses and sings opera and always makes me feel insecure, as though her family would have used mine as house help. The only thing I've ever liked about her is her name.

Anyway, we got past Thayer Street market, the small grocery store at the corner, and Clark's flower shop, and the Avon theatre and we were just about at the College Hill Bookstore, when Corinne jabbed me. "Eileen, look!" she whispered. Coming toward me was John and a group of people. I didn't have time to look the other way or think about what I'd say. I just stopped dead in my tracks a few feet away from him.

"Hi," he said, and he smiled but he kept walking, his group of people weaving through mine, everybody bumping shoulders. And as soon as he'd gone by, and I hadn't even been able to get a hi out, I noticed that his group of people was actually four, John and another guy, a preppie type, and two girls, both of them dressed in raccoon coats. Fur coats. I couldn't believe anybody close to my age would wear a fur coat. I kept walking, my legs like jello. I wanted to kill myself for not saying hello, and for turning around, for gawking at him.

And I wanted to kill him too, for being with somebody else, because he was obviously paired off with one of the girls, the blonde, the taller of the two. She wore bright red lipstick, for God's sake. And a god-damn fur coat.

"Who is she...with John?" Corinne asked, looking at me. I shook my head. I had completely lost my appetite, but by this time we were past the bus tunnel and at the Thayer St. Grill. Corinne pushed open the door, and a warm cloud of grease and French fries greeted me, and all I wanted to do was run back to the dorm. We took a small round table near the window, and I craned my neck to look out, but the sidewalk was empty.

Would he be at the Near concert, I kept wondering, as I waited for my dinner. Would he take the girl with him? The crowd kept building inside the restaurant, the noise grew too, the juke box blaring out Cat Stevens, "Tea for the Tillerman." Corinne was busy talking to Candace about some Classics course they had together, with Professor Workman. I ate my salad and kept thinking what a fool I had been all these weeks, counting on John, counting on seeing him, counting on somehow being with him again.

I cringed when I thought back to the one and only night we had spent together. Snow had fallen in the afternoon, had turned the hilly streets around campus perfect for sledding. John found me in the library and a bunch of us "borrowed" lunch trays from the cafeteria and used them as sleds. We did run after run, and a couple times, John spun out, flew off his tray. We just kept laughing and falling down in the snow, and getting up again, and throwing snowballs at each other, and trudging back to the top of the hill, and riding down again. I felt reckless, like a little kid. Studying for exams had unleashed some jittery energy in me. I didn't want the day to end.

John walked me back to my room. I put on Holly Near, lit a thick candle. I went down the hall to use the bathroom and when I came back, John had gone. I was crushed. I blew out the candle. Had my hand on the stereo, was about to change the music when I heard somebody hiccup, loud. I turned around and John had reappeared in dry clothes. Smiling, with a six-pack of Narragansett. He was holding up one can. "Cheers," he said, hiccuping again. He snapped opened another can for me.

Pretty soon, John's head was in my lap, and what happened next felt so natural, at least at the time. We undressed each other, made love, and just lay there wrapped up around each other until we fell asleep. We took such a long nap that we missed dinner. Ate strawberry waffles and whipped cream at the House of Pancakes about eleven. And the rest of that night we spent at his room. I left the next morning, in seventh heaven, had myself convinced this was the beginning of something that would last.

It took about a week before my bubble burst, before I got it through my fairy tale head that John and I weren't going to be a "thing" because of a single night together. We had gone sledding, and we had slid into bed. That was it. That was all. The snow had melted, the weather had changed, and John, for all I knew, was on to another girl. For all I knew, John took six girls to bed a week.

The waitress was setting down a hamburger dripping in grease. I lifted the limp lettuce, the pale tomato and the big white circles of onion from the plate onto the burger bun. Underneath was a pool of bloody meat juice, lots of fat. My stomach rolled.

I looked up. Candace and Corinne were sipping cokes, looking at me. "I can't," I said, softly, hoping only Corinne would hear.

Corinne frowned. "You can't what?

I shook my head. "I can't eat this."

"But you just said you were..."

"I know, I know I did...but that was back in the room." I gestured to the plate, as if it had a dead squirrel on it. "Now that I see it, I...just can't."

Candace looked at Corinne, and they laughed. Corinne reached for my fork and pushing aside the napkin, stabbed a French fry.

Meehan auditorium was pitch black, except for a large circle of light that flooded the stage in the center of the floor. Holly Near was holding the mike, her hair billowing out, a huge cloud of strawberry blonde. She wore bell bottom jeans and pointy boots, and her blouse had big puffy sleeves and was unbuttoned half way down her chest. A guy she called Jeff sat behind her playing a grand piano. Her voice soared out into the dark, floating above Jeff's piano chords, and I got a flood of goose bumps. As soon as she sang the first lyrics, my chest ached. She started with "Old Time Woman," the song I had been playing over and over again.

"Well I just found out this afternoon I've been carrying life for two..." The crowd, recognizing the song right away, erupted in cheers, whistles and applause. I was on the verge of tears. "I needed some conversation to know what I should do..." I closed my eyes, saw the album spinning slowly on the turntable in my room. I saw John and I felt him next to me on my narrow dorm bed. I saw the candle burning, side by side with the incense. I gazed into the darkness of Meehan. Somewhere out there, John was sitting with a red-lipped blonde in a raccoon coat. He wouldn't miss Holly Near. But he probably wouldn't remember that the album had played the night we spent together.

The crowd was clapping. Holly was introducing her next song, "Water Comes Down." As a kid, Holly Near lived on a farm in northern California, where she would play in the fields all summer and stand in the irrigation ditches, waiting for water to flood in. For me, the song conjures up blue skies, hot dry fields and a wild rush of cold water. Sitting in Meehan, the song seemed to be California calling to me, to come there, to live somewhere faraway and mysterious, under sun and blue sky.

"Children in the pastures where the water flows, sunshine turning shirtless backs to brown...summertime, the water's coming..." And now water was coming. I pulled a tissue from my backpack and blew my nose. I didn't want Candace or Corinne to see me crying.

March 26, 1972 Monday

It's 7:30. I woke up a few minutes ago feeling very groggy, not even sure where I was. But even before I was fully conscious, panic flooded me. I remembered I've got organic chemistry class in a few hours. We got home from the concert at twelve and stayed up talking until 2:30. Now, it's 7:30. Corinne's asleep and I am writing, writing all the time. I'm forever grateful to Corinne that she sent me the journal.

I swung my feet to the floor and grabbed my terrycloth robe. I forgot my slippers at home. The linoleum was cold. I grabbed my toilet bag, just like old times, and headed down the hall. One shower was in use. By the time I finished washing my face, the shower curtain swept open. I could see Candace in the steamy mirror reaching out to grab a towel off a hook.

"Hi," she said, and I grunted a reply.

"Incredible concert last night," she said, winding a second towel around her head. With her long neck and straight, aristocratic nose, her drowsy-looking eyes, she looks regal to me. Immediately I felt self-conscious about my old bathrobe, and my swell of belly.

"Yeah, that was great," I said, pulling out my toothbrush. I wanted Candace to clear out right away, so I could use the toilet in peace. And also, I didn't want to have to undress in front of her. But naturally, she seemed to have all the time in the world.

"Corinne tells me you're going to spend the summer in Berkeley," she said, stepping out of the shower. Her toenails were a deep pink, each nail a perfectly shaped rose petal.

"Yeah, well, it's an option." I crossed my arms in front of my chest. I really needed to shower, get dressed. I was thinking about Corinne, how she should keep her mouth shut.

"What about..." Candace wrinkled up her face. "Oh, you know, what's his name?"

I stared at her. I was not going to help her. "Russell. Isn't that your boyfriend's name?"

"I call him Rus or...Rusty." Nails. Like the nails. "But his real name is Paul."

"Right. What about him? Is he...does he...mind?" My face flushed the color of Candace's carefully enameled toes. In that moment, I wanted to scream or wrap my hands around Candace's regal neck and make *her* scream. But instead, I spoke in a whisper.

"No," I said, forcing a smile. "No, this isn't his decision. It's mine." And then I opened the belt of my robe and slowly let the robe fall to the floor. I raised the nightshirt over my head. Candace stopped toweling her hair. Her eyes fell, from my breasts to my belly.

Standing there, I realized that I held a peculiar power over Candace Patterson. Considering the look on her face, I was absolutely certain that she had never seen a pregnant woman naked before. My spirits soared. I pulled my shoulders back and, smiling, stepped confidently into the shower.

❦

Organic chemistry has never been my strong point, but this morning, as Professor Harrison scribbled formulas across the blackboard, I was completely lost. At some point, I stopped taking notes. I could hardly listen. I started to doodle across the top of my notebook, writing "BERZERKLEY" on every line. The professor's voice grew louder as he approached my seat. I put my pen to paper and looked up sweetly.

"Are you following this?" he asked me, pausing by my desk. I had explained my situation to him before class and, now, he was trying to be nice.

"Well...kind of," I said softly.

He continued with the lecture. Sitting there, my face and neck hot, it occurred to me that I was so far behind in this course that I might flunk. This became even more apparent after class, when Harrison told me I'd have to make up my labs.

"You have about six unknowns to identify," he said, and suddenly I felt as though someone was twisting my insides the way you might wring out a towel. I hate chemistry lab and I'm hardly competent at the work. To identify the unknown chemicals in the lab takes precision and patience. I don't have either. I licked my lips.

"What do you suggest?" I squeaked. Harrison was perched against the edge of the desk. He stared at me, and I was just waiting for his focus to drop to my waist. But it didn't. Maybe because I had on my bulky Equadoran sweater, and that has always made me look fat.

"Well, maybe you can find somebody who's been through the labs, say in last year's class? See if he or she would supervise you through the unknowns. You'll still have to do the identifications, but with somebody there who's been through it, it won't be so bad."

I shook my head. "Yeah, that's a great idea," I said. "I'll do that." And I knew exactly who that somebody would be.

❦

John lives off campus in a run-down duplex with three other guys. Two of them are artists, taking classes at the Rhode Island School of Design. John toys with art himself. Last year he started blowing glass at

RISD. He took me once to the cavernous dark room where the furnaces are set into one wall. When the doors open, they form a row of fiery eyes, glowing yellow. He told me that sometime I could watch him turn a hot molten glob at the end of a long pipe into a fragile piece of glass.

As I walked toward his house today, I remembered his kitchen. The walls are fluorescent orange, and on one side, John and his roommates painted life-size black shadows of themselves. One figure is crouching, hands covering his head, in the corner. Two look like they're stretching, or dancing. To me, the shadows are haunting, maybe because John said they painted them one night after dropping acid.

I walked street after street on the hill, one home more elegant than the next. Big porches, white pillars. Brick mansions rising three stories above me. Between me and the houses were towering wrought iron fences. Finally, the big houses disappeared and I was in the blue collar Portuguese neighborhood of Fox Point, where John lives. The houses are right up against the sidewalk. No yards, but plenty of cement. On one corner there's a Portuguese bakery, with nothing but plump round loaves of shiny sweetbread in the window. Each loaf glistens just like my mother's Easter bread.

Soon I was face to face with John's house. I banged on the door of his glassed-in porch. It was one o'clock in the afternoon, not a time most students are home. But that's exactly why I chose to go then. I was not expecting to see him; I just wanted to leave a note. I banged again and a third time, and then took a notebook out of my backpack.

John — How did you like Holly Near? Great, I thought. Anyway, I wanted to ask a favor. I have to make up six organic chemistry labs, identifying unknowns. Harrison said I could get help from someone who went through the course before. Would you consider being my guide? I'd really appreciate it. Also, if you can't, do you know anybody who can? Thanks much, Eileen. I stuck the folded note into the metal screen door and turned to go when I heard the door opening behind me.

"Hey wait up." I turned. John was standing in the open door, with sweatpants on. No shirt or shoes. Tan arms the color of coffee with milk. A tight swell of muscle at his stomach. My own stomach flipped.

"Hi." He bent to pick up the note which had fallen when he opened the door. He began unfolding it, keeping his eyes on me.

"What's this, a love note?" He grinned and instantly, I was angry that I'd come. He has this incredible way of humiliating me.

"No, it's not." I shifted my backpack to the other shoulder. "I'm in a fix."

He looked up at me and muttered, "Yeah, so I heard." My face caught fire. Who would have told him? Not Corinne, but...word has gotten around.

He began reading the note.

"Look, John, just forget it. I shouldn't have come. I just thought that since you'd been through the labs, you wouldn't mind..."

"I don't." He refolded the note.

I stared at him. He grinned back. "Want to come in?" I did, more than anything in the world, but I shook my head no.

"What's your schedule like? I told Harrison I would arrange some time in the lab."

John yawned, and stretched his arms overhead. A knot of hair the color of wet sand clung to the pit of each arm. His sweatpants dropped slightly, exposing still more of his stomach. I stared, certain that he was stretching for my benefit.

I bit my upper lip. "How's four on Thursday?"

"Sure."

"I'll tell Harrison. So I guess I'll see you there. At the lab. Thursday."

I can still see him, the way he was leaning against the doorframe, his muscled arms folded. That grin. That chest. I was wondering if he was cold and suddenly that got me thinking about the girl in the raccoon coat. Where had she come from? No doubt she was a wheatie, imported from Wheaton College.

"So, Eileen, you liked Holly Near?"

"Yeah. She was great." I turned to go.

"Hey...Eileen?"

"Yeah?"

"I really would love to have you come in." Some kind of warm liquid started rushing up and down my arms and legs. Then I got a vision of a raccoon coat lying on the floor and a slender naked woman on John's bed, her red lipstick smearing his pillowcase and sheet.

"No, I can't. I've....got class. But thanks." I turned, trembling, and hurried up the street.

March 27, 1972
It was crazy to think I could miss six or seven weeks of school right in the middle of the semester and make everything up. Maybe my mother

was right. Not about marrying Rus, but about going back to school. Maybe I should have bagged the semester and taken incompletes. The amount of work I have to do in the next month feels like punishment.

I went to the science library to study tonight. Going through the door, the familiar smell rose up through my nose. I think I'm subject to the same operant conditioning that makes a dog salivate at the appearance of a bone. All I know is that just walking inside the library and smelling that unmistakable odor of dusty books, and hearing the overwhelming silence of the place makes my insides roll and clench. For somebody who wants to be pre-med, I'm not much of a student.

My carrel is on the seventh floor, right next to one of the tall, skinny windows that rise up the side of the library. The window looks out over trees and the buildings of Providence proper. Outside tonight, there was a gorgeous sunset. A ridge on the horizon. Flaming red, and above it a gleaming strip of purple, then yellow. I could have stared at the sky all night. Instead, I pulled out my calculus book. The lecture today was on "Definite Integrals as Total Change." I started to read page 203: *differential calculus is the mathematical study of change.* Outside, just beyond the glass, a crow, no, a seagull, was flapping by. The sky was quickly losing its color, taking on that wonderful milky blue that follows sunset, a royal hue, diluted in silver light.

I turned back to the book, to read words that meant nothing to me: *There are three types of mathematical change we might consider: total change, average change, and marginal change.* The rest of the page was filled with equations and wavy lines in green and black. I stared at the graphs and functions, and my eyes froze. I hadn't gotten this in class and I certainly wasn't getting it now. I looked back out the window, out to the royal blue sky, streaked through with slivers of salmon.

The math book was wrong. There *are* more than three types of change. There is an infinite variety. Just look at the range of colors in the evening sky. Just look at the way day slips imperceptibly into night. What equation could we possibly write? I put the calculus book back in my bag and pulled out *Don Quixote.* It will take me the rest of the night to translate three pages.

Late Thursday.

I want to figure out how this mess happened to me. I'm in such pain now I can barely think...but I must write...a little. I am terribly frightened...

I got to the lab at four. John wasn't there, so I climbed onto the stool next to the black lab bench and waited. Harrison had left me a note at the station, along with the lab book with instructions for testing the unknown chemicals. The first one was in a clear glass beaker on the lab bench. I swirled the beaker around and put my face to the opening at the top. An odor like alcohol and vinegar rose up, pinching my nose. Harrison says there are any number of ways to go about testing a chemical. I was reading about a few of those ways when the door swung open. John waltzed in, wearing the same grey sweatpants as the day before.

"Hi." I slipped off the stool.

He threw his book bag on the floor, and straddled the stool across from mine as if he was in a saddle. "Hi."

"So," he said. "We're here to explore the great unknown. Or should I say, unknowns. Yours, in particular." He swiveled one complete revolution on the stool. No hands. Finished with a grin. In the wake of his spin, I got a rush of his cologne.

"Are you sure you're up to this?" I was asking him, but I was really asking myself.

"Of course."

"This isn't a joke, you know." I had the lab book open against my chest when I realized my breasts, my nipples, were hard and tingling. My face flushed warm. I forced myself to set the lab book calmly on the bench. I bent over it, tapped it with my pencil eraser. "Harrison left me the first one here in this beaker."

John jumped to his feet, reached for the beaker, letting his arm pass very close to my breast. He passed the beaker under his nose and smiled. "I can tell you what it is, if you want, just from the smell, and we can skip the rest." He started to laugh, his deep rolling laugh. I wanted to yell at him, "Don't be so cocky, you total know-it-all-son-of-a-bitch."

Instead, I frowned. "No. I've gotta show Harrison I did the tests. With all the proof."

"OK, OK." He crossed his arms. "So what do want me to do?"

"Just watch me, I guess. And let me know if you think I'm making a mistake."

"OK. I'm watching you. Except, one thing, before you start."

"What?" I turned and he pulled me swiftly toward him and kissed me on the mouth. I pulled back, my heart hammering as I spoke.

"John, why didn't you ever call me back?"

"When?"

"What do you mean, when? I called you six times."

He hoisted himself back on the stool, straddling it with his legs. "I guess I...I'm not into long distance relationships."

"I guess." I turned back to the lab bench and lit a match. My hand was shaking. I should have stopped while I was ahead. I should have gotten the hell out of there. But no, instead I lit the Bunsen burner, then turned back to him. "I'm sure what's her name, with the raccoon coat, doesn't live next door. Where's she from anyway, Wheaton? Smith?"

"Ha," he said. "That's Sarah. She's...she's like a cousin."

"Right."

"She is. Anyway, why should you care?"

"I don't."

"I don't believe that."

I turned the flame up on the Bunsen burner and set the beaker in a metal ring over the flame. "Believe what you want." I took a pair of rusted tongs in my hand and squeezed them. When the glass beaker gets hot, you have to pick it up with tongs. It's tricky. And you have to pay attention, concentrate. I wasn't concentrating.

"I do believe one thing though...I believe you're pregnant." He said it quietly, almost sadly. I whipped my head around, so the tongs were pointing right at his nose. Suddenly I had this notion of throwing something at him, a dangerous idea when you're standing in a room full of glass beakers, some more than a foot tall.

I turned back to the Bunsen burner. There was steam rising from the beaker.

"Well, are you?" Slowly, I looked back at him. I got this vision of myself undressing, right there in the lab, just as I had for Candace in the shower.

"If I am, I assure you it has nothing to do with you."

"I know that. But what will you do?" The liquid in the beaker was bubbling frantically now, reminding me it was time to place a thermometer inside to see what the boiling point of the unknown liquid was. I dropped one in. The mercury started shooting up.

"I've got a few ideas," I said. John laughed.

"Like?"

"Like I think come May, I'll go with Corinne to Berkeley, stay with her all summer."

John laughed again. "So then we'll be neighbors. Kind of. But then what? I mean in the fall? Where will you..." He didn't get to finish the question. At that moment, the bottom of the beaker cracked, and glass shattered all over the lab bench. Hot clear liquid shot out from the exploding glass. I jumped back, but not before the steaming liquid coated my right hand. I screeched, and John jumped to my side at the bench.

He pushed me to the nearest sink and turned the cold water on full blast, and held my hand underneath. I screamed louder. It felt as though somebody was holding a blowtorch to my skin.

"Keep your hand in the water," he yelled and ran from the room. I remember him sprinting out the door and I remember putting my head down on the lab bench. I saw nothing more. John was yelling for help and I was swimming, my eyes closed, in a blur of pain and raw flesh and endlessly splashing cold water.

PART TWO

EILEEN

March 30, 1972

Luckily, I write with my left hand, because my right hand is lying in my lap like a polar bear paw, bandaged in white gauze. Only the tips of my fingers stick out, four loose little breakfast sausages. The gauze winds almost up to my armpit.

If there is anything positive to come out of all this, it is the way John has been treating me since it happened. I'm seeing a side of him I never saw before. No more smart aleck. And he says the accident was his fault. "If I hadn't been distracting you with all those dumb questions..." Last night, he drove me home from the emergency room and insisted I stay at his place.

"No, no, I don't know, I don't think so," I kept saying, my head anchored against the headrest. It was nine o'clock, and I had only eaten the tea and toast John had brought to me in the ER. I was groggy from the pain medication they gave me, and so exhausted that I couldn't imagine being romantic.

"Look," he said, swinging the MG sharply over to the curb and turning to face me. "I'm not planning to seduce you. Believe me, I just want to keep an eye on you, period. Phil Rosier wouldn't have let you out of the ER tonight except for the fact that he was discharging you to me. I promised him I'd be the one changing the bandage in the morning and that I'd bring you back in two seconds flat if you needed to come."

I looked over at him. Was I dreaming? Could this really be John Darrow offering to be my personal physician and nursemaid all night? The pain medication was finally starting to take hold. The throbbing in my right arm felt like it was growing more distant. I had a picture in my mind: my arm floating on a pillow, no, a cloud, and the cloud rising high into the sky, drifting overhead. I wanted nothing more than a pillow for my arm, but also one for my head. I wanted to be lying in a warm bed. Smiling, I drifted toward him. As I did, I caught the sweet odor of his cologne again. The smell was comforting, and soon it caught me up, carried me into his cloud, and I floated silently away.

March 31, 1972

The next morning, pain sliced right through my sleep. I woke up sobbing, staring into the grey light, my arm throbbing and tears streaming down my face. I forced myself onto my left elbow. My right arm followed unwillingly, a searing hot torpedo. "John," I wailed. He had been beside me all night on his own side of the double mattress on the floor. "Oh God, John!"

He bolted upright, confused, looked around, then rubbed his face briskly with both palms. Fumbling, he found the brown bottle of pain pills.

"OK, OK, you should have had two of these at four, I'm sorry, it's my fault, I overslept." He shook two white tablets into his palm and handed them to me with half a glass of water. I gulped them down. He watched, then gently set his open palm on my forehead.

"No temp," he said, leaving his hand there a moment. Then, ever so gently, he let one finger drop, stroking the side of my face. "For somebody who's been to hell and back, you look pretty good." Normally, a comment like that would make me melt. Now, it just started me crying again. I lay back down on the bed. Moving closer to me, he kissed my face once and cradled an arm around my head.

When I woke up again, I could see a line of bright sunshine beneath the shade. The throbbing had receded, and I felt somewhat better, but terribly thirsty. I reached over for the glass. Only then did I realize John was gone. On his pillow, though, was a note.

Thought I'd catch my eight o'clock. Be back by nine fifteen. PLEASE stay in bed. Bringing you breakfast. Love, JD

I smiled. No, I wouldn't have intentionally burned my hand, even for this. But since it happened anyway...

Rolling onto my knees, I tried standing, so I could get to the bathroom. The walls tilted and circled my head. Sinking back to the floor, I slid on my butt across the room, my useless hand like a claw resting in my lap. As I slid down the hall, dust balls rose up around me. I reached the bathroom and came face to face with the toilet bowl, crusted yellow. This place was more disgusting than I remembered. I held my breath and kept my eyes closed until I was seated upright. When I was done, I got back on the floor, slid toward the door.

Digging my heels against the oak floor, I felt a tug in my belly. A reminder. Two whole days had gone by and I hadn't thought once about being pregnant. And then this thought followed: not only am I pregnant, but now I've got this charred hand. How can I possibly get by on my own at school?

Soon John was back with a warm loaf of Portuguese sweetbread from the bakery next door. He sliced it, made tea, and presented the food to me on a tray he'd stolen from the Rat, Brown's cafeteria. Something about the tray reminded me: two different men had brought me breakfast in bed within the same week.

"Orange juice?" he asked.

I nodded.

"Fresh-squeezed," he said, pouring me a glass of a pulpy orange liquid. "My grandmother spends winters in Palm Beach, so she sends me box after box of citrus." He drank his glass, sitting cross-legged on the bed.

"So," he said, reaching into the glass with two fingers to fish out orange flesh. "Are you gonna let me take a look?" He gestured with his head to the bandage on my arm.

"How bad will it be?" I said. "The pain, I mean?"

He leaned his elbows into his knees. "Well, look at it this way, it'll be a whole lot worse if you don't let me look."

I kept my eyes trained out the window as he unwound the gauze. Only at the very end did I glance down at my arm. The skin looked parboiled, the flesh pink as a raw wet ham.

"Not bad," he said. I shivered. Just the air touching the skin pressed in like sandpaper. I bit my lip, turned my head to face out the window. An older woman from the Portuguese neighborhood was walking by in a shapeless, black coat. She was carrying a black pocketbook and wearing the kind of scarf on her head that my mother always wears to church. I shivered again, but this time, it was because I was think-ing about my parents. I knew I was going to have to call them — soon.

For lunch, John fixed me a can of chicken soup and a BLT. I ate it in the kitchen, staring at the shadows painted on his walls. That's when the call came. John answered. "Yeah, sure," he said, handing me the phone. "Corinne," he said.

I swallowed a spoonful of soup and took the receiver.

"Why haven't you called?" She sounded unusually annoyed.

"I guess because I've been kind of out of it. I'm sorry. What's wrong?"

Corinne heaved a sigh on the other end. "Your parents called. Apparently, the University reported the accident to them and they're frantically trying to reach you. Didn't it occur to you that maybe you should call them?"

I closed my eyes. "Corinne, please, I don't need a lecture." I paused. "What did you tell them?"

"I told them you were at the health center having...I don't know...the bandage changed. But look, I can't lie for you. You've got to call them..." I cut her off.

"OK, OK, I'll call this afternoon." For a second, neither of us spoke. "Anyway, how are you?"

"I'm OK. Really, I'm fine." John left the kitchen.

"Yeah, so what about...what's going on with John?"

"Look, I'm fine," I said, talking as softly as I could into the phone.

"Are you coming back anytime soon? Or have you decided to move in with..."

"Corinne?"

"Yeah?"

"I can take care of myself," I said, raising my voice. "Honest I can."

"Sure, fine, whatever you say, I just wondered is all." She sounded hurt.

"Look, I'm sorry. You have a right to be pissed. I should have called you, I should have called my parents. I've been kind of...in a shell, completely dazed." I looked at the clock on the stove. "Anyway, I was planning to come over to the dorm later on...unless...would you come here? I mean would you mind bringing me clean clothes, I could tell you what to bring."

She sighed again. "No. I don't mind, but I'm beginning to wonder if I have a roommate anymore."

She brought a grocery bag full of clean clothes at about four. John had gone out to play racquetball, so she and I sat in his room on the mattress. Corinne held her knees to her chest and scanned the room. It was empty except for the mattress and a beat-up dresser. And some empty beer cans.

"He's not much of a decorator is he?" she said.

I laughed. "As if you and I are?" She turned her greenish blue eyes on me.

"Look, Eileen. This...this thing with you and John. What exactly is going on?"

I was tracing a finger over my bare toes. "Nothing's going on."

Corinne folded her arms over her chest. Her gaze narrowed.

"OK," I said. "I'm in love. Is that what you wanted to know?"

She leaned over, looked me in the eye. "I'm really glad for you, Eileen, except..."

"Except what?"

"It's just..." she inhaled, long and slow. "I guess I'm...oh God I don't know. I was going to say surprised, but I know that's not fair. I guess it just seems like it's all happening kind of...fast." She said the last word slowly, softly, then raised her eyebrows.

"Corinne I told you before, I can handle it. I really can."

She started bouncing her chin against one knee. "I'm sure you can. It's just..."

"Just what?"

She looked straight at me. "Well, it seems like you're handling kind of a lot...at once."

"Look, would it surprise you if I told you John and I haven't done a thing? I mean, last night, he slept on that side and I stayed on my side."

"Yeah well..." She shrugged, shook her head. "I guess that *would* surprise me."

"Well, believe it or not, I'm telling you the truth."

"Fine, let's say I believe you. But what do you plan to do? I mean, are you moving in? Are you coming back to the dorm or going home or..."

"I'm not going home, that's for sure."

"OK. I should have figured that. But..." she heaved a sigh. "I know it's none of my business, but I can't imagine how this thing with John is going to go anywhere now that...now that you're..." Her mouth hung open but nothing came out.

"Corinne?" I whispered.

"What?"

"Please. Don't finish that sentence. OK? Just don't. Don't say another word? I know what I'm doing. Alright?"

She smiled. "Yup." She stood. "I got it. Only..."

"Yeah?"

"Are you still thinking you'll come home with me in May?" I started to get up, and she put a hand under my good arm to help.

"More than ever," I said, when I was standing. "More than ever."

❦

For dinner, John bought fresh scallops in town and we cooked them in a thick garlicky butter sauce. His roommates were gone for the weekend, so we had the place to ourselves. He stuck half a candle in an old wine bottle and set it on the kitchen table and then opened a new bottle of white wine.

"I know the guy who made this wine," he said, pouring. The pale wine lapped at the inside of the glass.

"You know the person who made the wine?"

He smiled. He loves to impress me.

"Yeah, the guy who owns the vineyard in Napa is a college friend of my father's."

"And so, let me guess, you went to Napa every summer and helped harvest grapes..."

"Well, actually it was in the fall. And we didn't harvest. We went out there some years for Thanksgiving weekend."

"You just flew out there? For the weekend?"

He shrugged and smiled again. "Yeah. Not every year though."

I sighed. "It must be nice."

"It is." He was about to refill my glass, but I put my hand up.

"Just a little, I mean this much." He looked at me. I think John forgets sometimes that I'm pregnant. We were eating scallops and spaghetti and garlic bread and I was thinking about the fact that three weeks ago I couldn't eat anything but Cream of Wheat.

"So what's Napa Valley like?" I watched him pour himself more wine. The bottle was three-quarters empty.

He looked up. His face was flushed and his eyes were a little shiny and his lips had started to go soft.

"Napa...happens to be...unbelievable. I went there with Dad once in March and it was completely covered in this yellow mustard flower. Waves of it. Whenever we used to go, we'd hit Calistoga and the natural hot springs. We'd drink wine all afternoon and then just sit in the hot springs and soak it up."

"That sounds perfect."

"It was." He sat back in his chair. "It will be." He was studying me. "Again."

I looked down at my plate. "Yeah, I'm sure you'll be going back."

I was going to add "next fall," but something in me didn't want to say the words. Because it would define a time that could not be defined. At least not for me. So instead, I just smiled, ran my good hand through my hair.

John pushed his plate away and he was tipping back on his chair and sipping wine and rolling it around in his mouth. His eyes were wide and bright and he kept staring at me. I thought, *he's going to make a move toward me any time now.*

"Well, maybe I'll bring you along, to Napa."

I looked at him. "Maybe you will."

"I mean...if you're out there anyway..." He shrugged.

"Yeah. If." I brought my plate to the sink. I couldn't think straight. I hated these games we played. I hated feeling so desperate, so carried away that I would do anything to get him to touch me. I was at the sink with my back to him. I heard him set his glass on the table.

"Eileen I have...I want to ask you something."

"Sure. What?"

"I don't want to get into a big thing, though."

"OK, so we won't. What is it?" I was trembling. I washed my plate with my good hand. I hated myself for wanting him to want me. I kept seeing him hold me. I kept hearing him ask me if I would come out to San Francisco with him.

"Just one question."

"Sure." I turned from the sink. He's going to ask me when I'm going to San Francisco, or how I'm getting there, or where I plan to live. He's going to offer me a ride.

"Did you...did you ever think..." He got up, poured more wine into the glass, took a big drink. "I mean...why is it you decided not to get an abortion?"

The question landed like a grenade on the table.

"I...I didn't...I don't...I don't want to talk about it." I ran out of the kitchen.

"Eileen, come back!" he yelled. I was heading for his room but I realized that wasn't where I belonged. For the first time since the accident, it hit me: I didn't belong in his apartment at all. I grabbed up my clothes and threw them into the grocery bag Corinne had brought earlier. I told myself *don't cry, don't cry*, and I held my breath, and didn't. Until he opened the door.

"Look," he said, "I know it isn't any of my business, and I'm sorry...."

"You should be." My mouth was cottony and my throat felt bound in rope.

"OK, but it doesn't seem like you've got a hell of a lot of good options or that you've invested a hell of a lot in this kid..." I covered my ears but, still, I could hear him. I heard myself shriek and then instantly I stopped, embarrassed. He turned and left, slamming the bedroom door. I sank onto the mattress and sat there like a baby, sobbing so hard I felt like I might be sick. Why hadn't I listened to Corinne? Why had I been stupid enough to think he would want me to go with him to California? I stood up, grabbed the grocery bag and left the bedroom. I was putting my coat on when John came back, holding his wine glass. He leaned against the door.

"You will regret leaving and you know it," he said, his cocky self once more. But his tone wasn't menacing or mean. He was just quietly stating a fact, and he was so sure of it. And he was absolutely right.

"Move out of the way," I said, keeping my distance. I had the grocery bag full of dirty clothes shielding my chest. "John, please, are you going to move?"

"No, I'm not. Not until tomorrow morning anyway. We'll just spend the night by the door." He slid down to the floor holding the wineglass. He sipped the wine and stared back.

"John," I said quietly, keeping my eyes closed. "I really appreciate all you've done for me this week. I am in fact incredibly grateful. But I have to go back to the dorm. To get myself...oriented. I mean this has been wonderful but very confusing." I opened my eyes and to my surprise he was on his feet again, only an arm's distance away.

"I don't know what's so confusing about it," he said, very softly.

I stared back at him. "Sure you do," I said. "And a few minutes ago, you reminded me about it all over again." Tears streamed down both my cheeks. "You know exactly what my problem is. You can be so cruel."

He set the wine glass on the floor and lifted the bag out of my arms. He pulled me toward him and kissed my mouth. His face was hot and flushed and mine was hot and wet and I was trying to get something out, something like "No, John, no, don't. Stop, please, stop." But we weren't stopping. Instead we were dropping to the floor and he was cradling my bad arm with one hand and slipping his other hand deftly into my T-shirt and down my chest and suddenly I didn't speak another word. We came to rest in the corner, right in front of the door, and I let him move his hands wherever they wanted to go.

AUDREY X

Audrey comes home on crutches, arriving at Maple Hill shortly after noon in the wood-paneled station wagon. Marjory is driving, straining as she always does to see over the steering wheel. Her chin rides high above her arched neck, so that by the time she pulls into the driveway, her face is tense and the corners of her mouth are drawn down in a pout, and her chin is puckered. Big Martha, on the other hand, is in the back seat, relaxed and smiling, the crutches and her cowboy hat resting on her lap.

The car accelerates up the driveway, back tires scattering gravel. In the living room and the kitchen respectively, Pit and Francine hear the car. Candace hears it too, upstairs, where she's been for most of the morning, rolling white paint over the rosy sea on the wall.

Marjory opens the passenger door of the car and steps back. In a moment, Audrey's leg emerges, dangles outside the car. The leg ends in a short white cast, heel covered, toes exposed. On the good foot, which emerges next, Audrey wears her weathered sneaker. Big Martha is waiting with crutches. Audrey wedges them under her armpits and shifts side to side as she settles into the orange rubber saddles.

From the bedroom window upstairs, Candace is watching. What occupies her thoughts isn't her grandmother struggling to inch ahead through the mud and gravel on crutches. Instead, she has a view of Audrey just a few days before, when she took off across the dazzling white snow so confidently in her ridiculous sneakers. Nothing could stop her, nothing at all, Candace thought that morning, until of course something did, the next day, one wrong move in the early morning, one icy rock, one hole, one slight incline in the forest that the foot wasn't expecting. With one false step, the whole picture turned upside down. Now, Audrey can't walk, and won't be able to, for weeks.

Candace clamors down the stairs in time to see Audrey come through the back door.

"We're glad you're home," Francine says, reaching up, placing a kiss on Audrey's cheek. Pit kisses the other cheek and Candace touches Audrey's shoulder.

"Hi," Candace says brightly, and smiles at her grandmother, but the smile doesn't last. Audrey's hair — which is badly in need of washing — is tied in an unsightly ponytail, hanging down her back. The hairstyle and her worn face make Audrey look years older than she did just a few days before. Audrey moves methodically across the kitchen. Marjory and Big Martha tail right behind her, one on each side. When Audrey reaches the picnic table, they move ahead and cushion her elbows while she pivots, pale and winded, off the crutches onto the bench.

"So you stayed," Audrey says to Candace, a hand on each knee.

"Yup."

"Good. And Mark too." Barefoot, Mark is quietly standing in the corner of the kitchen. "I'm glad to see you. I am told you did the work of three people helping on pails. I appreciate that." Mark raises one hand in greeting, wiggles his fingers.

"What did your mother say to your staying on?" Audrey says, turning back to Candace. The question, Candace knew, had to come.

"I haven't called her." Candace raises her eyebrows, twists a strand of yellow hair around one finger, the same strand of hair that always gets twisted at moments like this. "Because, well, actually, Gram, we thought we'd probably leave later on today."

"Oh." Audrey narrows her eyes slightly, then her lips wrinkle. "That's too bad. I had thought to ask you to stay on, now that I'm half crippled here."

"I could," Candace says, her voice and spirits lifting. "If maybe you would call Eileen."

"No, no, it's probably best you go. I don't dare come between you and your mother." Audrey sets her crutches against the end of the table. "Besides, there are other able-bodied souls here who can help out." She reaches up to take the mail from Marjory. There are three or four colorful catalogues on the bottom of the pile, and a few windowed envelopes that look like bills.

"Are you ready for lunch?" Francine asks, tying on her apron. "I made tuna and egg salad, and there's lettuce and tomato..."

"No, no, thank you, they fed me before I left."

"If you call that food," Marjory mutters, settling beside Audrey on the bench.

"Food or no food, it filled me. But you all go ahead and eat." Francine opens the refrigerator. Audrey pulls a letter from a powder blue envelope. "Only, before you do, I want to..." she inhales again, "...to...share something with you." She looks up. "All of you."

Marjory reaches for Audrey's hand. "Can't this wait, Audrey, don't you think it..."

"No, no, certainly not. This definitely cannot wait." Marjory recoils, as if she's touched something hot. Audrey sits up straighter. She's got the letter in both hands, has it raised to her chest, as though it were a heavy pot with a lid. Candace can see the letter is typed, single-spaced, and across the top of the blue paper is a jagged line in dark purple ink—the profile of a mountain chain.

"We got three days' worth of mail this morning, and one thing was the tax notice, because, again, we're overdue." Audrey licks her bottom lip quickly. "But there was this, too." She stares around the room. Pit is sitting in her rocker, sipping a glass of orange juice. Francine is at the sink shaving a carrot. Big Martha is standing beside the open refrigerator, eating a square of cheese.

"How bad can it be?" Francine asks, "I mean, we're current on the mortgage and..."

"I didn't say it was bad," Audrey says, shortly, directing her gaze at Francine. "In fact, I think at least a few of you will think it's pretty good news. You'll be downright delighted." She holds the letter up a little higher. "Snowstack wants to expand. They want to add a whole new series of trails on this side of the mountain. They want to buy our land, or at least most of the ninety acres. They're willing to purchase the whole property." She pauses. "We have here a very decent offer."

Francine clears her throat, crosses her arms, slipping her hands under her armpits. Big Martha raises a hand to her double chin.

"How much do they offer?" Pit asks, her voice croaking.

Audrey surveys the group silently, then gazes down at the letter. "If they buy the whole place, the company is offering $560,000. Of course, they'll pay less if they don't take the house."

Francine whistles. Silence follows.

"But Grandma, you don't want to sell, do you? I mean all of you...this is your home, isn't it? And a place to do your work, too? You can't just sell it all, can you?" Candace asks, her voice thin and a little breathless, a whisper hovering over the room like mist. It settles lightly on each and every head.

Audrey folds the letter, slides it back into the envelope. "This clearly isn't a decision for me to make alone," she says, her voice even. "It's for the group to decide. Only..."

"Only what?" Francine asks.

"Only, we have to make the decision soon. Really soon. Snowstack says the offer only stands for the next ten days."

Audrey reaches for the crutches and hoists herself up. Marjory rises, stands beside her. "We have to talk," Audrey grunts. "All of us, together." She glances at her wristwatch. "How about we meet say, at 4:00?"

"Sure," Pit says. The others nod.

"Tea time," Big Martha jokes, but no one responds.

"Right now, I've lost all my starch," Audrey says. "I'm going upstairs, to rest." She hobbles from the kitchen and the others silently watch.

AUDREY X

"We can talk about this all night if you want to," Audrey is saying to Francine. "I promise you, Fran, I wasn't trying to cut you off. All I was saying was, I think eventually we do have to put it to some kind of a vote." She looks to the rest of the group gathered in the living room. Pit, who is between Marjory and Audrey on the sofa, nods in agreement.

"Yes, of course. Of course we have to vote," Pit says, her voice a rasp. "Maybe not today, not this afternoon. Or maybe we should, maybe we should have a series of votes, one now, and then one in a day or two." Pit pulls herself up to a straighter position, brings the afghan she's wrapped in high around her neck.

"But the way I see it," she continues, speaking slowly, "we wouldn't even be talking about this except for the tax money. And in a way that's kind of silly, isn't it? What is it, forty-six, forty-seven hundred dollars, more or less, that we need and some of that we have already. And the rest, well, I have savings, we all have some savings we could dip into if we needed to..."

"Well, no, not all of us do," Marjory says, quietly.

"Thank you, Marjory," Francine says, raising her voice. "I appreciate your saving me the embarrassment of having to say that myself." She turns to Pit. "Unlike you, I was never fortunate enough to be married to a banker. Unlike you, I don't have a dime to my name. Literally. Except for my share of the farm, I'm broke. And that's the truth."

"Well don't get me wrong, I'm not swimming in stocks and bonds," Pit responds. "I just think that among all of us, we can assemble the money if we have to. That's all."

"I'd like to add something," Big Martha says. "Pit, I think you're probably right that we shouldn't unload the farm just because we're having trouble paying taxes this year. But from my point of view, that's not the only reason. Some of us are getting...how should I put it? Oh hell, some of us are just getting too old for this routine. We have to work too hard to harvest the sugar. And we make too little money. I'm tired of money being so tight all the time."

Candace, lying on the floor, wants to say something inspiring, wants to remind the women about how it used to be while she was growing up at the farm. The summers she lived there, no one ever argued, or even spoke much about money, and surely it was in short supply then, too. But in the old days, when they ate dinners together, or breakfasts, or when they would hike together, or lie outside in the backyard in the sun, conversation focused on Audrey's latest sculpture, or Pit's, or the striking shadows in Big Martha's photographs, or the difficulty Marjory was having painting a haystack or a wagon or a barn. In those days, what mattered most was their work, not money. Candace sees now that a new reality, one that is cold and sharp and unforgiving, has taken hold, and that reality is breaking her heart.

"Money's always been tight," Marjory declares, as if she's just been reading Candace's mind. "I think this farm is worth fighting for." Candace has a vision of Marjory kneeling on the oak floor of her bedroom, holding a frame, and a staple gun, stretching a piece of canvas over strips of blond wood.

"I don't see what it is we're arguing about," Pit says. "I agree with you, Marjory."

"What we're arguing about is the future," Francine shoots back.

"Yeah," Big Martha adds. "And the present, too. This life in the woods is way too tough for an old broad like me. I've been seeing my chiropractor so much lately, I might as well move in with him."

"I don't disagree that things are getting harder," Pit says, her voice barely audible. "I mean come on, look at me. Things are..." She shakes her head, and with that, her voice trails off.

Marjory takes over. "Maybe what we need to be talking about isn't selling, but finding more creative ways to improve the harvest. Or more ways to market it. Remember I told you about that fancy grocery store I went to in Boston that sells those cute little bottles of sap, right next to the seltzer water and soda? One of the big sugar producers is selling bottled sap, as a beverage, for almost two bucks a bottle. It's crazy, but hey, if city people are silly enough to buy it, what the heck? And the same sugar bush is making salad dressing out of maple syrup too, we could do that, we could try..."

"Oh, for God's sake, Marjory," Francine snaps. "Do you really see us mixing huge vats of oil and vinegar here in the kitchen? And can you actually imagine us trying to distribute thousands of bottles of salad dressing? From the back of the station wagon? Honestly, that's just plain foolishness."

"Why must you always be so negative?" Pit says, her voice menacing, despite its low energy. Her blue eyes flash in their dark sockets. "Marjory is right on the mark," she says, and here, Candace notices that in her anger, Pit's British accent is more noticeable.

"Don't call me negative," Francine says hotly. "I am simply being practical. We can barely get these damn pails from the trees to the sugar house and here you two are dreaming up some fancy new marketing scheme. First you've got to have the syrup, which we don't have, at least not this year. And it isn't clear we will next year either."

"Would you both just quiet down?" Audrey says, her voice deliberate and slow. "Would you please?" She waits. Pit and Francine remain silent, and sullen. "Thank you. Now, believe it or not, I think you're both right. To a point. Francine, you really have a way of throwing cold water on an idea before it even has a chance to spark." Francine starts to protest but Audrey raises her hand to stop her. "No, please, I haven't finished." Audrey looks around the room. "Now. In fairness to Francine, however, she is absolutely right about our basic problem. That is, we don't have an efficient system, or anything close to it, for collecting sap. Not to blame anyone, but we have our difficulties hauling pails."

Candace closes her eyes and sees herself moving slowly between the trees, cold clear sap slopping out of the tops of the pails.

"What we need," Marjory says, "is gravity tubing. Is that what you're saying?"

"That would help, and..."

"But Marjory how much would that cost?" Francine asks. "Be realistic."

"Obviously, I think one or more of us would have to spend a little time researching that option." Audrey pauses and Candace wonders if she is waiting for someone to volunteer to do the research. No one does. "The point is, it's certainly possible to do tubes. Most other farms around here have gone that route for their bushes, with good results."

"Yeah, but you read about the problems," Big Martha says. "You read where the squirrels and the deer nibble at the tubes, or the tubing gets constipated, or it freezes or…"

"Nothing is going to be perfect, Martha," Marjory says.

"Selling the farm would be easy," Francine shoots back.

"Oh God, Francine, how absurd," Pit says. "Sure, selling is easy. At first. But then what? Where does everybody go? Where exactly would you move?"

Big Martha chuckles, sinks deeper into the couch and pulls a knee up in both hands. "Well, let me tell you. I'd take my eighty grand and head directly south, without passing go. Palm Beach, maybe, or even further south. I've heard the Everglades are just spectac…"

"I hate to tell you Martha, but eighty thousand dollars won't get you too far or last you too long even in Florida," Marjory says.

"And it's only eighty apiece if we sell the house, right Audrey?" Pit adds.

"Can I say something?" Candace says, sitting up. She can hardly believe she hears her own voice. But she knows if she doesn't say what's on her mind, she will regret it later.

"Of course dear," Audrey says. "You have a stake in all this too." Not only does Candace stand to inherit Audrey's share in the farm, she has, in her own name, a full share in the property. Audrey set aside Candace's one-sixth share in 1973 when she and the women legally divided the farm.

"Well, it just seems to me that none of you is even thinking about your own artistic work," she says, feeling her face turn hot as all the women turn to look at her. "I mean, what would happen to each of you, how would you keep going with your work, your photography, Martha, or Marjory, your painting? Or, Francine, your book, your writing? You can't forget about that, or at least, you have to think about it, don't you? And what about…what about the fact that this place has been…well a haven, a place to hide. I hope you're not going to say you can just throw all of this, all of these memories away…" Candace's voice evaporates. She shrugs her shoulders. Something is tugging behind her eyes.

"Of course, sweetie, that's all very important," Marjory says. "I know it sounds like we aren't concerned about our work, or about what we've had here, but maybe that's because it goes without saying that we care about it, about what brought us together in the first place."

"But maybe Candace has a point," Pit says. "If we look around this room," and now her blue eyes flash again scanning the group, "the two people who seem to be most interested in selling are the two people who are the least committed to doing their artwork..."

"Now hold on, Pit," Big Martha yells, anger erupting in her for the first time. "That is just not fair."

"There you go Pit," Francine protests, screaming and jumping up from the couch. "I knew it would come to this. I just knew it. As a matter of fact, Pit, I have sold probably three short stories for every piece of junk metal you've welded together. And just because I haven't had luck with the second novel doesn't mean..."

"You haven't written a word of fiction in three years and you know it," Pit says, raising her voice too. It looks like it takes every last bit of her energy to talk.

"Maybe the reason I'm not writing has something to do with the fact I do so much goddamn cooking for this crowd," Francine yells, inching forward toward Pit. Francince's eyes look like they could bore holes. "I get no appreciation for it in return. And anyway, who are you to talk? I haven't seen you down in the studio once in the last three or four months and you know..."

"Francine!" Audrey intervenes sharply. "That is *enough*."

"I would be doing the sculpture if I could and you know it," Pit whispers, getting up. Suddenly she stops, stares wide-eyed at each woman in turn. "It really doesn't matter what I think about all this. As far as this matter goes, as far as I'm concerned, I am, as they say, history." Her eyes wide and filled with tears, her voice dissolving, Pit covers her mouth with her long bony hand and continues slowly through the living room. Marjory follows and helps her up the stairs.

"How could you be so cruel?" Audrey says in disbelief. "Francine, I think I may have seen your worst side today. And I pray that when Pit's gone, you won't be tortured with guilt." Audrey shakes her head. "I just hope you will be able to live with yourself."

Francine's face remains stony. "You've always taken her side," she says coldly.

"Side? What side? Why, Francine, tell me, tell me why it is that there are two sides here?" Audrey is almost shrieking now, and fumbling up onto her crutches. "I cannot, I have not ever been able to understand why the two of you hate each other so much."

"She...she never liked me," Francine says.

"Oh Francine that's not true," Audrey says.

"It absolutely is true," Francine says, a new and far more potent wave of fury pouring forth. "She...she never liked me, or my writing. She said...." and now Francine looks desperate, "she said I...she read my novel, and...one night I was in the kitchen, I heard her, I heard her telling Marjory." Her voice drops into a whisper. "She was so mean. She said I was just wasting my time." Francine's last few words can barely be heard as sobbing overwhelms her. Hurrying to the kitchen, she opens the back door and runs, coatless, out into the pouring rain.

Audrey looks around the room, her face drained of color. Slowly, she sinks back into her chair.

CANDACE

Candace finds Mark lying on her bed, eyes closed, earphones on his head, his portable CD player resting on top of his chest. She drops beside him and buries her face in the blanket. Mark's eyes pop open, and he lifts one spongy earphone away from his ear. "What's going on downstairs?"

"Oh God, could you hear?"

"Just a little. I was switching from Coltrane to Thelonius Monk, and from the sounds of things, it was the beginning of the next World War."

"Whoof. It was," Candace says, still talking into the blankets. "It was...horrible." She pushes herself up. "I think...I think it's time to leave. Are you packed?"

"Yeah, all two sweatshirts, sure." He gets up. "Was anything decided?"

Candace laughs. "Yeah, one thing. At least two people in this place hate each other's guts. Look, Mark, before we leave, I need to talk to Grandma. It'll only take a few minutes."

"Whatever you say." He drops back on the bed and readjusts the headphones over his ears. "I'll be here, just soaking up the Monk."

Candace finds Audrey in the kitchen, face to face with Marjory at the picnic table. Neither woman is speaking and each is staring over a mug. Steam spirals up out of each cup.

"Can I come in?" Candace says, her voice tiptoeing into the kitchen.

"Sure," Audrey says, not looking up. "Of course you can, honey."

Sliding into the bench beside Audrey, Candace rests her arm over her grandmother's shoulders. "Has...has Francine come inside?" she asks just above a whisper.

"No," Audrey says. She brings the steaming cup to her lips.

"Would you...do you want me to look for her?"

"No, definitely not," Audrey says. She turns to Candace. "But thank you for asking."

As if she heard her name being spoken, Francine appears at the back door. Her face is dripping and her hair is hanging in strings, a wet mop glued to her shoulders. Her clothes are drenched. She pushes open the door and walks inside, shivering.

"You'd better get a hot bath right away," Audrey says.

Francine crosses the kitchen, leaving a trail of muddy footprints. "I plan to." She stops by the table, stands there shaking. "I also plan to move out as soon as I find a place."

"Now Francine don't go making any hasty decisions," Audrey says. "This was an argument, a disagreement, and that's all." Francine is shuddering, but then Candace realizes she is also shaking her head. Water droplets fly. A couple splatter Candace's eyes.

"No, it was an argument that really made me see," Francine says. "As much as I hate to admit it, Pit is right. I haven't been writing for years now. I let Pit, her opinion of my writing, destroy me. I let her stop me from doing what I most love. Mostly, though, I let myself grow stale living here. I have turned into a goddamned wife. Yes. That's all I am. A wife, a slave to all of you who continue to be creative."

"Francine, that's not true. You never..." Audrey starts, but Francine isn't through.

"Oh yes it *is* true," she interrupts. "I do nothing but cook, shop and clean up. I'm in such a horrible rut. And do you know why? Because I'm afraid, truly terrified of my own writing. I've grown to hate it, and myself, living here. And now I hate all of you too, for letting me dig myself into a hole, for letting me become the slave I've become."

"But Francine, nobody ever wanted you to be anything but..."

"Of course not," Francine says, with another shudder. "Nobody *made* me do anything. I realize that now. And Pit, you see, for all her cruelty, for all her mean words, she finally opened my eyes. She has shown me how, for my own sanity, I've got to get out. I see that now. So clearly. I must leave. I can. And I will."

There is silence for a few moments. "Where will you go?" Marjory asks finally.

"I don't know... maybe New York. I still have friends there. Maybe I could stay with my sister Joan until I get settled. All I know is that I've just got to be around writers again. I've got to find a way to...to be inspired."

She says the last few words in a light, practically inaudible voice, wiping her sleeve across her face as she does. Not all of what's dripping down her cheeks is rain. "It's just so hard to have something like this thrown in your face..." Her blue lips tremble. "I'm sorry, Audrey, but even if she's sick, even if she's half dead, Pit is still as cruel and hateful to me as she ever was." Francine turns and before anyone has a chance to say another word, she flees the kitchen, leaving behind a muddy puddle on the floor. She's left behind a vague odor, too, a smell of the outdoors, the smell of wind, cold spring rain.

Audrey is the first to speak. "She's right, of course, you know." She pauses.

"That Pit is cruel?" Marjory asks in surprise. Audrey eyes Marjory.

"No, I meant Francine is right that she has to leave. For her own sake, it's better." Audrey sighs. "She's absolutely right when she says that we've let her become our wife. Our slave." The three of them sit in uncomfortable silence. Finally, Audrey speaks. "It's ironic."

"What?" Marjory asks. "What's ironic?"

"That Francine is saying she's become a slave here." Audrey pauses. "Candace, do you remember my telling you why my great grandparents started this farm?"

Candace shrugs. "I don't know, Grandma. If you have, I guess I've forgotten."

"When my great grandfather, Boyd O'Malley, was a young man, he traveled a lot in the Caribbean, on an English cargo ship, and what he saw — black men, women, and children slaving endlessly under a broiling sun on the sugar plantations — appalled him."

Rising from the table, Audrey reaches out to her crutches. "Eventually he went back to England, married my great grandmother, Clara Wheeler, and the two of them made their way to Vermont. They settled here. Boyd became a minister. He and Clara were part of a group of early settlers who decided to protest the slave trade by starting a sugar farm. Clara took charge. According to her diary, which is no more than a daily record, they started in

1833. They planted the first trees in a religious dedication ceremony that Boyd led."

"That's...sort of...interesting," Candace says, wondering what it has to do with Francine's decision to leave the farm. She is about to ask, but before she can, Marjory does.

"Audrey, please, what's your point here? That we've made Francine our slave on a farm that was settled to defy slavery?"

Audrey starts to hobble across the kitchen. "It's not just Francine. I can't help thinking how ironic it is that my great grandparents came here, hell bent against slavery. And yet here we women have ended up slaves to this farm, sugaring. I wonder sometimes what dear Clara would say."

Marjory gets up from the table. "She'd probably remind us that she too broke her back. I wonder how much help she got from her husband. Anyway, Francine may be right to leave, but that just makes things more complicated for us."

"That's for sure," Audrey says, nearing the kitchen door. "I'm wondering if maybe we shouldn't all just leave too. Florida is beginning to sound mighty tempting. I keep asking myself, why *any* of us should continue slaving away, caring for these trees."

Candace gets up now. "But Grandma. I *love* these trees, this farm. I feel like I grew up here, at least in the summers. I don't know what I would have done if I couldn't have come here and stayed with all of you. I learned to do my drawing and painting here. Oh Grandma, I can't bear to lose all of this. It's everything to me. You must see that."

Audrey stares at Candace, frowning now. "I do, Candace," she says in a low voice. "I do see that very clearly, honey. But Francine's leaving is a blow."

"But why, Grandma? Why not just let Francine go?" Candace stands.

"Well, for one thing, Candace, we really have to pay Francine back her share when she goes. When each of the women came, they bought a one-sixth portion of the farm. I took a share for me, and one for you, and each of the others bought one too, or committed to paying it off in work. So now, by rights, we owe Francine for her share."

"Oh but Audrey, that's ridiculous," Marjory says. "What's Francine's share worth? What's anybody's worth? And who's to say if she's paid it off in work?"

Audrey's eyes flash. "After the way Francine spoke today, I'd say she's paid way more than her share. Being here has destroyed her, as an artist *and* a woman."

"OK, OK, but she can't expect a hunk of money now, not when we don't have it."

"Look, Marjory, Francine is miserable. She's got to get out and she's got to have money to do it, to get set up elsewhere." Silence descends. Candace ends it.

"Grandma, I think you're incredible for being so...so understanding of everybody, of their problems even when their decisions stand to hurt you. I want you to know that I have some money in the trust fund Mom set up for me when I was a baby, and I would gladly give it to you, all of it, to buy Francine's share. I'd do it in a second, because the farm is worth it, it's worth saving, it means so much to me..." Audrey is shaking her head before Candace can finish.

"No, Candace," she says, reaching over and touching the shank of hair that Candace is always twisting. "This is not *your* problem, sweetheart. Not at all. I don't expect anything from you, least of all money." She lowers her voice. "And don't you think you might need that trust fund yourself? Especially now?" Audrey points a finger at Candace, then starts down the hall. Marjory follows, leaving Candace all alone in the kitchen.

She settles back on the bench and traces her fingernail in the reddish grain of the table. She remembers staining this table. She remembers being seven or eight and being with all of the women one Saturday afternoon in June. The maples had the tender green leaves of spring. Wood for the table was scattered in the newly mown grass, and everybody had a job in the table assembly line. Candace's job was to dip a rag into a can of orange red stain, and then to rub it over each piece of wood. She remembers running the rag along the wood, thinking, this is the color of my hair. But when she was told to stain the underside of the picnic table, she protested. "Why do that? I mean, nobody's going to sit underneath the table, are they?" And then her face had burned pink, because the women had laughed at her remark.

Her face flushes again now. She had wanted to argue with Audrey, had wanted to insist that she be allowed to use her trust money to help. But she had said nothing. She let her grandmother walk away. Once again, Candace was silenced, reduced to feeling like a child.

She stands and slams her hand on the table. This time, she will not remain the helpless little girl. This time, she has a plan, an idea that will work. All she needs is her mother's approval to make it happen.

CANDACE

By the time Candace and Mark leave, the rain is spent, and the clouds are thinning rapidly. Only Audrey steps outside to the back porch to say goodbye. Candace stands beside the open door of the Toyota while Mark guns his motorcycle. The engine explodes in an ear-splitting roar, and smoke blasts from the tailpipe. As if disturbed by the noise, the clouds part, forming a blue hole in the white afternoon sky. Sunshine pours through to the backyard. Candace smiles and points, hoping Audrey will see. "Grandma, it's a sign, a sign," Candace calls out. The appearance of the sun, she wants to shout, is the next best thing to a rainbow. Audrey, however, is oblivious. Pale and slung between her crutches, she smiles wanly and lifts one hand briefly to wave goodbye. Then she turns and awkwardly reenters the house.

As she maneuvers the Toyota back down Undermountain Road, Candace glances frequently in the rear view at Mark, dodging bumps and ruts and zigzagging around puddles. At one point, the bike swerves and tips dangerously close to the road. Instantly, Mark is off the bike, pushing. Candace stops, but he signals her to go on, which she does, soon losing sight of him in the mirror. She reaches the corner and pulls over. In a moment, Mark appears, grinning, coated up to his thighs in mud.

The rest of the trip is uneventful. If she had to, Candace could make the drive from Vermont to Massachusetts blindfolded. All her life, she has divided her time between North Adams during the school year and Wilmont every summer. Making the trip home in

August was always a sad ordeal. Candace would wake up that final morning, see her packed suitcases, and inevitably go running downstairs to Audrey's room, sobbing. Sitting on Audrey's bed, the two of them would have their annual heart-to-heart talk about why it was better for Candace to live in North Adams during the school year.

Traditionally, Francine would make blueberry pancakes for Candace's last breakfast. All the women gathered, bringing Candace presents to ease her departure. One year, Marjory tie dyed her a T-shirt with glowing red and yellow maple leaves on the front. That same year, Big Martha photographed Candace's bare feet while she slept by the pond and then gave her the black and white photo, enlarged to poster size. Francine inevitably baked a tin of brownies for Candace. Pit would make her another beeswax candle. And Audrey almost always carved Candace a small forest animal. By the time she was twelve, Candace's collection included a squirrel, a chipmunk, an owl, a fox, a bear, and—best of all—a small fawn. Marjory had painted the fawn, adding a gentle splattering of white spots along its caramel-colored coat.

Driving home to North Adams, Candace would keep her eyes shut tight, and not speak right away to her father. Sitting quietly, she would count to herself the number of days until she would come back the next summer. She would examine each of her presents and eat a brownie from Francine's tin. Then she would sit there, barefoot, staring glumly out the window. A few minutes outside of North Adams, just after leaving Route 8, Rusty would reach under the seat of the truck and pull out her sneakers. "It's time," he'd say, dangling the canvas shoes.

That's when Candace knew the summer was behind her. No more lazy mornings lying in the hammock under a jewel blue sky. No more roaming at will around the farm, a sketchbook and charcoal pencil in hand. No more lying still in the tall grass by the pond and swimming in the green black water with the women. No more climbing Maple Hill and whispering this or that to Hannah. Instead, Candace faced another boring school year: a new teacher, a pair of stiff leather shoes, and those awful cotton dresses, handmade by Lucy out of green and blue plaid. Sometimes her grandmother bought her an outfit or two, but usually it was a box-pleated skirt with a white blouse, or a jumper and a navy blue sweater, an outfit that inevitably proved much too hot for September.

After Eileen got back from California, Candace's school wardrobe transformed dramatically: finally, she was allowed to wear T-shirts, blue jeans, and running shoes to school like all the other kids did. That first September, when she had just turned eleven, Eileen even bought her a stonewashed jean jacket. Despite this, though, Candace still wasn't happy leaving Vermont. Yes, she missed Eileen and yes, she was glad to see her mother after the summer. But Candace's heart was in Vermont with her sketchpad and pencils. Much to Eileen's dismay, Candace hated school and was never much of a student.

In exactly one hour and thirteen minutes — even now, Candace still clocks the trip — she is stopped for the light at Main and Orchard, three blocks from the house on Pleasant Street she shares with Eileen. The light turns green, and Candace swings left into Orchard and pulls off to the shoulder. A few minutes ago, just after they passed through the city limits, Candace lost sight of the motorcycle. Now she is waiting for Mark to catch up. It would be best, she thinks, if the two of them arrive as a team, confronting Eileen together.

She pops the tape with the song Mark wrote for her — "Only You Can-Do it for Me" — into the tape player. The way he sings it, "Can-Do" runs together so that her nickname, "Cand," emerges from the lyrics. She loves the song, and she loves the fact that it is the only piece on his new CD with lyrics. The agent representing the CD said the song definitely has "cross-over" potential. She told Mark she would try to sell the song to a pop recording artist.

Candace has played the tape two dozen times on this trip already. But she is playing it — and singing along at the top of her voice — once again when Mark accelerates through a yellow light and roars past her in the Toyota. He holds up a hand but looks straight ahead.

"I don't believe he did that," she yells, laying on the horn and accelerating. "Just what I need — mud man greeting Eileen." And yet, after Candace pulls in the driveway, and hurries into the house, she realizes that maybe Mark's arriving first, unannounced, was precisely the right idea. As she enters the kitchen by the back door, Mark — in dirty socks, minus boots — is facing Eileen and getting mud on her immaculately clean floor. And yet, Eileen doesn't seem to mind at all. She is leaning casually against the refrigerator, and amazingly enough, she is even smiling. Candace proceeds gingerly across the kitchen.

"Hi," Candace says, glancing from Mark to her mother. Mark winks, fingering his earring. He has magic, Candace thinks, he has some magic way of disarming Eileen.

"Well, hello there, stranger," Eileen says, pleasantly enough. "Mark has been telling me about the song he wrote for you, the one he says is going to skyrocket up the charts."

"Yeah, it's a great song." An awkward silence follows.

"Audrey called," Eileen says. "She told me how she fell." Candace studies her mother's face. There is no sign of rising wrath.

"Oh yeah, she's...she was in pretty rough shape."

"But it sounds like, considering everything, she's doing OK."

"Yeah, she's...she's just fine." Candace smiles enthusiastically, wondering what strange optimism has suddenly infected her mother.

"She came home from the hospital doing some complicated two-step on the back porch," Mark says. "You should see Audrey dancing with her crutches. Actually, now that I think of it, she was doing more of a four-step." He grins.

"Why don't you two get cleaned up?" Eileen says, pulling open the refrigerator. "I'll fix some dinner. Mark, you are welcome to two-step upstairs and take a shower."

"Thanks," he says, heading out of the kitchen. He pauses in front of Candace. "You've got my clean clothes in the trunk."

"Oh, sure, I'll get them," she says. A thought occurs to her. "Ma, I'll get the tape for you, too, of Mark's song. I think you'll like it a lot." When she returns from the car, carrying Mark's backpack and her own duffel, Eileen is washing lettuce at the sink. Candace pulls off her cowboy boots and is half way across the kitchen when she stops.

"Here's the tape," she says, laying it on the table. "And Ma, I...I just want you to know I'm really glad you gave me your journals to read," she says, carefully guarding her tone. She wants to sound sincere, because she is laying groundwork now, trying to soften her mother up for the pitch she is going to make a little later. Still, she has to be careful. She can't be too enthusiastic, can't be too nice, because that might backfire, might trigger her mother's suspicions. "I got to the part where you burned yourself. Boy, was that scary!"

"Oh, in the lab?"

"Yeah, the lab." Candace smiles. She considers asking a sympathetic question, or making a kind comment, something like "You had it tough, Mom," or, "I can see why you and Grandma Lucy and especially Papa Frank didn't get along." But she holds back, because she doesn't want to push her luck. In truth, what she really wants to say to her mother is something altogether different, something like, "Ma, I can't believe you slept around when you were pregnant with me." Or, "Wow Ma, you were pretty hot stuff way back in the old days."

"I'm glad you're reading them," Eileen says, tossing lettuce into a salad spinner.

"Me too," Candace says. She smiles and nods and continues tip-toeing across the kitchen. Just then, the last journal entry flashes across her mind: Eileen sinking to the floor in John what's-his-name's arms. Candace shudders. She was disgusted reading that part of the journal. Infuriated to think her mother would fool around with one guy when she was pregnant with another guy's baby, especially when the other guy was her father and the baby was none other than herself.

In the bedroom, Candace dumps the diaries out of the duffel and stares at the pile on the bed. She opens the book she's been reading, then slaps it shut again and hurls it across the floor. The journal hits the door at the same moment Mark knocks.

"Come in," Candace mutters. He opens the door, his hips bound tightly in a damp white towel. The dark curls on his chest sport a mass of water droplets that glitter in the light.

"Done already?"

"Yup," he says. "So what's all the noise?"

"I dropped something."

"Oh. I thought maybe you threw something at Eileen."

Candace sighs. "Sometimes I think I should. Then maybe I'd feel better."

Mark bounces down beside Candace on the bed. "So what's got you down now?"

"Oh, it's just so depressing reading these stupid diaries sometimes."

"Well, then, don't read them."

"It's not that simple." Mark doesn't reply, but lies back, hands clasped behind his head. Candace goes on. "I get depressed when I'm reading along, realizing how I got in her way, how I got in the way of her life." Candace's face is pinched. "I mean, it's hard to accept the fact that she didn't want me. It makes me...mad and..." Candace shrugs, "sad, too."

"So don't read the damn journals then," Mark says, stroking Candace's back. "You don't have to, honey. Just throw the books in a closet and forget about them."

Candace is silent a moment. "No. I'd feel too guilty doing that. I mean, she gave them to me so I'd see what she went through. So I'd be more sympathetic. And I am, I mean, I do feel for her...sometimes. When it comes to things my grandparents, my grandfather did. It's just other times, I get so angry — and disgusted. Basically, I guess I'd just rather not read about who my mother was screwing, especially when she was pregnant with me."

Mark raises one knee to his chest, then unfolds the leg. "I can see that."

"What are you doing?" Candace studies the thick muscle in the back of his thigh.

"I'm exercising my sciatic nerve," he says, grunting. "All that sitting night and day in the studio last month made my lower back act up."

Candace reaches out and gently glides her fingertips along the back of his thigh, just below his rump. He catches her hand. "Now you'd better stop that," he says, sitting up suddenly, his face flushed. "Or else you're going to have to go where it leads."

She laughs, leans her head against his chest. "I guess," she says, sighing, "I guess I go back and forth about my mother. Some days, I don't want to know anything she went through, and then sometimes, I want to know everything." She traces her finger up Mark's breastbone. "I keep wondering, though, do I really have a right to know about every single thing, like every time she had a goddamn orgasm? I mean, don't you think that's weird?"

"I don't think having an orgasm is weird at all," he says, kissing her eyes.

She pulls away. "Mark, come on, you know what I mean. It's weird to read about your own mother's sex life. Don't you think so?"

"My mother never had a sex life," Mark says, slipping his hands under Candace's T-shirt. She pushes his hands away.

"MARK, come on, be serious for a second." His shoulders slump. "OK. But just for a second. What is it?"

"Please. Put yourself in my place for a minute."

He smirks. "I keep trying to do that, but you won't let me."

"Mark?" Her face takes on a grave look.

"OK, OK," he says, raising his hands in defense. "I am now putting myself officially in your place. It feels great." He smiles.

"OK. So, now don't you think you'd feel weird reading about your mother...you know...going on and on about her sex life?"

He rolls his bottom lip out. "I would," he says. "I *definitely* would."

"And don't you think you would feel weird knowing every single gory detail?"

Mark studies her, seriously now. He lifts a piece of hair off her cheek, sets a single soft kiss on her temple, then whispers in her ear. "Did you ever think, my dear sweet Candace, that maybe you feel guilty for another reason?"

Candace frowns, pulls away. "What? Why? Guilty for what?"

He shrugs. "Maybe you feel guilty because, like you said, you feel like you ruined her life."

Candace is silent, then whispers. "Yeah, I suppose. I guess I do feel guilty for that."

"Ah, but that's where you're wrong," Mark declares. "Because you didn't do anything wrong. It's Eileen's fault she got pregnant, not yours. It was her problem. Period."

"Yeah, well." Candace looks sad. "I would have liked it better if things had been different. If when my mother had gotten pregnant with me, she'd been..." She shrugs.

"Ah, come here baby. Don't be sad." He gathers her closely to his chest and they rest that way together. Soon, Candace is facing his chest, kissing him. Suddenly, though, she pulls back, lifting a single curly hair from her lips. "Yuck," she says, giggling. In one swift move, she grabs the towel off his waist, exposing his front side.

"That kind of thing will get you into deep trouble," he says, wrestling to catch hold of both her wrists. He does, and she squeals, but then he covers her mouth with one hand. Rolling on top of her, he pins her down to the bed.

❦

Eileen hadn't expected Candace and Mark for dinner, but she prepares a huge meal nonetheless. Tortellini. Homemade spaghetti sauce. Garlic bread. Fresh spinach, steamed and drizzled with butter, the only way Candace will eat it. A huge salad. The three of them chat pleasantly enough through dinner. This can't last, Candace keeps thinking. This can't last, she tells herself as she sops up sauce from her plate with a chunk of bread. This can't last.

And it doesn't. As Eileen carries in two bowls of frozen tangerine sorbet and a plate of butter cookies and sets them on the table, she makes an abrupt announcement. "I don't want to bug you guys all night, but there has to be a time when we talk. Seriously. So you let me know when that will be." She glances at both of them. "I'll be doing the dishes." She smiles, but it's her typical smile, Candace thinks, the one that isn't at all convincing. She returns to the kitchen.

"Whoof," Mark says, under his breath. A mischievous smile crosses his lips.

"Shhh." Candace slaps his arm, chuckling. "But I am kind of glad she left."

"I'll say."

"No, I mean it gives us a chance to talk first."

Mark is wolfing down the sorbet. "Sure."

"I...I had this idea. You know I told you Francine is leaving."

"Yeah."

"Well, it occurred to me that I have that trust, a few thousand dollars probably, that's all, but I wanted to use it, to let Audrey use it for the farm."

"You really think that Audrey will take your money?" He is scraping his bowl clean with the spoon, then the side of his finger. "I kind of doubt it, Cand."

"I wouldn't be giving it to her," Candace says, pushing her untouched bowl toward Mark. "It would be a loan. I mean I'd be taking Francine's place, you know, at the farm."

"You mean living there? For good?" He eats a cookie, his spoon hovering in the air.

"Well, for a while. Yeah, I'd live there. What's wrong with that?"

Mark laughs. "Oh I don't know, I just can't imagine you living with a bunch of women three times your age." He raises his eyebrows. "*At least* three times your age." Then he frowns. "Anyway, how can you? I mean, with the baby?"

"I'd bring her, silly," Candace says. She has long since decided her baby is a girl.

"You're gonna raise our kid *there*?"

"Why not? Can you think of a better place?"

"Oh, I suppose it's perfect, from your perspective. You'd have lots of built-in babysitters, maybe. There's only one minor problem. Or two."

"What's that?"

"Me and you. When do I get to see you? And my kid, when would I see my son?"

"You mean your daughter. Well, you could visit. I mean, I didn't think you'd want to see us every day. I mean, you did kind of say that..."

"I said I didn't think I could handle having you two live with me. That's true. But Candace, of course I'm going to want to see you and my kid. It's *my* kid, remember? Just because I flipped out at first doesn't mean I'm a total blockhead."

Candace smiles and reaches her hand out to touch Mark's mouth. He kisses her cupped palm. "You could visit every weekend."

"Not enough," he says.

Candace gets up from the table. "It's got to be enough," she says, sighing. "What other choice is there?" At that, the swinging door to the kitchen squeaks. Candace looks up. She is face to face with her mother.

"Everything OK in here?" Eileen inquires.

"Oh...sure, just fine," Candace says.

"Fine," Mark nods. "Great dessert." He grins.

Eileen steps into the dining room and scoops up the two bowls, leaving the plate of cookies. She tucks the three straw place mats under one arm. "So, have you guys got a problem talking in say, twenty minutes?"

Candace glances at Mark and he raises his eyebrows and shoulders.

"Not me," Mark says. Eileen glances at Candace, who slowly shakes her head.

"OK. See you then."

❦

Candace and Mark are side by side on the sofa, watching Jeopardy, waiting, when half an hour later, Eileen joins them in the living room. Mark gets up from the couch and turns off the T.V. Eileen takes a seat in the bentwood rocker.

"So, I thought we should talk about your plans." She rocks forward. Mark is settled cross-legged on the couch.

For some reason, Candace flashes back to earlier in the day, when she sat at the picnic table with Audrey and Marjory, and Francine was crying and dripping wet. Candace wanted desperately to tell her grandmother how completely frustrated she was that she couldn't do anything to help.

Only maybe I can, she thinks now, maybe I really can.

She clears her throat. "Can I ask you something before we start?" Candace doesn't wait for Eileen to answer. "I wanted to ask if there is any way I might get to use my trust fund early."

Eileen laughs a single short laugh. "No. There's no way."

"Oh Mom come on, you can't just say...*no*." Already, things are going badly. Already Candace knows her voice is wrong. But that's because her mother just set her off.

"Of course I can say no. Look, Candace, that trust fund is set aside, how many times have I told you, for one thing, and one thing only, your education. I set it up that way, and that's the way it's going to stay. Anyway, there isn't that much money there. I assure you, it wouldn't get you very far."

"But Mom, what's the point of having money sitting around when I really need it?"

"Need it for what? How are you going to use it?"

"For the farm. Grandma got an offer from Snowstack to buy the farm, but I think it's a bad idea, to sell, and besides, it's the wrong time. And now Francine suddenly wants out, so Grandma's in a real bind so I thought I could help by..." She doesn't get to finish her sentence.

"Candace Candace Candace," Eileen says, laying one open hand across her eyes. "Here you are in your own pickle and you want to bail Audrey out? Come on."

"Mom, listen," Candace shouts, and instantly Eileen's eyes get that how-dare-you-use-that-tone-with-me look. Candace lowers her voice. "Mom, I really need to explain this to you. I really need you to listen. I want to invest my money in Grandma's farm, not just because she needs it, but because it's an investment in my future, in the land, land I love, and...and because I think if Mark agrees, I might live there, move there, me...and the baby."

Eileen's eyes go wide. Slowly, she shakes her head side to side. "I don't believe this, I don't believe this. Mark, I can't believe you would go along with this."

"I, well, I just kind of found out," Mark says, shrugging. "I haven't... thought it through. I mean, totally." He flashes a quick smile.

"Well, at least you admit it. Candace, here, hasn't either, that's clear, but she apparently thinks she has. She thinks it's just a *mahvelous* idea.."

It's the word marvelous that makes Candace yell. It's the word, but more than that, it's the way Eileen says it: mahvellous. It's Eileen's stupid, unnecessary theatrics that always get Candace crazy.

"Mom, just shut up," Candace says, standing. "Just shut up." She is trembling, angry at her mother, but also at herself, for getting hot and red in the face. For shaking her fist, and crying.

"That's enough, Candace. I don't want to hear any more of your..."

Candace stomps her feet. "*Mom* stop! Please, *stop!* You have *got* to hear me out on this, whether you want to or not. I want to give Audrey whatever is in that trust, because...because she deserves it. She deserves every penny. That farm means everything to me. Audrey and the others were always there for me, every single summer I lived there. It was because of them that I paint, and it's because I paint, and only because I paint, and draw, that I'm happy, and now, now that Grandma needs help, I want to be there for her. Like she always was for me. Besides, I'd live there. I mean, I'm an artist just like the rest of them. And I'm never going to go to any Ivy League college. You should know that by now. Instead I can get a business going, start doing some freelance graphic work, and I can bring in money."

Candace stops, realizes her mother hasn't interrupted, and that somehow calms her. She has stopped crying, too, and now, she is quivering, but she forces herself to speak in an even tone. "Don't you see, Mom, this really may be the answer for me. I can live with Grandma at the farm, I can paint, I can raise the baby, I can get help doing it. But most of all, I'll be living with the people I've grown up with, people who really are...my family."

Eileen looks down quickly. Candace drops back on the sofa. No one says a word. Finally, Eileen looks up. For a moment, Candace is convinced that her mother has softened, that she has for once heard and for once sees the perfect logic behind what she has said. Eileen's voice does goes soft, but her message is anything but.

"Candace, that trust doesn't legally become yours until you turn twenty one, which you won't do for another six months. Until then, it stays where it is. The trust isn't big, it would barely make a dent in supporting the farm. Besides, I don't think you belong in Vermont living with a bunch of old..." Here, Eileen pauses, sighs, then continues. "A bunch of older women. You certainly don't belong there with a brand new baby. Maybe between now and September, you will realize that it makes absolutely no sense."

Eileen rises from the rocking chair. "Meanwhile, there *was* something I wanted to say." She waits, and Candace, sobbing quietly, gets up and starts to walk away.

"Candace, stay *right* where you are." Eileen's eyes are fierce and her voice is a knife slicing the air. Candace crosses her arms.

"What I wanted to say — to *both* of you — is that since you've decided to keep this baby, I'm going to insist that you, Candace, see a doctor, preferably *my* doctor. You need to do that right away. Like tomorrow." She circles around to face Candace.

"Do you hear me?"

Candace turns the other direction, away from her mother.

"Candace!"

"I hear you."

"Good. I'll make the appointment in the morning." Eileen leaves the room and Candace stares after her. She isn't sure, but she thinks she hates her mother more today than she ever has before.

CANDACE

Because Eileen has connections, and because she uses them, Candace gets an appointment with the obstetrician, Dr. Riordan, within a week. He calculates her due date to be September 17th. "Of course, that's a moving target," Riordan says, pressing his fingers deeply into Candace's belly. "You're fairly big already. It's just possible that what you thought was your last period actually wasn't a period at all, but false bleeding." Riordan has a head full of neatly combed blond waves, waves that Candace studies now as he stretches a tape measure over her naked belly.

"I do this at every visit to keep track of where the top of the uterus is," he explains, holding the end of the tape below her navel. "That way, we make sure the fetus is growing." He replaces the tape measure with a small round device that turns out to be a kind of microphone. A strange noise rises up from Candace's abdomen, a noise that she will later describe to Mark as "a team of horses thundering across a plain."

"That, I'd say, is the sound of a healthy heartbeat," Riordan says, smiling for the first time during the visit. At that moment, Candace regrets the fact that Mark took an extra shift at the bakery and didn't come with her to the doctor. He has to come next time, she decides.

Later, after Candace is dressed and sitting across from Riordan at his desk, he lectures her about the need to eat well. "And I'm sure you've probably already had an earful from your Mom about getting enough rest, and staying away from alcohol and coffee...and, of course, there's not to be any drugs." Riordan pauses, pushes his wire rim glasses back up the bridge of his nose. He maintains a steady gaze at Candace, who has her tongue poking out the side of her cheek. She averts her eyes, gazes around the room, studies a long shelf of burgundy-colored reference books. Does he know, she wonders? Has Eileen taken Riordan aside and told him everything?

"So. Any questions?"

Candace shakes her head no. "OK, then I'll see you in a month." He scribbles something in her file.

A few days later, on Sunday morning, Candace locks her bedroom door and slips out of her nightshirt. Standing naked in front of the mirror, she takes up a pose facing the corner of the room. For her art class, she is supposed to submit a portfolio of self-portraits, done in any medium. It occurs to her now that she could do a series of charcoal sketches of herself in front of the mirror — and call them *pregnant* poses.

Draping one hand on her hip, she studies her profile, then turns slightly. Her hand falls to her side. In the corner of the bedroom is her easel. Candace moves it in front of the mirror and balances a new sketchpad on the shelf. With a charcoal pencil, she swiftly outlines her shape on paper, accentuating her vanished waistline. Pulling back from the sketch, she cocks her head, frowns, twists her hair tightly around her finger and snaps it.

"Ooh, this is awful," she whispers, catching her reflection in the mirror. She rips the drawing off the pad and tears it into little pieces. Tossing the pieces up in the air, they flutter down like paper snowflakes into the wastebasket. Pulling the belt of her bathrobe snug around her waist, Candace slips back into bed and pulls the covers over her head.

Almost two weeks have passed since she returned from Vermont. She has resumed her classes, and without much effort, has made up all of the work she missed while she was away. But still, she's been growing more and more frustrated with each passing day. Nothing she draws, nothing she paints, seems quite right.

A few days ago, she visited the Clark, the small art museum in nearby Williamstown known for its Impressionist collection. Four times during the semester, Candace's painting class visits the museum to study the work of a different painter. Last week, the instructor, a young Italian woman named Ana Baptista, discussed Renoir. Candace and the other students huddled around Baptista while she quietly lectured on his painting called 'The Blond Bather.'

"Oh my God," a student standing across from Candace interrupted. "Candace, she could be your sister." The student, Dawn Petrocella, blurted this out, pointing first at Candace and then at the painting. "I can't believe it. I mean, you look just like her."

It was true. Even Baptista, who didn't appreciate the interruption, acknowledged the remarkable resemblance, particularly in the shape of the face and the mouth. "And of course the hair," Dawn said. "It's exactly the same color." A round of *oohs* and *ahs* rose up from the other students. Candace blushed. The Renoir bather, after all, was perched on a swath of white sheet, completely naked. Her breasts were large and plump and the nipples protruded noticeably. Thankfully, Baptista brought the students' attention to another painting. Candace, meanwhile, moved away from the others and pretended to be inter-ested in Renoir's still-life painting of onions. Secretly, though, she was gazing back at Renoir's bather.

Candace brought Mark to the museum again a few days later. Without telling him why, she led him to the room where the Renoir hung. "People in my class say there's a painting here that looks just like me. I want to see if you can figure out which one it is." Mark started to circulate the room but didn't get even half-way around. He stopped in front of the bather, remained there. Candace joined him. "Her tits are too small," he said, smirking.

"Jerk," Candace said, slapping his arm. He grabbed her and kissed her face.

"It's pretty amazing, the resemblance, don't you think?" she whis-pered, as they stood staring at the painting together, his arms wrapped tightly around her. His hands lay flat over her belly and it felt good to have them there. It felt like protection.

"Oh, I suppose," Mark said. "But I think beautiful red heads all look alike."

A few days later, when Baptista asked each student to select a painting to copy, Candace chose the bather. Oddly enough, even though copying was something Candace could generally do without any difficulty, she found the Renoir impossible. She tried several times to capture the bather's hair, the way it fluttered out from the woman's head, the way it stood, pale orange and electrified by some invisible, airy force. But on Candace's canvas, the hair came out looking flat and lifeless. "Like an orange sponge," she told Mark later.

The next day, she switched focus and started painting the body. But the skin in her painting turned out mottled and sallow, completely unlike the creamy pinkish white skin in the Renoir. Finally, Candace did something that Baptista said was a mistake. She painted the background first: a misty blue green coastline that set the bather off.

"I am thinking that you may have trouble foregrounding the woman, now that you've got the backdrop so prominent," Baptista said, pausing behind Candace in class. Candace grimaced. Maybe I won't paint the woman, she wanted to say. Maybe I just want to do a landscape in this painting. Maybe I'm just not in the mood to do a silly copy at all.

Lying on her bed now, staring at the ceiling, Candace wonders why she should be so intensely frustrated painting the bather. And why was the rosy wall she tried painting at Audrey's such a disaster? And why was the self-portrait a few minutes ago so awful? Why, she wonders, have I begun to have more trouble with my work these last few weeks than ever before? She rolls over on her stomach. At that moment, Eileen pounds down the stairs, no doubt going off for her morning run.

Maybe it's her fault, Candace thinks now. Maybe she's the reason I can't draw or paint or focus clearly. She won't even let me do what I want with my own money. Candace grimaces. She's been feeling especially hateful toward Eileen lately, and she doesn't like it. And so she's begun to avoid her mother. Now, the front door opens, bangs shut, and there is no more sound. Pulling the kitten blanket up, Candace smothers her face in her pillow and tries to go back to sleep.

In the succeeding days, the weather gets warmer, and Candace takes to walking longer and longer distances from the house. By the end of April, she is regularly walking two miles out of town to the base of Mt. Greylock. One day, she collects pussy willows. The next, she collects an armful of forsythia. Sometimes, Mark swings by the house on the motorcycle. If her mother isn't around, Candace hops on the back for a ride. Inevitably, they end up on the road that snakes to the top of the mountain. Candace keeps her face plastered against Mark's back, and her arms belted tightly around the middle of his chest. One thumb knuckle always comes to rest on his zipper, and it's always slightly raw by the end of the ride. Meshed together, Candace's thighs against Mark's backside, they lunge through each curve as a unit, coming dangerously close to a horizontal position on the sharpest turns.

"This is nuts," she screams one day as they emerge from a particularly dangerous hairpin, one in which the road reverses direction completely and, at the same time, rises about forty-five degrees. The motorcycle drowns out her voice. Mark says nothing, but shakes his head up and down. Candace wonders if he's even heard. He is smiling. A thought of the baby passes briefly through Candace's mind. What does the baby hear or feel while I ride, she wonders. Does the motorcycle's buzz bother her, or the wild flipflops in the bike's position?

One afternoon, Mark brings the motorcycle to rest at the top of the mountain, in the visitor's parking lot.

"Want to get a view?" he says, cutting the engine.

"Sure." She pulls off her helmet and her hair unfolds on her shoulders. It glows orange in the sun. "Hey maybe we could hike the trail around the top," she says.

"Oh right." He swings his leg over the seat. "In your condition, it would take you a week."

"Not true," she says. "I bet I could do it in under two hours."

"Fat chance," he says. "You may think you're in peachy shape." He grabs her hand, helps her off the bike, "but you're...you're shaped more like a pear these days." He ducks as she swats him.

"Spare me your pathetic attempts at humor." She pulls away from him, intentionally trails behind as he crosses the parking lot.

"Come on," he yells. "Catch up."

"No," she yells back. He's reached the crest of the mountain, just above a bank of coin-operated telescopes. Staring up to where he is standing, Candace notices that a woman has set up an easel. Candace squints, shades her eyes, then hurries across the parking lot, passing Mark. Approaching the woman, she stops, yells out.

"Trish? Is that Trish Bosco?" The woman in front of the easel looks up. She has short black hair, spiked on top. Her face opens into a broad smile. She waves. Candace hurries toward the woman and the two of them embrace. Only then, when Candace is at Trish's side, does she notice the playpen a few feet away.

"And who's this?" Candace asks softly, dropping to the ground on one knee. She pokes her fingers through the netting on the playpen.

The child has her mother's wide face, but blond hair and emeralds for eyes.

"Meet Priscilla," Trish says, picking the child up. The baby reaches out to grab Candace's face. "Watch out, though, she likes noses." Priscilla takes one of Candace's fingers in her two hands, hands covered with slobber. The baby tries to put Candace's finger in her mouth, and Candace laughs.

"She's teething," Trish says, "so everything that gets within a few inches of her lips goes straight into the gum factory." Trish kisses the baby and sets her back into the playpen. Priscilla wails. Trish picks her up again, jostles her against her narrow hip. Candace smiles. How unlikely a mother figure Trish cuts: her hair is dyed purple in one spot, lime green in another. She has a ring in her eyebrow and a line of earrings piercing the rim of one ear. Her jeans and black leather jacket are covered with metal studs.

Candace spins around, glances at the partially-filled canvas on the easel. A mountain scene, in fluorescent shades, is emerging. "I see you've been able to work," Candace says. Trish smiles.

"Well, sort of. I've started coming up here since the weather got nice. Mostly, though, I set the easel up in my parent's basement. They watch pudgy here while I paint."

"So," Candace says, reaching toward the baby, "how is it? I mean, what's it like, having a baby?"

Trish laughs. "It's hell and heaven, all rolled into one." She hands Priscilla to Candace. The baby goes unwillingly, though, her chubby fingers grasping for her mother. "The first few months I was convinced I was cracking up. Pete, of course, was no help at all." Trish turns back to the easel. "But then, when I finally started painting again, oh, you know, just an hour or two a day, well, it helped. A lot. That and my sister, my little sister moved into my apartment with me. She's fourteen and great with the baby. And she was dying to have some space away from my folks, so it worked out. She babysits at night while I waitress."

Mark walks up behind Candace. "Hi," he says, taking the baby's hand and shaking it. "Nice to meet you."

"This is Mark," Candace says, "He's...um...well, actually, he's MY baby's father..." Candace squints into the sun. "I'm pregnant."

"You bitch! Congratulations, Candace." Trish throws one arm around Candace's shoulders. "And congratulations to you too." Trish turns to Mark.

"Thanks," he says. "But she's doing all the work." Candace frowns. "So far, I mean," he adds quickly.

"Look," Candace says, turning to Trish. "would you...would you mind if sometime I joined you up here? I would bring my own easel and..."

"Mind? I'd be thrilled," Trish says. "That is, if you don't mind my associate here. She has her moments..." Candace lays her face against the baby's pale cheek. It smells like baby powder, and something else, too, sour milk. Pulling back, Candace notices that Priscilla's face has the same pearly pink skin as Renoir's blond bather.

"I can't imagine anything nicer than an afternoon painting with Priscilla," Candace says. "But...promise me something?"

"What?" Trish says.

"You'll teach me how to change her diaper?"

"O-o-oh sure," Trish says, reaching into her diaper bag. "Judging by the smell of things, it's time for your first lesson right now."

❦

Over the next few weeks, the two women fall quickly into a routine. Candace has classes three days a week, and on the other two, Trish comes by in the morning to pick her up in a battered blue Ford station wagon. Most days, they pack a picnic lunch. Priscilla rides in the back in her car seat, lined in a plush pink and white pad.

"That thing looks like a throne," Candace says, as she slides her canvas into the car.

"Well, it should," Trish says. "She is, after all, my little princess." The baby has two fingers in her mouth, and drool glazes her chin. Candace looks at Trish, wants to ask her about the first year, why she said she thought she was cracking up. But she doesn't ask.

Trish pulls into the parking lot at the top of the mountain. The wind is whipping up debris. For the last two weeks, they've set up their easels a few feet away from the telescopes.

"I wonder...would you mind if we try someplace less windy and... maybe a little more private?" Trish asks. She winks, and Candace wonders why.

"No, that's fine by me."

"I know you'll have to start another canvas, but I packed an extra one..."

"Trish, really, it doesn't matter," Candace says. She gestures at the canvas she brought along. "That painting is really, well, let's put it this way: it wouldn't do any harm to start over. This gives me a good excuse."

Trish pauses before backing out of the parking lot. She glances at Candace. "I'm surprised, Cand. You never used to talk about your work that way."

"Yeah, well, I've never had so much trouble working before." She bites her lip. "It's not like me. I don't know, lately, I start stuff and I drop it. I just can't seem to focus, or really get into anything. I guess...maybe I'm just depressed."

"No, you're just pregnant," Trish says, smirking. "Junior in there is sucking every single drop of creative juice out of your brain. But it'll come back. I promise."

Candace is tempted to ask when, but something holds her back.

They drive down the mountain a quarter mile and park alongside the road. Candace carries both easels from the car about twenty yards into the woods, through to a clearing, where a breathtaking view opens up to the south. The sky is clear, and the landscape below is a quilt of green and brown farm fields. In the distance, two tractors are working opposite each other, tilling a long narrow swath of chocolate-colored farmland.

"Now I know why you wanted to come here," Candace says, delighted. "This is an incredible view." Trish places Priscilla on a blanket.

"Yeah, and completely private, too," Trish says, smiling. She heads back to the car for the diaper bag and playpen. For the next two hours, they take turns holding the baby and painting. Candace spends the morning doing what she calls "dribbling," testing small dabs of different colors on the canvas.

"Sometimes playing like inspires me," Candace says, frowning. But clearly, she thinks, it isn't working now. She drops her brush into a jar of grey water and flops down on the blanket, pulling Priscilla to her lap. While Trish paints, Candace feeds Priscilla little cubes of cheese, and Cheerios from a baggy. When Priscilla fusses, Candace gives her a small bottle of apple juice and rubs her back and hums to her until she falls asleep.

"Thank you," Trish says. "I thought I was the only one who could get her to nap."

"Oh sure," Candace says, pleased. "If I can't paint, at least I can practice being mom."

Trish pulls something small and flat out of her pocket. She takes a seat on the blanket next to Candace. In her hand is a small mirror catching the sunlight and reflecting in Candace's face. "What's that for?" Candace says, but she already knows. Trish has another baggy, and in this one is a small amount of white powder.

"Oh, I just brought along a bit of fun," Trish says. "It seems to me you could use it. And hell, I know I could." She holds the mirror flat, and again it flickers in Candace's eyes.

"You aren't really..." Candace says, quietly poking her fingers through Priscilla's tangled blond curls. The baby's face is as still as crystal, the pink mouth forming a tiny o.

"Sure I am." Trish lifts some powder out of the bag with her fingers and lays it carefully on the mirror.

"Trish, thanks, but I...I don't think I can," Candace says, picking Priscilla up off her stomach. "It's not that I wouldn't want to, but not...I know it's not good for...for the baby."

"Oh, forget that. You have living proof that a few snowflakes do indeed make for a fine little snowman." Trish smiles. "Look, Cand, I did coke once a week through most of my last trimester, and I tell you, I was better off for it."

"How do you figure that?" Candace's eyes widen. "How could you not get caught?"

"I made sure that just before the doctor's visit, I kept clean. And when I knew I had to give them pee," here Trish smiles slyly again, "I made sure I gave them somebody else's...usually my younger sister's." Candace's mouth drops. Trish has a line of powder on the mirror and she is blocking one nostril and inhaling the powder in deep snorts. A smile glides into her eyes. She holds out the mirror.

Glancing down, Candace catches the reflection of her own hair, and it brings the Renoir bather to mind. "Oh, no. I can't. I'll lose my hide if my mother finds out. I mean, God." She shakes her head. "Besides, I tried it once, but..."

"Yeah?"

"Well, it...I don't know, it was nice, I guess..."

"Come on. Do you honestly think a little bit will hurt the kid?"

"No. Well." Candace shrugs, looks out at the view. The sun is caught behind a cloud so everything is in shadow. For some reason, Candace feels like she might start to cry. "I've read that coke can make the baby be born smaller." She whispers the last sentence.

Trish laughs. "If I were you, I wouldn't worry about a few ounces here or there. You look like you're hosting a small moose already. Hell, if the baby turns out a little smaller, it'll be a whole lot easier to get the little devil out. Delivery, my friend, is no picnic."

"Well, I know, you've said."

Trish reclines on the blanket. "Yes, well let me tell you a few specifics sometime. I'll tell you for example what it feels like to push for six hours. You're dead. And then, just when you think you're home free, you see them heading toward your bare rear end with forceps."

Candace shudders. "They...they don't do that, do they? I mean, I am pretty sure they don't use forceps anymore. Or do they?"

"Ha. Who've you been talking to? The tooth fairy? They used two pairs on me."

Candace inhales, crosses her legs. Trish goes on.

"But hey, don't let me make your decision for you. It's just," and here Trish sits up, "I'm telling you this for your own good, Candace. Having a kid is a shit load harder than anybody will ever tell you. It really is a hell of a sacrifice. You'll see. You think it's all sweet and rosy stuff now, tiny T-shirts and pink dresses and baby powder and cute little party shoes and bows and all that crap. And yeah, that's true, the babies are cute and all, until you are so goddamn tired every morning you feel like somebody beat your head in with a baseball bat."

Trish points a finger at Candace's chest. "Remember, Candace, you've gotta take care of *Candace* too. You've gotta have a way to hang on is all, and if you need a little help now and then, hey, I say it's better for them in the long run." Trish quickly flattens the other nostril and snorts up the other line of powder. Candace licks her lips.

"You kept it all together, I mean you didn't get too hooked...?"

"*Me*? I couldn't afford to." The glaze in Trish's eyes reflect a patch of cornflower blue sky. "But I'll tell you, it's done wonders for my painting." She grins an unfocused grin, and lays the mirror and bag of powder on the blanket. Getting up, she returns to her easel. "If I were stuck, like you clearly are," Trish says, taking up a brush, "I'd give it some serious thought." She gives Candace a dreamy smile, and sets to work filling the canvas with wild oranges and blues in bold zigzag lines.

Candace shifts Priscilla aside, and covers the sleeping child with a blanket. She studies Trish's mirror. In it now she catches a glimpse of one of her own eyes. She sees a knot between her eyebrows, too.

Immediately she tries to smooth out her forehead. Then she notices something else: something she has never seen before in her own face: deep fatigue.

"I have rings," she says out loud. She has been waking up every morning about four, tossing and turning, unable to sleep. She mentioned the problem to Eileen, who just laughed.

"It happens to pregnant women," Eileen said calmly. "You're getting ready for night feedings." Candace repeats that to Trish now.

"Yeah, right. You just wait," Trish says. "You better get used to living with no sleep. There's this whole world you discover when you're up in the middle of the night." For the first time, Candace imagines having to function in the dark. The thought scares her. She has never been a night person before. She stares at Trish, who is whistling now, and literally throwing gobs of paint on the canvas, her face dominated by a silly-looking grin.

Candace walks over to her own easel, picks up a brush, begins dabbing it with paint. Her heart starts hammering. There is no way she can work today, and she knows it.

"Oh what the hell," she says, throwing the brush down and walking back to the blanket. Balancing the mirror on her knee, she unrolls the bag, and draws the powdery white crystals into a short line.

The results of the drug are dramatic. Candace stands at the easel for the rest of the afternoon, oblivious to Trish, and to Priscilla, and to absolutely everything else around her. She has a flood of color rushing by her eyes. What's more, she begins painting a quirky kind of self-portrait, combining some of the lines from the charcoal sketch, and some of the feeling she carried away from the Renoir. After an hour of painting, she realizes she is capturing the essence of the backdrop and the blond bather, but in her own terms. The image that appears on the canvas is a kind of human tree, combining her own face, her arms, her protruding middle, her brash orange hair, but all enveloped in a sea of vines entwined around her face.

"Amazing," Trish says at some point during the afternoon. She offers Candace a bag of Oreos, but Candace refuses. She feels she could keep working forever, not eating, not stopping to sleep. Priscilla is awake, whining, clamoring to get out of the playpen. Trish picks her up. "See what I mean? This stuff works wonders, doesn't it?"

Candace grins sheepishly. "I *am* having fun," she says, dabbing bright yellow ochre between burnt sienna. She sets to work defining the bather's face. She adds dark almond eyes, the pert cherry mouth. By the end of the day, the canvas is tropical, an exotic tree.

"Way cool," Trish says, dragging the second word out into two syllables. She packs the diaper bag. "I'd say there is definitely some greater power at work in your canvas, there."

Candace is wiping her brush, and liking what she sees. Strangely, though, she is feeling just a little let down. She doesn't want the afternoon light to fade, or the feeling of power, of infinite creative energy, to end. And she is beginning to be afraid of how she's going to face her mother. "Can we...come back soon?"

"Sure," Trish says. "Like. How about the day after tomorrow?"

"Great. And, Trish?"

"Yeah?" Trish collapses the playpen, leans it against a tree.

"Sometime, not today, but soon, I think I really need you to, you know, fill me in on...how a baby beats up your head. What you said before about having a baby being hard?"

"Oh sure. Look, Cand, I'm sorry if I scared you. But you really need to know."

"Yeah, sure I do. And nobody else will tell me." Candace glances at the canvas and another wave of good feeling surges through her. She grabs the canvas and goes to the car.

By the time Trish pulls up to Candace's house, Eileen's car is in the driveway. "I knew it," Candace says. "Just the person I least wanted to see."

"Yeah," Trish says, "I know the feeling. Are you planning to move out soon?"

"I'd love to," Candace says, collecting her gear from the front seat. "But so far, it doesn't look that way. Mark says he doesn't have room...and I'm kind of broke." She smiles, and sticks out her hand. "Thanks...for everything."

"See you Thursday," Trish says, taking Candace's hand and squeezing it in both of her own. Candace nods. It takes three trips to get her belongings inside. As she enters the living room with the last of her load, the canvas and easel, Eileen sticks her head out of the kitchen.

"So you *are* here. How about joining me for dinner? I've got homemade fettuccine with mushrooms." Candace considers the alternatives: refuse to eat, which is certain to irk her mother, and spark a lecture on "proper nutrition." Or face her mother over dinner, and endure her endless questions and scrutiny.

"Could I clean up, maybe take a nap first?" Candace figures she had better angle for extra time before she has to sit face to face across the table from Eileen. For one thing, she wants to study her eyes in the mirror, to make sure they aren't too glazed.

"Of course." Eileen smiles. "I'm glad you're taking care of yourself."

Candace throws her mother a quick grin and hurries upstairs. Once she is safely inside her bedroom, she sets the new painting on the easel. *The tree glows*, she decides. Then she glances into the full mirror. *Oh dear God*, Candace thinks. *My eyes glow too.*

Lying flat on the bed, she stares at the painting and brings her hand over her stomach. She wants to hear the baby's heartbeat again. She wants some reassurance that this afternoon's episode didn't do anything to interfere with the sound of pounding hooves.

There is no preparation for what comes next. The sensation, which is over before Candace realizes what has happened, is so unlike anything she's ever felt before that she isn't sure at first what she's feeling. It's as if a fish flickered through a pool deep beneath her navel. No, it's a wave, she thinks, gone almost as soon as it registered. She lays her hand flat on her stomach, waits, then presses in slightly. The ripple flows beneath her hand again, and tickles the underside of her palm. As soon as it's there, it's just as quickly gone.

Riordan told her to expect it sometime this month, probably, he said, around week twenty. And here it is, only week eighteen. The baby has moved.

For the next hour, Candace stays flat on the bed, too excited to sleep. Her hand is glued to her stomach, and every so often, she feels the same slight flicker of movement beneath her palm. She is completely calm. She is completely ecstatic. She lifts the telephone receiver and dials Mark's number.

"The baby is moving," she squeals into his answering machine. She even tells her mother at dinner. Eileen is lifting a second helping of fettuccine and mushrooms to her plate.

"Oh that's great, honey," Eileen says in a kind tone, taking extra mushrooms. She waits a moment before she starts eating. "And that explains things."

"What things?" Candace says, her chin lifting off the back of her hand.

"Oh, the fact you haven't touched your food, for one thing," Eileen says, between mouthfuls. "And the fact you've got this starry, faraway look in your eyes." Eileen studies Candace's face. Candace sits up straight and digs her fork into her cold fettucine.

❦

Had the baby not moved that afternoon, it is possible Candace would have refused Trish's next offer of cocaine. But in general, Candace is inclined to interpret events as signs. In her mind, the fact the baby moved is unmistakable proof that, despite what the doctor has said, an occasional indulgence isn't going to hurt the baby. To Candace's way of thinking, something good has come from the afternoon's drug escapade, for her and the baby.

The next morning she wakes in the dark, dreaming of fish, a huge school of slim glimmering minnow-like creatures that shine like silver paper clips. They all move together in formation and when the light shifts on the water, the fish change direction, taking on an iridescent glow. Candace switches on her light, wondering if she can take the watery image from her dream and transfer it to canvas. She throws off her covers, approaches the easel.

Part of the tree she painted earlier in the day looks like it is rising up from the surface of the canvas. Smiling, she takes another canvas from her closet, sets it on the easel, and takes up her slimmest paintbrush. Candace rushes to paint the fish, trying to keep in her eye the dream view, the fact that the ocean creatures are barely visible to the naked eye. Mixing cerulean blue, sky color, with the spring green she adores, she adds a dab of ochre and of white. From this mix comes an aquamarine shade suggestive of a lime-colored sea in sunlight. Gradually she builds up a series of lines out of this color, until there is a swarm of them gyrating on the canvas. To be right, that is, to be like the ocean creatures in her dream, the fish must look as though they cannot be seen except in certain slants of sunlight. Somehow, too, she thinks, I have to make the fish look like they change, like they depend for existence on the shifting cast of the sun's rays. They have to shimmer, just like they did in the dream. They have to flicker through liquid like light itself.

Candace is painting a fury. But then, with no warning, it all stops. She steps back. "Oh hell, this is awful," she mutters. Glancing out her window, she notices that the sky has brightened. She hears her mother in the bathroom, running her morning shower. Candace yawns, drops the paintbrush in water, and climbs into bed. Before her mother is out of the shower, Candace is asleep again.

The fish aren't any more cooperative later in the day. As soon as she gets home from class, Candace takes up the brush. She works for two hours, experimenting with different colors, but the lines never stop being lines. They never come close to being the mass of light slivers that shivered through her dream.

"I guess my heart's not in it," she tells Mark over the phone.

"I guess not," he says. "But I'll tell you, I was up all night writing this song. And it was your phone call about the baby that got me going. That message gave me goose bumps."

"Great," she says, feeling slightly jealous. She hasn't mentioned the cocaine to Mark. Until now, she hasn't wanted to. But now she wants to ask him if he thinks the drug might have had something to do with the baby moving. She wants to ask him if she was stupid to do it. Mostly, she wants to tell him what an incredible inspiration the drug gave her. Mark has done coke before, but Candace isn't sure whether he did it for fun or inspiration. Still, it's too risky to bring the subject up now, over the telephone.

Instead, she calls Audrey. "I thought you'd want to know, I felt the baby move."

"Oh, wow. And did you know I'm down to one crutch and a walking cast?"

"Oh, no, I didn't," Candace says flatly.

"Yes, I'm thrilled. I can't wait to get rid of the crutches altogether. But then I'll be on a cane, maybe for months."

"That must be awful hard for you, Grandma. What did you decide to do about the farm?"

"We voted not to sell. I hope to God we don't live to regret it. But not counting Francine, it ended up being a unanimous decision." Audrey pauses. "You see, Pit is terribly anxious to stay here until...well until she can't anymore. And then I woke up one night in a sweat. I had a nightmare the sugarbush was gone, carved up in ski trails."

"Oh God, Grandma, I'm so so glad you're staying. Did you know...well, of course you didn't...how could you? When I got home, I asked Mom if I could give you my trust, you know, I wanted to invest it, I still do, so that you'd have the money to pay Francine."

"Candace, I am really touched. But you know, dear, I'd never take your money. And anyway, Pit dug into savings and paid Francine."

"Well, what if I told you I wanted to join you, you know, move in, be part of the farm, as an artist, part of the group?"

Audrey chuckles. "If you told me that, I'd tell you to stay where you are. Or, at least, think long and hard about it. Once upon a time we thought we could make this dream come true. But, you know now how hard things are here now." Audrey sighs, loud. "No, dear, I don't think this is the place for you, or your baby."

Candace cuts off the conversation and immediately dials Trish. "Can I come over?"

Priscilla squalls in the background. "Be my guest," Trish yells. "But I'm warning you. I think the baby's coming down with something. She's been crying since breakfast."

When Candace arrives at Trish's apartment, the baby is lying on her side, fast asleep on the couch. She has two lines of green goo running out of her nose.

"Ooh, bad cold, huh?" Candace whispers, touching the child's feverish head.

"Whatever," Trish says. She is standing in front of a sink full of dirty dishes. "Have a seat," she says. "If you can find one."

Toys and shoes and bottles and dirty clothes are strewn all over the apartment. The ironing board is stacked with magazines. Candace sits on the couch, opposite the baby.

"I just had to get out of that house." Candace picks up a baby rattle. Shakes it.

"Hey, don't I know. Go ahead and stay as long as you want." Candace leans her head back on the sofa and feels something underneath her head. When she reaches back, her hand lands on a cold soggy diaper that never made it into the wastebasket. Instantly, she is off the sofa, staring at the diaper.

"Oh, God, sorry about that," Trish says, laughing and scooping the urine-soaked wad of plastic off the couch. Rolling the diaper into a tight ball, she shoots it toward the waste basket and misses. "I get it in about half the time," Trish says, smiling. She leaves the diaper where it landed and drops into a kitchen chair, where she lights up a cigarette.

Candace blinks. She stares at Trish, then the baby. Try as she might, she can't help thinking what Eileen would say if she were watching this display. Candace closes her eyes, tries to force her mother out of the room.

"You OK?"

"Oh sure," Candace says, opening her eyes. "Just a little tired is all."

"Yeah, well, just wait."

Candace stares blankly at the wall. Her eyes settle into something new. Something she has never seen before. All of a sudden, it hits her.

"Trish," Candace whispers, her eyes flooded in images. "I have to paint your wall!"

"Great," Trish says, sucking on her cigarette. "And while you're at it, fix the sink here, too. It leaks like crazy."

Candace stands. "No, no I mean it. I really need some space, some large space for a piece I have in mind. And your place, I mean it's perfect. Big walls. All I need is paint."

Trish laughs. "No problem. Paint I got plenty of. Maybe you want to start over there by the table. Cover that spot near Priscilla's high chair where she throws her carrots."

Candace decides to use a blunt table knife to apply the paint. She layers long strokes on the wall, applying paint as thick as butter on bread. All she can think of is Van Gogh's "The Starry Night." When Candace was in eleventh grade, Marjory took her to New York one weekend. They spent an entire afternoon at the Museum of Modern Art. Candace stood in front of the Van Gogh off and on for an hour. She was enthralled by the way the painting carried her eye in waves through the night sky. Always, her gaze came to rest in the right hand corner, where the orange crescent moon shone like a reflection in water. She tries now to paint the fish in the same way, laying thick strokes of different shades of light paint against a dark blue background.

"What exactly have you got in mind?" Trish asks, leaning against the doorframe in the hallway. She has just finished putting Priscilla to bed. Candace steps down from the kitchen chair and moves backward. The lower right hand corner of the wall is a squall of color, strokes of white, yellow and green all going in different directions. Candace frowns. The technique may have worked for Van Gogh, but in her own painting, it looks like a mess.

"Well," Candace says, sinking into the chair. "I woke up the other morning with this incredible image, a swarm of fish, all glowing and turning and catching the light. I want the paint to make the fish move, I want the whole thing to shift in different lights. I want the fish just to lift right off the surface." She shakes her head. "What I've got instead is a bunch of squishy-looking fish that look dead and dried out, like they've been left in the sun all day."

Suddenly Candace's eye is reflecting light. It isn't sun, though, but light from overhead. She turns to Trish, who has the small mirror in hand, the bag of white powder.

"Would a little of this help?" Trish has a devilish grin on her face.

Candace shuts her eyes, rests her chin on the back of the chair. Then she takes up her strand of hair, twists it tight around her finger. She opens her eyes, and Trish already has the mirror on the kitchen table. Candace reaches out and touches the mirror lightly.

It is her firm intention only to snort one line. But the first time she inhales, the drug seems to have no effect. She inhales again, and again she waits, all the while staring at the wall. "How did he do it?" she whispers.

"Say again? How did who do what?" Trish is lying on the couch.

"Van Gogh. You know, how did he get the paint to move across the canvas?"

"Oh, that's easy. He cut off his ear. It hurt so much he started running. He just kept his paintbrush moving with him."

"I'm serious, Trish. Did you ever see Starry Night up close? Or the Sunflowers? They blow me away. I mean, the way he layered the paint and it all swirled together. It really buzzes." As she says this, Candace has her chin in her hand, and she glances down, and she catches sight of her face in the mirror, and suddenly her face is buzzing, too, or more precisely, one nostril pulses, in and out and down, and her eye, it's alternately getting larger and smaller, and all the time Candace is thinking, my God, this drug must be taking effect. Soon she starts laughing, because it seems so silly that she ever worried that it wouldn't.

Rising from the chair, she takes up the butter knife. "I just want these damn fish to move," she says, not exactly to herself, but not exactly to Trish either. And now she realizes that the baby is moving, rather frantically, inside her belly, and that the room is moving too, all over. The walls suddenly have the same kind of waves that she remembers from the Van Gogh, enormous arms curling across the room, crashing into waves at the end of the arms, and now her own arms feel shaky, or numb, and her legs are wobbly, and she is tired and wide awake both at once, completely wired, completely ready to paint, and not ready at all, feeling like she's going to faint, or at least fall over. And her final mistake is that she attempts to step up onto the chair, only her foot doesn't make it, it places itself squarely into air only. Candace collapses and as she does, she screams out, and the last thing she thinks is this: how strange I never noticed before that Trish's floor is white and black squares, like a checkerboard, and how strange that I should be lying here, face down, as if I were one of the checkers.

PART THREE

EILEEN

April 1, 1972

I am sitting on John's back porch, my face full of sun, the air swarming with the smell of spring and rich warming earth and things growing. Below me, next to the sidewalk underneath John's porch, I can see purple and yellow crocuses. So pretty.

Oh God. I just remembered, today is Palm Sunday, meaning my mother will be carrying home palm fronds from Mass and later, she and Aunt Marie will sit at the kitchen table silently weaving the palms into those intricate cones, and then they'll tuck them behind the crucifix. Just thinking about church is enough to ruin this incredible good mood... I'll close my eyes and concentrate instead on John's face, lying on the pillow as he was so peacefully this morning. If only I could freeze time, if only I could stay here on John's porch inhaling spring air, forever staring at flowers, not caring about the future. In English class last fall we read T.S. Eliot's poem, "The Dry Salvages," and I memorized this: "Between midnight and dawn, before the morning watch when time stops and time is never ending; And the ground swell, that is and was from the beginning, clangs the bell..." Those last two words had their own line, which made me feel like I could hear the bell ringing. I loved the poem and I loved Eliot's idea of the still point in time, that is, time stopping.

How did I get onto the subject of poetry? I suppose because I'm so happy, and I want to freeze the feeling, I want to be this happy forever, I want it always to be the day after John and I spent the most incredible night together. I want to save this amazing feeling in a poem but know I cannot write one (I tried one this morning but ripped it up right away.)

I know this is crazy, I can't be in love with John but I am, and I want him to be in love with me. (Is he? Could he, considering how me is now me plus someone else?) I want to go with him to California and stay and after that, when it's time to…(can I say the word deliver? I'm going to have to say it sooner or later) oh shit, who cares what happens after that?

But now, of course, it is almost noon on Sunday and if I don't call home in the next couple of hours I'm afraid my parents might show up at the dorm. Sooooo. I'd better go call. Meanwhile, though, I'm feeling optimistic as can be, I can handle anything today, in this mood, in this weather. As they say, here goes nothing, here goes nothing at all.

Later today.

I can't believe my parents. I can't believe my parents did this to me. How could they? How could they?

They did it without asking, too. I screamed that over the phone. *"You did this without asking? Without even asking me once how I felt?"* I screamed that and they said nothing. Nothing at all, except for one little thing. "Come home."

They withdrew me from school. They called Dean Rogers Friday afternoon, after they weren't able to reach me all day. They told him I couldn't continue in school because of "circumstances," and they pulled me out. They told the Dean they wouldn't finish paying this semester's tuition. Officially, then, I am out. I AM OUT! I want to scream…tear their eyes out. I ran back here to the dorm to tell Corinne and she was gone. I am sitting here with no one to tell, with no one to yell at. I am sitting here, my hands shaking, my heart pounding, tears streaming down my face. John took off for the day, to see his uncle in Boston, a guy who teaches classics at Harvard. Wait till he finds out. Wait till Corinne finds out. Wait till she finds out she has no roommate anymore. She's out of a roommate and I'm out of a life. I have no place to live. I have no place here at school. They have erased me from Brown. They have taken it away. My life. They can't do it, but they have.

And of course I see at the top of this page it is April Fool's Day. It is. I knew that, or should have known, this morning.

April 6th Good ?? Friday

Who in the world came up with the name Good Friday anyway? Here we have the biggest murder in history on this day, a guy gets nailed (literally), and he's not just anybody, either, and he hangs on a cross for no crime at all and he bleeds to death from his hands and feet and a crown of thorns. And that's supposed to be a Good Friday? I want to see the Friday they call Bad. This is certainly not a good Friday for me. How could it be? I am back here, back home, confined to the second floor — 324 Pleasant — and as far as Lucy and my father are concerned, I have no future at all. I will show them, though, I have to keep telling myself that, I will show them. I got home Tuesday night, John drove me to Hartford and I got a bus to North Adams about six o'clock, and just before I stepped on the Greyhound, John took hold of me, kissed me on the mouth and swung his arms tightly around me, we swayed together side to side, he rocked me and whispered, "Look, it won't be that long," but of course all I could do was cry, act like a complete baby. And since I stepped inside this house, at ten o'clock that night, I have not spoken a single word to my parents. I won't either. I will show them. I will show them whose life this is. I may in fact already have a job, I went to Italo's Wednesday, I walked, I walked all the way to the South side of town, I told Art Italo I would waitress, hostess, I would work any day of the week.

"I have to get a job," I said.

"Aren't you the Rosetti girl who's...who's getting married?" His glance dropped, damn him, his eyes searched my waist. What did he expect to see, a bulging belly?

"No, no, the wedding's off," I said, "well, actually, it was never really on. My mom was, you know, kind of pushing me." I nodded, and he nodded. And he scratched the side of his head, and said, "Let me see, give me a couple days, I'll see if I can use you."

Then he glanced down again, but this time I realized he was staring at my left hand, pointing at the bandage peeking out from my shirt-sleeve. "So what's with your hand?"

"Oh, I burned it, but not bad," I said, waving the bandage in the air, showing him I could still carry a tray. "I...I uh, was taking something out of the stove. Bread. You know, I bake bread." He shook his head, and I smiled, wondering why I was lying to him. "Anyway, I'm going to get it taken off soon, the bandage, that is. Maybe even today." And now I'm praying that maybe today he'll call. Or if he doesn't, I will call him.

Meanwhile, I haven't eaten anything at all. For a few days, my mother was leaving trays by the bedroom door. But I kept letting the food go cold. Finally, last night, my father got mad. It was late when I heard him say something to my mother in the hall.

"She's getting outta hand," my father said. "Way outta hand. And I'm not gonna stand by for it. She's gonna see what happens when *I* get outta hand." I could hear dishes rattling as one of them picked up the tray. "No more trays," he bellowed to me through the door. "You wanna eat with us, then you get yourself downstairs. You wanna stay in your room all day and starve, then starve. You decide." He rattled the door handle, but I had it locked. Then he pounded once with his fist. "I tell you Eileen, you better watch out," he said. "Because you're pushing me too far. And you're pushing your mother, too."

My mother protested. "Oh, Frank, don't. Come on. Leave her be."

He spoke into the door again. "I'm warning you Eileen. You better watch it or you're gonna get a taste of something beside food from me. You hear me?"

"Frank, please," my mother said. "Take it easy." Her voice had the same sad, worried twist it always had. This morning, she came back to my room alone.

"Eileen?" she whispered through the door.

"What?" I had just woken up.

"Open up. Please!"

I did.

"Look, you know you gotta eat," she pleaded, her eyes pained. I remained silent, staring at my bare toes. "Come downstairs, I'll make you a bowl of oatmeal. Or a nice frittata. Come on now. Come downstairs and eat and stop acting so foolish."

"No, Ma." I was going to add, "See, Ma, it's Good Friday and I'm fasting." But I didn't want to get her get mad. I don't want to have anything to do with her or my father.

I will walk to town later, I will buy my one daily meal sometime this afternoon, at the diner. I walked there yesterday, in the morning, and who was walking out but Rusty.

"Whoa," he said, holding the door open for me. "When did you arrive?" I grimaced, and followed him back inside the diner. We sat in a booth facing the parking lot. I told him as much as I thought he should know. Which was not much.

I sat eating my omelet and home fries. "I'm getting a job, and as soon as school ends, Corinne and I are leaving for California." I didn't look up, but I didn't have to, I could see his eyes flash open. And I could hear him whistle in amazement. Silence followed. All we heard were dishes clanking, and bits and pieces of dull conversation floating back and forth between the waitress, the cook, and three ancient customers sitting at stools at the counter.

Rusty leaned way over the table, so close that I could smell his breath. You've been smoking again, I almost said. But before I could, he began talking. "So I guess the next thing I'm supposed to ask is where exactly you intend to have this baby?" He leaned back.

I ripped open the little plastic container of grape jelly, and spread it on my toast.

"Could I have some more coffee please?" I called out to the waitress.

"Sure thing," she yelled back.

"Eileen?" Rusty was waiting, not so patiently, for his answer.

I looked at my plate. "How can I possibly know that now? It's months away."

"But you must have thought about it? My God, Eileen, you must have some idea? Some place you have in mind? How can you not have a plan?"

I considered saying I planned to deliver the kid on the Golden Gate Bridge. Instead, I just spread more grape jelly on the other piece of toast.

"OK. I'll tell you what to say to me. Try this: Say, 'Hey, Rus, honey, I'll let you know. I will definitely let you know. I plan to keep in touch.'" He pauses, then gives me a big fake grin. "How about that?"

I wiped my mouth with the napkin. I looked up. Shrugged. The waitress was at my elbow, pouring coffee. "I just can't say, Rus."

And then, the waitress left and with no warning, Rusty slammed one fist down on the formica. His hand came down so hard that the table shook and coffee splashed out of my cup and into the saucer. All three of the customers at the counter turned to look at us at once. Then Rusty bounced up and walked out.

I'm left thinking now about something Corinne said. That I might be making a mistake treating Rusty as if he doesn't make a difference. "That isn't smart," she said one night in the dorm. "Who knows? There might come a time when you need him." And he has rights, Corinne said, he's got rights to the baby. And that's something I better consider, too.

CANDACE

Candace sits cross-legged on the braided rug cradling her mother's journal. Surrounding her on the bedroom floor are her backpack, her duffel, and two pieces of black nylon luggage. In her hand is an exacto knife. In her mind is a plan to destroy the black book in her lap. In half an hour, her father is supposed to arrive to pick her up. The plan, which Candace had no role in shaping, is for Rusty to drive her across the state to a small drug rehabilitation center north of Boston called Redfield Retreat.

Eileen announced the plan the very next morning after Candace was rushed to the emergency room from Trish Bosco's place. "Somebody at the clinic knew about Redfield, knew they were one of the very few residential treatment programs that would take a pregnant woman. They have an OK reputation. At least there you'll get some good counseling. And thank God it's a place where they'll take our health insurance."

"I don't need counseling," Candace said drily.

"Oh, but you do," Eileen replied calmly. She was paring carrots at the sink. Long shavings of pale orange carrot flesh, not so different from the color of Candace's hair, fell into the white porcelain. Eileen looked up. Her eyes had an icy look.

"You have a choice: go to Redfield for the remainder of the pregnancy, or I report you to the police. I'll ask them to press charges against you. I'll tell them I have proof that you have twice — at least — tried to endanger the life of your unborn child with cocaine." She paused. "And if you think I'm kidding, just try me. I've never been more serious in my life."

In the end, even Audrey and Rusty turned against her. Both took Eileen's side, insisting Candace get "help." And now, only a few minutes remain until Rusty arrives. A half hour to kill, Candace thinks, staring down at the black book. A half hour to kill or at least to mutilate the pages of this book. With the knife she took from her desk drawer, she sets to work, slicing strips an inch wide out of the book's pages. At first, she slices vertically, then she cuts horizontally, then she switches, savagely slicing several pages on the diagonal. Finally she plucks whole pages, at random, first from the front, then from the end of the book.

Taking up a pair of scissors, she cuts confetti-sized pieces, letting the paper drift this way and that, fluttering toward the floor. She smiles, thinking how her mother, coming into the bedroom with a vacuum cleaner a week or two hence, after Candace has been swallowed up in some kind of glorified hospital room, will find the pile of cut paper on the rug.

The snippets of paper contain words, words written in a bold black scrawl, all the inflated first letters unmistakable, all the product of her mother's hand. The name Italo's comes up over and over, and the months, April and May, June and even July. The year 1972 appears repeatedly, sometimes in black ink, sometimes in red, most often in blue. Occasionally, Candace encounters names: Rus and John and the first five letters of Corinne, or sometimes the middle letters, and sometimes the last. Pieces of "California" appear in all variety of combinations. Candace smirks, tosses the paper up, delighting in the destruction. Such a lot of unnecessary words, she thinks. Such a lot of nonsense her mother wrote, and now it's being swept — no cut — away.

After only a few minutes generating confetti like this, Candace begins to grow bored. There must be a more creative way of destroying the book, she thinks, a more appropriate way of obliterating her mother's tender concerns, so carefully laid down on paper. She takes the journal to her easel and, propping it open, proceeds to lay a thick coat of paint on page after page. Arbitrarily, she alternates the pages in black and red.

Her brush is thick, and so, too, is the paint, as thick as paste, so thick that it covers every trace of her mother's handwriting. In her haste, Candace slops paint on the floor. The mess doesn't stop her, or slow her down.

"It will give her something to clean up after I'm gone," Candace whispers, continuing her rampage through the book. "A pleasant little reminder of me." She continues passing the brush at will, now swirling, now zigzagging, now filling any white space she sees with intricate curlicues, all sluicing out of the thick wet wad of bristles in the brush. She does one page in nothing but large points, attacking with the tip of the brush. She does another page only in Xs, as though she was embroidering in thick yarn across the white paper.

It is while she is doing a line of Xs that she notices the word that puts an immediate halt to her destruction of the journal. She is on the right-hand page, and she has splashed three red Xs in a row, and suddenly, the word "SUICIDE" jumps out at her. Maybe because of how it is written, in huge block letters. Maybe because it is in all capitals. Maybe because it departs momentarily from the peculiar cursive scrawl. Or maybe because it is the one word she has never connected with her mother before.

She pauses, the brush hovering over the page. She reads the rest of the sentence, and then the one that follows, and then the one that follows that. Before she knows it, Candace is on the next page, hooked on what she is reading. At that moment, she hears a gentle knock.

"Hey, anybody alive in there?" Her father's voice presses at the door. Candace glances up. Tossing the paintbrush beneath the easel, she picks up the journal by the small clump of remaining clean pages and carries it to the rug, where she left the exacto knife.

"Coming," she yells out, using the knife to sever the unpainted pages from the journal. She tosses the mutilated book to the floor. It lands face down with a slap. A thick clot of red paint splatters the braided rug. Like blood, Candace thinks, smiling. Just like blood. She kneels, folds the clean pages in a thick wad and slides them into her backpack, beneath the next volume of the journal. Then, eyeing the journal she just abandoned on the rug, she gives it a sharp kick, sending it across the room. Bending, she picks up her duffel and opens the door, smiling.

EILEEN

June 13, 1972

This is how far I got: I had the tablets, long white, torpedo-shaped pills, cupped in my hand. (I got them from Lucy's top drawer, she needs them occasionally to sleep, or for what she calls her "worry spells.") Anyway, I stood and walked around her room awhile just holding the bottle, shaking it like a rattle, then I came downstairs to the kitchen table, why the kitchen table, God only knows, I just felt like I'd be better able to pull it off in the kitchen, and then, too, I thought how bad they'd feel when they found me slumped over on the kitchen floor. I shook the pills out into my hand, there must have been 25 or 30, I held them out in front of me, I can still see myself standing there, staring at them, like they were sitting on a platter, then I held them close to my chest. I sat down. It occurred to me to spell my name out of the pills. Yes, I thought, I will do that, and then I will swallow them, letter by letter, I'll see how many letters I get through before I go over.

I made an E, was just finishing the bottom part of the letter, when it occurred to me I hadn't written a note. But what could I write, I thought...I tried to remember what Sylvia Plath wrote the first time she tried suicide, but I couldn't; and then I thought, how stupid, what difference would that make anyway, I'm not Sylvia Plath. Then I thought how stupid any note I wrote would sound: "I want to die because I lost my lousy job, I'm pregnant, and my boss at the restaurant found out and the jerk fired me." Or: "I want to die because I'm pregnant and it's such a horrible *mistake, I've wrecked my life and I don't have enough money to leave home and all my parents do is keep telling me to get married."* The problem, I realized, is that nothing I could write would make anybody understand. I decided to keep on spelling my name. I laid out E—I—L—E—E and then I came to N, I didn't have quite enough pills for the N, I got about halfway through, so I thought that was my clue to do it.

Shivering, I picked up the first three pills, part of the E, carried them in my sweaty palm over to the sink, filled a glass with water. I could hear my heart beating in my ears. Oddly enough, I wasn't thinking about death, but about not being able to catch my breath. I thought about being underwater, about the time I tried scuba diving at Brown, I was at the bottom of that gigantic swimming pool with the awful feeling I couldn't get enough air. I came back to the table. Closing my eyes, I thought, it's now or never. I opened my mouth and threw the pills against the back of my throat, and quickly guzzled down the water. There, I thought. And for a while I just sat, calmly taking in air, drumming my fingers on the formica. And that brought me back to the day not so many weeks ago, when, sitting in this very spot with Ma, she described the rosemary chicken to me and I ran to the bathroom to vomit my guts out.

And maybe it was the power of suggestion, or maybe it was the tranquilizer itself, but suddenly I got so dizzy the room was doing circles. Lowering myself to the floor, I crawled, head spinning, over to the door. *Air*, I kept thinking, I am desperate for air, the door blurred, became two, I reached for the handle, I thought I saw it turn, for a second I thought I heard my parents, but that was absurd, they were out of town for a wedding. I got the door open a crack, the smell of sweet spring air, laden with flowers, seeped through, I pulled myself up to sit and the room spun faster, I rolled back to the floor, and that's when I thought *Oh my God I can't take this anymore*, just then, thankfully, I started throwing up, gigantic heaves just kept coming and coming until I was only heaving green. Then nothing, I was heaving dry. I lay there, completely wet, my face, my hands, my hair, I've never ever sweat like that before. I started immediately to cry, I felt so relieved, so thankful the stuff was out of me, so grateful I had been given a reprieve, a second chance to be alive. I felt free and light, and unbelievably relaxed and happy.

I reached for the door, shoved it open wide. Coming across me was a blanket of golden afternoon light. A slight breeze followed the light inside. I breathed it in, the air, the light. I knew I was still a little dizzy, so I lay there for a while more. Before long, I knew something else. It didn't matter if I had enough money for anything more than a ticket. Just as soon as I could, I would leave for California.

Audrey X

She hasn't walked the sugar bush since her fall on the forest floor, but today, the late May sun beckons Audrey out. Something else calls her too, the trees themselves, their branches glaring and stark, so bare as to be startling. For the last two weeks, she has occupied the rocking chair by her bedroom window, watching, waiting for the swollen buds to break open, to produce a canopy of new foliage. In all her years on the farm, Audrey can't remember a time when the trees bloomed so late. Every other year, it has happened all in a matter of days, the buds splayed apart, casting forth a new swarm of leaves. Fragile green, tinged red, the tiny leaves flutter from their nascent stems at tender, awkward angles, reminding Audrey of the tiny waving hands of a newborn infant. But gazing from the house in the last week, she's seen no sign of leaves at all. And then last night there was that peculiar dream, where all the buds had grown into large blistered sacs the size and shape of apples.

In the dream, it was night, and the moon shone full and creamy yellow, a disc of butter clinging to the dark sky. Moonlight lit up the strange translucent sacs, and when Audrey reached out to pluck one, the sac exploded, the blister oozing red and bloody in her hand. Inside were no leaves at all, just matted hair, a tooth or two, and a leering eye, staring up at her, so that when she threw the clear sac aside, and stepped back from the trees, horrified, she was greeted by hundreds of the same eyes, all gleaming down at her in the midnight sky.

Slapping a black fly against the milky skin of her neck, she pivots down the three steps of the back porch. The rubber sneakers and the soles of her crutches squeak on the wooden steps, steps which she notices now are badly in need of paint. Sometime this summer, she promises herself, she will hire that high school kid to come to the farm to scrape and paint the whole house.

The warm sun brings an immediate flush to her face as she lifts it toward the sky. She has braided her hair, coiled the braid into a tight bun. Stray hair forms a fine silver halo around her face. She pauses, lets the sun toast her cheeks. Leaning heavily into her crutches, she proceeds across the lawn. By rights, the cast should be gone by now, should have come off her ankle two weeks ago. But at the last visit, Dr. Dunbar said no, it had to go a few more weeks. So here she is, still clumsy, still depending on the crutches. Each time she takes a step, the rubber tips pierce deeply into the tender ground. As she pulls up from the soft grass, the holes left behind fill with muddy water.

She reaches the maples at the edge of the yard when Marjory appears, coming down the path. "Wow," Marjory calls. "How nice. You're up and out today. Hurray for that."

"Yes, well, I can't stay cooped up forever. Not in this weather."

"That's for sure. I was going to force you out anyway. I saw something just now I have to show you." Marjory pulls a branch to eye level. Audrey lumbers closer. "We've got a problem in these leaves, Audrey. Something, an insect, I think, eating the buds. Look, you can see it right here."

Audrey examines the branch. Where there would normally be a spray of tender new leaves is instead a knot of tree flesh, twisted green, brown and crisp.

"Crazy," she whispers, fingering the damaged leaf. "It looks...it almost looks like something ate the bud from the inside out."

"Have you ever seen ..."

"No," Audrey says quickly, "never. I've never seen anything like this in the maples. Not in my entire life." She inhales as she says the last few words, and the effect is startling. It's as if her words have been sucked away, as if the wind itself is swallowing her breath.

EILEEN

June 19, 1972

Flying definitely does not agree with this baby! He keeps poking me. Notice I said he. I've decided the baby is a boy. I intend to name him something bland like Kendall or Kenneth, a name for somebody who can fend for himself. A name for somebody who keeps on an even course. Ah, that's it! He doesn't like the rocky ride here up above the clouds. The turbulence was so severe a few minutes ago that the flight crew had to stop serving drinks and post-pone meal service. (No great loss.) For a while, I rode the swells by squeezing the armrests until my knuckles turned white and my wrists and hands felt completely numb. But then things went totally wild: the plane took a free pitch forward into nothingness. I snatched the small white bag out from the front net pocket of my seat and held it under my mouth. Meanwhile, Baby K decided to contract into a tight little ball and then he nose dived forward himself. I imagined him vaguely purple in color, his toes and fingernails poking out, scraping my insides like a row of toothpicks.

I suppose Baby K isn't thrilled with the idea of going to California. Not until this moment have I considered that possibility. *I promise you, Kenny, you're going to love California.* Every time I close my eyes, I see endless groves of sweet-smelling orange trees, tawny mountains, glittering ocean waves. I see actresses with slim tan legs and golden hair flowing to their shoulders, lying beside blue swimming pools as clear as if the water floated in sparkling glasses with stems.

You could lift those pools to your lips and sip the blue water from them, the way the actresses do their drinks.

Oops, more frantic side-to-side swooping of the plane. Out the window, the egg white clouds look so serene, like a sun-licked lemon meringue pie stretching forever into the sky. Everything looks so perfectly calm out there, while inside, it's another story. Every time the plane is sucked out of control by some mighty but invisible force, the plastic cabin pieces squeak under the strain. A couple minutes ago the overhead luggage compartments flew open and clothing and suitcases and shopping bags spilled out. At the worst moments, all of us passengers sit here in an eerie hush, terrified and humbled by the thought that this hunk of metal is hurling through the sky against the will of the heavens.

I keep thinking that this ride must be some kind of punishment, or a test. Sure you want to go to California, but just how badly do you want to go? I also keep thinking of my mother and father sitting stony-faced in the living room. Last night, I made a half-hearted attempt to say goodbye. Is it my fault that they just kept staring into the great blue hue of T.V., watching Mary Tyler Moore bicker with Lou Grant? I stood in the room, waiting for a commercial. When the Polydent commercial came on, and I saw the glass of water with the dirty dentures in it, and the dark stains bubbling away, I made my final plea.

"I'm leaving at seven," I said, quietly, but certainly loud enough for them to hear me over the T.V. No response. My father kept staring at the fake teeth. My mother glanced down at the crochet needle in her hands. She pulled up a little more yarn. Then my father slumped deeper into his chair. Fine, I said to myself. I left the room, went upstairs and showered, got ready for bed. I fell asleep with the radio on. Sometime in the middle of the night, I woke. The radio had gone to static. I leaned over to the night table, shut the radio, but couldn't get back to sleep. I crept downstairs, and ate some cornflakes.

I got up as soon as it was light enough to see. I had already laid out my maternity bluejeans (the ones with the stretchy panel; I've given in) and the bright yellow T-shirt that is big enough to be a maternity top. Blue and yellow. Colors for California. Corinne told me those are the colors of the state's license plates. Colors of sky and water and sun.

Anyway, I snapped my suitcase shut. I opened my bedroom door, hoping I wouldn't bump into one of my parents in the hall. I eased softly down the steps. The clock in the kitchen read 5:50. Any minute, I knew Ma would emerge from her bedroom, belting her terrycloth robe. Any minute, the cab I had ordered would be pulling up outside the front door. As I undid the lock, my heart was banging against my chest. Nobody appeared, though. Nobody said goodbye. I stepped out into the June sun, filled my lungs with the flower-scented air. Irises, growing in thick purple clumps, sitting beside the house. I set my suitcase down. I had a rush of nostalgia. I flashed back to the night of the senior prom, having my picture taken with Rusty in front of those irises. Thankfully, that thought didn't last long.

At 6:05 exactly, a run down cab careened around the corner, pulling into the driveway beside the pines. I got in, and never glanced back at the house. *Goodbye forever!* I wanted to scream. As I settled into the back seat, a seat without any springs left, I felt I must be dreaming. There I was, making my big break. It occurred to me then that I had made only one mistake: I had promised Rusty I would definitely come home to have the baby.

Out the window, the clouds have thinned. Below me is jagged blue rock splashed with snow. And now the pilot, speaking in his soft, off-handed tone, can be heard above the drone of the engines: "Ladies and gentlemen, out the left side of the aircraft you'll see we are passing over the Rocky Mountain chain just north of Park City, Utah." Chills go up my arms. John told me about hiking in Park City. He said he wants to take me there. For so long I've only dreamed about escaping. Now, I am. I'm on my way.

The seatbelt light has finally gone off. The plane is smoothing out. Two stewardesses in grey jackets with tiny metal wings pinned to their lapels came by a moment ago, zigzagging side to side down the aisle with the drink cart between them.

"Something to drink, miss?" The stewardess set a package of peanuts on my tray.

"Juice. Orange juice, please." The stewardess dipped a plastic glass into a bag of ice cubes, snapped open a small can of juice and started to pour.

"So how long do you have?" She set my glass, in a small napkin, on top of the tray.

I looked up, confused. How long? For what? The flight? She was asking *me*? I shook my head. She smiled, pointed to my stomach. Of course. My stomach. It was almost touching the tray table. "I, it's, I'm

due in August, the end, I think." The stewardess smiled briefly and
moved on to the passenger across the aisle. I set my head against the
window. Dear God! Do I have to spend the next few months telling
people how long I have?

The mountains have disappeared. The landscape is getting flat
now, a myriad of muted colors, light browns, pale purples, pinks and
blues. Of course, I think, glancing back at the map in the airline
magazine. We are fast approaching the Nevada desert.

❦

The plane is being held back by the airport tower. We are making big
lazy circles around San Francisco. The water in the bay is a deep blue,
sparkling in a thousand points in the sun. The pastel houses on the hills
look like piles of seashells cast up on shore. The bridge, *the* bridge, is not
golden at all, but a strange rusty red color. Beautiful just the same.

I wish I could magically make this belly disappear. Send it gift
wrapped to my parents, via UPS. I guess there are some women who just
don't feel any motherly instincts. To me, being pregnant is just a condition, an awkward bulging body that keeps on swelling, an occasional
backache, a few blue veins popping out of my thighs. I am continually
amazed that there is another person contained inside me. Actually, I am
not convinced at all that a person really will emerge. (Sorry, Ken.) This
isn't the way I'm supposed to feel, I know. A girl I met in the doctor's
office a few weeks ago told me how wildly excited she was when she first
"felt life." I sat there, listening carefully. I smiled a little at the end, nodded politely, thinking about how I feel: like a balloon slowly filling with
air. The scariest part is that soon, the balloon will have to burst. It makes
the future feel, ah, just a bit ominous. Everybody tells me I'll feel differently when the baby comes. They say I'll flip the first time I see it,
hold it in my arms. But I can't imagine my feelings changing. There just
isn't room in my life for a kid. Not now, not when there are so many
other things I want to do, like hike the Rockies with John.

The plane is making a sharp turn over a low set of golden hills. San
Francisco is just across the bay. The hills have the same honey color
as that Golden retriever Rusty once had, Bogie. So soft. We're heading for the airport now, getting ready to descend. In a few minutes, I'll
see Corinne; and I'll be walking around Berkeley and maybe talking
to John on the phone. At last, I am really going to be a California girl.

Eileen

June 21, 1972
California

I have been waiting since last night for John to call. I left a message with his roommate, who is, oddly enough, a woman. I hope there is a very good reason he is living with a woman. She said her name was Belle and that she, like John, will be a med student at UCSF in the fall. She sounded nice enough and said she would give him the message as soon as he got in. That was eight o'clock last night. And here it is nine o'clock the next morning.

All I know so far is that I love California. Corinne lives in a pale salmon stucco house way up in the hills of Oakland. The view from her living room window is spectacular. The whole Bay, and the Golden Gate Bridge, is at the edge of the horizon. Outside her house are gorgeous orange poppies and ivy and strange-smelling shrubs. Nutmeg, I told her. They smell like nutmeg to me. She tells me I'm crazy. Now and then you see a palm tree.

She took me walking down Telegraph Avenue yesterday as soon as I got off the plane. There were street vendors lined up, selling everything imaginable: bulky hand knit sweaters from Ecuador, dangling silver earrings, fancy redwood tables and chairs and mirrors, soft leather satchels and handbags, and lots of incense and candles. Oh, and lots of Indian gauze clothing, too, long flimsy dresses, gathered skirts, baggy pants with drawstrings at the waist and ankles. The rainbow-colored clothing hung on crowded racks on the sidewalk.

I took my sneakers off, walked barefoot with Corinne on the warm sidewalk. A parade of weird people passed by me. Men with pony tails down to the middle of their backs. Women in headbands, with babies in front packs strapped to their chests. Women in Indian skirts, with long hair, wearing a lot of beads and no bras. They had long hair growing in their armpits, too. Incense was burning everywhere, and I smelled something else, too — something called falafel, a Middle Eastern food in a cart just up the block. "I feel like I'm in a foreign country," I whispered to Corinne. She smiled. "You are."

At one point, we stopped, saw two brown smoldering sticks of incense propped in a small brass cup on the sidewalk. The smoke curled lazily upward. I stared at the cup, then smiled at the street vendor, who sat perfectly straight on a white mat, legs crossed in a lotus position. He had cinnamon-colored skin and long, jet black hair with a sheen. It was parted in the middle and it fell in waves over his shoulders like a veil. He was dressed in a baggy white shirt and pants. His face was perfectly calm, his smile saintly, his dark eyes blissful. He gestured with his hand, inviting us to look through his clothing.

We did. Soon I found a black shirt with embroidery across the bosom, a rainbow of reds, yellows, and purples.

"I want that," I said, nudging Corinne with my elbow. "I've got to have that shirt." Suddenly I felt self-conscious. I was carrying my sneakers by the heels. I had my maternity jeans rolled up to the knee, as if I were wading in shallow waves at the seashore. I was wearing the same outfit I had left home in only a few hours before, the same blue pants and yellow T-shirt that had seemed just right for California. Now, though, walking on Telegraph Avenue with its exotic array of street people, its foreign smells, I felt out of place.

"Try it on," Corinne said.

I bent over and spoke softly to the vendor, who continued to sit cross-legged and stare out peacefully at the passing crowd. His face still had that saintly smile pasted on. It occurred to me maybe he was meditating. Or taking drugs.

The man gently nodded his head up and down. I wondered if he understood what I had asked. Handing Corinne my purse, I squirmed into the black shirt. It smelled of incense. It fit my shoulders, and flared out enough to accomodate my belly. The embroidery shimmered in the sun.

"So?" I twirled around and the shirt flared out.

Corinne cocked her head to one side. "Nice, except..."

"What?"

"Well, it's just those pants. You look, well, you look like you belong in the suburbs." I looked down. The black shirt didn't cover the maternity panel of my blue jeans.

"You're right. These pants are awful." Corinne started rifling through a rack of baggy cotton pants. She pulled out a pair at the end of the rack. "Here, these should fit. Try them."

The sun was beating down on the black gauze of the shirt. I had on two shirts and I was starting to perspire. And now I would be wearing two pairs of pants. I pulled the drawstring snug, looked up. Corinne was smiling. "You look amazing," she said. "With that black hair of yours, and those clothes, you look like you belong in some ashram yourself."

I turned, and the street vendor was holding up a small ornate mirror.

"How much?" I pointed to my purse and then gestured to the blouse and pants.

"Ten, each ten," he said, in a heavy Indian accent. He brought his hands together at his chest as he spoke, as if he were praying. I looked at Corinne.

"I'm not sure." In my head, I was calculating how much money I had for the summer.

"Seven, then, seven," the vendor said, smiling and nodding. I slipped him two tens.

"OK." I turned to Corinne. "You realize I'm going to have to get a summer job?" I handed the man the money. "I hope you have a few ideas."

"My father might," Corinne said. The vendor handed me back my change.

"You will make a very fine mother," the vendor said, reaching toward me. Horrified, I thought at first he was about to touch my stomach. Complete strangers think they have some right to my belly these days, as if it's some kind of public property just because it sticks out in front of me. Instead of touching me, though, he took my hand. Into it he pressed a small card. It had a color picture of another dark-skinned man. He resembled the vendor, but his hair and his long flowing beard were both grey. Underneath the man's face were the words: Peace in the World Through Rami. On the back of the card, there was an address: 2033 Shattuck Avenue, Berkeley.

The vendor smiled. "Please come, see Rami," he said. I smiled. But Corinne was tugging at my elbow, urgently trying to drag me away from the vendor, up the crowded street.

EILEEN

July 7, 1972

I came home again today smelling of gasoline and
Corinne's mother and father met me at the back door. Dr. Rivers
had another fit. "I told you it's dangerous for a pregnant woman to
pump gas," he scolded. He was standing on the back patio, a couple
steps down from the front yard. The whole house sits on a steep hill
covered with California ivy. He was wearing an apron, with the words
"Je suis le sous chef" running diagonally across his chest and I was
vaguely staring at the words and wondering what sous meant. He was
holding up a metal spatula and pointing at me, sternly, at my black
and rainbow-colored shirt. It reeked of gasoline. It was truly an awful
smell, and I was so tired from walking, and standing, and from
pumping gas, and from hanging out in that stuffy little box where I
spend the day taking money and selling cigarettes that I started to
cry but I tried to pretend it was the smoke in my eyes from the
barbecue that was doing it. I rubbed my eyes and he waved the
smoke away with the spatula. He wasn't cooking burgers, at least not
the kind I'm used to. Corinne and her family never eat meat, instead
they barbecue slabs of tofu and brown rice veggie burgers; everybody out here eats them.
"I can't help it," I said.
"You can't help what?"
"I can't help the gasoline. I mean spilling it. I can't get used to
pumping gas." Ever since I got this job two weeks ago I've had gasoline

on my shirt every day. I wasn't supposed to have to pump gasoline, or do anything else dirty, only be a cashier, but the weasel who hired me didn't exactly tell the whole truth about the job. And of course when I spill the gas, it's always on my belly because that's the part that sticks out furthest.

"Look, Eileen, all I'm saying is you ought to get another job. I mean, try a bookstore, a grocery store, even a laundromat, just do something where you're not around chemicals."

I bit into my lip and watched him flip a veggie burger. One piece fell through the grill. Dr. Rivers, I wanted to say, do you know I've combed Berkeley looking for work? Do you know I spent four days walking and riding the bus up and down College Avenue in Oakland, asking for work at every single place I came to? Do I have to spell out for you the fact that without this job, I will shortly be running out of money?

"I have to have this job," I said quietly. "And I...I don't plan to work too long."

"How long?"

I glanced up. The Rivers have a huge eucalyptus tree in their backyard, right behind the patio, and it gives off the most amazing smell. It filled my nostrils just then.

"Oh, maybe six, seven, eight weeks at most."

"Too long." Dr. Rivers was shaking his head, hand on his hip, preparing to flip the tofu. A moment passed and then he looked up, and with no warning at all, his whole tone changed. "Why don't you go on in and get rid of those clothes. Have Nancy soak them. Get a shower and then we'll talk." He smiled in the controlled way he does. He's not a jerk, or unkind in the least. He's just...reserved.

I inhaled the eucalyptus again and walked inside. Corinne was at class (she is taking organic chemistry at Berkeley every day this summer), and Nancy, her mother, was making croutons for salad (out of home-made sourdough bread.) Funny how she and Ma both bake bread, and yet they're as different as they can be. Nancy also grows her own sprouts and makes her own yogurt. Oh, and she has something called a juicer and she is constantly making — and drinking — carrot juice.

Smelling the way I did, I didn't linger in the dazzling white-tiled kitchen where I've spent so much time the last couple weeks chatting with Nancy. I yelled a hello to her and bolted through the kitchen, covering my mouth so she wouldn't hear my crying. I've been in California three weeks and most of that time I've been cooped up in what amounts to a closet selling cigarettes and running credit cards through a machine. I come home smelling like a mechanic. I have grease under my fingernails and I even wear one of those hats with a visor.

When I get home from work, I'm usually too tired to go out since my shift starts at six a.m. and I have to be up at 4:45 so I can catch the 5:25 bus two blocks down from Corinne's house and then change in Oakland for the College Avenue bus.

The worst thing is I have to work weekends, so except for the first weekend I was here, when Corinne took me on a tour of San Francisco, I haven't gone anyplace or seen anything or anyone. Anyone, of course, being John. We've talked a few times and he keeps saying he'll rent a car and come over to the East Bay. But I still have not seen him! I have this suspicious feeling that Belle may be more than a roommate.

July 12, 1972

If I close my eyes now, I am still staring through the clear patio table. The surface is made of mottled plastic, so it looks like everything underneath is below water. I see Corinne's flowered shorts, and Nancy's skirt, and Dr. Rivers' dock siders and hairy legs. I hear the clink of forks and knives against clear glass salad plates, and Nancy slicing fresh sourdough bread.

My head is bowed, and I am picking at my brown rice. I quit the gas station last week. Or, I should say, I was asked to quit. It's all Dr. Rivers' fault; he forced me to confront the boss at the station about why it was I had to pump gas.

"Let me get this straight. You're asking me why you have to pump gas? Did you figure out yet that you are working at a gas station?" He had a huge box full of cigarette cartons at his feet, and he was filling the shelves over my head.

"Well, I just won't be able to pump anymore," I mumbled. He just laughed. "Because...I'm pregnant." He stopped laughing. His eyes dropped and landed on my belly.

"*What*? Why the hell didn't you tell me that when I hired you?" He had three cartons of cigarettes poised on a shelf in my cubby. There's only room for one person in there at a time, so I was standing outside with the door open. He stepped out to take a good look at me. "I figured you just liked wearing those stupid Cal sweatshirts," he said. "Or those ridiculous Indian shirts." I had two outfits for work: my rainbow shirt from Telegraph and my new U.C. Berkeley sweatshirt. Both of them disguised my stomach, more or less. Jeff, of course, is pretty young and not awfully bright. He slid a hand into his greasy hair.

"Look, you should have told me right away that you were...oh Jesus, I can't have you here anymore. I mean, that's it." And that was it. I untied the apron (I wore it thinking it might keep me from spilling more gasoline on myself) and caught the bus home.

"So now what?" Dr. Rivers was asking, as we sat at dinner. I hadn't touched the cold sesame pasta or grilled swordfish. Tears were taunting me.

"Maybe I'll try San Francisco," I said quietly. "They must have jobs over there."

Everyone was silent, maybe because the last thing I'd said was too stupid for words.

"Well it's just nobody likes to hire you to work across the Bay if you live here," Corinne said. "They think people will be late for work, tied up in traffic on the Bay Bridge."

Silence, again, only this time, I heard a voice in my head scream-ing, *Well what the hell, then? What the hell am I supposed to do? I tried, goddamit, I tried, so now what?* I closed my eyes and felt warm tears squeezing out from beneath my lids.

"I have a friend at Alta Bates Hospital," Dr. Rivers said, pushing his empty plate away. "He may be able to help." I turned to him. He had his arms folded across his chest. I wanted to ask him why he hadn't suggested his friend sooner. I wanted to yell at the top of my lungs: "Do you think this has been fun for me? Do you think I came to California to scramble around for three or four weeks looking for a fucking job?" But instead I stuck my fork into the swordfish. I cut a small chunk and tried to swallow it. It stuck in my throat. I gulped the fresh-squeezed lemonade, hoping it would push the fish down.

July 13

Friday the 13th turns out to be lucky for me. Alta Bates comes through. I will be a temporary ward clerk, handling charts, ordering tests, blood work, filing lab results. Dr. Rivers said I will fill in for people taking summer vacations. So I start Monday. I am actually excited about this job. I've said before that I want to be a doctor and now I'm going to get a chance to work in a hospital. Corinne and I are planning to celebrate tonight by going to San Francisco. I've been trying all afternoon to reach John, to see if by some miracle he wants to get together. It is almost four weeks since I arrived.

July 15

From the bedroom of John's apartment on Fulton, you can see a corner of Golden Gate Park, a few eucalyptus and a bay tree or two and one of those wonderful madrone trees that have tawny red bark. His house is stucco, painted creamy yellow and white (why are so many houses in San Francisco painted these same pastel colors?) Driving in, I saw all kinds of Victorians with gingerbread trim, all painted strange combinations: purple with grey, blue with lime green, yellow with orange and pink.

John has the upstairs apartment, and his bedroom is in front and that's where I am lying now, next to him on his mattress on the floor, looking out the window into the blue, blue sky. One thing about summer here: it's freezing. I wore shorts and a T-shirt Friday night, not expecting to stay at John's (certainly not two nights) so yesterday, I had to go out to an Army Navy store in the afternoon and buy a pair of huge overalls. (In this city it's Levi's).

"All you need now is a hoe and a pitchfork," John said, catching me around what remains of my waist. "And a straw for your two front teeth."

So he seems happy enough to see me. Friday night, when Corinne and I knocked on his door, he pulled me inside and danced me around the living room. He had Van Morrison on the stereo, which we both love, and even with Corinne there, in her penny loafers and white pants, standing with her Coach pocketbook on her shoulder looking awkward, trying not to stare, he did a long slow dance with me, we danced the whole song, Crazy Love, and at the end he held me close, my belly to his. All I kept thinking was, OK, where the hell is Belle?

Well, the bottom line is that Belle is *not* his belle (she has a boyfriend in L.A.) And anyway, John says he is too busy in the lab to be playing around.

What has most surprised me about John is that he isn't totally turned off by my present state. (I am wide and getting wider.) It may be in my head, but he almost seems to like me better this way. Maybe I should stay pregnant, if that's what he goes for.

At one point Friday night, I asked him if he was so thrilled to see me, then why did I have to come over to his side of the Bay? Oh, he said, he's tied up in the genetics lab every night including Fridays and sometimes even on Saturday he has to check the rats.

"I have a job at Alta Bates hospital starting Monday," I said proudly, and I could tell that he was genuinely impressed. It's a clerical thing; but still, a hospital job is a hospital job.

The first thing we did was drive across San Francisco to the ocean. We climbed the rocks and watched the sun set over the Pacific and then we went out to eat in an upscale Italian place called Vanessi's, where the waiters wear red jackets and mix Caesar salad in big bowls right at the table. We had zabaglione for dessert, a thick creamy pudding John said I should know about because I'm Italian. John treated, celebrating all of us being in California, my getting a job, his going to medical school, and Corinne almost finishing organic chemistry.

Corinne cornered me when John went to the bathroom. "Am I driving home alone or what?" I was stacking sugar cubes on the table with small silver tongs. I tried not to smile, but I'd had a glass of red wine, which is a lot for me, since the baby. My face felt hot and flushed.

"Would you mind?" I asked and she just rolled her eyes. I wanted to ask her if she thought I was nuts but it was too late. John was back, kissing my neck, secretly slipping his hand over my breast. Clearly I was going home — with him.

Suffice it to say after two days with John, I'm ready to stay here with him. Only what would I do come September? Have the baby in S.F.? Have John coach me through and then send the bundle U.P.S. back to North Adams? There would be ways, of course, to give up the baby here...except for one small detail. I promised Rus I'd go back. I told him he'd have some say about the way we worked things out. I said I wouldn't ignore the fact that he wants to try to be a father.

Still, there's no question but that I'd rather stay here. John just a minute ago rolled over on the bed and now he's licking my shoulder while I try to write. "We can't have sex," I yell, "it's three o'clock on a Sunday afternoon!" Oh, what the hell...

CANDACE

From the large brick dorm at Redfield Retreat, the walk to Skinny Pond is a quarter mile down a grassy hillside. After dark, when the moon is bright, the pond shimmers. An evening wind ruffles the water tonight, and light quivers across the surface. Candace glances skyward, guessing the moon to be two days away from full.

"I got smokes," Mary Finnerty whispers hoarsely as she follows behind Candace, opening a pack of cigarettes. Candace turns, considers the cigarette in Mary's hand. The cellophane wrapper glows blue in the moonlight.

"I better not tonight," she sighs, turning forward again. "And you better wait to light up till we get to the water." Her bare feet slap against her flip flops as she hurries downhill. Shrouded in the hood of the terry bathrobe, she could be a monk.

The two women move silently toward the pond. Residents at Redfield are expressly forbidden from swimming at night, and the last time Candace and Mary went to the pond for a midnight dip, they were caught. They lost television privileges for a week. Candace doesn't care, though. She is fond enough of swimming Skinny that she will take the risk.

They stop in the dark undergrowth just short of the pond. A thin fog hovers over the surface of the water, and the bullfrogs take turns bellowing. Crickets make a bleating noise that sounds extraterrestrial. Candace listens, inhales through her nose. The smell of water and dank earth and sweet summer vegetation takes her back to nights at

Crooked pond, the one at Maple Hill. There were summers when the women swam naked almost every night.

"Stop here," Candace says, shuffling out of her sandals. She drops onto the thin grassy area the girls call the beach. Mary crouches onto her haunches and hides her cigarette and lighted match from the wind. She rocks, then sits down, stretching each of her bony legs their full length on the ground. Mary is seventeen and four months pregnant. She reminds Candace of a younger version of Pit. Tall, lean, hollow-cheeked. But Mary has a cropped head of carrot-colored hair and a pierced tongue and three diamond chips in each earlobe and a face full of auburn freckles. Her problem, the one that landed her here at Redfield, is a terrible weakness for beer, wine, and almost any form of alcohol. The last time the police found her, she had passed out in a parking lot.

"So are you going to the funeral or not?" she asks, blowing smoke.

"It's up to my mother," Candace mutters. "But God help her if she says no." A clear picture of Pit comes into view, Pit at the kitchen table. To think, Pit will never sit at the kitchen table again. *Ever.* Candace rolls onto her side, pressing her wet eyes into her forearm. It's been two days since she had the call, and the reality just keeps finding new ways to sink in.

"And when you leave in September, who will I swim with then?" Mary moans.

Candace snorts. "Oh come on Mary. When I go in September you won't swim with anybody but the fish." She glances out to the center of the pond. A bass slices the water.

"Yeah, well, you know I'll miss ya."

"Yeah, but you'll fall in love again. Soon enough." Candace pauses. "Hey. Maybe with Myra." She reaches out and slaps Mary's bare leg and gives her a sly grin. Candace and Mary share a running joke, pretending — for the sake of the other residents — that they are lovers. To most of the other women, the game is a much-appreciated distraction. It has a particularly lascivious twist, since Candace and Myra are currently the only two pregnant women in residence at Redfield. But lately, the game has become the object of consternation for the administrators, who have been receiving regular complaints from Myra, who objects to the lesbian relationship.

"I wonder what Myra would do if I kissed her full on the lips some night, say when she was just lying there in her bed."

"She'd claw you with those ravaging red nails of hers, that's what she'd do," Candace says, yanking a blade of grass from the ground. She chews it, enjoys the sweet white bulb at the tip.

"Or she'd bite me and then I'd need rabies shots." Mary rolls on her hip, laughing.

"Whatever you do, pick somebody besides Myra. Please." Candace yawns. At that, a rustling noise rises out of the tall grass by the pond. Candace spits out the grass. The mention of rabies now tugs at her mind. A few nights ago, the news reported on a girl in a neighboring town who had caught rabies from some animal. She died. Candace gets to her feet, feeling her heart throb up in her throat.

"Who's there?" Candace calls out. It occurs to her that this might be one of the administrator's spies, checking for midnight swimmers.

"Me." The voice is familiar. A dark shape comes bolting out from the grass. Slowly, it grows into a small woman with a towel over her head.

"Celia?"

"Yeah, it's me." Celia lays her cold hands on Candace's face.

"Shit, I thought you were a raccoon," Candace says. The bullfrogs honk in earnest, one after another. Mary comes up behind Celia and spooks her ribs.

Yelping and jumping aside, Celia covers her mouth. Only fifteen years old, Celia has been hooked on crack for the last three years. This is her third time back to Redfield, and she almost always has the jitters. "Christ, Finnerty," Celia shouts, "grow up."

Mary collapses onto her knees in laughter. "You love it. You know you do."

"Yeah, you'll love it too when I report your ass to MacLish. Then I'll watch you squirm through six extra sessions with her bending your ear about fear and insecurity. Ha. You'll be beaming in self-esteem."

Candace unbelts her bathrobe, lets it drop to the ground. Her breasts hang like ripe melons on her chest and her belly is a gentle swell, luminous in the moonlight. "Look, ladies, I didn't risk my backside to come down here to listen to the two of you bicker. I'm heading in for my swim. Either of you sissies going to join me?"

Celia and Mary are silent. "Too cold," Celia says.

Mary lights up another cigarette. "No, you go," she says. "We'll do shore duty."

"You know, you two could spend a lot less time at our little pond outings smoking and a whole lot more time in the swim," Candace scolds, stepping gingerly into the dark, cold water. She picks her way over the rocks. Once she is hip deep in the pond, she stops, stands with her arms stretched up in the air. Reaching for the moon, she thinks. Reaching for the moon.

Celia and Mary sit riveted, staring at the giant teardrop that is Candace's body, a bottle-shaped swell tinted blue by the moonlight.

Candace twists her hair up off her back and knots it in on itself so it exposes her long slender neck. Then she brings her arms together overhead and arching, she dives, disappearing into the shimmering black skin of the pond.

"Just like a dolphin," Mary calls out. Celia smiles. Candace rises up from the water and cuts the surface with long lazy crawl strokes. She crosses the narrow pond and then returns to the middle, where a few minutes ago she saw a fish. Flipping over on her back, she assumes a floating position. Water slaps gently into her ears and around her cheeks. She can hear nothing now, only the lap and buzz of water. She gazes at her belly, which rises, a glistening mound floating in the moonlit water. She gazes up at the moon, its darkened patches making a mighty face at her. Against her backbone, she feels the baby roll, compressed in its tight internal space. A foot, or an elbow, or some other sharp human part presses through her internal organs. She smiles at the notion that the baby, too, has its own dark pool to swim in, a mysterious midnight flotation chamber. She closes her eyes and sees Pit, and immediately her heart tightens. Oh Pit, it isn't fair, she thinks, it isn't fair that there has to be something as awful as death. The forever of it makes her limbs go limp. But then out of nowhere she recalls that it was Pit who taught her the backstroke. She starts to cry, but simultaneously, she smiles and stretches her arms back, attacking the water in reverse. Soon enough, she is comforted, thinking that she and the baby have formed an alliance, a continuum with Pit, each of them swimming peacefully in a body of dark still water.

AUDREY X

It is March in deep July. Four days straight it has rained and now, on the morning of the fifth day, the day that they will bury Pit, the day that they will stand among the trees and say goodbye, the pouring has stopped. But the ring of raindrops on the roof is now replaced by raw and relentless winds. The few branches in the bush with a full fan of green leaves are scooping and whipping back, hissing, turning mean on themselves. *Questioning the necessity of events*, Audrey thinks. *Questioning the why of winter in July, the why of winter ever, the why of never and goodbye.*

Even the smell of summer is missing. She's come on crutches to the door, out to test the weather. She is wondering whether her heavy yellow sweater will be sufficient, or whether she should call upstairs to Marjory, tell her to bring down the grey wool coat. Audrey frowns. *That damn grey coat. I am likely to die in that damn grey coat.*

She stares sadly across the front porch, eyes the Mother tree. In an hour or two, Rusty will arrive, maybe bringing Candace, that is, if Eileen finally agreed to free her daughter for a day from captivity at Redfield. Candace pleaded for it. Pleaded that she be allowed to pay respects to her dear friend Pit. Audrey, in the end, called Eileen herself. In a choking voice, she too begged for a little leniency for Candace. Because even with Rusty, even with Candace, there would be so few to honor Pit's memory.

Audrey shudders now, sighs, squeaks her crutches across the porch. Stands into the stiffening wind, feels it like a hedge of pins coming through her sweater.

She is more depressed than she's been in years. Since Jack. She keeps blaming the lingering sadness on her injury. On the ankle that hasn't healed. A week ago, the day before they took Pit to the hospital in final distress, Audrey sat on a papered table at Dr. Dunbar's office, and he sawed and peeled the cast away and there were toes, fresh, raw and flecked with plaster; they were raw sausages, those toes. She wiggled them and as she did, her foot felt like a butterfly, free and light, emerging from a cocoon. All too soon, though, that feeling disappeared. As she set her newly exposed heel to the floor, the bones felt pinned together by jello. And when he got her fully off the table to test the leg, it failed miserably. She almost fell again, right there in the office.

"Is it going to heal or not?" she asked the doctor, near tears.

"You must be patient," he replied. And then he set to work replacing the cast, turning her leg into an even bigger mummy than before.

She's at the very edge of the porch now, seeing how badly the Mother Maple has been taken by the bugs, left without a mite of shade. Leaves normally bigger than a man's hand are shriveled dry and crisp, pitiful cripples. That young bearded man from Cooperative Extension, Chuck Parker, called the bug a pear thrips, *Taeniothrips inconsequens*. How silly those scientists and their names. Because this is no inconsequence at all. This thrips has tipped the balance not just at Maple Hill, but all across the state. A speck of an insect has brought forests of giant maples to their knees, leaf by leaf — the bug eating buds from inside out.

She is getting weepy. She keeps having the saddest thoughts: Pit dead. The trees bare of their leaves. Slipping a hanky from her pocket she blows her nose, one-handed. Squeaks across the porch and back inside. Closing the door, she hobbles to the bookshelf, where she stores the herbal remedy book that she inherited from her great grand-mother, Clara. Lowering herself to the sofa, Audrey considers the crack that nearly splits the black leather cover. Most of Clara's recipes Audrey has long since memorized, but there are days, like today, when she takes comfort simply seeing what prompted her ancestor to write.

Sniffling, she turns to the third page, where Clara offers her "Safe and Reliable Recipe for Wavering Spirits." Audrey stares at Clara's careful handwriting — a small, evenly slanted scrawl in midnight-colored ink. "Despite your best efforts to fill your days with pleasant, productive tasks, there will come to pass, like a veil descending, an occasional lonesome day. On those mornings or afternoons that you find yourself locked in blue thoughts, I rely on borage, which is always said to 'bring courage'." Take a generous handful of the tiny blue borage flower, toss them into salad. I use the leaves as well; cut into fine pieces and steamed, and eaten with a pat of butter; things will seem much better." Clara had added a small sketch of the star-shaped flowers on the page.

There was a time, years back, when Audrey grew borage — it reminded her of violets — right in the back yard; and she followed Clara's recipe enthusiastically until the time came when she realized the recipe didn't make her feel a bit better. Today, thoughts of the flower — and memories of filling a basket of them for Pit — just bring her lower. Her head drops to the arm of the sofa, and she cradles the book in her arms. Later, Marjory finds her, curled up on the couch, napping, the book still tucked against her chest. Marjory covers her with the blanket that was Pit's.

In an hour, Audrey awakens to the car, Rusty's wife's car, arriving on the gravel. It is the spit of tires and traveling voices that wakes her. She sits up, conscious of Pit's smell buried in the blanket. That begins her tears. What finishes them is the sight of Candace out the window, in a summery white and blue-flowered maternity dress. The wind whips up the bottom edge as Candace plods the stairs side by side with Rusty.

"Oh thank God you came," Audrey calls, struggling off the couch. Clutching one crutch and Candace, Audrey buries her face in her granddaughter's salmon hair. Lets Candace place her aging hand on a stomach made large and dense by baby.

Later, after returning red-rimmed and weepy from the cemetery, the five of them gather a few paces from the sugar house, around the oldest tree. Because Pit asked for that, she specifically wanted to be remembered in song at the Frieda tree. So they stand in a ring, hands clasped, circling the tree, and are circled themselves by an eternity of other trees. Their ring is simple: Rusty next to Candace who is beside Big Martha, and then, Marjory and Audrey holding hands. Audrey glances at the place — between Big Martha and Marjory — where Francine's face belongs. She looks away. Today she is in her long grey coat, and it is unbuttoned. And she hovers over crutches, staring dejectedly into the sugar bush at the paucity of life, at curled and withered leaves, at humbled trees, at a once-thriving community of women come undone.

The five of them sing, off key, "Amazing Grace." And in the midst of mourning Pit, Audrey lifts a wet face to Frieda and what comes to mind is a wild night many years before. More precisely, she sees an early morning, post-debauchery. Audrey had been sleeping all tangled up in clothes, hers and Marjory's, and when she woke that morning, the sky was a yolk, pink at the horizon. She rose and there was Marjory, already awake, standing stark naked, hugging Frieda. It was the strangest sight to Audrey: to see Marjory embrace the tree so tightly, pressing her breasts into the bark, as if Frieda were her lover.

Audrey joined her, she too held to the tree like a glove, let herself feel the rough bark against her bare stomach, her sagging breasts, her face, her triangle of pubic hair. All of her skin in touch with the tree tingled and when she pulled away, she laughed, because she was caught to the tree, bark to pubic hair. She looked to Marjory, who by then was laughing too. They came and held each other. Even now, Audrey can recall the warm softness of pliant flesh, the single becoming two, the most divine entwining she'd ever felt, the two of them sharing each other in a more profound way than they ever had before.

Shifting on her crutches now, her armpits sore on rubber saddles, Audrey thinks how long ago this was, how so much has been lost. But then she catches sight of Candace's face across the ring. The sadness lifts. Candace, in her maternity dress, has grown so much wider. And something else. Altogether, Candace looks more mature. A small portion of joy surges through Audrey as she thinks, well at least there is a baby to be born. At least there is this gift, a life to come.

EILEEN

July 25, 1972 7:45 a.m.

The sky is bright, ocean blue, like it has been every single day since I arrived. I never thought I'd live in a place filled with sun, sun, sun; but suddenly I am here and it is just wonderful.

Nutmeg. I am thinking of nutmeg. (I should say that I am writing this on the bus in a shaky, shaky, hand, my sentences are going up and downhill. I am going to work. Mornings, my commute to the hospital takes half an hour. Coming home at night, the trip is faster because there is a special express bus up into the hills from Alta Bates.) When I was waiting at the bus stop a few minutes ago there was that familiar smell, like nutmeg, but different, it's always there, some kind of shrub with shiny little leaves, it fills the air with a wonderful odor. One reason I love this place so much is that it's so unlike anything I have ever seen, I mean, I never get tired of seeing palm trees swaying overhead or ivy blooming up from the ground or beautiful red and yellow and salmon-colored hibiscus flowers. They make big splashes of color in people's yards. In front of Corinne's house, there are two madrone trees with huge branches, reddish brown; I imagine the trees to be bronzed dancers reaching out with lean, muscled arms.

Last Sunday, Corinne took me on a hike up Mount Diablo, a hulking golden mountain swelling out of the East Bay. I was reminded again of Bogie, Rus' honey-colored dog. The mountain was that same light gold, the grasses dry from lack of rain. The air was hot and dry, and the mountain was dotted with trees—cottonwood,

Corinne said — and the smell of sage and bay trees rose up my nose and made my chest tickle. To think that the bay leaves that Ma buys in a can back in Massachusetts actually grow on bay trees! Mount Diablo on Sunday made me think about Mt. Greylock. Only Diablo is so much more exotic, I mean the two mountains aren't much different in height, but on Diablo, my feet covered in reddish dust, I felt wildly excited. The West has some hold over me, my imagination, it makes me feel like I'm living at the edge, (I am, of course, on one coast) but more than that, there is some mystery, the landscape constantly presents a grand adventure.

And now, time out, to switch buses...

I think I will pick a bunch of leaves from a bay tree and put them in an envelope and send them home to Lucy. By the time they arrive, the leaves will be dry and ready for her weekly spaghetti sauce. (I see her there: Sunday morning, right after church, the Italian station playing on the radio, Lucy stirring sauce.) I have written exactly one postcard to her: "Got here fine. Have a good job (hospital clerk.) Adore it here, Eileen." She has my address and phone number but nothing has come, which is just fine with me.

There is a woman sitting right across the aisle from me. I see her at least four or five times a week on this bus. She is fascinating to me, a real flower child, sixteen sets of beads around her neck, a long gauzy skirt, an Indian headband and leather sandals, and a baby in a backpack. She gets off where I do, but I think she goes on to Berkeley, at least she heads up Telegraph in that direction, and I keep wondering who she is, what she does. Maybe she sells silver earrings on the street. (She has a new pair every day, dangling against her brown wavy hair.) I just looked over at her and she looked up and smiled. I pretended to be looking at the baby, fat-faced with gorgeous blue eyes.

Lunch break

My job is dreadful sometimes. I am frantically trying to read four different doctors' inscrutable orders for ten patients at once: intravenous antibiotics for one patient, a special inhalation therapy for another, six units of blood for a third going into surgery, T.V. and special diets and on and on. Combine this with answering phones ("Four West, Eileen Rosetti speaking,") six times a minute. Serious overload.

Now I sit here on a bench beside the hospital and lean my head back and let the sun bathe my face. I sweat more these days, I wake up at night soaking wet, even in a thin nightgown, the sheets drenched. Dr. Pave told me last week at my second visit: "It's hormones." Everything, it seems, is hormones. All my clothes are tighter; the only comfortable thing I own now are these two tent-shaped cotton jumpers, one navy, one red. I have blue on today, it's big and ugly and baggy, and I wear it with different blouses and T-shirts for variety. Even my precious rainbow shirt doesn't fit me anymore, though I bought it only four or five weeks ago.

I wore my support stockings for the first time this morning. Dr. Pave said I had to wear them day and night to keep my legs from swelling. Varicose veins are so ugly. (I inherited them from Lucy and Frank!) The stockings are hot and make my legs look bandaged up in surgical wrap, just like I'm a patient at the hospital.

Corinne called to ask if I would meet her in Berkeley at People's Park (*the* People's Park) for a rally tonight. Apparently, U.C. Berkeley has been making noises again about building a dorm or something in the park and so the protesters are coming back to show support. I'm excited about it, feeling finally like I really am part of this place. I have a job, a place to live (for a while). And now, a Berkeley event...

Later

Something amazing happened tonight. Or should I say someone. The world is small, all the time people say that, but now I know how small it is. That woman on the bus, the one with the baby and the earrings, turns out to be somebody I might have known all my life. When I got off work, she was waiting for the College Avenue bus (no baby.) We smiled and for a while we just sat on the bench together and finally she asked me when I was due. For the first time, I didn't mind somebody asking. August, I said, and she said, ooh, soon, huh? and she smiled again and that got us talking about her baby, when she had it and before I knew it I had her whole life story.

She is Barbara Cicero from Bridgeport, Connecticut, her family is Italian American, she was a nurse in Bridgeport before she got married at 21, then, when her husband started beating her up, she left him (married only a year) and she left Bridgeport with a friend. They moved to Berkeley five years ago in the heyday of hippiedom. She, too, worked at Alta Bates — first as a nurse, then she decided to go back to school in public health at Berkeley. She met this other student, a guy named Waldy (short for Waldo), a Vietnam vet who was working at the Berkeley free clinic as a kind of paramedic, and now they are living in the Oakland hills. She got pregnant a year or so ago and decided she wanted the baby.

I could listen to Barbara talk all night, which is kind of what I did tonight, sat right next to her on the ground (no grass in People's Park) as she also attended the rally. Only about fifty people came out, while a half dozen police cars lined Telegraph at the edge of the park (it looks more like an abandoned lot than a park). We all sang "Give Peace a Chance" and then "Give People's Park A Chance." Later, Barbara, Corinne and I went to look at Barbara's garden in the park and we helped her weed, and in return, she gave us some turnips and fresh celery and zucchini and a pile of red and white radishes, which I carried in the pockets of my blue jumper. As we kneeled on the ground getting our knees dirty, Barbara was laughing, her teeth so white and even, I felt like I had always had her as a friend. Corinne is going back to Brown come September, but I, well, I don't want to go back East at all, or, at least, I want to come back here just as soon as I can.

Later, as I watched the sky slip into that royal night color, light at the horizon, my favorite milky blue, I felt peace running through me. Never felt quite like that before. The world has opened up here — it has something to do with the air, the people, the sense of possibility.

August 7 (Lunch in the employee lounge)

Where I'm supposed to be and where I am now are suddenly 3,000 miles apart. I have just seen Dr. Pave this morning, and he says from here on, I should be back East (nesting, of all things) getting ready to deliver in North Adams, because originally that's where I told him I would have the baby.

"You know, most women get to this point and they're painting the nursery yellow and buying a layette and hanging curtains. You know, nesting," he said, a little smile curling his lower lip. The humor was lost on me. Heat crept up the sides of my face.

If I'd thought fast enough, I would have said, "Sorry, doctor, I guess I'm different from your other patients. I'm neither a duck nor a chicken." But all I managed to get out was: "I...I'm not ready to leave California yet." My voice quivering, I sat twisting the belt of my paper gown in my hands, which were now so sweaty they made the paper damp. The belt tore in half and the two sides of the gown moved apart, exposing my monstrous breasts and tight mountain of a belly.

"I've really just gotten here," I went on, "and I love it here and anyway, I've got another four weeks on my job, at least." I crossed my arms, pulling the gown around me.

At that, Dr. Pave pivoted on his small round stool. The chair squeaked and he rose. His lip had lost its curl and his eyes were stern and level with mine.

"Oh no. Absolutely not. You certainly don't have another four weeks, Miss Rosetti. You've got maybe two more weeks of work, preferably less. Your baby is well engaged and riding low, very low, which means he may show up well before your due date." Pave has never called me "miss" before and I found it offensive. I've been calling myself 'Ms.'

Anyway, he didn't need to say anything about this business of the baby being low. I know that already. I don't walk anymore, I scoot, I take baby steps. It takes me twice as long to make my way down the street to the bus stop these days. I've given up going outside for lunch breaks anymore, too. I walk the twenty yards to the employee lunchroom and drop onto this sofa, where I am writing now. Last weekend, when I stayed with John, I finally told him Saturday night I couldn't make love. "Could you...maybe...just hold me," I whispered. "I'm...I feel like I'm riding on a cantaloupe." I just blurted it out like that, and he leaned on his elbow and stared down at me.

"Now, you're sure it's a cantaloupe?" he asked, very seriously, the grim look on his face making him more attractive. "You're sure it's definitely not a watermelon or a honey dew?" He rolled off the mattress laughing. I felt foolish, and frustrated, too. (Never in my life did I think I would tell John I didn't want to make love with him.) But my body has taken over. I am now all baby, and baby oven. I told Corinne last week I feel like a human crockpot, timed to simmer for nine interminable months.

My mind isn't my own either. Lately there are times I get weepy even at work. Somebody comes along, like crazy Cavandella, he's the head anesthesiologist at Alta Bates, notorious for being nasty to everybody. Yesterday, about noon, I hadn't had lunch yet, and I was starting to get dizzy from hunger, when he dropped by the desk in his green surgical scrubs, his blue face mask still dangling around his chest. Before I realized it, he was telling me to do a dozen things at once, the shit head, and then he disappeared and I couldn't read his writing for at least six orders, all for these two patients going into surgery. I got scared, because both patients were due for triple by-pass.

Before I knew it, I was swimming in my own tears, blowing my nose, and slobbering to one of the nurses "I can't handle this." She patted me on the back and told me I should go get myself a drink of water.

I thought of asking for the afternoon off, but they would be nowhere without me, and besides, what would I do? Corinne and her family are camping at Big Sur for nearly two weeks, so I've been at home by myself. It feels spooky having that giant glass house all alone. I wake up at night frightened of an earthquake, trying to plot my escape if the house starts to shake. I get home at six or so, and make myself a yogurt shake with ice, strawberries and bananas, all in the blender. These yogurt shakes are called smoothies and aside from cappuccino, they're the rage out here. Then I take a little nap and make myself dinner. I usually end my exciting evening watching Johnny Carson. Before I actually fall asleep, I check all the doors and drink a mug of hot milk.

Tonight, Barbara Cicero has invited me for dinner. She said if it got late, I could stay over, since they wouldn't want me riding the bus home after dark. They live in a huge house with an empty third floor.

Now, about my mood swings. I am feeling much better after writing this. That seems to be how things go, up and down and up again. And of course, when I write, things almost always look brighter, despite the impending decision (will I really go home?) and my various aches and pains: awful heartburn, especially after spicy food; the varicose veins, wicked even with the ugly stockings on; and now, how horrible to mention, I have hemorrhoids.

Putting all the pains aside, though, I have this overall sense of possibility, of opportunity, of excitement about things, a general sense I can do amazing things on my own (like go back to school, maybe here in Berkeley, because it's cheaper than Brown, and I like the campus better). I attribute the good feelings to living here and writing this diary. It has given me some vague sense of being in command of myself and my life. Of course, there is that second life tucked inside me. If it's a she, I've decided to use the name Candace. To hell with you, Candace Patterson!

August 9 Sunday, sitting on Barbara's porch swing

At eye level are two palms, side by side, which is part of the reason why I am feeling so calm. The palms are stately, like two giant guards, standing watch in the front yard. As I swing, a gentle breeze passes over me. Maybe if I let go, push the swing to its furthest height, I

could lift off the porch, sail outward, touch the top of the palms with
my toes. There I could let go of the swing, settle into the graceful
fronds, and right at the crest of the tree, I could, yes, make a wonderful nest (oh yes, Dr. Pave, a nest), and in that nest, I imagine I
would be happy.

I stare at the sky and the palms and pretend I'm in Bermuda or
the Bahamas. And here it is just Berkeley, well, Oakland. Barbara
and Waldy live in Waldy's grandmother's house. She was quite
wealthy, and a year or so ago she died, and after Barbara had the
baby, his parents said the house was theirs, at least for the time
being. It's a tall white wooden house, unlike most others here, which
are stucco. It reminds me of a New England house. It has a beautiful
yard, a garden (artichokes with purple flowers, grow along the
fence) and a plum tree. The house is three stories high, and the porch
is on the top floor.

I have been here since Friday. I came for dinner — spaghetti and
tofu meatballs — and afterward, Barbara and I talked for three
hours straight while Waldy gave baby Garcia a bath. (Baby's name is
Garth, a family name, but Waldy and Barbara are both Dead heads).
About ten o'clock, I felt these strange twinges, tightening sensations,
low around my belly. At first I thought I had the worst stomach ache. I
casually mentioned the pains to Barbara, who smiled and said, "kid, you
may be in labor," which shocked me to no end, to think it could really
be happening already, I mean, right now? But wouldn't it be amazing,
I thought, if it just happened that way, the baby born here, on the West
coast, the baby making a statement. Barbara took out her stethoscope
and set it on my belly where she listened for a long time. Then she
took my blood pressure with one of those cuffs. She made me some
sleepy time tea and told me to have a few sips of wine, because if it
was false labor, the wine would probably stop the contractions.

"So this is what it feels like?" I asked Barbara. I wanted to know how
it went for her, and she stopped washing dishes, came in drying her
hands, and told me the story of Garcia's arrival, 36 hours of labor.
She and Waldy had a midwife in their old apartment in Berkeley, all
their friends came, candles and incense burning at the head of the
bed, Dead music playing. As Garcia finally made his entry, American
Beauty was playing, all Barbara can remember is "Sugar Magnolia"
and "Truckin," playing over and over, her face dripping, her hands
gripping her ankles, and the feeling, she said, "that I was delivering

the world, literally, that the earth was coming out my bottom, I was cracking in half, and it was hell, but in the end, out fell the truth." My mouth dropped open when she said that. Poetry, I thought.

She gave me a mini-lesson in Lamaze. In theory, it seems like a good idea, only the way she described the pain, I'd say breathing can't possibly do the trick, and I'd be surprised if I got through without drugs. I'm not sure I care to see it happen, either, not after Barbara showed me her pictures (yes, pictures). All that blood and slime. I couldn't look too long, but I remember Barbara lying there, naked, her hair floating everywhere. The bed covered in blood, the baby's head coming out, and Barbara with a look of agony on her face, pouting and grabbing her knees.

By the time I finished looking at the pictures, my pains were gone. Barbara put me to bed on the third floor, door open, and told me to call at a moment's notice. She said she would be delighted to catch my baby. She said the idea of somebody delivering a baby is kind of silly, most of the time doctors do nothing but catch the kid as it sails out. I fell asleep thinking about the baby like a rubbery football, shooting slippery and red across the room. Rusty, who played football his junior year, was grinning ear to ear when he made the catch.

Later Sunday

Scary, but the pains are getting worse. Barbara and Waldy said if they keep up much longer, they'll take me to Alta Bates. We put Garcia in his stroller and all of us took a very slow walk down the street and back, me smelling that nutmeg again. Barbara held my shoulders and breathed with me, holding one hand and tapping on my wrist to show me the timing of the little puffs. The pain then wasn't so much in my belly, but in my legs and back, which she said could mean the baby was turned around, posterior.

Back at the house, she made me lie down on the couch. She and Waldy said I should stay at their place. Waldy would even take me back to Corinne's to get my clothes.

I realized then that the idea of going back to the Rivers' house alone was terrifying. So in a few minutes we are going to Corinne's for my clothes. Now, though, I've started counting pains, timing how many minutes between contractions. Barbara says if it gets to be ten, we go right to the hospital.

August 11 Still at Corinne's

I spent yesterday at Alta Bates. As a patient. Waldy drove me in about one o'clock in the morning Sunday in the V.W. (a bright yellow bug with a hole in the floor, you can see the street rolling beneath as you drive). I realized then that I hardly know him at all. Barbara came in later in the morning, about eight, and sat with me in the labor room. I was concentrating on the sensation that someone was tugging two burning steel ropes together across my lower abdomen, pulling them tighter and tighter. I told Barbara "there's a freight train on fire and it's barreling through my lower half." She laughed and took my hand, and gently started tapping out a rhythm on my wrist, and breathing with me, her cheeks puffing out.

"Oh, so you're the coach," said a nurse who came in just after. Barbara and I walked the halls together a little later, me leaning on the wooden railing. Oddly enough, by 2:00 in the afternoon, I felt perfectly normal again. The resident (a young woman from India with a tiny red jewel in her forehead) checked me internally. "Young leddy you might as vell be on your vay home." She called it false labor. Just as we were leaving the labor room, in waltzes Dr. Pave with my chart in his hand.

"So, you've started in," he said, which confused me.

"I had some pains, pretty close..." I began, but then Barbara finished my sentence.

"...so we thought she ought to be checked," Barbara said, reaching her hand out to Pave. "Hi, I'm Barb Cicero, I'm an R.N., I used to head the med surg unit here." She spoke forcefully, in a sort of tough, professional voice I hadn't ever heard her use before. I felt protected.

"So then your friend has decided to stay here in Berkeley to have her baby?" Pave was talking as though I wasn't there. I glanced at Barb's face. Her forehead wrinkled ever so slightly.

"Has she decided that? I'm not sure," Barbara answered, and suddenly I was afraid maybe she would be angry with me, for being so flaky about my plans, for embarrassing her in front of the doctor. But she put her arm around my shoulders and pulled me close to her. I looked down, stared right into Barb's armpit, caught sight of the tuft of hair growing under her arm.

I was feeling silly. By now, I should have decided what the hell I'm doing. "Eileen told me today that if I was willing to coach her through, she'd stay and deliver here in Berkeley," Barb said. My head shot up and my mouth dropped, and Pave looked from one to the other of us without saying a word.

"Well, fine, then. That makes sense," he said quickly. He opened the chart and scribbled something down, even as he was already turning around. He told us to follow him down the hall. He pushed open the swinging doors leading into the delivery room. The walls were all grey and green tile. The floors were stainless steel, and they gleamed. Stacks of blue sterile cloths were folded neatly on shelves. "This is where you will actually be for delivery," he said. The room was so...surgical. Gloomy and cold. I shuddered. Over the narrow bed was a big light. Metal stirrups stuck up at one end.

I nodded, but inside, the worst dread came over me. This was really happening. I started imagining myself in this horrible, spooky room. Bleeding. Yelling out. I felt sweaty, and chilled, and even slightly dizzy. I turned to Barb.

"Will you take me home now?" I asked quietly.

I was lightheaded on the way to the car. "It's OK," Barb kept saying. "It's OK." I had this strange sensation, that nothing was familiar enough to me. I had the feeling I wanted to be under the covers, in bed. Suddenly the palm trees at the top of Ashby Avenue looked way too exotic to me, too tiring, too foreign. The strangest feeling came over me: I felt like I was shutting down, like I couldn't handle anything out of the ordinary around me. In that moment, I recalled a time when I was little, when I had gone to the circus with my parents in Springfield on a hot summer night. I got sick on something I ate and threw up. I remember loving the elephants, the tigers and lions. But by the time the trapeze act started, my head hurt, and I had a bad chill. I will never forget huddling against my mother, trying to get comfortable and warm. I kept pulling her skirt around my arms and saying, please, please, Mommy, please take me home.

Riding beside Barb in the car, I was feeling exactly the same way. I was tired, cold, uncomfortable. I wanted the vacation to be over. I had been roaming around in a strange place and loving it, but now I wasn't feeling well, and I had to get home. To somewhere familiar. To people who knew me. Even if that had to be Rus, and my parents. After all, here in California, I would be almost completely alone. Corinne was leaving in two or three weeks to go back to Brown. Barb would be my only friend. Where exactly would I be, after delivery, but in a town with hardly anybody I knew and nowhere to turn to.

"Barb, will you be angry if I go back East?" I whispered, looking through the hole in the V.W. floor. The road was whizzing by, and I didn't have the courage to look her in the eye.

"Oh, no, not at all. I kind of expected you'd go back." The car was starting to slow, because we were heading up into the Berkeley hills. I had my visor down, the light was so bright around me. In the mirror, I saw the beautiful blue bay, the Golden Gate Bridge. That view is always there, in the background, like a gem. But right then it was too much for me. I felt drained by all the beauty. Barb drove in silence. She was taking me back to Corinne's.

"So why did you tell Pave I would deliver in Berkeley?"

"Oh, just so he would get off your back," she said, lifting her right hand briefly off the steering wheel and twisting her bushy hair up and off her neck. Her elbow floated in the air, hair thick under her arm. Wind poured into the V.W. and over me and it felt good and cool as we rose higher into the hills. I got a whiff of nutmeg again, and I missed Corinne and the Rivers' house, it was the closest thing to home I had out here. Suddenly I saw what Pave meant about nesting. I wanted a place, a downy space, to rest in. I was beginning to realize I didn't have such a space here.

"It seems to me that you are ready to head East." She turned to me. I nodded.

"But I want to come back, really, really want to come back," I said, my voice catching. I was teary at the thought of saying goodbye to Barb, to the Bay, to my life in Berkeley. The summer had been so wonderful. Barb reached over, squeezed my hand. "Can I come back? I mean, could I maybe stay with you and Waldy, in the beginning, while I look for a place?"

Barbara didn't say anything at first, she just kept her eyes on the curving road, and smiled, and I thought maybe I had asked too big a favor. "You're heading into a tunnel," she said, and quickly I looked up thinking we were, actually, maybe the one that leads under the Berkeley hills. "The next few weeks and months are going to make you dizzy," she said. "They will amaze you: difficult and hellish and special. You won't be the same person after it is all over."

I winced, thinking she was casting a spell, trying to predict my future, telling me things she couldn't possibly know anything about. She went on. "But if you still want to come back, the third floor is yours," she said. "And it's big enough not only for you, but for Baby

Boo Boo too." (Barb coined that after I told her that getting pregnant is the only boo boo I've ever made in life. But what a big one.)
"Actually, the third floor is even big enough for three." I looked
down. Barb was being so kind I wanted to hug her. I wanted to say
something, to tell her yes, or no, or to thank her, or to explain why
it would never be three. I haven't told her much about Rusty, or
John. I had no words in my head and nothing at all coming out of
my mouth.

A few minutes ago, just before I sat down here on Corinne's patio
with a tall thin glass of iced chamomile tea, I called American and
reserved my return flight for Friday night on the "red eye." That's
three days from now. I called John and asked him if he could spend
one last day or two with me. All he said was *maybe*.

CANDACE

To counteract the boredom at Redfield, the days when she's tired of playing hearts with Mary Finnerty and Celia Kent, when she's tired of sitting on the lawn sketching, when she is fed up reading Stephen King, when she can't bring herself to write another letter to Audrey or Mark and when she can't stomach another page of Eileen's journals, at those moments when there is absolutely nothing else to do, nothing but three meals to look forward to, Candace lies in the sun with her eyes closed and counts the days, the weeks, the hours, and sometimes even the minutes and seconds remaining in her pregnancy.

At one such moment, early in September, when the Monarch butterflies are dancing across the blaze of yellow and orange mums at the top of the driveway, Candace is lying on a blanket in the thick grass behind Redfield's dining hall. She is once again calculating her dates: "Last period (December 17), back three months (September 17), add seven days (September 24); from today's date (September 7), 17 days to go, 408 hours, and, and...24,480 minutes and, and..." She sits up, is about to calculate the number of seconds, is about to multiply "24,480 x 60" on her sketch pad, when out of the corner of her eye she spies Mrs. MacLish. The hefty dorm supervisor is heading briskly for Redfield's back door, the door beside the dining hall, when she looks up and makes eye contact with Candace.

"Oh shit," Candace mutters, looking quickly to her sketchbook, pretending to be busy drawing. But MacLish is heading her way. Candace throws the pad aside, rolls over on the blanket and covers her head. Over her, she hears MacLish clear her throat.

"Candace?" MacLish has her fingers laced below her soft, ample belly.
"I'm resting," Candace says.

"Candace, please, I saw you a moment ago. Come out from under
the blanket." Candace does, looking disheveled. MacLish studies her.
Candace is wearing one of Mark's old shirts, white and tight across her
belly. The sleeves are rolled to her elbows. She has on the grey fleece
shorts she's been wearing all summer, stretched to their furthest reaches.

MacLish has a "wish list," that is, a list of ways she wishes "her
Redfield girls" would behave. Number one on the list is that the girls
dress neatly. Hardly anyone ever does.

"What are you up to today, besides resting, that is?" Another of
MacLish's wishes is that the girls be "purposefully engaged" at all times.

"I've got reading," Candace says, not moving her head, but pointing to the book resting beside her, the book she took out of the local
library just this morning. It is a volume on Van Gogh. Candace brought
the book along mostly so she would have it to show Mrs. MacLish, to
prove to her that she has something meaningful to do.

"Very good," Mrs. MacLish says. "So after studying Van Gogh,
maybe you'll paint?"

"No," Candace spits back. She pushes herself up onto her elbows
on the blanket she took from her dorm room an hour before. "No
way. You're the one who's always saying it's unhealthy for me to
paint. You must remember that?"

"No, Candace, I merely said no to oil paints or acrylics. Too many
toxins, dear. Cobalt blue, cadmium in reds and yellows, and of
course, lead in white. Awful stuff. And that thinner, not for a woman
in your condition. But you do recall I said you could use the..."

"I HATE WATERCOLORS," Candace yells. "How often do I have
to tell you that?"

"Candace, lower your voice." MacLish's tone is stern. Candace
rolls her eyes.

"Mrs. MacLish, I've told you six times at least that I don't want to work
in watercolors. I especially would never do Van Gogh in watercolors."

"Well, then, you might consider drawing. Surely, he did draw."

"I'm not in the mood to draw," Candace drops back to the blanket.
Her eyes flap shut.

MacLish presses her thumbs together, raises her head straighter.
"Well, I can see you're not in the mood to talk, either." She pauses.
"There is one thing, though."

"What?"

"Dr. Rahalia is asking if you will deliver here in town at the local hospital or if..."

"Tell him yes," Candace says impatiently.

"You're sure then?"

"No, of course I'm not sure, but tell him yes anyway." Candace has been avoiding a decision about where she will deliver. Eileen left the decision to her, saying Candace was welcome to come back home to North Adams Regional Hospital or she could stay in Redfield instead.

"Wherever you are, you know I'll come," Eileen said the last time they spoke.

"Who cares?" Candace had wanted to say. "Who cares whether you're there or not?" But she hadn't said either of those things, she hadn't had the chance, because Eileen was in a hurry to get to work and had cut the phone conversation short.

"Candace, it might help to visit the hospital, to see the pretty way they've done up the birthing room," Mrs. MacLish says pleasantly. "I'd be more than happy to drive you if..."

"Mary went for me," Candace says, cutting her off. "She told me all about it."

MacLish frowns. "Oh she did, huh?"

"Yup, she filled me in on all the pretty details," Candace mutters. "Let's see: one small rug, one cheap picture on the wall, one basket of plastic flowers. Wow, how homey!"

MacLish runs her tongue over her bottom lip. "If you change your mind young lady, let me know. Meanwhile, I will go ahead and phone Dr. Rahalia." MacLish turns abruptly and walks away, her departure accompanied by the slide of nylon stockings rubbing together.

Candace glares at her back. She and MacLish have locked horns again and again over the last four months, most recently over Candace's desire to paint in oil. Dozens of phone calls have gone back and forth between MacLish and Eileen. At one point, Candace tried hiding oil paints in Mary's room. MacLish threatened to send Mary back home to her mother if she didn't hand over Candace's paints. Mary did, and MacLish confiscated them, and now, Candace feels nothing but hatred for the woman. For weeks, Candace hasn't painted at all. She has fallen into a deep state of inertia, where it seems to take every bit of her energy just to change out of her nightgown into clothes.

It has never been Candace's plan to deliver at Redfield. It has always been her plan to phone Mark, to have him take her home at the very last moment. She has delighted in the idea that she would, at some late date in September, dump herself, nine swollen months pregnant, in Eileen's lap. In a perverse way, Candace has been looking forward to surprising Eileen. She liked the idea that she would catch her mother totally off-guard. Eileen would come home from work one day, tired, irritable, not sure which leftover to pop into the microwave for dinner and there in the kitchen, she would discover Candace, a bloated thing, spilled over in a chair, just lingering there, waiting to deliver.

Candace picks up the Van Gogh book, flips through the colorful pages. She is confronted in quick succession by 'The Sunflowers,' 'The Sower,' 'The Harvest,' all of them infused by greens, blues, and yellows that look so warm she wants to touch them. Grabbing at her favorite strand of hair, she lingers on 'The Sower.' It's the short brush strokes she loves, the way the artist stoked up an almost electric tension in the painting with harsh little dabs of glowing color. She runs her fingers lovingly along the painting's horizon. She pauses where the sun lingers over the standing wheat, then closes her eyes. For weeks and weeks, she has been suppressing her desire to paint. Seeing the Van Gogh, though, she now has a physical longing to hold her brushes, to play in rich warm colors. Yes, she thinks, my eyes have missed this, I have desperately missed this color. She hasn't been to a museum since she and Mark were at the Clark, standing before Renoir's 'Blond Bather.'

It occurs to Candace now that she would rather go to a museum than do just about anything else. She needs a total immersion in color to revive her lagging spirits. What better way to spend the last few days of her pregnancy than in a museum. For too long living at Redfield, all she's been doing is surviving day after dull day, enduring one boring group therapy session after another. She yielded to MacLish on the paints, and in doing so, she went numb, descended into a sort of limbo, where she suspended all feeling. Now she has started to feel erased. More and more, she is wallowing in her "condition," and dreading the labor she faces. Meanwhile, her painting and her relationship with Mark are on hold. Life has stopped being any fun.

Slapping the book shut, she stands, snatches up her sketchpad and blanket and heads for the dorm. *I have let myself be captive long enough,* she says to herself. *I won't wait until tomorrow night, or even tonight, to call Mark. I will call him right now.*

CANDACE

Mark arrives on his Harley about six forty-five in the morning, the motorcycle sputtering up Redfield's circular drive-way just as the sun is glancing orange in the small glass panes of the second-floor window where Candace has slept for the last four months. Candace is waiting outside, on the portico in front, trying to stay out of sight behind one thick white pillar. The pillar is wide, but Candace today is far wider.

The motorcycle drops into a gentle purr and comes to a halt next to the porch. Candace, her backpack slung over one shoulder, moves awk-wardly off the step. Without a word, she grabs the sleeve of Mark's black leather jacket and hoists her leg up and over the cycle's seat. Beneath her maternity bluejeans, the ones with the elasticized belly panel, her calves are swollen and riddled with varicose veins. Before she pulled the jeans on this morning, Candace spent a few moments running her fingers across the jelly-like flesh inside her left thigh. The veins there were pale blue and puffy, a knotted turquoise rope coiled beneath white skin.

In a moment, she is settled against the padded backrest of the motorcycle. She inhales deeply, sucking in the cool September air, washed of the remnants of summer. Exhaling, she opens her palms flat against each side of her swollen belly. Mark turns, gently runs a knuckle along her nose and cheek. Then he presses on her a blue helmet, speckled in flecks of gold and silver.

"Sorry, bud, no helmet for you," he says, chuckling, poking one thick forefinger into the maternity blouse that shrouds Candace's stomach. Candace is about to say, "Hey, bozo, get the name straight at least. It's not Bud, it's Gretchen." But then, before she can speak, Mark has turned to face forward again.

In a moment, the motorcycle is roaring, moving ahead.

"You know how thrilled Eileen will be when she hears," Candace shouts into Mark's back. By now, though, the Harley completely drowns her out. Candace has her arms under Mark's armpits and her hands locked together in front of his chest. The knuckles of her thumbs scrape against his zipper, the way they always do when Mark and Candace ride the long winding roadways up and around Mt. Greylock.

Today, though, Candace's belly is in the way, a dense sack jammed between their familiar bodies. Almost immediately, she is having trouble breathing. She tries sitting up straighter, but that leaves her belly hanging unsupported in front of her. The Harley's vibrations send a funny buzz through her abdomen, making the top of her belly tighten. Candace shifts a little to the left and then back to the right. Something the size of a grapefruit, or maybe, as Eileen's journal suggested, a cantaloupe, is pressing down on the floor of her pelvis. Her buttocks are sore and those horrible hemorrhoids are puffy and raw, a ring of fire at the core of her rump.

Mark glances over his shoulder, as if to ask why Candace can't get comfortable. She releases her grip on him and leans back, twisting her arms behind to grab the backrest. It is far more awkward, holding on this way, but at least the pressure is off her bottom and her stomach isn't riding in a vise anymore. There is far more space for her stomach to expand skyward. Candace closes her eyes, gets a whiff of chrysanthemums, and when she looks up, a thick row of the flowers rushes by in an orange and yellow blur.

The wind is whizzing by the bike, billowing Mark's jacket sleeves, and now, it snaps up Candace's maternity blouse and puffs it upward. For a moment, before she catches hold of the blouse and pulls it down, it floats a few inches over her belly, suspended like a blue flowered parachute drifting gently toward the earth.

Under normal circumstances, the trip across Massachusetts, from Redfield — just north of Boston — to Candace's home in North Adams would take about two and a half hours. That, however, would mean driving straight through on the Mass Pike. Mark rarely drives his bike on the highway, though, and today, with Candace in tow, he follows Route 2, the scenic back road that snakes its way across the northern part of the state.

Ordinarily, Candace loves the scenic route. She loves the way Mark handles the winding roads on the Harley, soaring into the straight-aways and then smoothly drawing back on the curves. Sometimes, when he is showing off, he will accelerate into the curves, bringing the speed of the Harley up to sixty, maybe even sixty-five. At those moments, Mark and Candace lean precariously close to the road, riding at an ungodly angle that by all rights seems an impossible viola-tion of whatever laws of physics govern a motorcycle's motion.

At those moments, Candace does something that Mark has strictly and repeatedly warned her not to do. Instead of keeping her eyes up, focusing on the blur of trees whizzing by, Candace purposely looks straight down, into the mottled black oblivion that is the asphalt flying by only a few inches from her face. Candace is petrified, but supremely pleased. She experiences, in those moments, an exhilaration that few other activities — even pulling the powdery white grains of coke through her nostrils — have ever supplied. Riding the cycle, Candace tastes mortal danger rushing and roaring so near and so fast by her face and vibrating so thoroughly through her arms and legs and back, that somehow she is calmed. After a few seconds, she always turns and buries her face in Mark's black leather jacket, shrinking her arms tighter around his chest. She loves the feeling that she has all she needs, right there on the bike.

This morning, however, Candace realizes that the ride won't be anything like what she is used to. They are only a half an hour out of Redfield, slowing down through some quaint little town where a white steepled church dominates a spacious square of green, when Candace tugs at Mark's arm. He brings the bike to a stop beside a sidewalk in front of a small cluster of Main Street stores, each with a striped awning of a different color. An older balding man with wire-rimmed glasses is sweeping. The noise of the motorcycle draws his gaze. His eyes come to rest on Candace. He stops sweeping and stares.

"I need a...just a short break," Candace yells over Mark's shoulder. The engine dies. Pressing into Mark's back, she sets one leg on the street and drags the other after her over the seat. Then she removes her helmet and bows her head, massaging the muscles in her neck. Candace's hair is bound in a French braid, and the crown of her head glistens wet with a ring of sweat left by the helmet. Mark lifts his own visor.

"Riding with you on back today is like trying to balance a tub of water," he says, smirking.

"Thanks, I needed that." She glares at him and wrinkles her lips. He's right, of course. She is swollen way out of this world. And she would be better straddling a fence post than trying to sit still on the bike.

"Look, Mark, maybe we could ride just a little further, out to the country somewhere, and then I can lie down," Candace says, massaging her lower back. "I just need a few minutes to get myself, you know, together."

"Cand, this whole damn thing, riding you home on the motorcycle, is beginning to look like a big mistake. You just say the word and we can call Eileen and have her come pick you up. I'll even contribute the quarter," he says, reaching into the front of his jeans. "I'll be outta here, no hard feelings, you know that."

Candace's eyes narrow and the look on her face isn't friendly. Taking in one long slow breath, she lifts her leg into place over the seat and snaps the helmet on her head. "Get going, you fart," she says into his leather back, settling against the metal rest. "And no more lectures."

They ride another half an hour, Candace forcing herself to stay put on the seat. Her buttocks are so sore they are numb, and her lower back is laced with ropes, each one dangling a cinder block. But she is determined not to give Mark another opportunity to lecture. They pass a series of small shopping malls, stopping for several lights. Soon the road enters open country. Instead of picking up speed, though, Mark keeps the bike relatively slow, as if he is looking for something. They come to a cornfield, and a narrow road leading off to the right. Mark takes the right turn.

Almost immediately, a pasture is in sight. In the distance, a handful of black belted cows are grazing. There is a small makeshift parking lot, with a couple of picnic tables and a rusted trash barrel beneath a few maple trees. He pulls over and cuts the engine.

"Rest stop, everybody out." He hops off the bike, turns, and helps Candace off. Lifting her helmet from her head, he takes hold of her chin, kisses it and her lips too. "You look so washed out," he says.

"No doubt. So where's the bathroom?" Candace places both hands on her back. Stomach thrust forward, she takes a few wide steps toward the closest picnic table, which is heavily splintered and carved deep with chunky initials. Mark supports one elbow while she eases herself onto the bench and places her head over her folded arms on the table.

Mark takes a seat across the table and from inside his leather jacket he brings a clear plastic sandwich bag, twisted closed at the top. "Maybe this'll help," he says, opening the baggie and digging into the contents with two fingers. He lays some marijuana on a thin sheet of white paper. He rolls a tight reefer, twisting both ends and then twirling each with a little saliva. In seconds, he has the reefer lit and he's inhaling. "Here, try it, you never know, it might help."

"Yeah, and it might land me in heavy duty labor," Candace mumbles, her head buried in her arms.

"So then I'll just buzz you to a hospital. You wanted me there all along, right?" He sucks in again, holding the smoke, then slowly letting it out through his nose.

Candace raises her head and Mark meets her gaze with an innocent look. She stares at him for another minute and then holds out her hand. Grinning, he places the reefer in her fingers. A car passes and Candace lowers the reefer and glances over her shoulder.

"All we need now is a cop," she says, bringing the smoldering reefer toward her lips. "Then I can deliver this kid in jail."

"Well, now, there's a thought," Mark says, and from the glaze in his eyes, and his soft tone, Candace knows the drug is taking hold. "If they have cribs, you might want to consider it. Better there than at Eileen's."

EILEEN

August 14-15, 1972

They call this flight the red eye but today they should call it the red sky, because what I'm staring at through the jet window is nothing short of an amazing blaze of color. The eastern sky is cherry red, bright orange in places, with long streaks in a shade I can only describe as pink lemonade. At the horizon, the morning sun is burning a hole the color of a bright egg yolk — which reminds me, I'm starving and they haven't served any breakfast. I have had less than three hours of sleep, and for now, that looks to be all I'll get. The man next to me (I'm way up front in the bulk head — they moved my seat up here when they took one look at my size) is snoring like a chainsaw. He's wearing a white shirt, and a copy of *The Wall Street Journal* is rolled up in his lap.

Corinne drove me to the airport in Oakland for my 9 o'clock flight, and all the way down the freeway, the windows were open and flooding us with night wind. Please Corinne, turn back, I wanted to scream. I was tempted to lie, to tell Corinne I couldn't fly home because my contractions had started up again, and that wouldn't have been altogether untrue. I have this steady pull, as if the muscles beneath my belly are sneaker laces and somebody is tugging them together. Tight. The feeling started two nights ago, after John and I spent ten hours together in bed. He took me, unbelievably, to the Claremont Hotel.

"Hell," he said as we pulled up in front of the monstrous white palace, palms shifting lazily against the bright blue sky, "we might as well say good bye in style." At which point I cringed, because he had said the word. "Is that what this is, then, goodbye?" I whispered, staring at blush red carnations growing along the driveway of the hotel. He shut the ignition, slumped over the steering wheel, and stared out the windshield.

"No, it's not goodbye. It's more like...see you, so long, hasta la vista...oh Christ, I don't know what it is. Shit, Eileen, you're gonna have a kid any day now, so let's not fight it. But I'm not dropping $150 for a room at this place tonight so I can stare at you pouting."

"You paid a hundred and fif..." I started, but he covered my mouth with his palm, came around to my side, and helped me out of the car. As we walked up to the front door of the Claremont, with no suitcase, holding hands, it occurred to me what a peculiar sight we made: John, me, and my nine-month belly. I belong in a hospital, not a hotel. In any case, we signed in, Mr. and Mrs. John Darrow, ha! And we heard not even a murmur of complaint from the woman at the desk. When we got to our room, I flopped immediately onto the king-sized bed. John had arranged for champagne, and when he released the cork, it shot a giant foamy spray at the mirror over the dresser. I went to clean it with a couple of tissues, but as I reached up to wipe, he reached around me, slid his hands up under my T-shirt (men's extra extra large).

"I would never have predicted I'd be so turned on by a pregnant woman," he mumbled, as he set his mouth to my neck. He unhooked my bra, and voila, there I was, loose, my breasts swinging like melons. He tossed my shirt aside, scooped up one breast in each hand and pushed me gently to the bed, where he set me down, burying his face in my endless flesh. He proceeded to undress me, and cover every square inch of me with his lips, and I did the same to him and that's how the night went; or I should say, the day, too. We arrived about two in the afternoon, skipped dinner, ordered room service about eleven p.m.

"Hey," I said to John, as I sipped champagne and dipped an ice cold shrimp into hot red cocktail sauce, "did you know this place sits squarely over the San Andreas fault?"

He had a champagne glass balanced on his chest, was trying to rest it there, but maybe because of all his golden hair, it kept wobbling. "No, actually, I did not happen to know that," he said, emptying the glass. "But maybe that explains why you are shaking the living daylights out of me every time you come." Which was true, I've never had sex like I did that night, and at one point, rocking away, I wondered what it felt like inside, I mean, it occurred to me to worry (briefly) about the baby. Probably, he kept busy trying to hide.

Sometime about two o'clock in the morning, we finished the food and champagne and said good night, and then started laughing and tickling each other, and then we started in again. And when it was all over, finally, I pressed my face into his chest, and inhaled and tried not to exhale, thinking I could hold him, or at least hold in the sweet soapy fragrance of his skin. The next thing I remember, which I'll never forget, is the sight of John as I woke the next morning, his breathing light, his face tan and placid and childlike. He was gently sucking in the world with each breath. I watched him until he twitched, and woke up, and then I kissed him again and again.

By eleven that morning, we began thinking about getting up. (If it weren't for the fact it would have cost us another $150, we might have stayed the rest of the day and another night too.) As I got out of bed, I glanced in the mirror at my face. Rubbing against John's slight beard all night had left my face looking like it had been sandpapered. I was bright pink. I showered, toweled my hair with a plush white Claremont towel, emblazoned with a burgundy satin C. As I wrapped myself in it, the C resting on my chest, I was reminded suddenly of Hester Prynne, and her scarlet A. My face went a darker pink. Here I was, on Wednesday night, screwing my heart out with John, and by Friday, I'd be flying home, where I'd be picked up at the airport by the father of my unborn child. (I had no choice but to call Rusty and ask for a ride.)

I decided to put all thoughts of the scarlet letter aside.

John dropped me off a couple blocks from Corinne's so that he wouldn't have to come in with me to the Rivers' house. When we said goodbye, I didn't cry at all. Quite calmly, I watched his car disappear between the sycamores. I waved, and threw him one long kiss, and thought, I love this man, I'll miss him, but I can live without him, too. That, for me, is certainly progress. For once, I feel I've got a life, of sorts, and a sense of who I am. All that, thanks to living on my own this summer (and maybe thanks to writing this journal too)! Being here in Berkeley, working, has made me more independent, has made me know myself, and what it is I want to do. Barb has been telling me about public health, and who knows, maybe I'll study that after college instead of going to medical school.

Meanwhile, though, how will I hang on to this "new me" when I get back East? I am so sorry to have to go "home" to deliver Ken or Candace and I'm scared as hell about what happens next. So here I sit, staring at the scarlet sky, thinking once again about Hester Prynne and the letter stitched to her chest. I thought when I read the book, and I think it now too, that it wasn't so bad that she had to wear the A. I mean, hey, in the end, she became something of a heroine. The townspeople stopped blaming her, they forgave her so-called sin, and they ended up even clamoring for her sympathy and attention.

Oh, great, the stewardess is bringing breakfast trays now (no doubt, soggy eggs and toast). Maybe after I eat, I'll try to stretch out my legs (that is, if my neighbor here ever stops snoring) and take a nap. I'm suddenly feeling awfully weird, like I'm wired, and I'm very tired, all at once.

CANDACE

Candace is asleep, her arms stretched across the grey splintered wood of the picnic table, her cheek resting on a page of her mother's journal. When she opens her eyes, the first thing to greet her is the lazy magic marker scrawl of Eileen's words. Instantly, she recalls the last entry — her mother's passionate escapades with her doctor friend John. Candace winces in disgust. Eileen had certainly chosen an odd time to be so wildly erotic. Beyond the blur of black words, there is the wavy grain of the wooden table. At eye level, the lighter sections of wood snake like a muddy river toward the perfectly flat horizon of the table's edge. She holds the view of the river for a moment, imagines a humid cloud of bluish air hanging over the breathlessly still water, then, abruptly, she pulls her head off the page. If Candace could see her cheek, she would see her mother's words, slightly smudged, in a mirrored imprint on the hot pink flesh of her freckled face.

The early morning was cool and breezy, but now, at midday, the sun is high and beating hot on her back. She and Mark shared two joints and then, Candace remembers pulling out Eileen's journal — the fourth of the six slim books — from her backpack. She remembers reading three or four pages with her chin in her hand, and then, she read a page — or was it a paragraph — with her face propped on the table. She doesn't remember anything after that. Clearly, the reefers put her to sleep. They also managed to calm the muscles that had been flickering tighter and tighter across her abdomen. She sets her hands behind her waist, pulls her shoulders up and tosses back her head. Her hair has come loose from its French braid and now it hangs in a shimmering blond blanket over her shoulders.

"You awake?" Mark grunts. He is lying on the narrow bench on the other side of the table beneath a ruby red tree. He has his hands tucked beneath his head. When Candace doesn't answer, he grabs the side of the table and pulls himself up to a sitting position. As he does, a sliver of wood from the table lodges in his palm. "Damn," he says under his breath. He puts his open palm to his mouth and uses his teeth to tweezer the wedge of wood out of his flesh. Blood flushes out of the hole where the sliver was lodged. Wiping the blood on his T-shirt, he spits the splinter on the ground.

"Hey, Goldilocks." He pivots off the picnic bench and comes to sit beside Candace. He slides an arm beneath her hair, supporting her back in the process. She sits up, giving him a sleepy look and leaving him to hold her massively wavy hair. "God I am so glad you got rid of that skanky orange dye," he whispers. He gathers up a handful and twists it into a thick wad.

"Why?" She yawns. "I liked it. A lot."

"Yeah, well it's gone and I hope it's not ever coming back. It made you look like a witch." He leans over her shoulder and kisses her pale neck. Then he lets her hair go and buries his face so deeply into it that he ends up kissing her shoulder.

"Mark, stop! You're tickling me." She giggles and he holds onto her. She shifts her legs onto the bench, and he lets her head go back onto his lap. "You know how much I love this two-tone hair of yours." He bends forward and sifts the top layer — strawberry red and as fine as corn silk — between his fingers. Then he drops into the bottom layer, right above her neck, the hair so blond that it looks white.

Candace closes her eyes and suddenly it is once again that winter night, four years ago, when they first slept together in his studio, the comforting warm aroma of baking bread and rolls drifting up to the apartment from the bakery below. They occupied a Salvation Army mattress in the corner opposite the grand piano. Candace was sprawled on the mattress face down, while Mark rubbed her shoulders and back. He swept her hair up and caressed her neck. And then he whistled, because he had discovered the two shades of hair.

She opens her eyes now. "I don't think I ever told you about when I was a kid, about that fat little boy named Gus who used to tease me about the two colors in my hair."

"No you never told me." He holds both her hands, then lets them go and begins to massage her shoulders. "Yeah, well, I would come home crying. My grandmother told me just to ignore him, but Papa Frank always said no, no. 'Tell him 'thank you Gus.' Tell him that only a princess can have hair with two colors.'"

"Oh so you're a princess then." Mark slides his hands over her breasts, rests them there, then bends and kisses the bridge of her nose. "And that makes me a prince, right?"

"No. Actually, that makes you a frog." He tries to tickle her but she catches his hands and goes on with the story. "So anyway, the next time I wore a ponytail to school and tubby little Gus teased me, I socked him in the face and I told him I was a princess and that my grandfather was going to beat him up if he tried to mess with me again."

"Ha!" Mark slaps one knee. "Good for you. So then he stopped bothering you?"

"Nope. I gave him a black eye though. But then I had to go to the principal's office and Lucy had to come in and sign for me." Candace sighs and twists a piece of her hair around one finger and holds it. "And it was that same summer my mother came home from California, and that's when I really started thinking that maybe Papa Frank was right, maybe I really was a princess, you know, maybe I had been abandoned, like Cinderella. I kept on thinking that even after Eileen showed up. I mean, when she was being nice to me, I used to pretend she was my fairy godmother. And when she was mean to me, I would pretend she was the evil stepmother..." Candace stares across Mark's shoulder into the orange and red maples. "You know, she has that jet black hair and all."

"Yeah, and the fangs," Mark says, bending over and licking her lips.

"Mark!" She slaps him but kisses him at the same time. The kiss is long and slow and warm, and then she lets go. "Anyway, I remember thinking that if I really was Cinderella, then I would live happily ever after. Just like Cinderella did. Only..."

"Only what?"

Candace frowns. "Only I just kept waiting. I guess in a way I'm still waiting."

Mark watches her in silence for a moment. Finally, Candace pulls herself up. The sun plays up the fiery highlights at the crown of her head. The wind rises, gusting up through her hair and the golden leaves of the trees. The sun sets the leaves, and Candace's hair, on fire.

"You won't believe what my mother writes here," Candace sighs, reaching across the picnic table and thumbing through Eileen's journal, which is lying open on the table. "I really have to read you some of this. I mean she is so horny it's unbelievable. I'm amazed that this is really my mother and that she could go with this guy to…" But Mark is swinging one leg across the bench and starting to get up.

"Cand, you better wait on that till later. We really gotta get a move on." He scoops up a couple of yellow maple leaves that have drifted down onto the table.

"Why?"

"Why what?"

"Why are we going?" She shrugs. "I mean, I'm in no hurry to see Eileen. Are you?" Mark doesn't answer. He kisses the top of her head and starts toward the bike.

"I just hope our kid has your hair," he yells back, jabbing one golden leaf into the dark curls behind his ear.

"Mark!?!" Candace screams at his back.

"Hey what?" He pulls the bike forward, off its kickstand, and steps astride it.

"I'm serious. Why are we going?"

"*Why?* Because I am not about to deliver your baby beneath a goddamn picnic table. That's why. We better move while you're still able to."

Candace frowns and puts her head back down on her arms. Neither of them speaks for several minutes. Mark shuffles his boots back and forth through the yellow leaves gathered against the bike. Then he dismounts and heads back to the picnic table, taking the seat next to her on the bench. He cradles one arm around her shoulders and sets the other hand on her bulging middle. Then he bends over and whispers into her belly. "Hey, Junior, why didn't you warn me that your mother would be such a pain in the butt?"

"Come on Mark, I just have to read you one thing," Candace says, opening the journal, but right away Mark reaches over and snaps the journal shut.

"Candace, look, I mean it now, cut the crap. We need to go."

Candace sits up straight. Her unhappy face is only an inch or two from Mark's. "But I don't want to go home." She shakes her head, a series of quick short thrusts that make her look like she's shivering. "You know my being at Eileen's won't work, you *know* it won't. I mean how could it, it's never worked my entire life, why should it be different now?" She sets her eyes on Mark, leaves them there. Abruptly, he stands and turns away.

"Candace, I know what you're thinking and that's not going to work either. I just can't do it, I can't have you live with me now. I mean, the studio is hardly big enough for my piano, let alone a crib, a highchair, a playpen."

Candace twists her hair and stares off. In her mind's eye, she is there in front of the piano at Mark's place, where she can see a row of handsome brick buildings lining the street outside his window. Candace has imagined — only vaguely, to be sure — sitting on that bench next to Mark, one hand rocking a small cradle while listening to him play piano, to that voice of his which reminds her a little of Stevie Wonder's, to him singing "Isn't It Wonderful?" — canned baby laughter in the background. Candace wants to describe this scene to Mark, has wanted to for months, and she wants to again now, but he isn't giving her a chance.

"Look, just as soon as you deliver, I'll help you get a place, I promise, wherever you want to live. If that's what you want. I'll spend as much time there as I can, wherever you go, I'll help you out, with money, whatever, you know I will as much as I can. But it's just not...I'm not ready for the whole family thing, having you and the kid moving into my place. Not now."

Candace sits silently, pressing her thumbs together. She feels the baby twist into a new position, arching. Something, a foot or maybe a toe or knee, pokes her. Candace lays her hand on the hard knob. The kid must have toenails, she thinks, as something sharp scrapes across the bottom of her pelvis.

"I've never once told you how to live this thing," Mark continues. "I've never pushed you. I let you take it exactly where you wanted to, all along. But for Christ's sake, Candace, don't make me out to be the bad guy now. You know I've done my best with this ever since...since day one..."

Day one. The words ring in Candace's head. Day one was the Sunday afternoon they spent together last December on Mark's mattress. It was a brittle cold morning. There had been an ice storm the night before, and Candace and Mark had woken up to find the trees and the telephone wires covered with icicles. When the wind blew, the branches and wires clattered together. The bakery was closed

that morning, so Mark's apartment was chilly. The two of them huddled under his sleeping bag for most of the morning, then got up
about 11:00, and wolfed down scrambled eggs and bagels.

Afterward, Candace asked Mark if she could draw him. She had
been doing the life drawing class at school all fall, and she was supposed to submit her final portfolio. Twice a week, she and six other
students, most of them art majors, would use charcoal to sketch a
man or woman posing in the nude on a white sheet.

That Sunday, Candace sketched Mark in the nude for about 15
minutes, while he read a magazine. She spent a lot of time trying to
get the dark curly hair on his chest and abdomen right. But then, as
she started to draw his penis, he looked up, saw what she was doing.
His penis started to stiffen. Smirking, he threw the magazine aside
and pulled her down on the mattress. She laughed, made a feeble
attempt to pull away, then tossed the sketchpad and charcoal to the
floor. They had done exactly what they were supposed to do: use a
condom. Who could have predicted it would break that day?
Candace was horrified when Mark withdrew, his penis red and
naked except for the condom's rubber ring. This much she knew:
she was half-way through her cycle, the absolute worst, most unsafe,
time of the month. Frantically reaching inside herself, she pulled
out the gooey shred of condom and shook the wet thing from her
fingers. It left her hand and landed on the bed in a wad. She stared
at it, nodded in disbelief. It lay there, looking harmless, like a crumpled
piece of Saran.

"Oh, shit," she moaned. "I can't believe it."

"Hey, where are you?" Mark is beside her on the picnic table, waiting for a response.

"I wanna go to the Clark," she blurts out, the words coming from
nowhere, taking even her by surprise.

Mark stares at her, incredulous. "You wanna do that NOW?"

Candace shakes her head yes. "Yeah, I do, I really really do."

"I don't get it," Mark says. "When you called me a day and a half
ago, you said, and I quote, 'You gotta come right away and take me
home.' As I recall, you didn't say anything about a detour through
the museum. Honest, Candace, I don't think this is really the time
to take in the Impressionist paintings."

"I do," Candace says simply. "Anyway, it would only be for an hour or
two." She smiles and strokes his face with the tips of her fingers. "And

then, I promise, you can take me right to Eileen's. I won't give you any more lip. Or maybe just a little." She puckers up her mouth and he kisses it. Then he catches her fingertips in his mouth and holds them there.

"Lip I like," he says, kissing her again. He bends over and speaks into her belly again, in a loud, exaggerated accent. "Hey juni-ah! You awake in deh? Ya moth-uh wants to show ya a little Monet. Maybe I'll find a piano and play ya some Chopin at the same time. Then we'll really give ya some cul-cha." Mark starts humming and soon he is drumming all ten fingers on Candace's stomach, as though he is playing piano. She smiles for the first time all afternoon.

"It's not Monet I have in mind," Candace says, clearing away his hands and rubbing her stomach with both of her own hands. "I want …the 'Blond Bather.' You remember."

"Sure, sure, of course I do." Mark helps her up from the picnic bench and puts his arms around her. Her belly is in the way. She turns sideways, then embraces him. "A couple hours at the museum will do us both good. But then, sweets, you're going straight home."

"Yeah, wherever home is." Candace is moseying toward the bike.

"Hey, somewhere it says you're supposed to be having a nesting instinct by now," Mark says, following her. "You're supposed to be putting baby clothes away in drawers, and washing floors, cleaning out closets, stuff like that."

Candace stops and turns around. "You dog you," she says smiling. "You've been reading." She points a finger at him, amazement in her voice. "You've been reading one of those books I told you about, the ones you said were so dippy. Admit it."

Mark pulls on the tiny gold earring in his left ear. Scratches the side of his face, just above his beard. "Let's just say somebody I know, this older musician I was recording with in Boston, sent me one," he says. "Along with a bag of diapers. His idea of a joke. But after you called me from Redfield, I pulled it out just so uh, you know, I'd know what to expect."

"So?" Candace says. "What do you expect?"

"I expect you, first thing tomorrow, to come over to my place and clean out my closets and wash my floor," he says. And now she is beating him on the arm and he is holding the arm up and away from his face as a kind of shield.

"You creep," she says, and she keeps swatting him. "There's no room for me to live there, but I'm supposed to clean up? You are a dog, a stray, a ratty, flea bitten stray."

"Oh don't I know," he says. Laughing, he catches both her hands and wraps them around his neck. Candace stops hitting, and goes limp, and Mark kisses her hard on the mouth.

"You know, sometimes I really hate you," she says, her head on his chest.

"Yeah, but the rest of the time you love me." After a moment, he turns her around, and holding both her shoulders, he steers her toward the motorcycle.

"And now, my little pretty, we better get rolling, so get this bloated bowling pin of a body back on the bike." She starts to give him a dirty look. "Sweetheart," he adds, grinning.

EILEEN

August 13, 1972

The gleam of the gym floor, I see the fine sheen on the old wood after Christmas break, when Mr. Spinelli would wax and polish the parquet. I smell the wax, as if I have my nose to the floor, or my teeth, but actually I'm right by the door of the gym as it swings open, revealing the varsity team, arms raised, channeling through the dull roar of the crowd. The team treads across the gym, no opponents in sight. I hear the regular bounce of the ball, the squeak of sneakers, the occasional whistle of the ref. The players dribble and trade, dribble and trade, shoot, shoot, shoot. The light reflects off their maroon satin shirts, which are soaking wet, like their faces, their hair. Sweat drips from their chins, their shoulder blades. The shorts, I see the shorts hanging loose over stalky legs. When they raise their arms, I see hair growing thick like it does in Barbara's armpits. Suddenly, it isn't the team I'm watching, but the audience, and I am the one clutching the ball. Only I don't wear shorts, just a long maternity T-shirt, my yellow shirt, but it shines, too, and I have a scarlet number on my chest, and my pale thighs wobble, and my high-tops are laced half-way up my calves. Realizing I have the ball, and the rest of the team is staring at me, heat rushes to my face. The crowd is clapping in time, melted into a throb like pulsing blood, and I'm leaning toward the gym floor, knowing I'm no damn good at basketball, but dribbling anyway, or trying. Somehow, though, the ball seems too hot, I can't seem to let go of it, and the heat is rising, strangely, from the floor, into my feet, my calves, and finally it settles in my gut, and the ball is getting bigger, too, swelling, getting more dense. It's still a basketball but it's not, it's a glowing orb, and I am trying to pass it, but it's stuck to me. I think, oh how silly, this makes no sense at all, so I try again to pass the ball, first to Rus, who's not there, then to Dave Barth, a kid I went to high school with, finally to Billy Spence, another guy in my high school class, but as soon as I pass the ball, the person I pass to disappears. THIS BALL IS ALL MINE, ALL MINE, I yell, and the rest of the team fades back. The ball has melted, has glued itself in place right into my belly. The heat gives way to hurt, the ball hurts, it is pulsing in steel cords, and pulling, and the crowd has disappeared, and I'm crouched over the ball, turning my head side to side, take it away, take it away, I scream, but the pain stays. A hand lands gently on my shoulder, and I think it must be the coach, but no, I see it's the stewardess, and she is saying, "Are you OK? Are you OK?" I can't answer. I hold tight to my middle, my belly as tight as a drum, and it is pulsing and cramping, in a severe but regular rhythm, waves of pain are shooting through me and I'm moaning. I look down, and see the tops of the trees, and I see my knees, and I think, please let me get down, please, please let this plane land, let somebody help me, let somebody stop the pain.

CANDACE

She is riding, helmet sealed against Mark's jacket, and she is convinced that today could very well be the day she delivers her daughter. She is thinking that if this is the day, then she must remember every detail. She must remember the tangy smell of rotting leaves, the odor of foliage fermenting into an earthy autumn wine. She must remember the warm Indian summer afternoon, the pale blue sky, the chalky haze hanging over the mountains as she and Mark snake across the state. She must paint in her mind the stark orange leaves cascading in long lazy spirals from the trees lining the side of the road. She must create a permanent image of the chalky tint of the clouds, and of the leaves, how they spin in gold, ruby and russet spirals up from the asphalt in the wake of car wheels shooting by. Mostly, though, she must remember the wind and the sun, how they catch and play with the leaves, how they toss them one to the other, how the leaves dance and glow as if they are charged by a mysterious electrical force.

Her surroundings seem vibrant enough as to be cinematic, some kind of living filmstrip in which she is both participant and observer. How much this is because of the dope she smoked with Mark at midday, she isn't sure. Even before the joints, she had the feeling she was under the influence of a powerful drug, one, perhaps, of her body's own making. Trish Bosco had warned her she would "go ozone" when it was time to deliver. Could it be she is now? Could this be her body's way of getting her through the inhuman ordeal that lay ahead? All day, Candace has been feeling slightly out of touch, "spacey," as she told Mark after getting back on the bike. Time was going in slow motion, as if her body was slipping out of gear with her mind, as if she were getting ready for an experience in which reality would be temporarily suspended, out of step, when her sense of what is normal, what is possible, would be swallowed up by events over which she would have no control.

"I'm starving," Mark yells back to her only a few miles after they are back on Route 2.

"Well, I'd kill to use a bathroom, so stop." Mark steers the bike into the first gas station, swerving close to a glass door that opens into a small convenience store. He helps Candace from the bike and leads the way in.

"You got a bathroom?" he asks the young woman at the cash register. She is snapping gum and wearing a Boston Red Sox hat. Mark roots for the Yankees.

"Not for people who don't buy gas." The woman's eyes widen when she notices Candace.

"Then I'll take two dollars worth of regular." He pulls a worn, brown leather wallet from his back pocket and throws two limp bills on the counter. "Just give me the key to the bathroom." The woman snatches up the bills and passes him a single key attached to a large piece of chewed up wood.

Candace grabs the key. "Get me a quart of juice, grapefruit. No, make it cranberry." She walks, legs wide, to the back of the store.

The toilet is filthy, so bad that Candace does something she never usually does, something Eileen always used to insist on when they used a public restroom. Unwinding a long strip of toilet paper out of the holder, she lays it around the perimeter of the seat. "For you, Mom," she says, smiling and pulling down her jeans. Light pink blood stains her underpants, blood mixed with a thick wad of mucous. The physician at Redfield told her there would be blood just as she went into labor. "Unless it's bright red, don't panic," he told her that day she sat on the examining table, covered in a rustling paper gown.

She pulls another long strip of toilet paper out of the holder and folds it over several times in a makeshift pad. Then she tucks it into her panties. As she stands and pulls her jeans into place, Candace feels pain scissor across her middle. It isn't intolerable. In fact, in a strange way it brings her pleasure. Candace is glad for the cramps, glad that the muscles are finally beginning to kick in. The question, of course, is whether to tell Mark that the time has come. He would panic, no doubt, and insist on taking her straight to one or another hospital. And first labors, she has read repeatedly, can and often do go on for hours, days, even. She isn't about to spend the rest of this glorious fall day in some antiseptic hospital. She wants to be outdoors. She wants to get at least an hour in at the Clark, too.

Mark is leaning against a shelf of boxed bakery goods and eating a triangular pre-wrapped ham and cheese sandwich when Candace emerges from the bathroom. He stuffs the last chunk of white bread in his mouth and crumples the plastic wrapper and cardboard into a ball. Gulping open-mouthed from the quart of cranberry juice, he swipes his arm across his mouth and passes the bottle to Candace. She takes it in both hands and tips it delicately to her mouth several times. The physician at Redfield cautioned her to stick to liquids once she knew she was in labor. She has no appetite now anyway.

❦

Candace has never before been what Mark called a "problem rider," someone who insists on trying to sit up straight even as the bike and the driver lean into the turn. But as they wind through the steep hairpin curves leading to North Adams, Mark has to turn around several times, and once he even yells at her to "cut it out." Candace can feel herself losing confidence in the bike's motion. She is pulling up when Mark is easing down. She is tensing. Coming through the mountains, a few curves are so steep and change direction so sharply that she thinks her knees will surely scrape the road.

The reason, of course, is that her contractions are turning fierce. They started to worsen just as she left the bathroom at the convenience store. They still aren't impossible to endure. But they seem to be heading in a certain direction, they are starting to reach up, now and then grabbing and twisting her diaphragm, depriving her of breath. It occurs to Candace, and it gives her a shudder, that the pain may turn to agony before the ordeal is over.

As they enter North Adams, Mark leaves Route 2 and circles into the narrow one-way street where he has his apartment above Molly's Bakery. With the motorcycle running, he anchors his boot on the curb. "How about a rest?" he yells back. Candace needs a rest, badly.

"No, the Clark's going to close in an hour. I can rest there, you know, lay on the lawn." If Candace weren't wearing a helmet, Mark would see that her normally pale complexion is flushed pink, that heat is rising through her hair, gathering wet under her helmet. Candace can feel herself sweating. And she can feel that the flowered blouse beneath her sweater is soaked through and sticking to her skin.

The Clark is in Williamstown, only five miles east of North Adams and the highway is straight and flat. Mark makes it through all but one of the lights without stopping. The trip takes less than 15 minutes. The entrance drive into the museum is lined by thick white birch, their yellow leaves fluttering in the wind and glowing in the late afternoon sun. Mark circles in front of the museum's north annex, a modern structure built out of blocks of red granite. He takes the motorcycle as close as he can to the entrance, next to the handicap ramp in a section of the lot reserved for bicycles.

Candace has the sensation that she is melting into the backrest. Her thighs are wet, glued to the seat of the bike. *Mark can't have any idea how bad I'm hurting,* she thinks, as the bike goes quiet and he hoists his leg up. Nonchalantly, he turns and waits for her to dismount on her own. She lifts her left thigh and drags it across the seat, letting her knee come first. Both legs drop to the ground. "Give me a boost," she says, holding her hands out to Mark. Her words come haltingly and she is breathless. Mark looks into her eyes.

"You're totally glazed over," he says. "Are you sure you're..."

"I'm fine," she interrupts, smiling. The smile, though, fades as searing pain zigzags across her bottom. This one crumples her forward. "Just get me inside, so I'm not, so I can...sit," she says, leaning into Mark's chest. She forces her legs, now feeling water logged, to inch forward. Mark laces his arm around her shoulder and practically pushes through the door. "If only you came with wheels," he says, chuckling, sliding her through the entrance. He pays for two tickets. "Maybe we'll need three before we leave," she whispers into his armpit. The smile on his face disappears.

They get off the elevator and walk through a long glass corridor. Candace is concentrating on breathing, and staring at cracks in the slate floor. At the end of the walkway, just before the entrance to the galleries, stands a large bronze sculpture: a jubilant female holding a baby aloft like a prize.

Mark lowers his lips to Candace's ear. "That's a statue of Supermom, just after delivery, as she races through the hospital raving about what a wonderful experience labor is." Candace's head is braced against Mark's chest, her hand against her lower back. She glances up, winces, smiles to acknowledge the statue. A middle-aged couple in identical yellow sweaters and khaki slacks and penny loafers stop, look briefly at the statue, then stare at Candace. *My hair,* Candace thinks briefly. *My hair must look like wet straw and my face has a day's worth of road dust and grease.* But those concerns dissolve as another contraction gathers strength, erupts, inflicts a flood of pain.

"I...I need to sit," she mumbles. Mark opens the glass door of the gallery and they move toward a mahogany bench in front of a Monet. Meadows and trees in the painting come to life in a multitude of pastel colors. Candace crumples against Mark's arm, seizes his elbow. "I want to get to the other side of the room, to...to the bather," she whispers.

"Why don't you just stay on this side of the room for a few minutes," he says, anchoring her shoulders with a firm grip. "Look, there's a Renoir. You can stare at his onions for a few minutes." Candace glances at the onions momentarily, then her eyes close. Exhaling, she drapes herself against his chest. "Here comes a doozy," she whines, the words oozing out, squeezed by the anguished breath accompanying the contraction. Air explodes from her mouth in a series of short forceful breaths, all directed at Mark's chest. When the claw of pain clenches even more tightly, she turns toward a statue right next to the bench, a bronze Degas of a dancer, her leg poised beneath a skirt of metal netting. Candace glares at the rumpled ruffles and wrenches both of Mark's hands so tightly, his fingertips go white. Finally, the contraction passes, and Candace releases her grip. "As soon as you can walk, we're out of here," Mark says. "I never should have listened..."

"Look, I'm really OK, just let me up," she says, filling her lungs. She chuckles. "The doctor said this kind of thing could go on for hours. So let's just enjoy the art."

"For chrissake, Candace, don't be ridiculous." Mark reaches for her elbow, but she slips from his grasp and stands. Bracing both hands against her back, she steers awkwardly across the wooden floor of the gallery. She knows exactly where she is headed, to the right corner, the 'Blond Bather,' and she is not going to be moved off course. She approaches the Renoir on unsteady feet, gazes at the milky skin of the young woman's face, the voluptuous breasts, the feathery head of strawberry hair. Once again, her eyes delight in the way the sun plays lightly on the rocks, the ragged shore, the way the woman's hair has a life of its own, as if it's electrified, as if at any moment it might lift up and float away. The bather's skin is flawless, the skin of a baby, and her breasts and belly are swollen as if she could be in the early stages of pregnancy.

"Renoir gave you your hair," Mark whispers. He is standing behind Candace. She manages a smile, sinking back against his chest as they study the painting together. She has the same sensation she did the last time she saw it, namely, that she isn't looking so much at a painting, but into a mirror at her own image. She is riveted now on the small enchanting eyes, slivers of brown almonds set delicately in the creamy face. The woman's full form is commanding yet calming, a woman who is both in charge of her body, yet ready to yield it up to the ethereal forces of nature. Vulnerable because she is exposed, yet strengthened by the exposure.

"She's so incredibly peaceful," Candace says. It occurs to her now that the bather is peaceful because she is resolved. This woman has a plan, Candace thinks. She knows her mind and that resolve is reflected in her body. It's clear from her eyes, the delicate point of her chin, and also in her mouth, the way the full pink lips are set and ever so slightly twisted.

Staring at the mouth now, an ashen-faced Candace realizes that her own lips are twisted too, into a grimace, as a contraction, worse than any that have come before, crashes viciously through her body. Candace's head drops to her chest and she catches her hands together under her belly as if to support it, or the infant inside. Another fiery pain comes roaring through her, and this one shuts her down, savagely seizing at her legs, pushing her forward with unbearable force. With no warning, Candace drops away from Mark's chest. He grabs awkwardly for her arm just as her knees are buckling and she is flying off, sinking into the floor.

DELIVERY

The mother. *Becoming that creature takes exactly nine months, in one sense, maybe a lifetime, in another. But it really happens in still a third time, in that instantaneous stop clock of labor and delivery, when the brand of motherhood becomes burned remembrance in the flesh. That instant of utterly sweet abandon, birth, the pain unwinding long and drawn out as mother-not-quite-yet mother and baby suspended forever. Every mother never forgets it, the joy of pain beyond agony, even decades later, they remember together at the baby showers, legs in nylons, neatly crossed, they trade the war stories that made them mothers, speaking freely over steaming cups of tea in white porcelain cups, china decorated with strawberries, delicate silver spoons resting comfortably on gold-rimmed saucers on bellied laps.*

Years later, mother, whoever she is, smiles proud to tell her day, a day more important even than her own birthday, its weather, every detail fresh in her mind, flesh recollection being perfect. The mother calmly recalls for anyone who will listen all about the labor she had, all the early signs, the trip to the hospital, but most of all, the birth itself, if she was awake, or what she remembers just before they put her to sleep, because in those days, it happened, some of them, poor things, were put to twilight, and they were best off that way, because they were alone, no men allowed, no coaches.

Usually who listens to these gory tales is only another mother, an aunt or sister, usually another mother who is only waiting to share her own story, to come clean, years later, of the triumph, the blood and ooze she slid through. To the woman who endures it, the birth is an event of heroine proportions, a miracle unmatched in man, far more grand than war or flight or levitation, the body of woman playing God, creating life, earning a badge of honor from the eternally wondrous Mother Nature simply for doing what She has dictated. Those who have not gone through it may listen crossing and uncrossing legs, a few of the youngest will surely clear their throats or step away, out of ear shot, waiting nervously for the gruesome baby tales to end. The others, the veterans, sail along discussing, but still marveling, wondering the same thing: how does this impossible thing happen?

This is how it happens, in a final push, there being no way to avoid the burn, burn, burn, even sometimes a tear, a rip of the tenderest rim of skin imaginable, that of the lip of the canal. The limits of human flesh are in that moment learned forever, are burned forever, into the birth canal, will be recalled as a big bowling ball split, an impossible fit, even later, the idea terrifies, but in the end it happens, you do it to make someone to live after you. "I can't, I'm I'm going to, it will break me," is how it comes screaming out in words from Candace's mouth, the words emerging exactly at the same moment as that first tiny lemon wedge of wet red hair appears, matted flat, between Candace's legs. Mark says a single syllable, "Wow," but Candace doesn't hear that, nor does she see what Mark sees now, which is a baby coming.

He has just pulled off Candace's short black boots, tugged her jeans down, unrolled them practically — all blood-soaked at the crotch — and has taken the socks off too; Mark thinking, how God damned thoughtful of me to see that the bare flesh of her feet making contact with the wooden floor beneath this Renoir might help. The bare feet might help to give Candace a grip, because so little else really would, give her or anyone else a grip on this most inhumane of human experiences. And all the while, above and watching, those dark almond eyes of the bare blond bather. There she sits, demurely posed, belly and breasts permanently swollen, on a pure white sheet that looks like satin. What I would do now, Mark thinks, to have that sheet on this floor.

"I can't do this," Candace screams, taking both hands to her crotch, now bare of clothing, only there now is blood and wild hair. She is trying to pull herself wider open. She is panting, hyperventilating, the twist of pain like nothing she has ever known before. And down on the floor beside her, Mark is kneeling, trying to get hold of both her hands, to pull them away from her, not sure what she might be about to do, but afraid that she may actually be trying to keep the baby from coming out. Mark wonders whether he will have to fight Candace's hands away, whether he will have to pull the baby out himself.

Only minutes before, in what already seems like hours, Mark shook a guard alert, told the dumbfounded woman in uniform staring open-mouthed at Candace sprawled on the floor to use the damn two-way to call for help right away. An ambulance, something.

❦

And in still another place and time, another ambulance is being called, is streaking a blue flashing light across an airport tarmac, converging on the sleek white whale nose of a DC-10, a whale which has yet to swim to a complete halt on the runway. The jet's engines are still searing hot, shimmering the air before them, and the wings of the jet have yet to sluice their moisture, beads of firmament cling to them and the wings are still moving, still swinging around in the final motions attendant on landing. The ambulance arrows to its goal, while simultaneously, a set of stairs is moving swiftly toward the belly of the aircraft, where inside hell is having its way with the belly and womb of a dark-eyed woman. Sunrise is hardly an hour old, a milky blue engulfs the sky, a flood of gold is poured and resting at the horizon, all sky motion seems suspended in a cup, caught up in honor of the event inside.

Stretched four airplane seats across, all armrests flipped up and aside, Eileen now lies legs wide, sucking in the stale air of the cabin, that warm dank air that reeks of airplane, that odor so peculiar to flying. Eileen is staring at her bare feet, bearing down into the future in order that a baby to be known as Candace will emerge. And 20 years later, Candace is sharing with her mother of 20 years before nothing whatsoever in looks, not the face, nor the color of the skin or hair, but almost exactly the same expression of absolute incomprehensible terror streaked with sweat and agony painted across the lips and brow.

"I'm having, it's coming," Eileen barks out, short and hoarse and gasping, to a total stranger, a nurse named Paula, a stout black woman in a sleeveless white blouse, her knock knees peaking out below coral bermuda shorts. Paula, riding all the way from Oakland only two rows behind Eileen, can now be seen with her large hands separated, one planted on Eileen's forehead, the other anchored on Eileen's knee, and she is speaking, softly, into Eileen's ear, saying that the baby's head is crowning, as if Candace would emerge a princess or a queen.

"So honey when I say so, you gonna take a breath, you gonna take a big breath, a mama-sized breath, and you gonna hold it, and honey, then you push down, I mean just as hard you can, that's right, honey, take a breath, now hold it, hold it hold it hold it now PUSH, PUSH THAT BABY INTO

THE AISLE, that's right, the aisle," where, staring into Eileen's gore is a wide-eyed blond stewardess, her makeup frosty and sublime, the stewardess pressed into service by the nurse, the stewardess' only knowledge of delivery being the vaguely remembered details she learned birthing her own two children more than a decade and a half before. The stewardess' grey cotton blouse is rolled to the elbow, her wool jacket, airline wings pinned to the pocket, cast aside so it won't get splattered with blood.

Paula, all the while, Paula, patiently standing, then kneeling by Eileen's side, whispering a monologue to her ear, trying to allay Eileen's fears, trying to rehearse Eileen as she goes, trying to convince Eileen that help is only a siren away, telling Eileen that she, Paula, has delivered many a baby in her day, but no, none in an airplane before, but still, Eileen is doing swell, just fine, she's done most of the hard part already, and all by herself, hell, Paula says, this baby's head is half-way to college, before you know it, hon, one more, one more big push, you'll be done, that baby will be sailing out, a big breath now, that's right, a big breath, we'll have it, can you, can you, OK, breathe, breathe, big breath, big breath, now hold it, now PUSH, PUSH, PUSH, PUSH, push, push, push.

For so many months, pregnancy has been for Eileen an idea, a bad one, to be sure, an idea that only made Eileen fat and cranky, made her legs hurt, her life hurt, her ankles swell. But still and all, it was constantly and only a condition, not permanent the pregnancy, only a way station in the line to parenthood, the far more serious state of matter, the pregnancy being physical but almost completely mental too, mostly an idea safely embedded although growing within the body of a future mother. But now baby the possible is quickly coming soon to be baby the absolutely real, born through the eye of a human needle, poking out from the flesh with a push of a major muscle called uterus, you ter us, you turn us, you do, you turn us inside out and laugh and then make us mothers. And one especially, at this moment, Eileen, with her dungaree jumper up around her rib cage, her blood-soaked panties cast to the floor, where, a few hours later, a horrified member of the plane's clean-up crew will discover them, wedged safely beneath the seat. Dangling them on one finger, she will stare at them, shudder to see there is indeed some hair stuck to the lace. At a loss for what to do with them, she'll toss them quickly into a plastic garbage bag, she will feel a mixture of shame and guilt, wonder and disgust, almost as if she's discovered a bloody knife or a smoking gun after a murder, incontrovertible proof that a horrible or essential miracle has really taken place.

And so babies are born in blood and guts, no glamour, nothing but sweat and screams, no amount of practised rhythmic breathing can take the place *of the blast of full steam ahead, a loss of control, a primal abandon that Eileen discovers quickly enough lodged into the seat of a plane, and Candace finds out on the art gallery floor, each suddenly converted to the most real life labor and delivery rooms. If you don't let go, let the split of skin happen, get on and out with it, stretch and break the crotch until it feels like it will never be the same stitched or not again, unless you are willing to do that, to go right through with it to the other side of the tunnel, take it to the end of self-hood and beyond into something else, then you will never accommodate a head of some uncertain size. Only that feeling of giving way to the stretch, the split in half, my God, the blind push that never ends the pain, only in that long moment can it come to be the baby. Now, indeed.*

Paula says as much to Eileen, "Honey you have to let it go, relax that tush all out, now, just let that baby loose, that's our only hope, the only way to get this gal out, we'll have that baby bouncing to the ambulance if I have anything to say about it, OK, now I can see you're trying...OK, yes, here it goes, the medics are here, are you with me Eileen, here we go, take a breath and this one is it, now keep track of my eyes, that's right, stare right at me, honey push that child, sweet Jesus get that baby to me in some neat kind of football pass, just pass it out and I'll catch. All this kindly babble coming from a nurse who was on her way home to visit her mother in a shored-up duplex apartment in Hartford, Connecticut.

"I...can't...do....this," Eileen shrieks, pulling on Paula's hand, reaching for the nurse's knee, setting her teeth into the flesh of Paula's kneecap. And at Eileen's other end, she is blood-splattered, splayed, bent legs spread as wide as the wings of the plane, and there at the bloody center slit, a little head is tearing her mother, almost already hanging out. "If you just catch your breath, you gonna see we got something now, girl, we got that head, we've got the head, WE GOT IT see," and now Paula lifts Eileen by the armpits, wedges her shoulders up, so she can see the mighty progress. "And the medics are here, now, hon, now show 'em what you can do, we got that beautiful baby's head, now all's we need is one, two more pushes from you, that's all, spread and give me two more, a shoulder, each one a shoulder, you'll be done, all done, honey, those shoulders will slither to us like snakes in wet grass." The nurse is speaking thus, Eileen is pushing and all the while a medic is making his way to the scene with an oxygen mask.

When Eileen thrusts again, when she is through, there is inside and out, at least two reasons to rejoice. Outside the tiny airplane window, a shiver of lavender streaks the western sky, it spreads like paint and holds, and spreads some more, a color never seen before. Meanwhile, inside, Eileen's baby lies, new-eyed, howling, stiff arms startled, reaching wide.

 Paula apologizes for being in the way, for not having that baby out sooner, for having to see this young woman suffer it out in the narrow space of an airplane seat. "But oh God, we got ourselves some magnificent baby now," she squeals, the shrieking child slithering like a human cork in the medic's blanket, coated in slime, hard and purplish blue, the cord white, the hands wrinkled and purplish, much too big, compared to the rest of the body, the fingers look gigantic, they are hands from outer space. And the face, the face is red and squashed and to Eileen's sudden horror, it can be traced, this face is a tiny version of her father, Frank. Thankfully, her horror doesn't last, it passes as the medic, bespectacled, with thinning hair, passes her the baby platter-style, he serves it, her, a little girl, Ma'am, you have a daughter, down onto Eileen's plenty bloody stomach, and now, Eileen crying reaches up for the kid who is screeching and so too is each member of the flight crew yelling, cheering, all of them sandwiched in the cockpit, coming up one or two at a time to try to see, clapping, unable to see a thing beyond the medics, the nurse, and the bewildered stewardess, unable to see the blood and ooze and tears that coat the child, but concluding from the yelp that the child must be doing fine.

 Twenty years later, that very same child, now in a body completely over-grown, is flat on the floor of an art gallery yelling, bleeding again, pleading for help. Legs spread, she is ready to shoot forth her own issue, another human special delivery package coming straight through the same sliver, one generation squeezing its way into the light of the next and the next and so on, mother into daughter into mother and forever into future again and again. But this time, not so neatly, the problem is a whitish cord wrapped snug around the baby's throat, wrapped once around enough to turn this baby more purple than eggplant, the squeeze upon her throat a most unsuitable way to emerge. Attempts to deliver such babies do not always fail, but always make for complications, particularly for a never-yet father, particularly on the floor of an art museum, where all color and form is assumed to be plainly ideal, but now, plainly, is knot.

 Not ideal either is Mark alone here, no doctor in the house, not a bit of help coming from any corner quick enough. Gaping is one uniformed woman, the guard, guarding only that no one else should gape, she finally thinks to bring out some kind of canvas drop cloth from inside the bowels of the muse-um's back room, something that Mark drapes beneath Candace's oozing lower half. "I...I...oh God, get this, I can't, get this, help me," Candace yells, thrashing, mired in motherly misery, Candace only wanting to be told that the agony, the pain, will soon be done.

Mark finds out now how being in the becoming-mother condition can make for highly indelicate expression, can produce sudden violent attacks upon the male, his anatomy, the female saying things like stay away, I'll kill you, help me, don't, if you ever come near me again, damn you fuck you and your penis all the way to help me, you have got to, Mark, help me. Candace, push now, I see it coming, now, Candace, right, go, go, go, help, now, go, go, push, I can't believe, baby, baby, it's coming, MARK I'M BREAKING IN HALF, No, No, Cand, you're not, burning, burning, right in half, God, Candace, it's coming, baby, it's...it's GOD IT HURTS, now, now, CANDACE THE HEAD IS OUT, I don't believe it all the red hair, and the face, he thinks, silent suddenly, and worried, why is the baby's face so purple?

Mark can see both the color and the cord, and wonders what connection. He hasn't ever seen a cord before nor does he know exactly where or when it's supposed to end or how it will come out, before or after, he only sees the whitish thing snugly like a collar ring, as Candace huffs and puffs and holds his hands. He has pulled her ever so slightly up toward a sit in order for her to see what it is that is making him so happy, that red head hanging out. With Mark Candace is holding hands and almost now the two of them are dancing together they are holding sway, pushing moving close and away, she gently drops her head, it arches, she flops back down, into another mother posture and then a push. Now push again, he says, and now the baby sashays out and forward, out and back, but the dance is interrupted every time by the cord pulling at the baby's throat. Instinct guides whatever thinking he does next, because life commands it, I have to loose I have to get this baby born, the noose must go.

"Try again. Push hard, let me get this, I'll try and pull it..." and Mark reaches right in for the cord, he pulls, she pushes, he gets his finger wedged beneath the cord, the slippery rope, the slope, he gets the cord ahold and tugs and lifts it around the head and dancing loop de loop around the neck his daughter, he loosens it around and Candace pushing hard again the head goes through the loop in a straight passage right and tight inside the needle hole.

And now the head comes through, and again the shoulders, plump and blue and suddenly Mark is dancing with his daughter too, slippery in bloody fluid and chicken-like, arms stiff and reaching out to each parent in a separate place, her face a spiral squawl, and all that Mark can say is "Hey Candace she has red hair." He cries that out, and on his face is wonder, relief, total disbelief that without a doubt, a child of his now exists. In the midst of this the ambulance arrives, shifts Candace to a stretcher (as Eileen too was moved, 20 years before). The baby rides along, on a bloody swollen belly, inside of which the placenta hides. Mark strokes the baby with a single finger, bends to Candace and lets his lips linger on hers, lets his tears mix freely with the gallery lights playing down on Candace's hair.

Staring at her, staring at the baby, he is numbed, a little dumb-founded, unable to comprehend what's just happened, that a new life has begun thanks in part to him, that a red-headed baby now exists where there was no red-headed baby before. Mark kisses each of Candace's hands and her sweaty forehead. And only then, when the stretcher is being wheeled away, does Mark notice that standing guard behind him is an early 20th century Steinway, a dandy museum piece made of delicate red mahogany and rosewood. On the old piano stands a small sign saying "1913. Do Not Touch Piano."

With hands still bearing baby blood and mother's too, with medics, guards and museum staff busy seeing Candace to the waiting ambulance, Mark pauses, lifts the piano cover, and, justified by this — I must do it, because I am now delivered, a brand new father — he sets his scarlet fingers to the keys. He plays quickly, a strain or two of Chopin, and then the refrain Candace loves from Stevie Wonder. And as he abandons the piano, and hurries to the ambulance, he sings out, "Isn't she lovely, isn't she wonderful..." because he knows she is, and because this song of his is just what the doctor ordered.

EILEEN

August 17, 1972

I keep reliving the plane ride, I call it the trip to agony, the day I came inside out. The last thing I remember is reaching up for the overhead luggage compartment, because I was chilled and wanted my sweater, but already I was in awful pain, so just as the luggage door floated upward, I slumped down onto my side, collapsing against the carpeted bulkhead. Everything hurt, particularly from the waist down, even my wrists, which had taken the brunt of my fall, and my knees, burned from scraping the carpet, but still I got up onto all fours. At that point, a stewardess crouched down beside me, a blond woman with pale pink iced lips and a smell about her like spring flowers, or sweet bath powder, and I heard her ask me what she could do to help, her nylons rubbed together between her knees, and I gasped, feeling fluid gushing out from between my own knees, a flood bathed my calves and thighs. I rolled onto my back, thinking it might be blood, and if it was, it occurred to me that I might black out, which at that moment I longed to do, because I realized that if this indeed was the real thing, labor was beginning, then I'd just as soon go out cold, have the baby the old-fashioned way, wake up waving to a swaddled bundle across the room.

At that moment, a black woman's face appeared over the blond stewardess' shoulder. "I'm a nurse, so maybe I can help," she said, squeezing behind the stewardess and scooping her hand beneath my head. "Oh, Lordy, honey, hold on now, your water's gone and busted, so we got to get you onto these seats." She took my shoulders and the stewardess grabbed my ankles, and the two of them tried to hoist me, but my backside felt glued to the floor, all the while cramps kept exploding more and more ferociously up and down my lower back and girdling my middle.

"No, no, no, don't," I moaned, at which point the stewardess yelled and a pilot emerged out of nowhere; and seeing the dilemma, he helped the two women. The three of them together, grunting, managed to set me lengthwise onto three or four seats. The nurse, whose named turned out to be Paula, pushed on my ankles until my knees bent, and then kneeling beside me, she came close to my ear. I had the sense she was praying, the way she spoke was as low and soothing as a chant, she spoke only slightly above a whisper, but I could hear her clear as day, and I could see her thick dark fingers above my brow, and her damp cheek stayed so close to mine that her skin — it had an oily sheen — nearly stuck to my own.

The rest is, well, history. Except for the kindness of complete strangers, I'm not sure I want to remember it at all, particularly my own wailing. I will forever recall seeing Paula's wide face, one side of it anyway, I can see her chocolate eyes, floating in their white pools, and I can hear her say *"Now push that baby into the aisle!"* Mostly I scowled, but at the point she said that I smiled, the thought of my kid being delivered in a row of airplane seats tickled me somehow. One other thing I remember, besides great ocean waves of pain, a whole freight train of pain, was Paula saying the head was "half-way to college." I nearly laughed, I would have if I weren't so near tears, but what I was thinking in my delirium was about that bus tunnel that starts in downtown Providence and empties onto Thayer Street right next to the Brown campus, how I used to walk to class, peer down that tunnel, a mysterious dark hole tempting and terrifying me all at once, and now here I was riding through my own tunnel, not convinced I'd ever deliver a baby or surface whole on the other side.

"I...can't...do...this," I screamed, pulling on Paula's hand, and suddenly I was twisted toward her and tasting the salt of her knee, her leg flesh was up against my teeth, thick and sour, and in that moment, I wanted to sink my teeth into her leg, inflict pain, bring blood, transfer agony to someone else so I wouldn't have to bear it all myself. I believe at that point I was reaching rock bottom, coming to some kind of moment of truth. Paula grabbed my shoulders and forced me to see the baby's head hanging out, just hanging there between my legs, a mess of hair and blood and a picayune little monkey face; and that sight gave me a second wind, I lay there in the plane, in a pool of sweat and ooze and clots of blood and gore and felt myself cracking in half, and yet that view of the head covered in black hair and hanging out of the tunnel, right in the air, and the blond stewardess staring at it open-mouthed, that was enough to get me through, it gave me some new hope, some sense of energy that I could last. And when Paula asked for a few more pushes, I gave them to her. I pushed until the ache in my neck felt worse than the rip in my rear, I felt unzipped from head to toe, and at that moment, when I knew I didn't have a bit left, not one more ounce, I felt the baby slither out, a hard knot of flesh escaped the tunnel into daylight, and soon I heard a piercing scream. *My baby.*

All of it seems like a dream, one of the worst, and I guess too, the best I ever had. I suppose I'm glad I was awake, because now I know I have what it takes to deliver a baby. It takes guts. I think of myself as a wounded soldier. I saw battle. Like a good soldier, I was brave, but the whole time, I was scared as hell.

Having a baby isn't exactly like going to war, but then again, I think it is. Women do battle, too. Only theirs is one that produces life not death. Something else comes to mind now too: having a baby, like going to war, has always been a glamorous everybody-has-to-do-it kind of thing. I mean in the old days guys went to war, and women had babies without even thinking. That's what life was all about: you served in the Army (or Navy) if you were a man, *or*, you got married and had a family, four or five kids, and served your husband, if you were a woman. End of story. Everybody did it and lived happily ever after. Right. But that was clearly the old days. God, have things changed. I mean Vietnam is hardly what you'd call a place of glory. Nobody with brains goes to war anymore. And so, in the same way, I don't want to be anybody's little stay-at-home wife (certainly not Rusty's!) I don't want to be stuck with a baby, living in a stifling little town like North Adams. I want to go places, do things, be somebody. I want a career. I would gladly erase the last nine months if I could. I would never have had this baby if I'd had a *real* choice, if I could have done what Corinne wanted. I guess that choice scares me.

I hear the baby carts being pushed up the hall. The funny thing is, even after all I just wrote about this baby being a big mistake, I can honestly say I am in love with the creature that just came out of me. I love holding and touching her. I love her smell. Sometimes I want to be her mother, and sometimes I wish there were someone else around, the baby's *real* mother. That would surely have to be another woman, because I can never be that, a real mother. I can't do that and still be the person I want to be, somebody who leads an exciting life in the world. And now look what I've done! I've begun crying, I get this way whenever I think I don't have a life anymore, now that I have this baby. I get scared thinking how trapped I am. Tears are falling right onto this page, making the magic marker puddle up. I cannot control my emotions these days. I cry over everything...

Later.

They have taken the babies away, and I am resting in my freshly-made hospital bed, and feeling a little better. I told the nurse how I felt, trapped, confused, and she was, bless her, understanding. She offered to change my sheets and she fluffed up my pillow, and then she told me I will feel better in a few days, after my hormones have settled down. I hope she's right. Besides my bottom being sore, the muscles in the back of my neck are killing me. The nurses say it's because I pushed so hard. They massage me every night, using baby oil. I have just been told I will be allowed to spend an extra day in the hospital because I bled so much, I suppose because I delivered in the plane. I am going to have the baby in my room again soon, so that every two hours I can nurse. I have been trying already, without much success. Instead, I give her small bottles of sugar water, and I hold her, and kiss her little nose, and touch her wrinkled hands and count fingers and toes, and once, in the middle of the night, I cried when she yawned and opened her eyes. I swear she smiled. First I smiled, and then she did, but my roommate (mother of four!) laughed and said that the smile was only gas.

Apparently my milk hasn't left the starting gate, that is, I have had no "let down," as they say, but today being the third day, the nurses said my milk should come in any time, and that's why I'm supposed to try feeding her every two hours. My boobs are certainly big enough to do the job, for God's sake each one is bigger than the baby's head!

Rusty has been in each day, he just sits here, neither of us saying much, he just keeps touching the baby's hands, or he walks, holding her against his shoulder until she falls asleep. He hasn't asked a thing about what I did this summer. He keeps talking about his work, he told me that he built the first of the solar houses, the one they'll use as a demo. He's been working outside so much that his face and neck and arms are dark and his strawberry hair is bleached blond. I'm fond of this guy, he's sweet and kind and good-looking. But I cannot imagine us as a couple, together, ever again. When I try to, I get this slightly queasy feeling in my stomach, or maybe it's in my head. I dread the times he comes in and stands next to the bed, staring down at me while I'm trying to feed the baby. I don't want him that close, especially when I'm totally exposed trying to get my huge breast into her tiny mouth.

It's strange to see him holding the baby, to think we created it together. The thought we are connected by this bundle makes me, well, uncomfortable. Nothing seems quite real, either. I feel as if I'm back in California, only God knows I'm not, I have got to face the reality of this child, this child who still has no name. Only one name rises from the deep, Candace, I love that name, despite Candace Patterson, the rich bitch who rode horses and played viola and had gorgeous hair and flawless skin and was double majoring in Chinese and International Studies. I felt so insecure and stupid around her. So why name my baby after somebody I'd rather forget? I guess the answer to that is I just love the name. And also, maybe I'm hoping that my daughter won't grow up like me, full of insecurity and self-doubt. Instead I want her to be confident and sure of herself and successful, too, and who knows, maybe even wealthy. When I asked Rusty what he thought about the name today, he smiled, and looked at the baby very sweetly and for a second I thought he would cry. He didn't though. He just whispered the name, "Candace." Then he said he had to get going home, and he left.

PART FOUR

CANDACE

When Gretchen isn't sleeping, and these days, she isn't sleeping much, she is instantly wide awake and wailing. Hot and pink and pinch-faced she howls, the sound piercing and incessant, a car alarm blaring from the cradle, careering across the kitchen, sailing out of the bedroom or down the hall, wherever Candace has carried her, the baby usually hooked belly down over her mother's shoulder like a sack of wet flour. Hour after hour, Candace paces, holding Gretchen's heels, and the agony of sound follows, muffled only slightly by the fact that the baby is buried in the loose, carrot-colored hair that flares around her mother's shoulders. Riding astride Candace in this fashion, the infant siren gives off one stinging wave after another, each wave winding higher, impossibly higher, tighter, clutching more insistently than the last, the total effect like that of a snarl of bees swarming over Candace's aching frame.

This afternoon, Candace has the baby cradled in her lap, in the rocking chair in the living room, and she is attempting once again to feed her. The baby's eyes are tiny, sunken slits, squeezed shut, the face twisted and damp, the eyelashes flooded and glistening. The pitch of her crying is steady but relentless, the act of bawling turning the small body deep pink. Even Gretchen's scalp, her whole skull, gets red when she cries, the flush extending all the way into the shock of pinkish blond hair. When Gretchen bawls like this, which she has since she came home from the hospital nearly seven weeks ago, even her narrow heels blush deep in color, and her feet beat the air like the wings of a wounded bird and Candace paces or rocks or jostles the baby in gathering frustration until, finally, her nerves bristling, she stares off into space, dissolving into tears herself.

Now the baby's lips come to Candace's breast, and hook over the brown puckered nipple, latch on, but after only a moment or two, the mouth goes slack and drops away, the delicate lips still pooled with milk. This is Gretchen's routine, to suck for a few minutes and then, as if disgusted, to spit the tit and the milk aside. Then, heaving a brief sigh as if gathering her diminutive resources, she retracts her knees and kicks out, crying again. The doctor called it colic, said it would pass in a matter of months, but to Candace it is interminable and it has a better name: hell on earth. The incessant screams raise her to a new understanding of pain, the baby's and her own. Candace is convinced that the baby needs something when she cries, some kind of saving or salving, something which Candace dearly would like to identify and would love more than anything in the world to deliver.

Clearly, though, she cannot, and nobody else can either, certainly not Mark, who has stayed around the clock many nights coaxing the baby to sleep and then fighting to keep her that way. Eileen, too, has tried, valiantly, in brief spurts. She has given Gretchen her own brand of serious, albeit high-strung, attention. But nothing and no one has been able to help, and lately, Candace has come more and more often to her own tears, flooded by doubts about her limited abilities as a mother, blurred by fears that she can't love a creature that cannot be comforted, frightened by her growing realization that this baby is more wretched a reality than she ever dreamed possible. (Her ideal, of course, never will exist.)

Compounding the problem is the fact that after seven weeks, Candace has hardly slept more than a three-hour stretch and she isn't eating right, and the ragged tear in her rump is raw and still oozing and infected. She can walk only so far before she has to pause, sit, endure the frying pain.

Gazing at the baby now as it lies face down on her knees, Candace tries something that one of Eileen's friends suggested: rolling the baby back and forth so as to put gentle pressure on the child's stomach.

"The idea," Candace whispers to her daughter, "is to force gas out of that bony little ass of yours." While Candace tries this, she has still another depressing thought: that maybe the baby book was right, that maybe it was the cocaine that produced the colic, that maybe

Candace herself brought on the baby's agony, and indirectly, now, her own punishment. Candace aches with this thought, convinced of her mistake, and with that, another thought quickly follows: she has no clear fix on her daughter's eyes or on her face, how it would look with the crying erased from the features, because in seven weeks, she has seen the baby's eyes only shut, when Gretchen succumbs to utter exhaustion. Awake, the eyes are inevitably wrenched by tears. There has not been one moment, Candace thinks, in which to gaze placid and uninterrupted into her baby's face, awake and at peace. And now it occurs to Candace what Trish Bosco said after the first week, the day she brought bright yellow and purple mums, Candace's favorite fall flowers. Sore and deplorably tired, Candace told Trish she was more burned out than she had ever thought possible.

"Sure you are," Trish said, smiling sympathetically. "What you need is a lift." Candace had looked at Trish in alarm then. She was half afraid — and half wishing — that Trish was referring to drugs, that in addition to the tiny pink dress, that maybe Trish had brought along a baggy of cocaine. But no, that wasn't what she meant.

"You just wait," Trish went on, "you'll get a big boost within a few weeks. You'll get that first smile from Gretchen and I promise you, that one peek will be pure heaven."

Candace mindlessly runs her fingers along Gretchen's fragile ribs now, numbering the rounded knobs of cartilage with the side of her thumb, numbering too how many weeks it's been since Gretchen arrived: seven; seven, and no, Trish, she thinks, I'm not anywhere closer to heaven. In another week, it will be two months, and still, there has been nothing resembling a smile. And now, Candace's head falls, and tears drip from her dark-circled eyes. Why me, she weeps silently, touching the bird-like back bones protruding from the top of Gretchen's neck. Why should such a horrible child have come from within me?

Lately, Mark has taken to coming over evenings, arriving about eight to walk the floor with Gretchen, or, when Candace is feeding, or trying to, he strums his handmade Spanish guitar. Lately, he's been playing in the classical style, his left foot raised and resting on a stool, his wrist cocked to the right, his hand positioned in an awkward-looking sway, fingers purposely perpendicular to the strings.

Tonight when he arrives, Candace has the baby sleeping on her lap, face down. Candace is wearing a flannel nightgown, rocking back and forth, the chair creaking, the living room floor squeaking underneath, and in that comforting rhythm of wood, she has created a small space of peace. But Candace's face tells another story, her cheeks are pale, slightly shrunken in, and there is a growing flimsy about her look. Mark places a palm on the crown of her head and lowers his lips to her hair, then lifts the baby away, lays her gently in the cradle Rusty made, the cradle that stands in the center of the braided rug. Gretchen stirs, her face contracts and for a moment, Mark flutters his fingers up and down her back, stroking, and whistling, because whistling occasionally seems to help, it cuts into Gretchen's crying, calms her, or like now, it helps keep her asleep.

This gives Candace half an hour to take a shower. Here it is 8:00 at night and she is only now getting to that simple thing she used to take for granted at 8:00 in the morning. Meanwhile, sitting on the couch downstairs, Mark plays "Greensleeves," and various Spanish folksongs, and a Malaguena, a fast melodic dance; and in time, Candace descends, hair dripping and making a wet ring around her T-shirt. She is holding a glass half-filled with milk. She dips her eyes at the baby, sips the milk, and settles into the rocking chair, but not until she's placed a flattened pillow on the seat to ease the pinch in her bottom. When Mark has finished the Bourree and ventured into the Catalonian song, one of Candace's favorites, she begins to rock, wide-legged. After a day in her nightgown, she has changed into a clean pair of jeans. She has lost so much weight that the legs of the jeans hang loose.

Eyes closed, letting both feet meet the rug, she wants nothing more than to hear Mark play, more folksongs, more dances, the rich guitar mixing with the creak of the chair and the floor. The music lulls Candace into a trance, which, under normal circumstances, would lead her into gentle sleep. And it would now, too, if only her internal clock weren't so tightly wound, set to go off at any moment, at the least little sound from the baby. Candace has the new mother's mind, stretched tight between feedings. She craves sleep, and yet, when presented with the opportunity to relax, she can't shut down, is burdened to stay awake by the endless responsibilities attendant on the new child.

Mark switches off all but one small light, making the living room dark, and Candace ceases rocking, having slipped now into a mindless state, the final slump before sleep, thoroughly stilled, numbed by the music. Mark has begun just a gentle strumming, and he hums, and occasionally taps the toe of his boot against the stool. The knocking of his foot prompts in Candace a vision of a dancer, perhaps even herself, wearing a shocking black and scarlet dress, a mantilla to match. She sees a set of lips, glazed red, her hair tightly coiled at the back of her head, the swirl of a ruffle, the lift of her dress, a flash of white thigh, a swish of hips, a knee, a click of metal heels in perfect rhythm against the floor.

At that very moment, when she is dancing, or would be, if she had the dress, the shoes, the shawl, the strength, at that moment, the baby screams, the sound that was bound to come back, does now, slicing like a razor, bone deep. The wail rips Candace out of sleep, her eyes flap open, glazed, and nervously, she lifts the glass of milk from the floor and drains it.

"I never got dinner," she says, hoarsely, fingering the empty glass. Mark has continued playing, switching, though, to Kemp's jig, a nervous little melody, but now, at the mention of food, the fact she hasn't had any, his guitar stutters, peters out.

"I'll make you something." He lays the guitar aside. Candace rises, stumbles across the room to the cradle, her feet clumsy in over-sized slippers. For a moment, she stares inside, then rocks the cradle rapidly back and forth. The baby squawls louder and finally, Candace picks her up.

"I'm going to feed you and put you in the backpack and take you out for a walk." She places Gretchen lengthwise astride her arm, the feet flailing, the belly and chest supported firmly on her open hand. Drool and clotted milk drip from the baby onto Candace's jeans, dribble to the floor.

"Ooh, Ms. Spit," Mark says, making room for Candace on the couch.

"Yeah, you said it." Candace has a steady supply of kleenex for wiping tucked in her sleeve, she takes a wad now to rub spit from her leg, then swipes the floor with the toe of her slipper. Dropping to the couch, she raises her T-shirt to expose her nursing bra, a mammoth white contraption with flaps. Mark watches the baby's cheek, watches the mouth root purposely for the enlarged nipple. Gretchen latches on, sucks. Generally, she feeds long enough to fill a thimble. This time, though, the pink mouth holds on for a full five minutes before it releases, and when it does, the milk pooling and drooling, the face is poised in a silent ugly shock. No sound emerges, as if the tape player is stalled, as if the baby somehow is unable to add audio to her grimace of pain.

A moment passes, and with no warning, a wide white spray of milk shoots from the baby's mouth. The warm white liquid coats Mark's chest and hands. He jumps back but not before curdles of white cream attach to the curly hair of his arms, and milk lands on the sleek reddish wood of the guitar.

"Oh Christ, watch out," he says, holding his dripping hands aloft, and the sight of him, and the bovine smell, the sweet cheesy odor of whole mother's milk, kid-curdled, makes Candace laugh. This being her first real laugh in weeks, a long loud guffaw that goes on and on, belly-felt, she gives in, leans over the baby, and when she sits up straight again, she is not prepared for what comes next. Sobs. Her laughter sinks imperceptibly into wallowing tears, the depth of her crying equal to the bold thrust of laughter that preceded it, both coming out of the same well of misery. Candace's crying gets Gretchen going. But oddly enough, the baby this time had a moment of peace after her show of milk, a moment when, burping loudly after her projectile, she actually looked around, and made no sound. If Candace had been paying attention, she might have seen the deep blue irises, creased in black, that are her baby's eyes.

Candace is still crying when she hears a familiar sound, that of tires compressing gravel in the driveway outside. And then two voices. Candace winces, knowing it's Eileen and her new "friend," Jorge Vencedor, the handsome Dominican physician she's been dating for a couple of months.

"Oh Lord," Candace groans. The last thing she needs in her present state is a visitor. "Take her, would you," she says, holding Gretchen up to Mark, the baby's bowed legs cycling below her pink plastic diaper. He takes Gretchen along with the wad of kleenex, and one-handed, begins sopping up the milk. Candace, meanwhile, attempts to hurry up the stairs, but is held back by the pinch of tender skin as she raises each leg. She reaches the second floor just in time, just as Eileen and Jorge enter the living room.

"Ooooh, Gretchen, you were crying when I left this morning," Eileen says, standing over Mark at the couch. "And here you are, silly baby, still crying at the end of a long day." Eileen throws aside her purse, kicks off her low pumps, and reaches down for the baby. "Mark, you've met Jorge, haven't you?"

"Sure," Mark says, reaching for Jorge's hand. Eileen makes a slow circuit of the braided rug, cradling the baby, bringing the child's downy forehead to her lips. She stops, flops the baby onto her chest, and for a few moments, the crying ceases.

"She's been puking all day," Mark says, raising the bottom edge of his wet T-shirt to his nose. "So I smell like butter. I think Candace feeds this kid Ben and Jerry's on the sly."

"There, there," Eileen says, swaying, patting the baby on the back. She turns to Jorge. "Bonita, si?"

"Oh si," Jorge whispers, fondling Gretchen's cheek. Suddenly, out of the baby's backside comes a loud squirting sound, not unlike whipped cream rushing from a can. Instantly, Eileen pulls the baby away from her chest, but not before one arm and part of her hand are covered in a pasty poop, the color and consistency of mashed butternut squash.

"Oh Lord," Eileen yells, as the baby's kicking leg smears feces onto her white blouse. Gretchen begins bellowing again. "Candace! Oh God, Candace!" Eileen holds the baby aloft, arms extended. "Mark, tell Candace I need help, a clean diaper, wipes, a changing cloth. Right away."

Mark bolts upstairs and Eileen walks the baby toward Jorge, who takes an exaggerated sidestep away, laughing. Eileen is laughing too, now holding the baby over the cradle as if dangling a small boulder over the side of a cliff.

Candace descends, her hair neatly clipped back. Her lips are firmly compressed, her eyes cast down, and without a word, she takes the baby from Eileen and rests her on a changing cloth on the floor beside the couch. Kneeling, she rips the plastic tabs on the diaper.

"For God's sake, Mom, you'd think she was a leper the way you had her there. She's got a dirty diaper, not a disease."

Eileen is wiping her soiled blouse. At Candace's comment, she pauses. "I know very well she's got a dirty diaper. I've got plenty of evidence here to prove it." She stands over Candace. "You know, Candace, I change diapers all the time. I change them here for you and I do them, too, for some of my clients at the clinic. It's just in this case, she got me, that's all." Candace finishes wiping the baby's cookie-sized buttocks and slips a clean diaper between the scrawny red legs.

Eileen crouches down, her knees cracking. She covers Candace's shoulder with her hand. "Honey, can you say hello to Jorge?"

Eyes closed, Candace forces up a grin. "Hi, Jorge. How are you?"

"I'm fine." Jorge nods kindly. "And you have a beautiful little baby." He crouches, cradles a caramel-colored hand over Gretchen's head. "She keeps you busy."

"Yeah," Candace mutters, her voice cracking. "You've got that right." She stands, lifts the baby abruptly and walks away.

Eileen follows, speaking in a low tone. "Are you OK, honey?"

"I'm fine," Candace says, pulling away, her voice nasal. "I'm...it's just...allergies. I'm stuffed up is all."

Eileen sticks her lower lip out. "Look, Candace, I know that's not all. I know that..." her voice lowers, "I know very well what this is like..." Her words trail off, and she brings her knuckles up against her mouth. "This baby," she says, quietly, firmly, "this bawling all day is tough. Very tough. It could land anybody in a padded room."

Candace's eyes flash. "Nobody here needs any goddamn padded room." She holds the baby protectively near her face. "Look, Mom, I told you, I'm fine, and I *am* fine. Mark and I were just thinking about taking the baby out for a walk."

"At 9:30 at night?"

"Why not? I'll bundle her up, and the fresh air will do everybody good. Maybe by some amazing miracle she'll even sleep."

"Hey, how about I keep the baby while you two go out? Jorge and I were just going to hang out anyway, right Jorge?" He nods agreeably. "So it would work out fine for us to..."

"No." Candace cuts her mother off, sharply. She slides Gretchen off her shoulder and clutches her to her chest, pressing her there defensively. Maybe because of the jerkiness, the urgency of Candace's motions, Gretchen heaves a sigh. Her eyes flutter and she stops crying. Instinctively, Candace brings the baby a bit tighter, holding her like a shield. "Thanks, though," Candace says, her voice relaxing a little. She manages a weak smile. "Maybe...maybe you'd take her another time. I'd like that and I'm sure Mark would." Candace calls up the stairs to Mark.

"Would you bring down a sweatshirt for me and a sleeper for the baby and her yellow corduroy hat?"

Mark comes down the steps grinning, carrying Candace's sweatshirt and the baby's things. He's even remembered the denim front pack and now he is showing it off, dangling it from two fingers. "In your dreams," Mark says, "did you ever think I'd be such a perfect father?" He kisses Candace, but she just looks at him oddly.

Outside, October's chill has cleared the dark sky. Stars are not visible, though, because the moon is almost full and rising, a giant white disc slicing its way above the horizon.

Gravel crunches as Mark and Candace cross the driveway. They hold hands, loosely, and Gretchen hangs heavy and long on her mother's breast, drooling into a white swath of flannel sewed into the pack. Candace likes to walk the baby this way, although it pulls a drawstring of pain across her lower back. At least, in this position, the baby's ear pressed against her mother's heartbeat, there is a better than even chance she'll be quiet. The air, maybe its chill, seems to still her.

They walk four blocks to the dead end, where the road withers, disappears into a hillside. Mark stops. "She certainly is a quiet little thing outdoors. I guess she really does go for the fresh air."

"Yeah, maybe the two of us should just move outdoors to a tent."

They proceed up a path that leads through the trees, a path they have walked often before, summer and winter. From time to time, especially when Candace was still in high school, they went "picnicking" on the hill, meaning they told Eileen they were packing a lunch and then, once there, they stripped naked and made love between the boulders of a stone outcropping a couple hundred yards up, leaving their lunch untouched. In the winter, once or twice, they tried following the path on cross-country skis, but the ice and the pitch made it treacherous. Candace recalls coming down the path on her backside, snapping one ski pole and losing the other, watching it skate across the crusty snow into oblivion.

"You won't want to hear what I'm going to say," Mark begins. He has a flashlight and he's spraying it ahead of him, and holding Candace by the hand, leading her up the path.

"So then, why say it?" Candace is breathing hard. Her bottom hurts, and feels so wet that she wonders if she hasn't started bleeding again. She tries to focus on her breath, the Lamaze way, though she doesn't know why she should, since it didn't work when she was having the baby. She listens to the long low howl of a dog, and pretends for a moment that it's a wolf. That crooning sound, and the light of the moon, and the smell of decaying leaves, all that helps somehow to soothe her ragged nerves.

"Well I guess I'll say it because you're going nuts and I can't stand by and watch." Mark's flashlight reveals the first boulder in a long straggling line, a line that leads up to the stone outcropping. Candace has the sense she can't lift her leg, so she stops, momentarily, breathes deep again, and when the pain eases in her crotch, she hoists the leg slowly. It goes where she wants it to but she has to drop Mark's hand. He shines the light on her footsteps.

"Take it easy there." A limb is within reach, and Candace uses it as a handle, lifting herself to the next rock.

"Out of shape. That's what I am, out of shape."

Mark stops. "Yeah. And that's not all. You've lost too much weight, and you haven't slept and you're not eating. You're totally strung out." He waits another moment and says, "Are you...oh, forget it, of course you're not."

"Am I what?"

"Oh, nothing."

"Mark, what?"

"No, it was dumb, really a stupid ass question best left unsaid." They continue climbing, slowly, stopping once, twice more, and Candace looks back into the darkness that has closed behind them. She hears the dog crooning again, it gives her goosebumps to hear it so clearly, to be out here, so exposed, holding the baby. She sets both hands under Gretchen's bony behind and watches the moon, wonders if it will cast its dim glow over the outcropping, which lies just ahead. Turning back to the climb, Candace has a rush of memories of the rocks, of her and Mark lying together there, huddled on a warm blanket, completely bare. On the warmest days, their bodies would stick together, wet with sweat.

"So I know what it is you wanted to ask."

"No you don't." They have reached one of the largest rocks of the outcropping, right above the broad mossy spot where they used to spread the blanket and make love. Mark sits down on the rock and directs the flashlight briskly over the green moss, the spot they used to refer to as their "carpet." Candace sits gingerly on the rock, her hands beneath Gretchen's backside, tightly bound by the denim of the front pack.

"You wanted to ask me whether I was ready to screw again." She runs the toe of her shoe back and forth on the moss, dislodging some of it from the rock.

Mark stands abruptly, turns the flashlight so it floods her chin. "You're nuts. You are totally and absolutely nuts. I wasn't thinking that at all. Not at all."

"Oh, right. You told me yourself you were horny as a toad last week."

"So maybe I am, I'm not going to deny that. But you don't get it. What I'm worried about right now, I promise you, is not my overzealous dick. I'm horny 99 percent of the time, with or without you. But that's *not* what I was going to ask you." He kicks at a rock and sends it tripping down the hillside.

"So?" Candace falls quiet, her voice chastened. "So what is it then?"

"I was going to ask if you felt ready to start painting again, or even if you had the energy to start thinking about it. Because I know that doing something besides taking care of this cranky kid is what you need. And you know that just as well as I do." He shuts the flashlight off and smacks it against his hand.

For a long time, Candace doesn't say anything. And then Mark does, in a hush.

"Baby, I'm really worried about you. I've been wanting to say it for weeks but I keep holding back because I'm afraid you'll freak out. But now I'll say it anyway...and so don't go getting pissed off at me until I'm finished talking. OK, so maybe, just maybe, you need to think about some other arrangement, maybe somebody to help, or somebody else to take the baby for a while, just a week or two until you get yourself togeth..."

"No," Candace screams, and the scream is loud enough so that Mark is sure that it can be heard in the road below. "No, no, no!"

He tries to put his hand over her mouth, and immediately she tries to bite him. He shakes her. "Candace," he barks, a harsh, throaty whisper, "stop it." She goes limp and begins to cry. He holds her by the shoulders, until, like a rag doll, she leans into him. "Candace, you want the cops up here for chrissake? Now look. I know you don't want to hear this, but for God's sake, you've got to. I think this baby is too much for you alone, even with me coming over. I told you I was worried, and now I'm more worried than before. We've got to get you some help, or something. Even if it means you going away, or the baby going away, maybe Eileen can tell us somebody who..." She is shaking her head, stiffening again, pulling back from him. "Candace you have got to consider it."

"No," she says, sobbing, dragging one wrist under her runny nose, wishing she'd brought her kleenex. Before Mark can stop her, Candace is up, starting down the path without the flashlight. Her voice trails back to him. "No, I don't care what happens to me, or what you say I should be doing. Nobody, nobody else is going to take care of this baby but me."

EILEEN

August 24, 1972

Home not even a week and already I'm nuts. Nuts! My homecoming, as it was, occurred in utter silence. There I was, bringing a new baby into my parents' house, and it was as though I'd carried an illness, or that we were gathered for a wake. I suspect that the two of them have spent this whole summer vowing to get even. In their eyes I guess I've ruined everybody's lives. Mostly, I think they're angry and terribly ashamed. After all, I've embarrassed them to no end, not so much by getting pregnant, although that was bad enough, but by going away, abandoning Rusty. I suppose I am the family scandal...

I came home from the hospital on a Tuesday. It was a hot, humid day, the sort you get at the end of August, when the heat hangs in a kind of blur over the trees, it lays on the mountain, too, clinging to the horizon. Everything feels suspended, the air sucked breathless, you can't inflate your lungs or keep your face dry. And you hear that snake of sound as the cicadas make their deathly rattle.

Rusty picked us up at the hospital about eleven in the morning. When he walked into the hospital room, I was just putting Candace into a stretch suit. She had her fists in her mouth, hungry again, so I fed her (formula, I'm losing patience with nursing, I don't get it, at least not yet) and then I wrapped her in the blanket that I had Rusty buy for me. It's downy soft, a beautiful pale pink, satin-edged, something that you imagine a little kid holding while she's sucking her thumb and rubbing her ear and falling asleep. Last week, I asked him to go to Walter's department store for the blanket and a few other essentials, the so-called "layette," T-shirts and night things, and also, a sun bonnet because Candace is so fair. (Her hair is the finest red color I have ever seen and her eyes are a watery blue green.)

"You are not going to need that blanket today," Rusty said. "It's got to be at least 95 out there already."

"Yeah, but they told me I've got to keep her warm."

At that moment, I noticed that he was trying to hide something behind his back. I pretended not to see, but soon enough, he thrust them at me. A dozen yellow roses with red tips. I choked up, which happens easily these days (the other night I cried when a nurse didn't tuck in the bottom sheet of my bed tightly enough.) The roses smelled like heaven, but I didn't hold them even a minute, because he should have known better than to bring them, because I told him again just the other day, things are *not* going to be that way between us. I still can't bring myself to tell him what happened in California.

All of that with John seems unreal, like a dream, far, far behind me — nothing, not a letter or even a postcard from John. For now, though, that's OK, I'm living here, and clearly I can't leave, not yet. But I also can't forget that I had a whole different life there, a life that made me feel like I was in control. I thanked Rus for the roses but shook my head quickly and handed them right back, said I couldn't carry Candace and a bouquet of flowers, too. Thank God the nurse arrived at that moment, pushing the wheelchair that would take us downstairs.

We left the hospital in that beastly heat, hot wind pouring into the truck (no air conditioning). Candace slept, and woke, and her face flushed so pink in the heat that I decided I had better take the stretch suit off. She lay there in the open air with a diaper and T-shirt. I leaned over and spoke softly to her and held her up and kissed her forehead, and my insides melted. I have never felt this way before — I love this baby more than anything I have ever seen.

"Look at her eyelids," I said to Rusty, and he did, he glanced over. "You see her eyelashes haven't even grown in yet!" And as if she knew, at that moment her eyes fluttered, so dreamily, all the while her little hands rested on her belly. I wanted to tell Rusty something then, something like "thanks for coming to pick me up," or actually, "thanks for helping me to have this beautiful baby," but I figured I should just leave well enough alone. Instead, I kissed her head and rubbed the bottoms of her feet, and felt her toes, like a row of tender pink peas, and she opened her eyes and looked straight at me. I felt so blissful that I almost started to cry, because here was my daughter, the most beautiful, and peaceful creature I had ever laid eyes on.

"She's never gonna get any sleep if you keep nudging her awake like that," Rusty said, jolting me out of my reverie. We were headed up Orchard Street. I told him she slept more in the hospital than any baby should and so it was time she woke up. I have since regretted that remark, as what she did in the hospital has nothing at all to do with what she does at home. The last three nights she has woken me up at least four or five times every night, bawling her head off. It's so bad that when darkness falls, I start to get frightened thinking I have to go through another sleepless night of being constantly "on call." Anyway, that first day, when we pulled in the driveway, Rusty asked if he could come in and hold her. "Sure," I said, feeling mellow, my spirits lifted so much that I was very close to telling him I would take the yellow roses after all.

When he opened the front door of the house, and I carried the baby inside, I smelled sauce cooking, and something fried, probably homemade pizza, and in my heightened emotional state, that made me feel like crying. Bizarre. I yelled hello, but the house was dark, the windows closed, the shades pulled to the sills. Often on the hottest days, my mother will shut everything up, trying to keep the house cool. But that day, the house felt more like a funeral home.

"Here, let me take her," Rusty said, and I handed Candace over to him, and immediately, he kissed her head, rubbed his lips lightly in her strawberry hair. Meanwhile, I began to search the downstairs, and not hearing a sound when I yelled hello again, I took it for granted that no one was there. Which was fine with me. Except, they *were* there, upstairs, the whole time! I know this baby, in their eyes, was born in sin, but for God's sake, she is precious and as sweet as her name, Candace, full of honey-pink hair, the blue eyes, her coloring so much like Rusty's and so different from my own. She is an absolute angel. And she is their flesh and blood too. You would think they might have figured that out for themselves.

When my parents finally showed their faces, after an hour or so, Rusty and I were sitting on the couch, taking turns holding her. They came downstairs, and Dad shook Rusty's hand, but to me, he said nothing. He didn't speak a single goddamn word nor did he glance at Candace. The two of them looked like they had been sucking on stone. Not a smile, or even a hello for me, and they didn't even ask to see the baby. You would have thought I had brought home a freak, or that I belonged in a cage in the zoo. They talked with Rusty a minute or two, then walked to the kitchen, where I assume they ate their lunch, not offering any to either of us. We stayed in the living room, and they went out, saying they'd be back around dinner. We ate cold leftover spaghetti later, after Candace fell asleep.

That day, we let her sleep on the couch, surrounded in pillows, but I told Rusty we'd have to get a crib. "Yeah, and that's not all," he said, as he dug into a his spaghetti. He reached into his shirt pocket and with two fingers he lifted out a slip of paper with a scribbled list. He had called Audrey in Boston and asked her what to get. "Highchair, play pen, stroller, changing table, bottles, pacifier, bibs." I couldn't help laughing when he read the list because he sounded so domestic.

"Wait, wait, wait," I said, interrupting. "Some things I can borrow." One of my cousins had phoned me in the hospital to say her baby was three now and she would be glad to lend me anything I needed. We finished lunch and washed dishes like an old married couple, which felt peculiar. I asked Rusty if he didn't have to get back to work.

"I figure I can afford to take one day off...for my brand new daughter," he said, wiping the last plate. He hung the towel on the stove, neatly folded, and, turning to me, dropped his head. Through his bleached blond hair, all curly on top, I saw his scalp had gone a mixture of tan and red and freckled from so many hours of working outside.

"I want to...we need to talk," he said, as I finished sponging up. We walked into the living room and sat down on the other end of the couch from where Candace lay in the same position we'd left her. She wasn't making a sound (I put my finger under her nose just to make sure she was still breathing because I've read about crib death, kids can just die in their sleep for no apparent reason.) Rusty was sitting, his work boot resting on his opposite knee.

"I want to feel free to come here, to see her," he said. I told him that I wanted him to come too, as often as he wanted, because clearly he would be an incredibly good father. At that he brightened and stopped rubbing his chin. I was about to say something else, about how he could take her out sometimes too, but he interrupted. He had taken what I'd said the wrong way.

"I had a feeling you might start to come around once the baby was born." He leaned over and touched my chin with the side of his finger, nothing much, just grazed the edge of my jaw with the slightest (and I will admit, the most sensuous) touch. But even that was too much. My heart started pounding and my face flushed red.

"Rus, no," I said sharply, pulling away and shaking my head. "I didn't mean *that*." I was pissed, as much as anything at myself, and of course, at him and at my parents, whose mood was still in my hair. I stood up and asked him to "cool it," just like that. Then he told me I was acting like the real bitch again, he even said something he used to say to me in the old days.

"You've always got to have things just your way..." He took in a big breath, and stood, keeping his hands on his hips, and his lips and his lower jaw jutted out, in a kind of quivering pout. I told him then it might be better if he left. He gave me a hateful look and walked by the baby, leaned over and gently brushed her head. And then he went. That night he phoned and sort of apologized, or at least he explained. "I get frightened when I think you're going to cut me off."

My parents, meanwhile, have remained more or less stone-faced all week. I certainly wasn't expecting them to be enthusiastic or welcoming to me, or to "forgive" me for going to live in California and giving birth to their grandchild on an airplane. But somehow, I figured they would want to make peace. They haven't. Oh they're softening toward the baby, all right. Ma asks to hold her all the time, and I must say, I'm more than happy to hand my little squalling bundle over. I even caught my father holding the baby once or twice, when he didn't think I was around. As soon as I appeared, though, he quickly handed Candace back to Ma and his face turned icy.

For all of Ma's maddening ways, at least she came to see me in the hospital. My father never once visited. The nurses told me that he went to the nursery every afternoon, but he never came to my room, even after I bowed low and asked my mother to see if he would come.

There is one spot of genuine warmth in the events of the last week, though. My mother, bless her grey soul, crocheted Candace a doll out of bright yellow and white yarn, with a bonnet. The doll has a rubber face and is fashioned in such a way that the doll's blanket is attached to the skirt, so you can wrap it up tight. The night she

brought it, she had it in a clear plastic bag, tied with a little pink ribbon, and she kind of lifted it up and then dropped it onto my lap. I
opened the bag and touched the doll's soft head and almost cried,
because I had a vague recollection of my own doll, the one she had
made me so many years before. I alway used to bring my doll outside
and sit her on a pine bough, or rock her on my knee. I lost my doll
when I went to school, but I remember calling her Dollcake, and
now, here was Dollcake Number Two, a new one, and it is, in spite
of everything, incredibly special to me. That night, I fed Candace
her bottle of formula and held Dollcake on my lap too. I thought
about Ma then, I wanted to remind her that I am her daughter, and
that she is my mother. I wanted to remind her of all those times
growing up, when I would curl up on Ma's lap, and she would call
me "ma bella gella," her beautiful girl, and she would stroke my hair
and trace all the letters of the alphabet on my back.

CANDACE

Candace takes a three-hour, fumy bus ride to Wilmont, and Gretchen sleeps most of the way. With one arm hooked through the arched handle of the infant seat, Candace falls asleep herself; she is so deep in slumber that when the baby's crying slices into her nap, she doesn't at first connect with the sound. For a few disjointed moments as she's coming awake, Candace can't imagine why screeching rises and surrounds her. And why it won't stop. Even after her eyes drift open, the blank and unfocused state persists. She isn't quite sure where she is, or why, or how she came to be travelling with a baby on a bus. Soon enough, though, she remembers.

"Shhhhh," Candace croons. Glancing around, she tries to gauge the effect of the baby's wailing on the other passengers. Thankfully, she engages no other eyes. Lifting Gretchen from her infant seat, Candace cuddles the baby's backside. One leg of the yellow stretch-suit is warm and soaked through. The odor of urine rises into the space above the seat. Holding her breath, Candace lays the baby on her knees. The baby's crying intensifies, taking on the insistence of a fire alarm. But when Candace removes the diaper, exposing Gretchen's bottom, the fury of crying eases.

In the last two weeks, Candace has noticed a curious thing: Gretchen is charmed by being naked. When stripped of her diaper, and allowed to cycle her legs freely in the air, she goes perfectly silent. Once she even stayed on the bed long enough for Candace to shower and wash her hair.

There is great progress in this, Candace has decided, if for no other reason than it has now become possible, during the diaperless interludes, to gaze into Gretchen's blueberry eyes. Candace is convinced, moreover, that this new behavior is something of a reward, earned by Candace for her devotion to the baby. The breaks in crying first began the morning after Mark suggested — and Candace angrily rejected — the notion that she find someone, a babysitter, or a nanny, perhaps, to help care for the baby.

"He should see you now," Candace says, beaming over Gretchen's belly. She sets her fingertips on either side of the infant's protruding navel. The skin surrounding the tiny stump of flesh that is the belly button is softer than that anything in Candace's memory. Leaning closer to the baby's face, Candace focuses on Gretchen's eyes, eyes that recall Audrey's: glittering blue irises with black streaks, and even the same white flecks.

"Your daddy should be as stuck on you as I am," she whispers, and when she says this, her throat sticks, and her eyes water, because she hasn't seen Mark since the night they argued in the moonlight up on the hillside. She has spent the last ten days trying not to count the time that's passed, trying not to be angry with him over his prolonged absence. She has tried, too, not to feel guilty, but that has been unavoidable: she knows full well that it was her outburst that made things between them go wrong.

The night of the argument, after Candace yelled, Mark trailed her silently down the moonlit path until they reached the house. By that time, the baby was awake and beginning to wail. "Should I come in?" Mark asked, hopeful. "I'd be happy to walk her to sleep if you..."

"No," Candace barked back, slamming the door before he could say anymore. It was the very next morning that the baby lay undiapered on her changing table, silently gazing around the bedroom. A jubilant Candace was tempted to call Mark right away to tell him the good news. She wanted to tell him, too, that the baby had slept five hours straight during the night. Candace felt buoyant, and almost as rested as she used to feel after sleeping eight hours straight. She came close to calling Mark. She picked up the baby, and then the phone, and touched the first three number pads. She even heard herself rehearse what she'd say: get on that damn motorcycle of yours and get your butt over here, ASAP, so that you can see your daughter's blueberry eyes for yourself.

Before she finished dialing the number, though, the baby began crying again. Candace nursed, and Gretchen spit up the entire feeding. Candace had to wipe up the floor and change her shirt because it reeked of sour milk. By that time, she had lost all desire to phone Mark. She was recalling all over again why it was she was so angry at him: because he had suggested she get some stranger to help care for the baby, a stranger who would cost money, when instead, she was hoping that he himself would volunteer to carry more of the burden. Why would she possibly want anyone but him to help care for Gretchen?

The good day quickly slipped away, and a not-so-good night followed. Gretchen was up nursing every two hours, and the morning after that, Candace was so exhausted she could hardly drag herself out of bed. She lay on the couch for most of the day, feeling ragged, lifting her shirt endlessly, letting Gretchen nurse as often as she wanted. By afternoon, Candace was thoroughly "milked out," as she told Trish Bosco over the phone. "Don't worry, I know, I've been there," Trish said. But somehow, Candace was not consoled.

Zombie-like, Candace had paced the second floor of the house, carrying the baby in the denim front pack. Finally, about four in the afternoon, the baby dozed off, at which point Candace collapsed on the couch. She lay there, wide-eyed, too tired to sleep. She could sense that awful hollow feeling taking hold again, a feeling that by now was becoming familiar. It was a mixture of fear, desperation, total exhaustion, and growing self-doubt. It generally came on in the late afternoon, when Candace was so completely spent, so tired out, that she kept forgetting things, simple things, from one minute to the next. She would change Gretchen and then, a few minutes later, wonder if she had put a clean diaper on. She would pour a glass of milk or fix herself a piece of toast and then wander off, forgetting where she had set the food down. She would ask herself over and over, "Have I taken my vitamin and iron pill today?" And worst of all, she would say to herself, "What did I finally decide to do about giving Gretchen a middle name? Did I write down 'Grace' in that space on the birth certificate form? Or did I write it down and then erase it?"

Mark would know, he would remember exactly what she had done, Candace was sure of that. But she was also sure she didn't want to call him. She didn't want him to know how crazy she was going. Or how angry she was at him. Angry that he'd stayed away for ten whole days. "I suspect he probably just wants to be asked back," Eileen had said at breakfast this morning before Candace left on the bus for Vermont. "I mean, honey, he's called you twice."

"Yeah, great, so he's called twice, big deal. I'm the one who's up every night, all night, pacing the frigging floor."

"Candace, I think you're being unfair. All he did was suggest you get some help, somebody maybe to come in a few hours a day, so you can nap. I happen to think that's a great idea too, honey." Eileen pushed her plate of toast aside and wiped her fingers and mouth with a napkin. "And I told you that I would help pay. I think these last two months have been too much, way too much for Mark, and certainly much too much for y..."

"Mom," Candace interrupted, trembling as she rose from the table. "Just shut up." Eileen's mouth froze around the word "you." "Just shut up, do you hear? Just because you couldn't take care of a baby doesn't mean..." Catching sight of Eileen's flashing eyes, Candace cut herself off. "Look. All I mean is that this is none of your business, OK? I really don't care what you think and I really and truly don't want to know what you want. Alright?" Candace ran from the kitchen and up the stairs, slamming the bedroom door.

The bus is slowing down now, groaning louder as it does. As if reflecting her mother's dark thoughts, Gretchen's face shrivels tight and red, in preparation for another round of bawling. Soon the awful sound fills the bus seat, spills over, wraps Candace, tucks itself in the taut muscles that are pulling tight behind her neck.

"Wilmont, next stop Wilmont," the driver calls, and in a moment, Candace is sliding a fresh diaper under Gretchen's backside.

Marjory is waiting at the station. "Audrey would have come too, but she went and ordered six million bulbs," Marjory says, slipping Candace's suitcase into the back seat. "She got this notion a couple weeks ago that what we need is a zillion spring flowers. But how she thought she was going to plant them I don't know. Because of course she can't."

"But why did she want so many bulbs?"

"She said she just had to have an immense spring garden in place this year, or she wouldn't get through the winter." Marjory inhales, holds her breath, then lets it out. "Anyway, I've been planting like a madwoman and today she's got your father digging."

"Oh, so Dad's here," Candace says, staring out the window. She last saw her father the week after the baby was born, when he drove to North Adams to surprise Candace with the cherry cradle he had built, designed with the same bowed back and slender spindles as the Russell rocker. Since that afternoon, Candace has only talked to him by phone.

"Oh yes, he's here. That poor guy has put more holes in the ground than a whole family of moles." Marjory shakes her head, which Candace notices now is cropped shorter than ever before. The last sprinkling of black hair is gone and all that's left is white frizz.

They ride in silence along Route 35, with Candace examining the blank trees.

"Is this part of the area that's infested?"

"Well it is, but of course you can't tell, now that all the leaves have fallen. But you can see when you look closely at the piles of leaves. They're just tiny shriveled things, hardly the size of a quarter. We had no fall foliage at all." Another silence follows, and then Marjory laughs. "At least it kept us from having so much to rake." She slows the car, takes a careful right turn onto Undermountain Road. Only two miles to go, Candace thinks to herself.

"You know, that darling baby is making a liar of you," Marjory says, gesturing with her thumb to the back seat. "I mean, she hasn't made a peep since you strapped her in."

"Just wait," Candace says. "She always naps in the car. But you'll hear from her big time just as soon as we stop and she wants to eat. I call her Queen Bee."

"Oh?"

"Yeah, because when she cries, she sounds like she's leading a whole hive of bees."

The moment they arrive, in fact, Gretchen comes alive, red-faced and crabby, rooting side to side in a frenzied search for her mother's breast. Candace takes the squawling bundle out of the car seat and follows Marjory to the back yard, where Audrey is sitting in a lawn chair, draped in an afghan.

"Well, she's blessed with plenty of lung power, I'll say that," Audrey calls out from her chair. As Candace nears, Audrey reaches up, cups her palm lovingly around Candace's cheek, then reaches toward Gretchen. "Oh, my dear, when you said she was beautiful, you didn't tell me this," Audrey whispers. She gazes from Candace to the baby, and back, and then at Rusty, who is approaching from the side of the house with a shovel. "You know, of course, that she is completely our side of the family, through and through. Just look, the coloring she inherited from you. I'm afraid your mother doesn't show up in this child."

Candace is about to say, "Well, but she does have Mom's bad temper," when she stops herself. Her father has placed his soiled hand over Candace's shoulder, and now he's kissing her cheek, too. She can smell him, a familiar mixture of sweat and soil, and she feels the brush of his mustache dust her jaw.

"Hey, you wanna dig a hole, kid?" Rusty raises his voice to a soft pitch and tucks a grimy finger under the baby's chin. The wind comes up sharply just then, reminding Candace that the baby needs her bonnet. She digs into her jacket pocket and pulls out a corduroy hat.

"Dad, she's all yours, believe me, just as soon as I tie this under her chin."

"Oh no, great grandma gets to hold her first," Audrey declares, reaching up with both hands. Candace lays the baby in the folds of Audrey's afghan, but the crying only intensifies.

"Hey, is this any way to say hello to your great granny?" Audrey bounces the baby gently against her chest. "Come on now, sweetie. Hush up." But the crying persists, grows, takes on a raw edge, becoming so sharp finally that Candace intervenes.

"Oh, Gram, she bawls all the time," Candace moans, taking Gretchen back. "I'll try and feed her inside, and after she's done crying her eyes out, maybe by some miracle she'll nap in your lap." Candace smiles weakly and trudges to the house.

Inside the kitchen, Big Martha has whole wheat bread and an apple pie in the oven. And for dinner, she is assembling "cassoulet" using one of Pit's old recipes. "Please God that it works," Martha says, hugging Candace's shoulders with one arm. She turns to the baby. "I hope she's half as sweet as you when she grows up." Martha strokes Gretchen's head.

"I just hope...she grows up..." Candace says, settling onto the bench. Lifting her denim jacket and T-shirt, she attaches the baby to her nipple. Martha resumes her stirring.

"I'm glad to see that she likes her meals, just like Great Aunt Martha," she says, chuckling.

"OK, so what's cassoulet anyway?" Candace asks.

"Beans, lots of different beans, mostly," Martha replies. "And then of course there's goose and lamb, and beef mixed in, too. The important thing is to let it simmer all afternoon. Of course, your grandma would just as soon eat tofu and broccoli and brown rice, but when you're around me, kiddo, you know you are going to eat meat."

Candace closes her eyes, inhales the delightful aromas — baking bread, pie, the rich stew. It hits her now just how incredibly hungry she is, and how tired too. The pleasing mix of kitchen smells convinces her of something else: that she's made the right decision coming to the farm. Here at Maple Hill, Candace feels secure; she has people who care for her and the baby. Surely, these women — women she has been connected to all her life — will be able to help her with this difficult child. Even if they can't put a stop to the crying, they will be there to spell Candace, to take care of Gretchen for a few hours at a time, so that Candace can take a break. Candace is convinced that Gretchen will thrive in this supportive climate. And that Candace herself will improve, even recover. At the very least, Candace feels certain that she will finally get the rest she desperately needs.

She doesn't get any that afternoon, however. Audrey takes Gretchen in the rocking chair with her for a few minutes on the front porch. She tries a variety of positions, but still the baby keeps crying.

"Candace, you better come," Audrey calls. Candace is kneeling on the ground around the side of the house, placing daffodil bulbs into a trench her father has just dug around three slender birches.

"I'm coming, I'm coming," Candace replies, stabbing the soil with her trowel. She has enjoyed even this small space of time she's had outside, playing in the dirt. Of course, this couldn't last, she thinks, rising. She starts toward Audrey's chair, noticing that the sky has grown darker. The temperature is diving, too, and cold air is driving right through her jacket.

"Hey," Rusty calls out after her, "how about you keep digging, Candace, and I'll take Little Gretch?" Candace turns, shocked. Her *father* is offering to take the baby?

"Little Gretch, huh?" Candace smiles. When she was a child, Rusty was always coming up with ridiculous names. Candace Jean, for years, was Sweetie Pants, until Candace, at age fourteen, put her foot down. But this name, Little Gretch, has a certain appeal. It fits.

"Sure. Like a Little Witch, only different." Rusty drops his shovel and now he is tugging off his work gloves and wiping his hands on the back of his overalls. "I'd be happy to take her, unless it's feeding time of course, in which case, she's all yours."

"No, no, she's fed all she needs to. You can have her." Candace goes back to digging, placing daffodil bulbs in groups of three or four in the trench, careful to have the points face upward. Cupping one bulb in her hand, Candace watches her father disappear around the corner of the house, hunched protectively over the bundle in his arms. Wouldn't that be amazing, she thinks, if he were the one who succeeded in calming Gretchen down.

No more than five minutes later, Rusty comes trotting around the side of the house pushing the deep red wheelbarrow. It takes Candace a moment to comprehend that her father has got Gretchen riding inside. The baby is snuggled into Audrey's hunter green afghan, and she is wearing the grey papoose-style snowsuit that Eileen bought, one that looks like a tiny sleeping bag with two feet. Rusty yells to Candace over his shoulder.

"She loves it. Come see." Candace hurries to catch up with her father. When she does, and sees the baby bouncing up and down in the belly of the wheelbarrow, she reaches out, nervously trying to lay a hand on Gretchen.

"Slow down, Dad, or she'll flip out onto the ground." Candace is panting.

"Oh she's just fine, look at her. She's not going anywhere, and I swear, she loves it. Look at those eyes, she's taking in the whole sky." The baby in fact has a look of shock about her, as if the wheelbarrow ride snapped her eyes wide open and now has frozen them that way. Rusty runs the wheelbarrow three or four times around the backyard, up toward the trees, and down again. Finally, he stops, breathing hard. He is smiling proudly. The baby peers out of the sleeping bag, gazing side to side. Her eyes, now smoky blue, look large and unfocused.

"I always knew you were nuts," Audrey chuckles. She is leaning on her crutches, watching from the back porch. "Candace, what you need is a nice new wheelbarrow of your own."

"Oh right, instead of a stroller." Candace laughs. But when the baby's face screws up into the pucker that always precedes her crying, Candace quickly takes the handles of the wheelbarrow and moves it awkwardly around the yard. The side yard is smoother, so she pushes it there and then to the front yard, where she circles the Mother tree. The baby is quiet.

"See, it works," Rusty calls, joining her. "Maybe we ought to run her up the road."

"Oh, sure, Dad, like a load of top soil or something." Secretly, though, Candace is delighted to think her father has turned this time with Gretchen into one of his games. It's so typical of him. Rusty would always take a break from construction work when she was a kid and play something ridiculous. Often he would lay a two by four between two sawhorses and let Candace pretend she was a circus performer crossing the "high wire."

And so they proceed down the road together, jogging, walking, and pushing the baby-laden wheelbarrow along the rutted road. They laugh to see Gretchen's expression, one of pure confusion, when Rusty tries zigzagging quickly back and forth across a section of the road that is particularly rutted. By this time, Candace has lost all her fear that the baby will bounce out of the deep belly of the wheelbarrow. Soon after the bumpy ride, in fact, Gretchen starts yawning. Finally, she falls asleep.

The three of them continue up the road, Candace and Rusty taking turns walking the wheelbarrow and talking, mostly about the furniture business. Rusty doesn't ask any probing questions about the baby, and Candace doesn't offer anything, about the baby or herself, certainly nothing that would reveal how depressed she's been lately.

They are outdoors until late afternoon. When they finally push the wheelbarrow up the gravel driveway and into the barn, the sky is a smudged grey color, and the wind bites at Candace's ears. She hears the winter wind howl and she shivers.

"I smell snow," she whispers, lifting a sleeping Gretchen from the wheelbarrow. As she carries the baby, wrapped in the afghan, into the house, Candace has a depressing thought: she will pay dearly for the peace she's had this afternoon. If Gretchen has slept two or three hours and is still sleeping now, she is almost certain to be wide awake later, either after dinner, or worse, in the middle of the night.

Coming into the kitchen, Candace is greeted by the warm smell of food. Her mood recovers. She settles Gretchen in her infant seat, and takes a stem glass full of red wine from Marjory. The wine is clear and golden, and it feels sharp and refreshing as it passes, tingling, down her throat. She seats herself at the picnic table. Gulping deeply from the glass a second time, Candace realizes her lips are wind-burned from being outdoors; the baby, meanwhile, has raspberry color in both cheeks.

Dinner is a celebration of sorts, or at least it is to start. The women begin by thanking Martha for cooking dinner. And they thank Pit up in heaven for providing the cassoulet recipe. Then Marjory lifts her wineglass and welcomes Candace and the baby to the farm. Audrey thanks Rusty and Marjory for planting bulbs. These remarks, and the wine, start a flood of warm feeling pumping through Candace's arms. Another flood follows when Audrey goes to the trouble of standing up and placing Gretchen's infant seat in the middle of the table. Then she makes a long elaborate toast to Gretchen's arrival into the world.

"And let's not forget," Audrey says when she's concluded Gretchen's toast and replaced the infant seat back on the floor, "let's not forget a thanks to God — or to whomever, male or female, is hanging out up there keeping watch — for the last few days of decent weather. Now that my bulbs are in, I say bring the snow on, we're ready for anything."

"Or we're as ready as we can be," Marjory adds quietly.

"Well, at least we're all here, all together," Candace interjects happily. The warm flood from the second glass of wine is now turning her arms and legs numb. And with the alcohol, her tongue comes alive. "I'm just so thrilled to be here, you know with the baby and all. Maybe now, finally, she will start to sleep through the night."

From behind Candace's head comes a plate of food, set down in front of her with a slight clatter on the table. She glances at the stew Martha spent the whole day cooking. Next to it is butternut squash, the center tub floating in butter and maple syrup. Steam spirals from the food toward her chin. She eats in silence, and when she's finished her first plate, she asks for more.

"I guess the cold gave you an appetite," Rusty says, filling her plate again. She finishes it all, scraping every shred of squash off its skin. She has two pieces of bread, too, slathered in butter, and as she swallows the last bites, she begins anticipating apple pie.

And when Audrey wants to refill her wineglass, a third, and then a fourth time, Candace readily accepts. The wine makes her head swim, which is fine, because that means the rest of the dinner conversation passes over her, virtually unheeded. She feels no pressure at all to participate, or even to follow what Audrey is saying about the potter in Marlboro who is building all by herself and by hand, a 21-foot kiln. And by the time the conversation turns to politics, and Marjory is expounding on whether the new Governor will allow development in the northern-most forests of the state, Candace has quietly slipped away from the table.

Maybe it's the wine that does it, because otherwise, Candace is helpless to explain her change in mood after dinner. It happens just after she carries Gretchen upstairs and lays the sleeping child in her seat in a darkened corner of the bedroom. When she looks up, the first thing to greet her eye is the wall she tried painting in the spring. It has been five months since she touched a brush or a tube of paint, five months since Mrs. MacLish forbade her to work in oils at Redfield. After the baby came, she hardly thought about painting, except once or twice — that time Trish Bosco prodded her, asking if she didn't indeed long for her brush and canvas, and when Mark asked her, just a few days ago.

Candace has been so disconnected from her painting since Gretchen was born that she couldn't imagine ever picking up a brush again and just the thought of stretching a canvas exhausted her. Tonight, though, something has changed. Clearly she's still tired, and probably more so because of the wine. But the alcohol has relaxed her, too, and set a tingling going up her arms and legs, and that tingling has translated into a surge of creative energy. Staring at the wall, she decides to try painting it again. She reaches under the bed for the shallow card-board box that contains her paints and brushes and the palette her father fashioned for her years ago out of a huge birch he cut down in Audrey's backyard. Most of the tubes of paint are wrinkled and dry.

"Just black and white are left," Candace sighs, uncapping the only two tubes plump with paint. She rolls up the sleeves of her flannel shirt. Somewhere she used to have a smock, and there is that old T-shirt she could throw on, the one she wore when she first painted the wall while pregnant. But her memory is cloudy, and she doesn't dare take the time to look for the shirts, since the baby will be awake in no time. "No time," Candace whispers aloud now, glancing down at Gretchen sleeping in her seat. Squirting a small blob of black paint the consistency of toothpaste on her palette, Candace climbs on the bed and begins. She is smiling, and humming an old nursery song.

Soon, a black tree emerges, its upper branches thin and tapering. Another tree follows, a thinner one, and another, and before long, she has painted a stark winter forest, a throng of severe-looking black trees against a backdrop of snow. It's restful, Candace thinks, and it's a perfect setting for...she smiles...for an egg. As she sets to work again, the song she's been humming takes on words, and the egg takes its place nestled in the crook of one large bare bough, which vaguely resembles an oversized human elbow. In the next instant, Candace knows that this is no longer just an egg, but a face, too, a face connected to a small bundle. The bundle is a baby swaddled in a white blanket. With two quick black lines, Candace paints the baby's eyes as tiny slivers, almond eyes in an angelic face that crudely resembles Gretchen's own sleeping countenance.

With no announcement, the song Candace is humming comes fully alive, making itself known to her. "Rock a bye baby," Candace croons, "on the tree top, when the wind blows the cradle will..." and with that, her attention falls to the infant seat, which is now starting to rock. Her eyes firmly shut, Gretchen is squirming and thrashing, screwing up her face, and mouthing both fists. Any moment now, she will pour forth her first scream.

Candace's song drops off. Sighing, she lays her paint brush and palette aside and takes the baby on the bed, trying to nestle her at the nipple. At first, the baby acts hungry, even ravenous, and Candace, still flushed from painting, imagines feeding her and laying her peacefully back down, lulling her to sleep. That would be perfect, Candace decides: the child fills her stomach and then, thoroughly satisfied, she falls asleep, leaving her mother to work through the night on her painting.

Soon enough the trouble starts, though. The baby pushes the nipple away, spits the milk out, and bawls. She pulls her knees sharply up to her belly, and swings her head side to side, her face compressed in pain. One blushing cheek is smudged in black paint. Why, Candace wants to scream, why this, why me, why now, why is it things just seem to get worse and worse and worse? "This baby is a curse," she cries, her good mood evaporating.

Glancing at the wall, she decides that painting was clearly a mistake tonight, because for an hour or two, it made her feel quite sweet, truly happy, and now she aches with the loss of that good, right feeling. How could she have stayed away from painting for so long? How could she have thought she wouldn't return to this work, work that is as necessary to her as breathing?

She glares at the baby. It's all her fault I'm not painting, Candace thinks ruefully. Half-heartedly, she tries putting Gretchen back to her breast. A flood of hateful feelings rises up in Candace, an ugly flood of resentment that now begs for release. Staring at the bawling child, Candace wants only to drown out the sound. If there were only a way out, she thinks, blinking back the tears, if only I had someone here I could hand Gretchen over to, someone who could be trusted not to despise her as much as I do every time she screams.

Once more, she tries shoving the nipple into the baby's mouth, but the baby won't have it. Her mouth wide, Gretchen has fallen into a kind of stupor, a blind squalling worse than Candace has ever heard before, a regular razor of sound. Frightened by the cry, Candace lays the baby over her shoulder. The child's stomach is taut, and her legs are pulled back. "Oh goddamn you, I wish I'd never had you!" Candace shrieks, trembling now, immediately regretting her words. She is angry at herself for what she just said, for all the bad feelings that fill her, but she's glad too, glad that she has finally let it out.

Resting the baby against her chest, Candace kisses Gretchen's head. And now instead of anger she feels guilt, because she realizes that the reason the baby is acting so up much tonight is because she has gas, and the reason the baby has gas is because Candace ate two plates of Martha's bean stew. Taking a breath, Candace makes a valiant attempt to walk the floor, tries to calm the crying child so that all those sleeping in the house won't be wakened at 3:00 or 4:00 or whatever time of the morning it is. She paces back and forth across the room, staring each time at the painting on the wall. The tall tree that holds the egg reaches almost to the ceiling. Candace throws her head back and focuses on the uppermost branch. Only now does she see that the tree has a human shape, that its branches reach out like arms, and that the smallest branches at the tip of the bough extend like long bony fingers.

She walks the floor for more than half an hour, jostling the baby. The screaming keeps on. Stopping by the window, Candace separates the curtains. Snow is falling gently to the ground at a steady angle. Candace is mesmerized. Suddenly, she has an idea. Turning abruptly, she leaves the room and creeps downstairs, muffling the baby's crying against her chest.

She bundles the baby in the grey papoose, throws on a down jacket, and slips into Audrey's oversized boots. She grabs Audrey's afghan, too, and a flashlight and bracing the baby in one arm, she exits the house through the back door. Snow pelts her face in icy needles, melting almost immediately on her skin. Cold air fills her mouth. She hurries toward the barn, and setting Gretchen momentarily into the snow, she tugs at the heavy sliding door. It yields. She sprays the flashlight side to side and a snatch of red metal comes into view. Candace places Gretchen in the wheelbarrow, and soon enough, the two of them are lumbering down the bumpy road in the dark through the swiftly collecting snow.

Once again, the wheelbarrow works its wonders. Either that, Candace thinks, or the baby is buried in the afghan and has suffocated. Setting the handles down, Candace shines the flashlight into the dark hollow of the wheelbarrow. The light casts a ghostly glow over the baby's face. Two dark eyes, shocked by light, and a tiny pink mouth come into view, nestled into the green blanket.

"Rock a bye baby," Candace sings, her voice breathy as she pushes the wheelbarrow through the snow. As she finishes one round of the familiar lullaby, suddenly she is wondering something: why does this old song end the way it does? Why should a baby end up falling from a broken tree? The thought of the perverse ending puts a smile on her lips. "Somebody whose kid had colic must have written that song," she says, chuckling. With the word 'song,' Mark comes to mind, as does the song he wrote for her, and instantly, her throat catches. She misses Mark like crazy, especially now, in the middle of the night. Shivering, she grips the handles of the wheelbarrow tighter, pushes it faster. Jogging in the oversized boots is tiring, and soon she slows. As she does, though, the baby begins to cry again.

"Oh dear God, please stop," Candace screams, resuming the faster pace. She races as hard as she can, hopping along, her boots skating through the wet snow. Leaning forward, she gets the wheelbarrow going full speed, her heart pumping, her breath spewing white from her mouth. She is only going to go a few more feet, in fact, she has decided to turn back, she's thinking about how she'll maneuver the wheelbarrow around, when the deadly sound comes, the front wheel butts up against a rock or a rut in the road.

Instantly, the wheelbarrow pitches forward and to the side, disgorging the afghan and the infant. Candace is thrown forward. She lands on her side, her weight twisting her wrist so far back that her knuckles practically graze her arm. The ground smacks her knees together and her teeth clamp down hard on her tongue.

Candace screams, tasting blood as she cradles her wrist to her chest. Slowly, she rolls, tries to raise herself out of the snow. Pain cramps her wrist. Her mind blanks, and then she has a picture: the baby lies crushed and motionless beneath the wheelbarrow.

"Gretchen," she whispers, salty tears and snow and blood mixing all together now on her lips, and clouding her eyes. The skin on her face stings, burned by the frigid snow. There isn't a sound out of the wheelbarrow. Rising to her knees, Candace creeps along on one hand, clutching her other like a wounded paw below her breast.

"Where...where are you?" she whispers, sliding her good hand back and forth through the snow. In the time it takes to locate the afghan, she envisions the baby again. The image is disturbing, yet decidedly appealing too. The baby is lying peacefully in the snow, her tiny hands crossed over her chest. In this vision, Gretchen isn't injured at all. Instead, she is comforted by the carpet of snow on the dark forest floor. She looks like Mother Nature's dream child from a page out of a lullaby book, her cheeks rosy and glowing, her honey-colored eyelashes curled, a sweet smile calming her saintly little face.

Candace's hand bumps into the afghan and the flashlight, and as she struggles to snap it on, she collapses again on her side. Light floods the afghan, and in that moment the peaceful image she had a moment ago of the baby cradled and happy in the snow is erased, replaced by the horror of what's happened. "Where are you?" she cries out, and in that moment a muffled cry emerges from one lump of the afghan. Candace pushes through the blanket, thrashing her hand back and forth to try to locate the grey papoose. Candace is bawling hysterically now, her breath short and shallow, her face flushed in tears. She can see only two horrible possibilities: the baby suffocated or cracked her skull on the ground. Her crying turns wild, and in that moment, her hand passes over a curve of warm flesh.

"Oh God," she says, grabbing up the grey papoose to her lap with one hand. She sets her lips on Gretchen's forehead and kisses the soft skin over and over, all the while whispering "Are you? Are you...alive?" And then it seems the baby was saving up her crying, because Gretchen bursts forth in sound, her bawling emerges more raw and insistent than ever, seeming to suck in the whole world with every new round of tears. If health were measured in sound, then Gretchen's tumble to the soft snow on the ground did nothing but improve her, make her even better at crying. Clutching the grey papoose under her good arm, Candace rises to her knees and rolls slowly upward, holding her head low to anchor the baby to her chest. With her injured hand dangling at a peculiar angle at her side, she walks the baby back to the house, taking each step as though she

were walking on ice, and holding the baby as though she were a
piece of fragile Venetian glass.

EILEEN

September 9, 1972

Wine for breakfast!?? Wine for breakfast. Instead of orange juice, I poured myself a tumbler of red Burgundy at six o'clock this morning. I gulped the whole thing down. An hour later, I took the bottle back out and poured a second glass. I lay down. It's now almost eight thirty but I still haven't fallen asleep. So now I've just poured a third glass.

I hope the alcohol starts to work soon. Candace is asleep, so I need to be sleeping too. Because before long, she'll be awake. This couple of hours is my big and only break. I know that. But still I can't will myself to sleep. Maybe because I was up walking her most of the night. At one point, she was crying every fifteen minutes, or so it seemed. I had to fight to stay awake all night long. And now I can't let go of the fighting. I'm a wreck. In my worst dreams, I never thought having the baby would be like this.

Since I arrived home from the hospital last month, Candace has kept me up at least half of every night. I've stopped looking in the mirror because the last time I did, I looked just frightful, dark baggy circles, puffy eyes, and pale skin. It looks like I've been living holed up in a dark box. Which, when I think about it, describes my bedroom lately. The shades are always pulled down, and the room is chock full of my stuff, plus the baby's crib and cradle, a swing, a rocking chair, and a changing table.

I've got a routine. As soon as she wakes up, I sit with her in the rocking chair and turn off all the lights. I hold her against my shoulder.

I hum. I sing. I try everything I can think of: I pat her bottom, I rub her back. I gently massage her head. Sometimes I lay her face down over my knee. I rub her toes between my fingers. I massage her legs. Most of all, I try to remain calm, because the book I have says that babies pick up on their mother's nerves. When none of these things work, I tie her into the front of my bathrobe, tight against my chest, and walk back and forth beside the crib. She sleeps, but never for very long.

The last few days, I've decided something must be wrong. No baby should be awake so much. Yesterday I got so fed up, I called the doctor. First I spoke to his nurse. I told her I couldn't get the baby to stay asleep. She didn't say a word. Then I heard what I thought was someone laughing softly in the background. Still the nurse didn't speak. Finally, she said, "I'm sorry, dear, that you're having so much trouble. Would you like to bring the baby in?" I did, later in the morning. Dr. Fitch was polite, asked me if Candace was eating. I told him yes, six bottles of formula a day. He asked which formula, and I told him, Enfamil. He laid the stethoscope on her chest. He checked her ears, poked her belly. Then he spoke.

"I'm sure you'll be glad to know that there is only one thing wrong with your baby," he said, calmly playing with Candace's toes. My ears perked up. "The problem," he continued," is that your baby isn't even a month old." I looked at him, confused. "You see, most babies don't adopt a good sleeping pattern until they're at least two to three months."

But she won't sleep at all, I protested, and I could hear the whine in my voice. I felt like I might start sobbing right there in the pediatrician's office. I ran my hand through my hair, which needed washing. He shook his head. "I guess no one told you that new babies are notorious for not giving their moms much sleep?" He glanced down at my hand. Everybody looks for the diamond ring and the wedding band. I folded my fingers together. He was trying to be understanding, but it didn't help a bit.

"You have a lot to shoulder on your own," he said. "Sometimes new parents have a hard time keeping things together. They feel like they're drowning in responsibility." He slipped a bootie on one of Candace's feet. "Is there somebody in your family, somebody more experienced with babies, who can give you a hand?" At that, Candace started into a shrill scream. She saved me from doing it myself. Dr. Fitch, I wanted to yell, family help has not exactly been pouring forth. My father hasn't even touched the baby. My mother has held her twice.

I asked Ma the other morning if she didn't want to watch me give Candace a bath.

"Oh, that would be nice," she said, drying her hands. I could tell she really was dying to hold her. But just as I spread out the bath towel on the kitchen counter and laid Candace down, my father appeared at the back door. He glared at my mother as he walked in, and that's all he had to do. She turned away, just up and left the room. Later that morning, at the kitchen table, I could tell Ma had been crying.

"Do you want to hold her?" I whispered. Ma twisted a kitchen towel into a tight ring.

"Oh, you know I have so many things to do..." She pulled a lump of rumpled Kleenex from her pocket and blew her nose. I realized then how hard this is for Ma, too, what my father is doing. Basically, he has forbidden her to come near me. His strategy is to isolate me, to give me no help at all. Then he thinks maybe I'll come crawling for help. Or maybe he thinks I'll be so desperate I'll finally give in and tell Rusty that I want to get married. My father is nuts. He should open his eyes, realize that Rusty isn't exactly busting down the door helping me take care of Candace. Sure, he comes over every few days. He keeps me and the baby company, especially in the evening after dinner. And he says how much he wants to see Candace grow up. But down deep, I don't think he really wants to get too involved in the day to day headaches of raising her. He can see for himself that she doesn't even let me sleep.

Last night, after I told Rusty what Dr. Fitch said, he just shook his head. He told me he didn't know how I stay up night after night. I wanted to throw something at him. Instead, I said something that got us into a terrible fight. I asked him if he could possibly give me more money. He paid my hospital bill, but now all he's giving me is $25 a week. I told him I can barely squeak by on that. I mean formula alone costs a small fortune. "Rusty, twenty five bucks is peanuts," I said. His face got red and he crossed his arms over his chest.

"I'm not exactly rolling in dough," he yelled.

I should have held my tongue at that moment, but well, I didn't. I had to go on.

"You would be," I said quietly, "if you'd give up building those damn solar houses that don't sell. You could go out and get a real construction job."

That did it. He blew up. "Who the hell are you to tell me where to work?" he sputtered, turning crimson. I've never seen him so angry. "Goddammit, Eileen, I am not your doormat any more."

I got off my bed and went to check the baby. It was amazing that she could sleep through his thundering voice. But there she was, peaceful, a line of dribble leaking out of her mouth, forming a wet circle on the crib sheet. When I turned around, Rusty was half-way out the bedroom door. "I've gotta go," he said. But then he stopped.

"Look," he said, holding the door. "I'm sorry for getting mad. It's just, lately, I can't stand anybody else hounding me for money." I leaned against the crib. He went on. "You know, my father being out of work, he's driving me nuts about working harder. I keep telling him 'Dad, I've got a job. And I love it. So please, leave me alone.'" Rusty paused, looked at the floor, then up at me. "You know Eileen, the solar house thing is a whole new world for me. And I need to do it now...because..." he swallowed, hard, and looked out the door, then straight back at me, "because it's the only thing, besides the baby, that makes me happy."

"Sure," I said quietly. Ashamed, I wanted to apologize, to tell him how unfair it was of me to bug him for more money. Because clearly, he was doing the best he could.

The baby stirred in the crib. I leaned over, stroked her damp, red head. I started to say something but he was already talking.

"I'll see if there's a way I can pay you more, but I'm not promising anything."

"That's OK, Rus," I answered softly. I picked up Candace and laid her against my shoulder. "Don't worry about it. You've done enough." In that moment, I flashed on the two of us, Rus and I, when we were in high school, so carefree, so incredibly happy. We drove everywhere together in the red truck, Beatles music blaring from the radio. How much older we were now. I felt my throat swell. I wanted to cry. Maybe Rusty could tell, because suddenly he was walking toward me, with a funny look on his face. He reached out. For a second I thought he was going to hug me. I was half-wishing he would. But I think he got nervous. I looked away, and he just stood there. Finally, he laid his hand on Candace's back, briefly. Then he turned and left without saying goodbye.

I've lost my chance to sleep. Candace has the hiccups, which she often does. When that happens, it's only a matter of minutes before she wakes up. I want to cover my ears with a pillow. Or better yet, I want to fill a suitcase, head out, go anyplace. Leave the baby to my mother. No, when I think about it, I'd rather leave the little squalling bundle to my father.

CANDACE

It isn't morning, it isn't even close, when Candace reaches the driveway, clutching the baby awkwardly to her chest. The lights are on in the kitchen, and Candace finds a measure of relief in the familiar yellow glow coming from the windows. She is even more relieved when she notices movement. Somebody — Marjory, maybe — shifts, throwing a shadow across the kitchen window. Candace moves quickly to the back porch. The snow swallows the sound of her steps, muffling all noise, just as the dark has practically erased her face.

Exhausted, she reaches for the door before it occurs to her that she's using the wrong hand. "Oh Jesus," she groans, her injured left hand going limp. Pain coils to her armpit. Shifting the baby to her right hip, she lifts one knee to support the papoose tightly from beneath. Then she quickly flicks the door handle and enters the mud room.

Marjory, her forehead creased in worry, is peering through the window of the kitchen door. Her mouth drops. "God almighty, Candace, where have you been with that child?" She swings the door wide, clutching her robe close to her throat.

"Out," Candace mumbles. "I've been out." Her boots slop snow onto the farmhouse floor as she plods past Marjory and sets Gretchen on the picnic table in a sprinkling of snowflakes. Almost right away, the snow melts into miniscule puddles. Gretchen, her face pink, is sleeping, her eyelashes crusted over, her mouth appearing to be frozen open. Candace brings her right hand to her own face. It feels stiff and cold and wet. Her jaw hurts, too, and both knees ache where they smacked together on the ground.

In the next instant, she sinks to the bench and lays her forehead on the table. *How can I say what happened? How can I explain, so somebody understands, why it is I took Gretchen out in the snow, why I let her go spilling out from the wheelbarrow onto the ground in the middle of the night? No,* she thinks, pulling off her gloves, staring at her hands, bright pink, *this isn't going to make any sense.*

"My heavens, Candace, she's frozen," Marjory says, placing the back of her fingers against the baby's cheek. "What ever possessed you to...." Marjory shakes her head.

Candace glances up. The sight of the baby's face, so still, so cold, fills her with new dread. Is it possible that the baby was hurt after all tonight? Is it possible that she suffered some kind of head injury, a concussion? She bends close over the baby's face. Ice clings to her miniscule eyelashes.

"Oh, she is freezing," Candace whispers. Instinctively, she tries breathing warm air over Gretchen's statuesque little face.

"Candace, for God's sake, tell me what happened," Marjory says, taking hold of Candace's shoulder, as if to shake something, some explanation, out. Candace pushes Marjory away. She unzips the grey papoose. Then she turns, holds her injured hand up.

"I fell and I'm going to need help getting her out," she says matter-of-factly. Somehow, the sound of her own quiet words light some emotion in her, bring on the feeling she will start to cry. "I...I wasn't intending to...to hurt her." Candace begins, but she stops, the words choked off by tears.

"Oh, dear, now don't go getting so upset," Marjory says, taking over the papoose. When Gretchen is free of the bulky snowsuit, Marjory grabs an afghan and wraps the baby snug. Then she helps Candace off with her jacket and guides her to the living room and into Pit's rocking chair. She sets the baby in Candace's lap. "Here, just rock for a while, and I'll get you some warm milk. Audrey is feeling ill upstairs, so I have to check on her."

"What's wrong with Grandma?" Candace asks, settling back, conscious of her wet hair against the back of the chair.

"I'm not sure. She woke up a few minutes ago very nauseous. She says her stomach hurts. She must be coming down with something. I was just getting her some Pepto Bismol when you came in."

Candace sets her chilled feet on the lip of the wood stove, and for the next few minutes, while Marjory is in the kitchen heating milk, she closes her eyes and rocks, silently comforting the baby, piled high in the afghan, in her right arm. Gradually, the intense warmth of the stove, combined with her deep fatigue, calms her. Maybe, she decides, maybe it's safe to tell Marjory what happened after all. Maybe she could tell her about being up painting all night, and about how she decided, on the spur of the moment, to take Gretchen on the wheelbarrow ride, never expecting that she would fall.

Candace is just about to call Marjory back, to ask her to sit down, so she can explain the accident, when a strange combination of sounds arises. The noises are different, coming out of two places, but they find one home in Candace. Inside the afghan there is the familiar crackle, the baby's typical way of coming out of sleep. Candace is wired to this ragged sound, it has hounded her now for two months; but in this instant, Candace is thankful because it signals that the baby is actually awake, and sounding the way she normally does. And maybe that means she suffered no lasting effects from the fall.

In the same moment she is feeling a flood of relief, though, her attention switches focus to the other noise, the one drifting down the stairs. There is no doubt now that the second sound is coming from Audrey: a high-pitched whine, alternating with a piercing howl that might be from an animal in distress. The sound prickles Candace's neck. Marjory hears it too, because she rushes through the living room from the kitchen, pausing only long enough to lay the mug of milk on the wood stove. Then she hurries toward the stairs.

"Audrey," Marjory yells, pulling her maroon bathrobe up almost to her knees and taking the steps two at a time. "Audrey are you OK? Are you...oh...oh dear God Audrey why did you try to get up?" There is a crash, a loud thud. "Oh, Audrey, oh please Candace, Martha somebody, please please come quick!"

EILEEN

September 29, 1972

It is sometime about 3 a.m., dark, dark all around me except for this small circle of light I am writing in. Somewhere I read that sleep deprivation can make you crazy, and it has me surely, I'm not quite right because a few minutes ago, when Candace finally fell asleep and I set her in the crib, I laid my hand on the back of her head, which I often do — I love the curve it makes precisely beneath the palm of my hand, warm, the hair clinging sleek to her skull. (I dread writing this, but this is the truth, so I'll do it anyway.) I was gazing at the fine crown of golden red hair on her skull, I was watching the way it sparkles in the light, the v-shaped line pointing to the base of her neck, and I thought, (this is awful to write but all these nights for who knows how long I've been thinking it) I thought: this tiny, fragile baby's head could so easily be crushed by a boot, a foot, a heavy rock, a car tire, oh God imagine, a large truck; I could imagine the head squashed like a bloody pumpkin on the road. All I keep seeing is pieces of crushed skull...a puddle of grey brain...this is totally insane, I am completely *fucked* up, here I am squashing my own baby's head...maybe because I am in bed dead tired at three o'clock in the morning, after being up since five yesterday. And soon it will be time to rise again, another day, I've lost track of where one starts and one ends. So is it any wonder that here I am secretly wanting to do away with her, she feels like such an immense burden, too much for me. Maybe the best thing is just not to touch her head...

11 p.m. same day

After last night I needed a day like today, even if I did end up saying/doing one of the stupidest things of my whole life. When I woke at seven after four hours of sleep I decided that, considering my frightening feelings last night, I'd better get right up this morning, get out as soon as I could. The leaves were gold, crimson, orange, the sky blue blue blue and so much wind was in the air, it whisked right through me. It made me feel, for a few minutes at least, that the breeze was going to wash bare all bad feeling.

I think it was eight-thirty when I dressed Candace in a pink sweater suit and put on her matching hat, and bundled her in a blanket. I went to the garage, where my mother's friend, Viola DeMaggio, had left a carriage for me. It's been stored there for weeks, but when I first peaked at it I thought, Jesus, who would ever want to use that monster, it looks like a white hearse. Four feet long, and waist high, it's got a shiny exterior and big rusted wheels bouncing on immense curved springs. Vi and her baby used to strut around the neighborhood with that thing twenty years ago. It fit Vi, who's always been a big woman, but I'm not sure it fits me.

Today, though, I was really desperate to get out, so I laid Candace inside, surrounded her with the blanket, and backed the carriage out to the gravel drive. We walked right into the center of town. With the sun shining down, it felt warm, and by nine, my spirits were picking up, so I decided to stop at the little diner near Grey's and have a cup of coffee. I parked the little hearse, and off we went into the diner. Of course, every head at the counter there spun around. I thought I recognized some guy my father knows, puffing away on a cigarette, but he didn't show any signs of knowing me, so I decided to go about my own business.

I ordered coffee, and then the smell of bacon and maple syrup made me hungry. I splurged, ordered French toast, sausage patties, but of course just as the food came, Candace woke up. I ate fast, bouncing her all the while in my left arm, which is why I guess I ended up spilling the orange juice, because my left elbow knocked into the plate and the plate tipped the glass. So there I was, as embarrassed as I could be, covered in juice, the thighs and crotch of my jeans soaked, and I had to get up, my ass all wet, with Candace squalling the whole time, and dry myself off with a napkin. I paid the bill, and grabbed one last square of French toast. This whole time nobody had talked to me, except for the waitress, but now as I walked past the counter red-faced, heading toward the door, the guy my father knows leaned back on his stool for a second and muttered something to me, and pointed.

I thought he was pointing at my chest, and for a moment I thought what he said was, "You forgot with babies you can't do that," which seemed strange: why would this guy say something so personal. It stopped me, and for one bizarre instant, connecting him to my father, I got paranoid, I actually thought maybe he was there as my father's spy.

"Look, I can do anything I want to," I said, my cheeks blazing. I didn't think I was that loud, but it was clearly loud enough, because suddenly the whole diner fell silent. That got me feeling bolder, I was just about to set this guy straight, I was going to say, "Hey, if I want to eat breakfast in a goddamn diner with my baby, I will and nobody can stop me."

Fortunately, though, I kept my mouth shut. The guy's eyes narrowed, and he looked confused and then he shook his head and pointed again and said, a little louder this time: "Lady, what I said was, you forgot the baby's hat." My eyes dropped to the floor and I hurried back for the pink hat, muttering a quick "Thank you" on my way out the door. And as the hearse and I rushed back up the street, I wanted to die, shout, vomit, scream, put wings on my feet, take off somewhere, fly someplace far away, much farther than California.

CANDACE

Morning comes to itself in a pure white solid, snow meeting snow against a blank sky. Candace, blank herself, sits beside the window, rocking, legs and lips flaccid and parted, cheeks chapped, streaked and teary, eyes attached to the short flakes passing at a steady angle outside the window. Her wrist is lying in her lap, a swollen ring of blue and yellow pain. Her mother's journal is face down on her knees. She cringes at the thought of reading one more word of Eileen's journal; and yet, something continues to pull her through the pages.

Gretchen is asleep now, in her infant chair, the first time all morning. It took nearly two hours to settle her down after the commotion of the early hours, when Marjory and Big Martha tried to hoist Audrey up, to carry her fireman style, because she'd fallen to the floor. But when it became clear that they needed more help, that Audrey, in agony with some kind of abdominal pain, needed immediate medical attention, Marjory called for an ambulance, which took nearly a half hour; all the while Candace listened to Audrey upstairs alternately moaning and yelling out for relief. Finally, the siren roared up and blue lights twinkled against the ceiling. The siren outside stoked up the siren within, so that while the stretcher passed through the living room carried by two men in oversized blue jackets, the baby screeched and Candace, one wrist useless, was all but helpless to quiet her back down. At one moment, it occurred to Candace to stop the EMTs, to hold up her wrist, to show them that she, too, needed medical attention. But when the men in blue brought Audrey through the living room, Candace only squeezed her grandmother's hand.

Holding a wailing Gretchen in one arm, Candace watched Marjory and Martha silently follow the stretcher out the front door. Marjory, looking tinier than ever, wore her bathrobe under her down jacket. Big Martha wore her cowboy boots, a bulky Ecuadoran sweater over her red long johns, and over all of that, a flared black cape.

Only when the house was empty again, when the clots of snow from the EMTs' boots melted into puddles on the rug, when the last of the siren evaporated in the white drifts surrounding the house, and Candace was peering out into a night gradually giving way to a day of grey nothingness, only then could Candace turn her attention fully to quieting Gretchen down. She paced with the baby around the braided rug. Then she tried nursing her, to no avail, tried jostling her, tried rocking her, tried settling her in the baby seat, and finally, in desperation, decided to sling her one-handed up and over her shoulder, in what suddenly seemed so appropriately named "the dead baby carry." Candace, by then, was sobbing every time a vision of Audrey's face, distorted by pain, came into view.

Mindlessly, Candace lowered a crying Gretchen onto the rug and removed a diaper that was soaked hard and cold with urine. With her left hand useless, she had to rely on her teeth to open the tabs on the clean diaper. Raising herself into the rocking chair, Candace placed the diapered Gretchen face down across her knees, bounced them and simultaneously drummed on the child's back, trying to ease the baby free of hiccups. It was in that position, on her belly, that Gretchen fell asleep, and woke, and fell asleep again. Finally Candace felt the baby's body go limp, slump into the dead weight of deep sleep. She lifted the child into the infant chair, and with her boot, nosed the chair across the rug closer to the wood stove.

"How will I manage with this baby alone?" she asked out loud, gingerly testing the puffy bruised flesh of her wrist. The movement sent a shock of pain up her arm. She knew the best thing would be to take Tylenol and try to sleep, because she hadn't had any rest all night, and because the baby might wake again at any time. But she couldn't, because every time she closed her eyes, Audrey's white face would arise there, and Candace would get scared. "Oh, God, please, let Grandma be OK," she whispered. "Please, please, let everything be all right."

Staring out the window, Candace sits now in the rocker, wondering where the women are, how far they've gotten, how beastly a drive it was for Martha, who would have had to maneuver the old station wagon through the unplowed snow. There are two hospitals, equally far away, one in Bennington and the other in Brattleboro. Knowing her grandmother's preference for the latter, Candace is sure that Audrey directed the ambulance there, where she is probably lying now in the emergency room.

"Promise you'll call as soon as you know something," Candace had yelled out to Marjory as she trailed Audrey on the stretcher. When she got no response the first time, Candace screamed louder at the back of the tiny figure.

"Marjory!"

"Yes, yes, of course I'll call," Marjory screamed back, and without even turning, she disappeared into the boxy white ambulance.

Candace is clutching a ball of Kleenex now, holding it up to her runny nose. She seems more alone than she ever has in her life. She has a chill, a stomach ache, maybe a fever too, and worse of all, the wrist pain is growing more intense. With Audrey and the others away, it will be at least tomorrow before Candace can see a doctor or get an X ray. Ordinarily, she could call her father. But he has gone to New York City to do a custom cabinet job, and will be out of town for at least three days. That leaves only two people to call: Mark or Eileen. Candace hovers in indecision between them, trying to decide which one of the two she minds calling less.

"I guess I'll just wait," she mutters finally, and begins shivering. Sinking deeper into the rocker, she brings her good arm up across her wet eyes and leaves her arm over her hot brow. Closing her eyes, she's got a vision of bare white snow, and the wheelbarrow, tipping over. Candace runs her hand through her hair, and thinks vaguely about getting up out of the chair, going upstairs for two Tylenol. All I really need is sleep, she says, or at least rest. Maybe the best way to fall asleep is to read. She picks up her mother's diary from the floor, and lies on the couch, where she reads a few pages, and then sleeps, soundly, for most of an hour.

EILEEN

October 9, 1972

I've got three letters in my lap, all arrived today, all saying the same thing, in one way or the other: come back to California. And I've got the atlas open to a map of San Francisco Bay, because John wrote me that he moved to Sausalito, of all places, he's living there right on the water. It's a mystery to me how he commutes to school in San Francisco. Maybe he's sailing back and forth to school; after all, he did say he's living on a boat, a boat, for God's sake, he is actually living on a boat. He's no fool. I can just see him floating out on the open water, face and feet up in the hot sun, sipping beer, improving his tan while staring at a pathology textbook under a clear blue sky.

And here I am, fighting for two lousy minutes a day to comb my hair or ten minutes to take a shower. I have turned into a feeding machine, too tired to think, too tired to do anything but eat, drink and catch a few winks of sleep whenever I can. Face it, I am chained to twelve pounds of baby flesh. And I hate it, not her, but *it*, the being chained, the horrible boring routine: I put the food in and then wait to wipe up what comes out the other end.

These are a few of the things I've grown to detest: the nasty buzz of the clothes dryer, the washing machine spinning, the odor of bleach in laundry, my mother frying onions and garlic in sputtering oil at the stove, and last, but not least, of course, the baby's incessant crying. Some days (and nights) I want to scream, kick, swear, shout, cry, throw things, and lately, I have. I smashed some dishes the other day, just because they were in the way. And the worst thing was, my father didn't say a thing. I know he saw me, and heard, because he burst into the kitchen right after I started cursing at the top of my lungs over and over again, as if I were singing an aria. When I saw my father's shocked face, I began flinging plates into the sink, two-handed, sent them crashing down. I looked around. He stared at me, his chin jutting out the way it does, and I glared back, and he raised a fist at me, shook it in my face. Then he left, holding the newspaper he had been reading, folded to the sports page.

I'm on the brink of doing something awful. I have had it, I have had it, I would be glad to go anywhere, I cannot stay here, because it is clear I will kill myself or someone else if I do. Who knew things could be this bad, who knew being a mother would drive me totally out of my mind. If I had, I would have done anything (yes, Corinne, anything) to avoid it. I feel a little sad writing this, but it's true. Becoming a mother means giving up everything you've got, or ever had, or ever wanted to be, all for the sake of somebody else, for another human being. In this case, it's twelve pounds of crabby, crappy flesh. That sounds terribly selfish, I know, but how could anybody choose to be chained the way I am now? The question is not whether I go, but how soon, and do I dare take her with me? Because if I don't, I'll probably miss her night and day. (She is, after all, twelve pounds of crabby flesh that came from me.) But if she comes along, then what? I will surely end up nuts, taking care of Candace and working full-time. An unbearable load, for sure. But at least I still have a job if I want it…the second letter was from Alta Bates, the guy I worked for at the hospital writing to say he hoped I would be coming back. He was counting on me to return to my job as a ward clerk.

And at least, if I go, I know I have a place to live. Barbara Cicero will take me in, her letter was the third, saying as much. She mailed it from San Jose, where she was attending some conference for nurses and midwives. Reading the letter, I began longing immediately for Berkeley — her tall, white wooden house, the two stately palms, the quiet, fragrant yard, the plum trees, the artichokes with the purple flowers in the garden. I could see Barbara's face, and I wanted so much to be back with her and Waldy and their baby. The letter was short, but very caring, and when I got to the last part, I read it over and over and practically cried. It said: "I know you think we weren't serious when we said you could come back, could move into our third floor, but the offer still stands, the door is always open, consider our place yours." I read the words and they went straight to my heart, I thought, yes, I will, I will go, I will show my father, and he and my mother can go to...and then, suddenly I heard the baby crying and my insides went all tight and still, because I can't imagine leaving her, and I can't imagine taking her and God knows what I will do.

I just read the letter from John for the fifth time. He wrote it on the boat. I can feel the waves rocking him around, slapping up against the shiny teak side as he floats. What can I say, he's the very same John, acting the same way he did in the old days, descending into my life from out of the blue, never failing to bring me goose-bumps. I love him for always being ready to whisk me off on some crazy adventure, sailing on the ocean, biking, driving to Newport or Maine in the middle of the night. Well here it's been months, and not a word from him, ever since the night at the Claremont. And even after I wrote a month or so ago, to tell him about the baby being born, I didn't hear a word. So I thought, end of story, I gave him up for good. But now he writes, says he sorry he's been so busy or he would have gotten in touch before. "But I'm glad the baby thing went OK, not too painful or gory, (be assured, working at the hospital I've seen my share of births, for what it's worth, I wouldn't do it in a million years), but clearly you did fine, not too much yelling I take it? Anyway, now that it's over, what are you doing for fun? And when do I get to see you again?"

For fun, John? For fun I would take a gun and blast my way out of this place. For fun, I would erase the last eight months and start over. Fun, John, isn't a word I remember anymore. It isn't part of my vocabulary. Not right now. But it will be again. Soon. Very, very soon.

EILEEN

October 13, 1972

He found me. He found this. He found this book beneath my mattress. How could he? How could he? How could he read me? He read some parts out loud. He screamed them, he plowed them into me like sticks. He ripped pages. He read them, I heard him shout my words out loud.

My eye, beneath my eye that's swollen shut, beneath my eye rises a rainbow of bruised flesh: yellow, blue, purple, white, a tinge of green.

He hit me. He hit me. He wouldn't give my journal back to me.

I cannot cry. I cannot cry. Not anymore. I am lying on the floor. I have the baby next to me. I have the baby next to me. I have the door locked.

I wasn't ever going to hurt her. I didn't mean to try. I...I cry to think...I tried to make him think I could.

But I...he came at me. I found him in the kitchen reading me. He was reading every page, every word of me. Rage was shaking through my hands, bellowing up, my body throbbing...a fire erupted out of me.

I was lying there, lying on the page. I was lying there, completely naked, my whole was pasted bare. I still see him there, sitting nonchalantly at the table. I came in, completely unaware. I had Candace sleeping in my arms. I came in to get her bottle. I touch the handle of the refrigerator door, I see him...turning pages, some book, some kind of black book. I pay no mind. But then I hear him swear. *Crap*, he says. *What a lot of crap.* I look up, and there...he's reading where

I slept with John…I am looking at my book, *my* book…my own father is reading me. My father is seeing me my journal he is read-ing everything I lived thoughtsaid livedthoughtsaid he has read it all.

I scream my blood wants to boil out.

Where where where did you get I can't I…get breath…sound I grab, he pulls the book away I can't…no words come out no breath.

My it's *mine* it's MY book. *Give me my book* he looks around at me. I see a snake in him, boring, an eye is boring into me.

He waves the book the pages flutter

I. I. It. It. I. Eye. Eye see a knife. I…a small knife is lying on the counter on a cutting board.

Give it back to me, I whisper. I whisper, croak, my throat hurts. *Give it!* I scream I scream a scream of breath is all. Candace cries. I drop the bottle falls and shatters shatters.

GIVE IT TO ME NOW. I lunge he pulls away. I gouge his arm he slaps my face he holds the book I scream *GIVE IT TO ME* I bite I grab the knife. I grab the knife I grab I say

ILLL KILLL YOUUU he jumps away I say *NO ILL KILL YOU* he's at the door.

put it down.

give me my book

put the knife down

give it to me.

put it down and put the baby down too.

WHY? YOU THINK I MIGHT HURT HER? I scream, I seem… some-body else is streaming through me. A red river of fire is in me. I hold the baby and a knife. I hold the baby, my baby, I could…her life is in my…her head, her head is so…I hear how hard she's crying. My mother is all black by the back door. Holding a bag of groceries. Coat. Kerchief tied. Sagging chin. Her mouth opens in the window. Terror widens her eyes. Furrows her brow how sad how sad she's had to live with him I will gladly kill him for her for me. GLADLY.

I glance away and instantly he lurches across the kitchen at me, cracks my wrist and smacks my eye. I oh I oh eye ohmygod I *HURRRTTT.*

the knife falls, sticks point-first into the linoleum floor.

ohmygod, I yell he yells

You go to hell you whore.

I hold the baby I hold the baby she cries my mother screams I hold the baby I am sitting on the floor he drops the black book at my feet.

You goddamn whore!
No, Frank, my mother yells. No more, Frank, please.

Some pages, ripped free, shredded, he lets them dance freely down on me. My mother is yelling *jesusmaryandjosephpleasegod please Frank nomore of this please she's your daughter* she's at the back door *jesusmothermary and joseph please no more.*

I gather pieces. Me in papered shreds. I gather me in pieces and crying, I surprise myself by throwing up all over, I swim in it, a pool of my own vomit on the floor. Still. I am still. I stuff me, all my vomity pieces I stuff me what's left in pockets. I pick me up, my head, I try to, I try to...I must be too sick to...

I lie down. I lie down. I cry, I want to drown the sounds around me. My mother crying, my mother praying *jesusmary and joseph please no* more my mother screaming my father screaming louder WHORE, *she's a goddam good for nothing slut a WHORE.*

me? Is he saying me? She is crying begging *no more Frank please no no more.*

I lie here on the floor. I have locked the bedroom door. I kiss the baby's head. She needs me. She needs me. She is sweetly eating. She needs me, plain, simply, she needs me to feed her a bottle.

FLIGHT

When Candace wakes, it isn't because the baby has been crying, but because she herself has been moaning, bellowing in her sleep, first yelling the word "water" over and over, and then, just as she is coming to, she switches to "hot...hot...oh god I'm so...hot." Indeed, she is rolling side to side in a puddle of her own making, sweat pooled inside her flannel shirt. Her cheeks are raw, gritty, her throat aches and her mouth is cottony and dry. When she opens her eyes, she realizes her head is pounding, too, as if somebody were driving giant screws right into her eye sockets.

She drags herself upright, supporting her swollen wrist. Leaning back on the couch, she opens her mouth, licks her cracked lips. Flu, she thinks, I ache so much, I must have the flu. She runs her good hand through her hair, then traces her thumb back and forth across the line of pain in her head. Closing her eyes, she sees a sky twinkling in bright red. She presses one finger against each of her lids, and the spots go blue. She tries to focus, to figure out what to do. Glancing to the floor, she sees the diary, recalls vaguely the scene in which her mother threatened to hurt her with a knife.

She shudders, raises herself from the couch, makes her way upstairs. Settling herself on the closed toilet seat, she searches the cabinet beneath the sink. A plastic basin. A toilet plunger. A can of cleanser. A couple damp sponges. A few twisted, soiled rags. She pulls open every drawer, and finally, in the last one, finds Tylenol. Opening the bottle, she pops three tablets in her mouth, cups her good hand under the faucet, then gulps the medication down. She studies the back of the bottle, and then pops three more. Cupping her hand again, she splashes icy water on her perspiring face.

Candace catches sight of herself in the mirror. She winces. Skin the color of dishwater. Stringy yellow hair, glued to her head like matted straw. Glassy eyes encased in black shadows. Raw cracked lips. The lips part, and suddenly, she laughs. "A face to scare the wolves away," *she whispers, then covers her mouth with her chapped hand. Her dark eyes look haunted. She stares at herself, recalling a day some months back when she stood naked before her bedroom mirror at home. That's before, she thinks, counting the months back. That's before, when the baby was safe inside, when the baby was nothing but my pride and joy, when she (because I was sure it wasn't a he) was still an ideal, my very own thought, nothing more, nothing more than art, a perfect mental form just swirling in my mind waiting to be born.*

Pressing a towel to her face, Candace hears the loud, disconnected whimpering that precedes the baby's cry. Oh God. Once, just once, why couldn't she just stay asleep? Candace drags herself downstairs and stands, feeling strange, almost dizzy, watching the weeping child squirm in her infant chair. The feet in tiny pink socks, the scrawny legs pump, the pumping limbs soon forcing the chair into motion. The baby's face is bright red, her scalp, her whole head is flushed pink beneath a thin net of golden hair. Tears, large and clear and as round as beads, slip down her cheeks.

You need to feed her, Candace tells herself. You need to feed her. Oh yes, sure. Of course I do. She's hungry. I need to feed her. I do. But even as she is thinking how she will proceed, how she will somehow manage to find the strength to pull the child into her lap, how she will struggle, one-handed, to unfasten her nursing bra, how she will attach the child to her breast, how she will give her fluid she isn't sure is there, even as she is mentally going through each step in the whole familiar routine, something altogether new is taking over in Candace. She has the feeling that she herself is fading away, that her mind isn't there, or if it is, that it is thoroughly bare, disconnected from all sense of feeling. She can't focus, nor is she able to heed completely the baby's cry. Nor can she hear clearly anymore the voice insisting on the baby's need for food. Candace drops to the couch, eyes shut, head swirling, her good hand against her forehead. Suddenly, above the baby's howling, she hears a different voice, a drone, an insistent monotone. "Choose," *the voice says.* "You've got to choose."

Candace stares at Gretchen from a growing distance, stares at the tiny rocking chair, now bouncing back and forth, the baby's legs flailing wildly in the air. A movie. That's what this is, Candace decides, a movie, and it's in me and around me. I am within it but watching it too. Candace focuses on the baby's face, her head, now bologna pink beneath her hair. How long, she wonders idly, how long will this baby scream? How long will the mother in the movie allow the baby to cry? How long will the movie flash across the screen? The questions are curious, irrelevant. The baby's screaming has taken on an academic twist, as if Candace is observing Gretchen in a painting, or reading about her in a book.

How long she sits there, staring at the baby, it is hard to say. In Candace's state, it could be a minute, an hour, three, a whole day. The phone rings. Candace reaches for the receiver, but when she picks it up, she doesn't say hello. Finally, the other voice, her mother's, calls from far far away, from deep beneath the baby's screams. "Hello?"

"Hi," Candace says, her voice as small as she's ever heard it before.

"Candace? Honey is that you? Are you OK? Why is the baby screaming like that?"

Candace sniffles, gazes down at her wrist. Gazes down at the baby, too, her twisted little face wet and almost as purple as the wrist. Gretchen is screaming like a hyena, and rocking so hard that her little chair looks ready to tip over. "I..." Candace tries to speak, but can't.

"Candace, what's wrong? Where's Audrey? Who's there with you?"

"No one," Candace whimpers, swallowing, feeling something clot her throat. "Candace, you've got to talk to me honey. Do you want me to come up? I could. I..."

Oh God then she would see me, Candace thinks. Then she would see me. See me like this! Candace shrinks, whispers no. No, Mom, she says, calmly placing the receiver back in its cradle, just as Eileen is saying something more, "I can be there in no time I..."

Candace slides onto the living room floor. The baby is quiet, has cried herself to sleep. Candace touches the infant seat, idly rocks it once or twice, then places her hand on the baby's face. Gretchen, too, is burning hot. Maybe, Candace thinks, maybe she too has a fever. The flu. Maybe she got it from me. A dark thought, like a shadow, passes across Candace's mind. For a moment, she is clouded by confusion: I am the baby's mother. There is no other person here. Clearly, she is sick. She has a fever. And I...there is something I should do. But what? Wiping her eyes, Candace yawns. Lies down. Sidles up to the infant seat. Cupping her hurt hand to her chest, she curls into a fetal position on the floor.

Across a span of twenty years, through a door of time, another mother is herself fetal on a bedroom floor. Her hair is black and thick in waves. It may

be a trick of the light, but today the highlights look more blue than brown. When she raises her head, the shroud of hair parts, and one wet swollen eye emerges: it too, like the hair, is black and vaguely blue. She kisses the baby sleeping pressed against her chest. Heaving, she drops back to the floor. She thinks to herself, I can't cry anymore. Her hands are joined, as if in prayer, around a book, which is even blacker than her hair.

Suddenly, a fury erupts at the bedroom door. Someone rattles the handle. Pounds.

"Open up. Please, Eileen." The handle rattles. Then silence. The voice resumes, plaintive. "Eileen, honey, please. You can't stay in there forever. You gotta eat. Think about the baby, she's gotta eat. Please, please open up. Don't let your father come up...don't..." The woman's voice falls off. A man's voice replaces it.

"You come out of there right now or I'll break the goddamm door down."

"Frank, no, please, oh, God, what...what is that? What are you...Dear God, not that. Oh, Frank, please, don't..." the woman wails, crying now.

"You just stay out of the way and be quiet," the man says. The woman lets out a small sharp scream, and there is a scuffling at the door. Then a thump to the floor, followed by silence. "Get up. Get up." The woman is crying louder. "Lucy, get up. Get off the floor." The woman cries harder, her voice sharper, in more agony. "OK, then, sit there if you want. Look, she's been in there almost three days and all you can do is stand there and tell her she's gotta eat? You think she's gonna listen to you? She's nuts. She's not gonna listen to you. But she's gonna listen to me." The woman's crying is muffled. The pounding starts up again, harder, and with it, the man's voice comes roaring through the door. "Look, you goddamn whore." The woman cries out again, her voice near the floor, her voice creeping under the door like smoke, reaching Eileen where she lays, her one eye swollen, the other eye wide open.

"I'm gonna give you exactly five minutes to get your ass off that floor and open this door. You hear me? Because if you don't, you're gonna see this ax chop the door in half. And if you think I'm kidding, try me." The ax comes crashing through the wood. Eileen cringes, her swollen eye opens a crack. She sees the wood splinter, sees the edge of a shiny blade poking through the door. She doesn't move.

❦

But Candace does. Gretchen is awake, her cry raging, piercing, incessant. Candace has been watching Gretchen for an undetermined amount of time. But *now, it seems the noise, or perhaps the reddish purple color of the baby's face, prods her into action, or at least, it prompts her to change her point of view. Candace stands, glances out the window. Oh, she says out loud, ohmygosh, how lovely. Her voice is unnaturally light, sweet. Oh my, just look at the snow. How beautiful. The snow in fact has stopped falling. The sun is casting a dazzling bright light on the white yard around the farmhouse. The sky is the purest blue. On the Mother tree, a few bright yellow leaves, leftovers of autumn, swivel from one branch. How I'd love to paint them, Candace thinks. One leaf comes unhinged in the wind, cascades gently into the soft white snow below.*

Again, though, the sound is all around her. The baby, her sharp, escalating cry. Candace frowns, glances down. Eyes the infant chair, rocking madly. Candace scoops the grey papoose off the coat rack, kneels, and manages one-handed to maneuver the baby out of the chair and into the papoose. Gretchen's crying falls off, is replaced by shuddering sighs, an occasional hiccup. The baby's face is tulip pink, plastered wet in tears. Candace zips the bag, tightens the string, leaving only the child's swollen eyes and her mouth exposed. Candace cups her hands over her mouth, rocks, rocks, rocks back on her heels, then comes forward onto her knees and lays her forehead right on the floor. When she comes up again, she is teary. "Time to go," she says. "Time to get out of here."

Candace slips into boots, a jacket, wincing as the sleeve passes over her injured wrist. She finds mittens, a hat. Curiously, the baby eyes her quietly from the table the whole time Candace gets dressed. When Gretchen is back in the infant seat, Candace opens the door. A crisp wind sweeps up her nose, bringing a whiff of wood smoke from the stove. Candace gazes over the backyard, trying hard to focus. The yard is enveloped in golden light. She inhales, feels slightly dizzy, confused. Exactly why did I come outside, she wonders. Exactly what am I supposed to do? Something. Something. I know I have to do something. A ring of heat rises around her neck, up through her cheeks. She shudders, feels sweat collecting, drop by drop in the hollows beneath her armpits.

Slowly, she descends the steps, the infant seat hooked on her arm. Bent by the weight of the baby, Candace proceeds around the yard. She makes a large circuit around the birch trees, then retraces the circle, twice more, each time placing her boots in the same footprints she made before. On the third trip, she reels slightly, and raises her face toward the trees. She squints as something drips onto her forehead. She looks up. A layer of snow on the branch is melting, drop by drop. Shifting slightly, Candace opens her mouth, lets the snow water in. One...two...three...four drops fall. Then nothing. Then two more cool drops. One drop smack in the eye. She takes a step backward. She realizes her headache has all but gone away.

And then she remembers. I'm sick. I've got the flu. I ache. And the baby. Yes, Gretchen, too, is sick. She sets her teeth into her bottom lip. She takes a step forward once more, feels another drop of water, this time in the center of her forehead. At that second, an ungodly scream pours out of Gretchen's mouth. Startled, Candace stares down at the child's face. The baby's eyes are covered by the papoose. Everything in the baby is erased except for her mouth, and that is opened wide.

Oh, dear. Oh god. Please no. No more of this. Candace covers her ears, overwhelmed with the desire to hide. But no, no. I've got to go for help. She walks slowly around the yard. She stops, considers how far it would be to walk the length of Undermountain Road. Two miles, maybe three. No. I can't do that with you, she thinks, staring at the baby in the chair. I can't do that at all, but especially not with you.

Suddenly, she is staring at the Mother tree, its branches stately, dominating the front yard. The lowest limbs, layered in snow, look to be arms draped in something, something soft, something cottony white, a shawl, or better yet, something comforting, safe, a white blanket and a pillow. The snow is melting evenly. Water drips steadily from the warming bark. The sight of it hearkens Candace back to spring, to snow melting, to sap steadily filling up the pails.

Slowly, she carves a trail of footsteps toward the tree. Maybe you could help me, she whispers, placing her face against the grey rivulets of bark. Maybe you could do something for me, for me and Gretchen, because she's sick, and I am too, and I…I can't quite, no I can't quiet her…you see…she is crying and she won't ever ever stop, and I can't…if I could…if I don't leave, I mean, I can't go for help and carry her too. I wouldn't do this, leave her, unless I had to. But I have to go, so…if you could, if you wouldn't mind… Stepping back, Candace hooks the infant seat securely over the lowest limb. The seat swings, and Gretchen rocks, and screams. Candace doesn't say another thing. She turns, a peaceful smile tying her lips. The sound of the baby's crying already seems distant as she hurries out of the yard.

❦

The door shatters rather easily. It's painted white, and it is quite dry, actually brittle, and the ax comes through in a few strong blows. Staring at the splintered wood, Eileen thinks that blade could hurt you, that blade, *glinting in the wood, it could really hurt you. She pulls the baby tighter. Eyes closed, she hugs the black book, and the baby, tightly with both arms.*

But another arm, shadowed by curly grey hair, squeezes through the door. Thick callused fingers fumble with the lock. The handle turns, the door kicks open, shuddering as it does. Eileen can't help herself. She laughs. She laughs, and immediately, she shrieks. She tries to hold the baby with all her might. But her arms are wrenched apart, her wrists twisted hot. She shouts out. "No, No, Noooooooooooo don't take her, you can't, you can't, you...she's miiiiiine..." She shouts, but already he has the child in his own arms. As he steps away, his black boot lands sharply in her ribs. She screams. But not because of the kick. Because the heavy boot that nearly cracks her rib is nothing compared to what she feels inside.

CANDACE

She is sluggish, hot, her cheeks blushed in two spots of cherry pink. She is taking small steps, proceeding slowly up the road. The November light is milky lemon, the color of crystallized honey, of bleached sun. One of the colors in her own hair. She has her favorite strand of that hair knotted tightly around her little finger. The finger dangles, the tip pinched white, practically strangled. She stops on the slushy road, looks up, her eyes numbly following a grey squirrel hopping from one tree branch to another. Occasionally, she stops, riveted by a sound, a hoot, a rustle, a crack, the sharp trill of a bird.

I know that bird, she thinks. I've heard these notes before. She thinks: oriole. No. Chickadee. No. Rufus-sided towhee. No. Before. I know I knew this bird. Before. She lingers a moment longer, frowning. The song is gone. She walks on, occasionally talking to herself. A car might come. A car. A truck. I've gone this far. I've got so far to go. She stops again. She jerks her pinky finger downward, snapping the strand of hair. She waves the pinky, then touches it to the hot blue and yellow ring now bulging around her wrist. She can't move the fingers of the injured hand. She can't begin to make a fist.

She hears a crack of branches, a heavy shuffling in the snowy leaves. She turns. Not even twenty feet away, a deer stands alert. One grey ear twitches. Candace stares. Two eyes stare back at her. Large brown pools. She takes a step off the road, taking great care to plant her boot. A second step. She is about to take a third when the tail flickers, a furry white flag waving goodbye.

Deer hooves are carved sharply in the snow. She follows. The light is to her liking as she goes. Lush. Lemon. Honey. Milk. The sun is painting without a brush. It turns the trees into long lazy lines, networks of smoky blue shadows in the snow. In places, the snow is gone. The leaves beneath are wet, soggy, matted, dank. More light. More light. The sun is low, glowing too brightly. Weary, Candace settles on a rock. She locks her arms around her knees. She smells the breeze. It brings a whiff of leaves around her.

Ahead, a ring of birches. One branch with tiny golden leaves. Leaves dancing and waving in the purest golden light. The sight reminds Candace of the other tree, the Mother Maple in the yard. Frowning, she has a vision of the tree. The baby seat, swinging gently from the lowest limb. The leaves, dangling, coming unhinged, cascading gently to the snow. Cringing, she sees the seat itself unhinged, the baby crashing. No, Candace shakes her head. No. But the vision hangs, is slow to go away. Another takes its place. The leaves, golden, more golden, are far too bright. The leaves catch fire, each leaf becomes a flaming blue and orange kite. The kites, dancing on the breeze, kiss each other, the tree is set ablaze, fire consuming every branch. The grey papoose, the grey bark, all of it is burning. The baby's skin, her hair, is singed, charring, turning into blackened flesh. Consumed by fire, the child is dying in her seat. Screaming, the child is screaming, the child is screaming, choking on the smoke and heat.

Screaming. Candace too is screaming while she rubs her eyes. Her face burns. Her neck is stiff. Beneath her jacket, a pool of sweat. She rubs her eyes again, and through the trees, she has another vision. Audrey approaching calmly, wearing the long grey coat hanging almost to her feet. Her hair is loose and lying wavy on her shoulders, a silver cloud, and balanced on her shoulders there is a huge wooden yoke, heavier and far larger than any a man might have to carry. Attached to the yoke, on either side, and in perfect balance, Audrey is carrying two magnificent silver pails. Water, or sap, or both, are sloshing out the sides. Open-mouthed, thirsty, Candace cries out. "Over here, Grandma. Over here." Here? But why here? Candace hears herself, instantly has a vision of the burning tree, the flames. *No,* she shakes her head. *No. Not here.* "*There, Grandma. Back there. At the house. The tree. The tree is on fire back there.*" Candace rises to her feet. The seat of her pants is soaking wet, cold, from sitting on the rock. But in her haste to meet Audrey, to lead her back, Candace doesn't notice being wet. She is racing now between the trees, kicking snow aside, hurrying for the road.

She is thinking get there, get there, I've just got to get there, and she is running, or trying to, her hair bouncing on her shoulders as she claws her way through the forest. Her boots are clumsy, sinking deep into the soggy underbrush, sinking, forming black puddles in the spongy ground. All around twigs slap and scratch her face. Her chest burns every time she heaves a breath, and a sickly taste keeps rising in her mouth. Her ears ring and her eyes won't stop tearing. Still she plows ahead, clearing branches aside, trying to block her face with her good hand, and when a thorn catches the sleeve of her down jacket at one point, snagging the jacket just like a claw, she yanks so hard to get it free that she rips a long gash in the nylon. Glancing back she glimpses a swatch of bright blue nylon fluttering from the point of the thorn like a tiny flag.

She hurries through a tangle of vines, and she is almost into a small grove of white pines when suddenly she stops dead. Panting, she looks around. She is completely confused. Which direction has she come from? Which direction should she head? She is slippery with sweat. Her face is streaked and one cheek has a long bloody scratch. Where was it she saw Audrey a few minutes ago, where was it Audrey went, and how can she get back there, because that's the direction she wants to go.

Confused and weary, she is tempted just to sit down. But driving her forward is the vision, the flaming tree, the baby engulfed by fire, the baby crying and coughing and choking in smoke and flames so thick so black it is impossible to see. If only Audrey would reappear with the silver pails. If only she would give me some clue, Candace thinks, if only she'd point me the right way. Closing her eyes, Candace tries to picture Audrey again, tries to make the vision arise. Nothing. Nothing but bright yellow spots, now blue, blue patches fading into red. Nothing comes to mind at all. Except. What's that ahead? A sound, something in the distance, at ground level. The familiar deep growl of a vehicle maneuvering up the final hill of Audrey's road. Opening her eyes, Candace listens closely, then turns, places one foot down, the next, the next, and soon she is pushing branches aside, moving toward the sound. Follow it, follow the sound, and Candace does, until the deep growl of the car has almost died, has faded to a barely audible buzz. Candace keeps walking straight ahead. Before long, the trees spread. In the distance, she sees an open swath of road.

It's only when she has reached the road's edge, when she is gazing into the deep tire prints winding through the snow, that this thought occurs to her: somebody is driving up to Audrey's. Somebody else will find the burning tree. Somebody else will find the baby. Somebody else will surely see that she, Candace, wasn't there to care for her baby. Somebody else is going to discover that she left her precious Gretchen, swinging from a tree.

If only her thoughts could carry her now. If only she could move half as fast as her frenzied mind wants to. As it is, she seems to go in slow motion, seems to be running with someone holding her legs, seems to be dreaming this act of running, this never-ending motion up the road, her legs and arms flying forward, her mouth hung open, gasping for air. She has never run this fast before, or that's what she thinks, she can't possibly run one step more, but she does, she keeps going, pouring sweat, not getting there, breathing so hard it hurts, one leg chasing the other, her face screaming red with heat. When she can't go another step, she slows to a walk, starts talking out loud again.

"They'll see. I'll be there. They'll see I was coming back. I'll tell them I went for help...I did, I was..." and then she pictures the tree again, in flames, and then she sees the baby dead, and then she sees herself to blame. Because, she gasps, I am guilty. It's all my fault that she will die. Running again now, her thighs burning, she comes around the last bend, and up the rise, and there, barely visible now, is the big maple in front of Audrey's house.

Nobody is dousing it with water. And nowhere is there smoke. Or flame. Nor any sign of the baby seat, nor the baby. Nor does Candace hear any crying. Not a cough or any sound of choking. Only the tree, its bare limbs standing stately, tall, all exactly as she left it, all as it has always been. Except for one thing: in the driveway is Eileen's car, the driver's door open, the front seat empty. Candace, chest heaving, approaches the house. She reaches the front porch, the front door. She tries the handle. It's locked. She thinks of knocking, ringing the bell, but that seems silly. Instead, she decides to go around back. Just as she steps off the front porch, though, just as she turns the corner of the house, she practically bumps into Eileen, Eileen rushing toward her, the baby cradled to her chest.

"Ma, you're…you're here. I…I can't believe you're here." Candace's voice comes out both weak and hoarse, a mumble that barely rises above a croak.

"Of course I'm here Candace. I knew something was wrong. Oh my God, Candace, look at your, your wrist." Eileen gasps, stares at Candace as if she's seeing a ghost.

Candace has her arms out for the baby. Her wrist, purple, yellow, black and blue, is swollen to twice its normal size. "My God Candace how did this happen?"

Candace nods, shrugs, ignores the question. "Ma, is she…is Gretchen OK?"

Eileen sighs, turns Candace toward the car. "I don't know. Her color is terrible and so is her breathing. We'd better get this wet snowsuit off and warm her up right away."

Candace drops her arms, lets Eileen steer her into the front seat. Gretchen she puts in back. In seconds the grey papoose is off and Gretchen is wrapped in the green blanket Eileen has pulled from the trunk. For a moment Eileen stands and cuddles the baby against her cheek, but then, frowning, she places her back on the seat and brings her own face down on top of Gretchen's. Over and over, Eileen blows into Gretchen's mouth, and using her fingers, she massages the infant's chest. Finally, Eileen delivers Gretchen to Candace in front.

"Hold her as close as you can, honey, and warm her, warm her as much as possible," Eileen says, her voice panicky. "We'd better get her to the ER right away."

Candace nods and in seconds they are driving, driving fast, faster than Candace has ever seen her mother drive before. Heat is pouring from the vents full blast. Candace feels Gretchen cool against her cheek, and so Candace keeps breathing on her, pouring out her own breath, mimicking the car's heater, trying to defeat the blue in Gretchen's face with her own steamy breath. Soon she feels lightheaded, though, so she stops, glances out the window. The grey road, the bare trees, whiz by. A few brown leaves flutter down around the speeding car. All of it is a blur of dull color; all of it feels suddenly far away. Eileen is saying something, something about the baby, her color or her breathing or maybe both, but Candace can't hear now. Like the brown leaves, Eileen's words come down around Candace in silence, fluttering noiselessly, collecting in quiet piles on her lap.

PART FIVE

CANDACE

Four months later.

Now, at least, there is night and there is day. In the beginning, she had no way of telling the difference. There was just a deadly grey mixture, an interminable between time, a medicated state that loomed, spread, lead nowhere, day after day after day. Now, at least, there is light separating the nights, one from the next, even if those nights loom like dreaded black holes, even if she rolls on her bed inside them, moaning, or wanders in tight circles around the room, hugging herself, wearing the long white T-shirt they have to rip from her body to wash, and the blue foam slippers and shapeless blue robe without a sash.

If she wanders the room too long, or if she makes too much noise stamping, or if she sings too loudly, particularly if she sings to the baby the nursery song, then they shatter black time with glaring yellow white, a rectangle of hall light floods the untouched bed, and she shakes her head over and over and backs away. "I don't need it, I don't need it, I'm telling you I don't need..." but by then, she can say whatever she likes, she can scream "I've got to feed the baby," she can try that, like she used to at first, but now she knows better, now she knows that only makes things worse, it will bring them down quicker, pouncing from either side. Two will hold her down, one will pin her ankles, the other her wrists, and the third will draw medication into the syringe. And the syringe will stand, taut and erect, and as she lies there, muffled, sweating, her head going side to side,

Candace will stare at the shadow of the needle rising against the wall and all of a sudden she will see that it looks vaguely like a penis, one that is stalking her.

After the shot, she always sleeps, a dead sleep thankfully devoid of dreams. Day breaks, foggy at the window. Some time later she rises, groggy, thick, her lids heavy, her lips dry, her head aching so badly it feels like it will split. Through slitted eyes, she sees the same bare tree, the single old oak, standing outside her window in the same sloping yard. It is hard to remember what day it is, and it is hard to remember the way it used to be, when she was free to come and go as she pleased, before they took Gretchen away, before the baby's tiny face closed up into a pale little rosebud in Candace's mind.

Today Candace is leaning against the window, clinging to a shred of yellow blanket, the one from so many years ago. She holds the blanket against her cheek, glad now she told Eileen to bring it. Eileen wanted to bring Dollcake, too, but Candace said no. DC2, she knew, was really always Eileen's doll, and besides, she didn't want a silly doll, she wanted Gretchen.

Setting her lips to the windowpane, she watches now how the snow is falling outside the window, wonders why it always descends at the same steady slant. She closes her eyes, exhales a warm cloud, a protective white space on the glass. She erases the circle away with the edge of the ragged blanket. If only she could wipe away the years, if only things could be as they once were, if only she could be a child again, wake up sheltered, living in the space of leafy trees offered by Audrey, or the clean, orderly place supplied by Lucy.

Instead, she lives here in this godawful sterile shell, day after day, watching old T.V. movies, game shows, sit coms. She is fed from brown plastic trays. Once a week, she's led to the grey and white showers. They smell of mold, mildew, and urine. An aide scours her scalp, raking sharp nails over her head. Other days, Candace satisfies the nurse with what the staff calls a birdbath, splashing her face, neck and armpits at the sink. Or she doesn't wash at all. Once in the beginning Candace heard her mother's voice ring out down the hall. "She hasn't changed in a week. For God's sake, she stinks." After that, right before her mother's visit, they yanked the T-shirt over her head, pulling her hair, all the while Candace swore and kicked, screaming, "It's mine, dammit, this shirt's mine and it's fine the way it is."

Candace shivers now, pulls away from the glass. Her tears begin, but just as they do, a commotion erupts down the hall, somebody is having a fit, raving behind a door, not wanting a shot, or yelping because they just got one. The noise dies, and Candace sponges her eyes with her peculiar little blanket. Sighing, she turns back to the center of the common room, to the T.V., to the morning game show she was watching a few minutes ago with the other blank faces.

There is the black woman named Bev, who wears a baggy yellow shift, sleeveless, and tiny red and blue beads threaded into the many braids of her hair. There is the fat woman, Frieda, who keeps yelling out, for no apparent reason, "Not fair! Not fair!" And there is the older woman named Moe, who has two earrings in one ear and one droopy eye, and a massive tattoo cloaking her back, and a very slow, kind way of talking. She wears her hair in a butch cut, dyed Kool Aid red. Maybe it's the hair, Candace thinks, or the fact she freely gives away grape bubble gum, or the fact she vaguely resembles Pit. Whatever it is, Candace likes Moe best.

"So when's your mama coming?" Moe asks now, the T.V. blaring an ad for a boxy jeep bouncing perilously close to the edge of an orange canyon.

"Today. She always comes on Saturday." Moe smiles, and her chipped front tooth shows, and then she waits a while, inhales, her lips closing slow and tight around her cigarette. She blows out a lazy circle of grey smoke before she asks the next question.

"So what good stuff is your mama bringing you today?"

"I don't know," Candace says. "I don't know. She didn't say."

She knows what she's asked for, though. Diapers. Bottles, too. Every week she asks. Because if Eileen brings diapers and bottles, then maybe, Candace thinks, she will also bring the baby. Every week when Eileen arrives, and before she's even had a chance to unbutton her coat, the first thing Candace does is dive into the grocery bag, looking. The bag inevitably is filled with apples and oranges, a few magazines, a round tin of chocolate chip cookies. Last week, a new hairbrush, a brand new game of Scrabble, a toothbrush, a loaf of banana bread. No diapers, though. And no bottles.

"You know why I don't bring you those things," Eileen says quietly, "because you know you don't need them here." Eileen says the words firmly, speaking very slowly and very cautiously, using the same measured tone every time. Candace has heard the words, the tone, before. Every time she sees Dr. Betz, the same words pour out: "Candace, you don't need diapers here or bottles either and I know you know that and I know you know why." Sitting across from Dr. Betz, Candace eyes the doctor dully, eyes the doctor's face, her brown hair, her maroon leather chair, the small metal studs that go nowhere but in circles. She says simply, quietly, "But I do need diapers, or I will, I've got to have them for Gretchen and also, I'll need them when the new baby arrives."

Today when Eileen comes, Candace rifles through the bag, and when she doesn't find what she's looking for, she stomps out of the room, infuriated. Doesn't return for half an hour. Hides all that time in the shower, behind the mildewed curtain. Finally, the aide finds her, drags her back to her room. Candace refuses to speak to her mother for most of the afternoon. Eileen relaxes in an armchair, flipping through a magazine. Candace lies on the bed, her hands on her chest, imagining the baby growing inside. Eileen makes conversation.

"Did I tell you Audrey is now walking half an hour on the beach every morning? She absolutely adores the place they found near Fort Myers." Candace is silent, watching a ladybug crawl along the ceiling. Four inches to the white fixture. Three inches to the white fixture. "And now that the sale has gone through on the land, they won't have to come back up north until the closing this spring."

Closing this spring. Closing this spring. She thinks about how the words would sound if she were to sing them. She opens her mouth, then abruptly brings herself to a sitting position. She has to pee. She has half a mind to wet her bed, the way she did in the beginning. When she would scream out of her drugged stupor, "I need a diaper and I need it now." And how they wouldn't bring her one. And then she'd go, right there in bed. Now, though, she heads for the toilet in the closet-sized bathroom adjacent to her room.

When she returns, Eileen lays the magazine aside. She stands beside the window.

"Candace," she says. "How would you like it if I brought your paints next time?"

Candace looks up, surprised. She smiles. Stays quiet.

"I take that to be a yes then," Eileen says. Silence. "OK. Now do something for me."

"What?" Candace plops back down on the edge of the bed.

"Get dressed. Put on some nice clothes. Comb your hair. Wash your face. Come downstairs with me, eat your dinner there with…" Before she finishes, Candace is yelling

"No! No! I won't eat there. I told you, I won't eat with a bunch of morons." She hasn't left the floor for almost four months. She hasn't gotten further then the common room since last November. It is now the 6th of March.

"You can't do this, honey, you can't just stay all cooped up in your…"

"I can do what I want. Anyway why should you care? You don't care…"

"Candace!" Her mother's tone turns sharp. "I love you honey and you know I am doing absolutely everything I possibly can to help you."

"Yeah, so if you care so much, where's my baby, huh? Why can't I see her? Huh?"

Eileen approaches the bed. "Candace, look at me honey. Please."

"No." Candace drops back on the bed and rolls over to face the wall.

"Honey. Please." Eilen's tone is soft, easy, as light as the snowflakes falling outside the window. "You know why I can't bring the baby here. You know full well how terribly sick Gretchen has been. I don't have to tell you that because I know somewhere inside, you know. So. I'll just repeat my request. All I'm asking you to do is to get dressed. That's not so much to ask now, is it? Please? Because I know Dr. Betz thinks it's best if you get up and…"

Candace grabs her yellow shred, pulls it and her pillow over her head, and then, when that's not enough, when she can still hear Eileen speaking, she drags the bedcovers over too. And when that's still not enough, she sings, booming as loud as she can, "Closing this spring. Closing this spring." With that, she succeeds in drowning out her mother's voice. But nothing helps her forget what it is her mother said about the baby.

Eileen promised to bring the paints the following Saturday. Which is good, because the days are too white. The snow keeps falling at that unrelenting angle outside the window. And the only color inside Candace's room is the pale blue of the limp curtains, the faded lime green of the bedspread. Sometimes the sheer whiteness terrifies Candace, scares her even more than the black hole she descends into at night. She said just that to Dr. Betz last week. She tried to tell the doctor how it feels, how she's not sure she is real anymore, how living here, she feels as though she is going blank, just like the white walls, how she has all but disappeared.

Somehow Dr. Betz didn't seem to hear. Or understand. Somehow Candace wasn't able to make herself clear: it's the hospital that's making her sick. The doctor just sat there, not caring, like everybody else. Wearing her glasses tied on a string around her neck. Nodding, her hands folded together, saying things like, "So you do miss painting then?" And when Candace said, "I guess," then the doctor replied, "Well, good, that's progress." To which Candace screamed, "But what I miss more is being outside, somewhere real, a real house, and people. *Real* people…" Candace thought of Mark then, thought about his visit, thought about how good it felt when he held her, how good he smelled, too, how she loved his new cologne, the one he called "Azure." Everything was going well too until Candace tried to explain how she felt, being pregnant again, how she was waiting patiently for the new baby to arrive. "I've got to do better this time," she whispered to him. "I've just got to." At which point, Mark's face crumpled and he looked as if he might start to cry and she felt sad because Mark hardly ever cried. She hugged him then and he just cried harder, and then she cried too, and then he left.

"I miss Mark," she told the doctor last Thursday. "I miss my baby and I miss Mark."

At which point the doctor sat back and sighed. "Of course you miss Mark," she said softly. "And of course you miss Gretchen. And you can see both of them, as soon as you're ready. But first we need to talk…we need to discuss the way in which Gretchen got hurt." Candace cringed. Those words, *Gretchen got hurt*, make her shake inside. Make her feel as though she is made of the same yellow and red jello that they serve for lunch.

"No," Candace replied. "I keep telling you no. And I mean no." She rose to leave.

"Candace?" The doctor called. "Candace, the longer you put this off, the longer…"

Growling, Candace slammed the door behind her. At dinner, she stood each piece of broccoli upright in her mashed potatoes. She stirred her peas into her butterscotch pudding. She drank all her milk, because she needs it, she will need it to feed the new baby. After she drained the glass, though, she let it go crashing to the floor. The glass shattered, and before she could even bend down, an aide was looming over her, wielding a broom.

EILEEN

When the phone rings at nine fifteen on Sunday morning, Eileen is curled up behind Jorge, her face pasted against his muscular brown back. The phone pulls her out of a surface dream, one about Candace, one that seems all too real. Candace has a sharp stick in her hand, and she keeps stabbing at a black snake, and then, when Eileen takes the stick away, Candace finds a rock and tries to smash it down on a bird. A red winged blackbird.

Rolling over, Eileen reaches out for the receiver. "Hello," she whispers.

"Eileen? Is that you? It's me. Audrey."

Eileen sits up, eyes Jorge dragging the covers over his ears. The two of them stayed awake, drinking Chilean wine and making love, until three thirty in the morning. And here it is now not even six hours later. Grabbing her bathrobe, Eileen gets up out of bed, her feet landing in their slippers. The sunlight pouring in the window hurts her eyes.

"Yes, hi Audrey. Yes, it's me." She tiptoes out of the bedroom and down the stairs.

"I'm sorry if I woke you," Audrey says. "It's just I…I have just spoken to Candace."

"Yes, oh, so you called her?"

"No, no, she called me. And that's the thing. That's why I'm calling. I was so surprised. And happy. I mean this is the first time she's called since she went into the hospital."

"Well, that's wonderful," Eileen says, reaching the kitchen, running cold water for coffee. It occurs to her that Audrey could have waited until eleven, maybe even noon, to share this news, but, oh well. She understands Audrey's excitement.

"She sounded good," Audrey said. "Better, I mean…well, almost like her old self."

"Yes, yes, she is better," Eileen said, reaching to the shelf for the coffee filters. "She's going to let me bring her paints next week."

"She told me," Audrey says excitedly. "I think that's wonderful. "I guess what I'm wondering is, why I called is, is it possible she might be well enough to be released soon?"

"Oh." Eileen has the freezer door open. She stands with the coffee bag in her hand. "No, Audrey, I'm afraid not. It's…it's too soon. She is making progress, though. She hasn't had medication during the day in weeks. But still…Dr. Betz says it will be a while until…"

"Oh." Audrey's voice has dropped a register. "It's just…she sounded so good."

"Well, now and then yes. But she has yet to deal with things. With…you know…"

"You mean… the baby… ."

"Yes." Eileen closes the freezer. "Dr. Betz says Candace can't face up to Gretchen's coma until she is ready to deal with what she did wrong."

"I see." Audrey sighs so loudly that Eileen can hear. "But I thought with the baby being so much better, I thought that would make it easier for Candace to…"

"Yes, well," Eileen replies, dropping into a chair. "Things with the baby are better, much better, but even with that, a coma is very serious, and, of course, she had the hypothermia too. The pediatrician says it's going to be a long haul for Gretchen. All we know is that the coma and the seizures that followed left some damage. And while she may end up OK, there is no way to know that for sure now."

Audrey lets out a long sigh. "How much longer will the baby be in Boston?"

"I'm not sure. But she's getting the best possible care there, the most advanced therapy. That long term care center is set up just for kids, it's one of the best anywhere."

"All I know, Eileen, is that I'd like to see both of them out of those hospitals today." Audrey's voice shakes. "If I could make a miracle…or two…I would. Every night, I lay in bed praying and saying I'm sorry for what happened." Audrey goes silent.

"Look, Audrey, I know how much you're beating yourself up about all this. But you've got to stop blaming yourself. What happened to Gretchen at the farm wasn't your fault, not at all."

"Yes, well, it's fine for you to say that, but if somebody had been there that day…"

"Yes, well, but you didn't choose to have a kidney stone that night, did you? And you didn't choose to fall again, right? I mean, when you and the others went rushing off to the hospital, how could you possibly have known that Candace was in so much trouble?"

Audrey sighs again.

Eileen is standing now, the coffee forgotten. "Look, Audrey, I've spent the last four months trying to figure out what *I* might have done differently. I keep thinking if only I'd kept her home. If only I'd gotten up to the farm sooner, or if only I'd called a few hours before I did. If only I'd realized she was going to leave that kid. Some nights, I lie in bed just going nuts."

"Oh, but she was at my house Eileen. *My* house, not yours."

"Yes, well. Maybe that's true. But honestly, Audrey, we both did the best we could."

"Yes, well, our best wasn't good enough." Audrey is practically whispering now.

Eileen pauses. "That's right. And that's the hardest thing to accept — believe me, I know. The fact that I've been less than the perfect mother to my daughter is…" Eileen goes silent. "If anybody is to blame here, you know in the end it has to be me. Candace is in the predicament she's in today mostly because of me."

Audrey says nothing. Eileen hears Marjory in the background. Then Audrey is sniffling, blowing her nose. "I guess," she says, "I guess sooner or later we all have to make peace with our shortcomings, don't we?"

"You got that right." Eileen circles the kitchen, stands at the counter in front of the sink, puts one foot on top of the other. Speaks slowly. "I think, I really think that forgiveness is…it's key. We have to give ourselves credit for what we've done, not blame ourselves for what we…"

"Well, yes, Eileen, that's right. You know what everybody has said, all the doctors, that dear baby would have been dead if you hadn't done the CPR, rescued her when you did."

"Yes, well," Eileen sighs. "I tried. When I think what might have happened that day. So you're right. I tried. I did my best. But God knows, *God knows*, I've made mistakes."

"We all have," Audrey says.

Eileen starts circling the kitchen again. "I think that's exactly what Candace has to come to understand, too. That's the struggle for her...for her recovery."

Neither of them speak. Then Eileen does. "Hey, I just want to say that your letters have really helped. I think both you and Rusty are wonderful to write her every week."

"Oh. Well. That's the least I can do. I just wish I could be there to...to hug her."

"Oh you will. You will. Right now we're a team. Like you said last fall, we have to be a team, all of us loving Candace and Gretchen back to health. And now, I think we are getting closer."

"You really think so?"

"I do, Audrey. Candace seems better. And..." here Eileen sighs, clears her throat. "Dr. Betz sent me back into therapy, too, just so I'll be better ready to help Candace through this tough part. Because I'm at the heart of what Candace has to work through."

"Yes," Audrey says blandly. "I guess so. That's good, Eileen. That's very good. So would you keep me posted? I mean would you call me with any changes at all?"

"Of course," Eileen says kindly. "You are on my mind a lot you know."

"Really?"

"Well sure. I keep thinking of you lying down there in that white sand. I keep thinking of *me* lying in that white sand. My face warming in the sun. I'm jealous of you."

Audrey snorts. "Yeah, well, you wouldn't be jealous of this old body. God what aches and pains I have. Look, Eileen, I was serious when I said you should visit."

"And I was serious when I said I'd come." Eileen's thoughts rise immediately to Jorge in the warm bed upstairs. Should she tell Audrey the news? That he's going to move in?

"Well, do keep me posted about Candace. And Gretchen."

"Yes, and you take care down there. Mud season is here...far too many grey skies."

Audrey sighs. "Oh, I don't miss March at all."

"I don't blame you there. Just enjoy the sun. OK?" For now, she will keep Jorge's move a secret.

"I will. You take care of yourself, Eileen."

After the conversation between them ends, Eileen begins scooping dark Brazilian coffee into the fluted filter. Then she hears a sound. She turns. There, stretching and smiling, is Jorge, wearing just boxers. "Que pasa?" he mumbles, shuffling toward her. He slips his coffee-colored face into her robe, into the space between her naked breasts. She holds him there and forgets the coffee.

CANDACE

As promised, Eileen brings the paint, the brushes, the palette, even the easel and three canvases, all stretched and primed with white. The following day, Candace takes up a position in a corner of the common room. Nervously, she faces the empty white space of the canvas. She selects yellow, feels the tube smooth in her hand. Licking her upper lip, she turns to face the window. The snow, finally, has stopped falling. For a moment, it occurs to her that she could paint a sun, the way she used to, when as a child of seven, she and Marjory would stand side by side behind the farm-house, painting together. In those days, she always started by laying a yellow glob of color in one corner, like an egg yolk. Then she would spread it with a brush, add a smaller gob of orange, swirl the colors together. Finally, she would drag the paint out in wobbly lines, each ray of sunshine a brush stroke radiating from the center.

She is half-tempted to start that way now, because she is totally without inspiration. In the old days, all she had to do was pick up a brush, gaze at the lush colors before her. Almost instantly, an image would begin to take hold. Now, though, she is frozen in indecision. She has absolutely no inspiration, not the least inkling of a vision. She glances over her shoulder. Certainly part of her problem this morning is the fact that she's got an overly eager audience. Moe, Bev, and Frieda are sitting in a small circle of chairs, all in awe, all silently staring at her, because, as Bev says, "we never saw a real painter paint before." Moe smokes. Frieda keeps poking her finger at the canvas, asking what Candace is going to paint.

"Give her a break," Bev says, rattling the beads in her hair. "How's she supposed to know before she even gets going?"

And that in fact is the problem. With people watching, nothing flows. Candace is losing heart, becoming self-conscious. For the first time in memory, she is feeling pressured to paint, feeling as though she had better hurry up and think of something, if for no other reason than she has to make an impression on her friends. Picking up a tube of red, she unscrews the cap, stares at the deep crimson hue.

"You could paint me," Frieda offers, standing now. "I'd make a good subject."

"Sit down," Bev says impatiently. Frieda drops back into her seat.

A few minutes of silence follow. Freida bends over, whispers into Moe's ear. "I thought artists wore berets," she says. Moe, exhaling smoke rings, shrugs.

A nurse approaches, carrying a tray with tiny white paper cups, filled with the day's drugs. "Pills, ladies," says nurse Harrison.

"I'll pass," says Moe, bending over, busying herself by retying her sneaker.

"Yeah, well, you talk to Dr. Ashby about that," the nurse says, flatly, setting a cup on the wooden arm of Moe's chair.

"Hey, not fair, not fair, you gave her first," Frieda says, standing again.

Harrison, tall and thin, waits for the three women to take their meds. "Good news, Candace," the nurse says, collecting the empty cups. "None for you today."

The nurse walks away. Candace doesn't say anything. She passes a thick brush back and forth across the palm of her hand. The clean bristles, short, soft, evenly cut, remind her of an animal's tail, or long ago, the tip of one of her own reddish blonde braids. The last time she looked in the mirror, though, the color of her hair, like her face, seemed to be fading away.

"I..uh...I'm not sure I can paint today," she says, suddenly turning to face the three women. In unison, as if they had been rehearsing together, they simultaneously protest. "Oh...no...Candace, please!" Frieda stands, more agitated than before. "You gotta paint, Candace, you're the artist," she says, poking her finger at the canvas again.

"OK, OK," Candace says, gazing from one to the other of the women. Tickling the tip of the brush against her bottom lip, she turns back to the canvas. The three women fall silent. Candace squeezes red onto the palette, dips the brush in water, and squashes the bristles into the glistening glob. Laying the brush on the canvas, she forms a petal-like shape.

"Oh, good, I knew she would paint a flower," Frieda says.

"Hush, you," Bev replies, slapping Frieda's hand. "Who told you it was a flower?" Candace looks briefly from Bev to Frieda, frowning. Squeezing yellow, and a ring of white, side by side on the palette, she swipes the brush through both and smears the outer edges of the red petals. Reaching for blue, she paints bold, rough strokes of the dark hue at the base of each petal, then fans blue into yellow, orange, and red. Her head tipped, she licks her lips, starts to see what she's painting, is about to paint more, when suddenly Frieda shouts out.

"You're painting fire," she cries, pointing and clapping her hands in excitement.

"Yes," Candace says, setting brush to canvas again. "You're right, Frieda, I am."

She paints for the next hour, adding layer after layer of flames. Soon, though, it is lunchtime and an aide brings the women their trays.

"Hey, Candace, time to eat," Frieda says.

"I want to finish this," Candace replies, ignoring her tray. "Anyway, I'm not hungry."

"Well, I am," Bev says. "All this painting is making me famished." She slurps up a spoonful of chicken noodle soup.

"You really oughtta take a break," Moe says, biting into a piece of buttered bread. "Come sit here with us. Then you can see it from a distance."

"OK," Candace sighs, slipping her brush into a jar of water. "If you say I should, Moe, then I will." She picks up her tray and joins the others, calmly eating lunch. Sticking her straw into her milk carton, she sips. Then she butters her bread, and folds the piece in half.

Frieda, suddenly, gasps and shouts out. "Look," she cries, pointing to the painting. "There's a face hiding there in the fire. And really scary eyes. Really scary."

Candace looks up, and at first, all she sees are the wild flames. But soon she realizes that Frieda is right. The white tips of two adjacent flames form a pointed pair of glittering eyes. A long orange swath takes on the shape of an oddly-curved nose. A mouth with thin lips leers out of the dark purple. In the center of the mouth is a small black *o*.

"Did you mean to paint that creepy thing?" Bev whispers, pointing with her teaspoon.

"No," Candace says, staring, mesmerized by the face in the painting. "I had no idea."

"Well, so, you gonna erase it then or what?" Bev asks in her raspy voice.

"Oh, stupid, you can't erase paint," Frieda says.

"Stupid, you can too," Bev says angrily. "You paint over it, right, Candace honey?"

"Right, right," Candace says now, transfixed by the glowing face, which is taking on a diabolical look the longer she stares at it. She has put aside her lunch.

"Well, it's spooky if you ask me," Frieda says. "I'd be scared to death if I painted something ugly as that." She squirms in her seat. Candace rises, walks back to the canvas, hugs herself with both arms. She holds her breath and stares.

"I didn't know I was painting a face," Candace says.

"Maybe," Bev says, following her, laying an arm around Candace's shoulder, "maybe it's like one of those tests, where they fold a paper in half, with ink inside, and then you have to decide what it is when they open the paper. I took one once. Maybe that's what's happening for you. You're painting on automatic."

"Maybe," Candace says, still hugging herself.

"Maybe," Moe says, speaking slowly, "maybe you ought to just take a break, hon. If you want, sweetie, I'll ask Harrison to make you some nice hot orange spice tea, just like you love."

"Fine," Candace says, shivering now, not quite focusing on what Moe is saying. "Fine. Have her make me some right away."

How she should proceed now, Candace is not sure. It occurs to her that if she hadn't had the company of her three friends, she might never have known about the face. She might even have proceeded to paint right over it, "erase" it, as Frieda said. But now that she sees the face, she wonders where it came from. And what else she hasn't seen. More importantly, she wonders what to do. Keep painting? Or stop, put the canvas aside, try something else? Candace is about to pick up the brush when Harrison brings the tea.

"Thank you," Candace says, taking the steaming mug. The orange scent floats up.

"Are you done painting for the day?" Harrison asks, eyeing the canvas.

"Uh, I don't know," Candace replies numbly, pressing her thumbs on the hot mug.

"Well, it looks to me like you're done." Harrison turns and Candace glares.

"Well I'm *not*," she barks at the nurse's back. "I have a lot more work to do today."

Harrison gives her another hour, during which Candace addresses the edges of the canvas, adding bright strokes of orange and yellow and white.

The three women, meanwhile, wander off, sit side by side on the common room couch and watch the soaps. About 3:30, Moe walks over to Candace standing at her easel.

"Hey, that's swell." The older woman nods, her eyes sparkling. Candace steps back, eyes her work. By using yellow and orange at the edges, she has defined the face even more.

She frowns. "I'm not sure what to do with the face," she says, collapsing into a chair.

"Just leave it there," Moe says, pulling out her grape bubble gum and holding a piece out to Candace. "Anyway, where did you learn to paint so good?"

"Oh, I painted as a kid. At my grandmother's. Her friend Marjory paints. And then in high school I took art. In college too."

"Well, you keep it up," Moe says, bringing one finger close to the surface of the canvas. "You got good pictures locked up inside your head. Excellent pictures, like ones in a museum. Or like movies that ain't run at any theaters yet."

"You think so?" Candace smiles at Moe, hoping she will go on. She does.

"Yeah I do," Moe says, sticking a second stick of gum into her mouth. "I'd say you got a gift. And when you got a gift, you better know it, and you better know how to get the hell out of the way and let it show itself. Your gift shows." Moe blows a huge grape bubble.

Candace blushes and busies herself unwrapping a piece of gum.

Later, lying in the dark that night, Candace tosses and turns. Moe's words are burning in her head. So too is the face in the painting, the face in the flames, the face she now thinks she should have erased. Except, she thinks in the very next moment, rolling to face the moonlit wall, it wouldn't matter. She could have destroyed the canvas altogether, but the face would remain etched forever in her brain. The question was no longer did she see it, but where else would it appear. Getting out of bed, she goes to the window, looks up at the moon. A bright buttery disc, almost full. She is watching the moon, noticing the way the light turns the snowy landscape a milky blue, when suddenly she hears herself say, "I will paint right now." The words come out in a faint whisper, as if someone else is talking through her.

Turning back to the inside of the room, she adjusts her eyes to the semi-darkness. She will paint by moonlight, in total silence. If she turns on even one light, she might drag a legion of staff to her side. And if she were caught awake at this late hour, she would almost certainly get a shot. She cannot be caught. She cannot be caught. She pulls out the duffel bag Eileen brought her, the one full of tubes of paint. She takes out yellow and red. Something in her head tells her that these two are enough. She shoves the duffel bag roughly aside, and stepping up onto her bed, she sets to work on the wall over her pillow.

For who knows how long, she paints into the night, the brush for a long time making the same faint scratching sounds as she passes it lightly over the wall, making rounded strokes on the cold white plaster. She is painting in yellow at first, but soon switches to red. The moon adds its own blue hue. More flames, she thinks. At least, she begins by painting flames. But soon, she loses awareness of her own aims. She has drifted off somewhere, her conscious mind has escaped, and the wall is taking on a strange new landscape, one that reflects her deepest mind's own making. At first, she sees what she thinks are trees, a forest of them, all protruding arms and legs and short twigs, all the branches wavy and fiery yellow and red. But then a pool gathers at the floor of this strange forest, and slowly, Candace sees that these aren't trees at all, but strange fleshy forms, forms with no heads.

Gradually, she is aware of herself painting a large sac to contain the fleshy trees, and the pool underneath, and now she wonders if this watery red substance is cool. So she touches it, puts her hand into the wet, and it is warm, and it is now swarming over her, swallowing the brush, her arm, until all of her is sucked in. Suddenly, she seems no longer to be painting. She seems instead to be dreaming, and yet awake, unable to make sense of where she is, except it is a violent sea, and she thinks "it is within me." The sea is moving in rapid circular motion, a swirling red broth, as if heading madly toward a giant bathtub drain. In the next moment, she is certain the pool is filled with blood and mucous. "It is within all of us," she thinks: me, Audrey, Eileen, and it is circling all the time. At that point she stops thinking, because she is straining, grasping, gasping for breath. She has all she can do to swim. And in the distance now, coming toward her in the pool, is the grey papoose, floating in the waves.

Thank God for the papoose, Candace thinks, because it helps her to float, it's saving her. "Gretchen," she calls, "Oh, Gretchen," but her voice is lost, and in the next moment she is tossed, swallowed in the cuff of a wave. Still she struggles to swim to the infant, intent on saving her. Finally she is there, beside the baby, so close she can see the red hair, when suddenly she is overcome by another wave, the flood of it, the blood of it fills her mouth, all salty and sour, and she goes under, comes up, looks for the grey, prays she will see it again. And there it is, across the pool, so Candace dog paddles across, all but exhausted now, and when she gets close enough to reach, she does, she grabs at the string, starts pulling the papoose toward her, when suddenly the string breaks, the papoose spills open, and the baby, naked, her flesh a strange shade of moonlight blue, goes under the blood, the last thing Candace sees is blood engorging the rosebud mouth. Candace grabs for the baby, latches onto a finger, a slippery toe, and then, she lets go of both, and the baby slips away, carried into the whorl that is carrying the flood of blood waters into the deepest layers of the pool.

"No, no," Candace cries, diving underneath, her eyes greeted by an impenetrable layer of red, the blood, the flood clouding any possible view of the infant. And now she is screaming "I drowned her, I drowned her, I laid her down, I let her drown." The sound of her own voice awakens her, and in that instant she sees that moonlight has given way to the steel white of day, and she herself is naked except for her underpants. Glancing down, she sees her hands, her arms, are covered in red paint, and her underpants are soaked in blood. And this much she knows: that she has her period, her first since the baby was born. And the sight of her own blood smeared between her thighs is ghastly to her eyes. She slips out of the bloody pants, and wipes them against the wall, shrieking now, adding her own blood to the red of the pool. And all the while she is wailing, *"NO, NO, I drowned her, I drowned her, oh God, oh Audrey, I drowned her."*

In moments, four staff people burst through the door, instantly convinced that what they see can only be a suicide in the making.

EILEEN

Eileen keeps a four-day vigil, staying with Candace around the clock, sleeping in a cot beside her bed. On this, the third night, the doctor has reduced the sedation, and now Candace is not sleeping so well, she keeps groaning and occasionally calling out, "*oh no don't...please, please don't drown.*" Each time Candace screams, Eileen gets up off her rickety cot and strokes her daughter's arm. Or she places her hand on Candace's colorless forehead and puts her lips next to Candace's ear, whispering calm reassuring words into the milky moonlight.

"It's OK, honey. I'm here. I'm not leaving. I'm here and I'm staying and nobody is going to drown. Do you hear me Candace? Nobody is going to drown." The last time Candace woke, Eileen was so exhausted, so totally spent, that when Candace didn't fall back to sleep right away, Eileen lay down on her own cot and rolled onto her stomach and took Candace's hand. And so Eileen and Candace fell asleep that way, their hands linked, their arms forming a sturdy little bridge stretching across the small space between mother's and daughter's beds.

Sometime after six a.m., Eileen wakes, and it takes her a few minutes to remember where she is. She does, though, and almost right away, she also knows this isn't going to be a good day. Because not only is her throat sore, but also, when she goes to sit up, pain scissors from her calf up through her butt and thigh. Meaning her sciatic nerve is acting up, no doubt because she's been sitting for far too many hours, and sleeping on the cot, four nights in a row.

And if that weren't enough, as Eileen rises unsteadily off the cot, she also feels the beginnings of one of her headaches, small knots of pain dancing across both temples. It's at that moment she begins to wonder how long she can hold up. It's at that moment she begins to yield to the gloom that has been gathering for three days. Only then does she think maybe she will have to take a break tonight, leave Candace alone here in the hospital so that she can go to a motel and get a decent night's sleep. Only then does she think that maybe she should have taken Audrey up on her offer to fly up from Florida to help out as she clearly wanted, to share the burden of taking turns sitting and sleeping by Candace's bed.

Three nights ago, when Eileen called Audrey from a pay phone at the hospital, trying to sound upbeat about Candace's condition, she told Audrey to stay put. "I know you want to come, but Dr. Betz says she believes that this may very well be our breakthrough, that Candace may improve quickly now. So by the time you get a flight up to Boston, Candace will probably be out of the woods." Now, though, Eileen wonders if she didn't make a mistake. She wonders if she shouldn't call Audrey back, beg her to come just as soon as she can book a flight. After all, how many more nights can she go without sleep?

"Come home today," Jorge keeps saying on the phone. "Sleep with me and rest. Then you can go back refreshed." Laughing, Eileen tells him he's wrong: if she sleeps with him, she certainly *won't* rest. And besides, she tells him in a more serious tone, she's afraid to leave, afraid to go two hours home and then find out Candace needs her here at the hospital.

Eileen stares down at Candace now, watching her daughter frown in her sleep. Candace's face looks pitifully thin and colorless and so small. To Eileen now, Candace looks altogether like a child lying there on the pillow. Her forehead is damp, her hair, stringy and limp. "Some breakthrough," Eileen whispers, biting into her lower lip. "Some breakthrough this is." Her mind slips back to the call that came at the crack of dawn four mornings ago. Candace…up all night painting the walls…completely disoriented, covered in red paint and…blood. At first, everybody thought the worst. Later, though, a second call came. Dr. Betz reassured Eileen: Candace had not tried suicide, she had simply soiled herself and the wall after getting her first period in more than a year.

Eileen wasn't convinced. Even now, four days later, she's still not sure that Candace hadn't at the very least *considered* taking her life. She still thinks that if her daughter had continued alone in her room another few minutes, then she might have done something even more rash...maybe smashed a window...taken a piece of broken glass, and...God only knows.

Tying the sash of her bathrobe, Eileen checks Candace once more, then slips out the door and wobbles down the hall holding the small of her back. The clock over the nurse's station reads 6:40, too early for nurse Harrison to be on duty. A younger nurse is doing charts.

"Excuse me," Eileen starts, clearing her throat. The young nurse looks up. "I woke up with such a wicked backache today I can hardly walk. I wonder, would it be OK if I used the common room to do some yoga this morning?" She smiles.

The nurse smiles back. "Sure," she says. "No one goes in there before about eight."

"Thanks." Eileen goes back to the room and quickly changes into sweats. After checking to see Candace is still asleep, she creeps out, walking barefoot down the hall, her legs as stiff as canes.

Before she begins her salute to the sun, Eileen sits in the corner, the same corner where Candace set her easel a few days before. Closing her eyes, she tries to clear her head. Tries to empty herself of thoughts. Tries to achieve what her yoga teacher calls the "zero mind." Slowly, she breathes in, concentrates on the air filling her lungs and then, the air going back out again. Usually, she can't keep thoughts away for more than a few seconds. But it doesn't matter. Even if she never finds the zero mind, the meditation is always relaxing.

"Hi." Eileen's eyes fly open. There, standing before her, is a fiftyish woman with a droopy eye, and a butch hair cut, dyed bright red. She has a cigarette in one hand.

"Hi....oh, hello. You're Moe, right?"

"Yup. I'm Moe. And you're Candace's ma."

"Yes. I'm Eileen." Eileen gets up off the floor and they shake hands.

"So...how's Candace? I mean, I was really worried when I heard."

Eileen wonders what she's heard. But she doesn't ask. "She's OK. Thanks." Eileen sighs. "I'd like to be able to say she's fine. But..."

"But that'd be a lie, huh? I guess she wouldn't be here then."

"No," Eileen says, shaking her head slowly. "I guess not."

"Hey, so what were you doing just then? Praying for her?"

"No, well, I was doing yoga. And...I meditate."

Moe smiles. Takes a deep drag on her cigarette. "I've never med-itated before," she says, circling her lips and puffing smoke through them. "I'm more the praying type myself."

"Oh?"

"Yup. I pray for different people. I mean, if they need it. I pray for me, too, so that maybe some day I'll get out of here. And lately I've been praying for Candace." Moe pulls a piece of grape bubble gum from her pocket.

"Really? That's awfully sweet of you, Moe. I'm sure Candace would be so grateful."

Moe shrugs. "Want a stick?"

Eileen is tempted to say no, but something makes her take the gum. "Sure."

"I figured doing yoga, you wouldn't go for cigarettes. Or would you? I got some."

"Oh, no, that's OK. Hey, this gum is fine." She smiles at Moe and Moe smiles back.

"Well, I better go," Moe says, blowing a big pale purple bubble. "I mean, to let you do your yoga. Or could I watch?"

"Well, actually, I don't mean to hurt your feelings, but I think I would do better alone." Moe smiles and nods. Eileen can now understand why Candace likes her.

"Well OK then. So have a good time." Moe turns and starts to leave the room. But then, just when she is almost out the door, she turns again, eyes Eileen. "When I pray, I think of a light, a light shining out of my heart. Then I let the words float right out on that light."

Eileen smiles. "That's lovely," she says, nodding.

"I don't think God is way up above us in the clouds," Moe goes on, blowing another bubble. It pops. "I think God is just..." She stops chewing. "Just light." She starts another bubble. Stops. "I love light. Don't you?"

"Right," Eileen says, starting to feel uneasy. She bites her lip. "I do."

"So anyway, take care. And maybe try that...try praying sometime. You know, pray for somebody you love."

"Sure," Eileen says, waving. "Maybe sometime I will."

Eileen isn't expecting to try it this morning. But somehow, after she finishes all of her poses, after she does the salute to the sun, and the half moon and the warrior and the hero and the tortoise and the plow, she finds herself back on the floor in her meditation pose once more. And what comes to mind right away is Moe, Moe blowing smoke rings and big grape bubbles. Moe lecturing to her on God and light and praying and love. Moe and her simple, slow way of talking. "I wonder how Moe prays," Eileen says out loud now. And in the next moment, she hears the older woman's mellow voice in her head, hears how words flow out of Moe's mouth, as easily as smoke from her cigarette. "Please let Candace get better. Please let Candace get..." Eileen stops. Opens her eyes. Feels dopey. It's one thing to meditate, she thinks. It's quite another thing to...to pray.

But then Moe comes to mind again: what she was saying about the light, about her heart in light. Eileen closes her eyes once more and this time she thinks of her own heart that way, surrounded by light. Right away, something happens. Eileen's chest softens; feels warm, exceedingly relaxed, almost as if her heart is glowing. She enjoys the feeling, and then she realizes: Moe said you just let the words float out. Eileen shudders. It's crazy, she thinks. I'm not the praying type. And yet, she can't let the idea go. There was something so comfortable about Moe this morning. Something so reassuring in the way she stood there, saying simply that God was light. That's all. Just light.

"I guess I might as well try," Eileen says, heaving a sigh. And so she does. She begins. "I know I shouldn't be asking for anything because...because I don't have the right. But Dear God, I am asking anyway. I am praying today because...I have to. Because I need help with something...with someone I love, with something I started a long time ago and messed up *so* badly." She pauses. Her throat closes, but she goes on. "I am sorry for that. Deeply sorry. And now I am praying because I need strength I don't have. I...my daughter is ill. Please help her. Please help me help her." She stops again, and then the words Hail Mary come to mind and she thinks, No. I can't say that prayer. And then the words Our Father come to mind and she rejects that too. But then four other words come to mind, words she's heard more times than she can count. And those words are OK. "Thy will be done," she whispers. "Thy will be done."

❧

Later, Eileen thinks back to her prayers. There she is, straightening Candace's bed. Candace is sitting up, groggy from sedation, and

Eileen is pulling up sheets and blankets and going on and on, talking as she does to Candace lately, talking for both of them, because Candace is too tired to hold up her end of the conversation. Eileen is saying how warm it is, how March may go out like a lamb after all, how if it's still warm later, maybe they can sit together on the porch.

Candace nods, but then her face changes, as if she's seen a ghost. "Oh God," she cries, her eyes as wide as they can be. She points and tries to get out of bed.

Alarmed, Eileen whips around. And then a sound comes out of her mouth, a small shriek of joy, and in that moment, she knows her prayers were answered. Because there at the door is Audrey, leaning on a cane, her face streaming with tears. Holding one of Audrey's elbows is Rusty, and he too is crying, and then they are all crying together.

Later, Audrey and Eileen help Candace down the hall, where they bathe her and wash her hair for the first time in two weeks. Audrey kneels by the tub and supports Candace's back while Eileen soaps and shampoos Candace, rinsing her daughter, pouring water wherever there is soap. And when Candace is finally clean and lying in fresh rinse water, her salmon hair streaming out in all directions, she smiles, really smiles, for the first time in months. "Thank you," she says. "Thank you both so much."

Eileen and Audrey grin and shake hands across Candace's emaciated rib cage. Then they wrap her in white towels. Audrey sets the first towel over Candace's head and just as the white fluff swallows up the strawberry red blanket that is Candace's hair, Eileen pauses and considers her daughter's lightly freckled face. At that moment Eileen decides she must go off by herself later and say another prayer. This time, though, she will only say two words: "Thank you." And then one more: Amen.

CANDACE

(*maroon leather chair, sun glancing on brown hair, dust dancing in afternoon light*)

—*she was drowning, she was drowning...* (*Candace nodding, looking down*)

And you were trying to get to her then, to rescue her?

—*I...I kept wanting to* (*grey carpet, tree shadows playing*)

And?

—*I tried, I reached down for her, I tried, I grabbed her finger...her toe...and then...*

And then?

—*I...she was so slippery...I...I let go* (*thumbs together, nails chewed frightfully short*)

She was slippery?

—*It was wet.*

It was water? You were swimming in water?

—*No.* (*lip quivering*) *It was red...blood or mucous or...or something slimy...*

And so you tried to reach her, but...

—*But there were waves...and they were too high. I couldn't get there...or hold on...*

Hold on? You said you were swimming...What was there to hold onto?

—*I told you, I was trying to hold onto her, my daughter*

And did you see anyone who could help you?

—*I...I saw...I thought of Audrey and Eileen, but...*

But what?

—*(shaking head)...it was so strange...I saw the pool inside me, and me inside it, and I thought it was in Eileen and in Audrey, too.*
So you were alone?
—*I was. And trying to swim...but....(tears now tears now tears) there was blood...*
Blood?
—*Or whatever the red was...*
And?
—*And it was in my mouth, I kept trying to shout, "GRETCHEN, GRETCHEN" and every time I did, I choked, I felt like I was choking...I couldn't get the blood out. (the arm of the chair, hairs of grey white and brown, grey and white and brown, deer colors)*
So you were trying to rescue her? Your daughter?
—*Yes. Yes, her, and me, too, I wanted to rescue me...*
You wanted to rescue yourself?
—*(head up and down, no voice, no sound) Yes. I wanted to, but...I...I was...so scared.*
Why?
—*BECAUSE.*
Tell me, Candace, why were you so scared?
—*Because...(pressure in chest)...because I was, I knew I was supposed to...*
You were supposed to what?
—*I wanted to...(looking up, crying) I wanted to...all my life I wanted to...*
Wanted what Candace? What did you want all your life?
—*(voice light) I wanted to...(inhaling) I wanted to show my mother how I could...*
How you could what?
—*(crying, crying harder, tissues passing across desk, blowing nose)*
—*STOP, I WANT TO STOP...*
We can stop in a little while.
—*I WANT TO STOP NOW...*
You want to stop what?
—*Talking. Talking about this...*
Why?
—*Because...because it's...I hate it...(breath in) I...I hate her*
You hate her?
—*Sometimes. Sometimes I still do. Sometimes I hate my mother*

Why?

—*Because. I've told you before. Because she wasn't there. When I was little, she wasn't there. I've told you that a million times before. And still you keep asking me why.*

OK, so you hate your mother sometimes. And?

—*And I wish she was dead...*

Right. Tell me Candace, when did all that start? That you hated your mother?

—*(head hurts, hand over eyes, window, blue rectangles, eight: one, two, three, four, five, six, seven, eight) I...I wished she was dead when I was little, or...or later...why does it matter? I hated her sometimes, that's all...*

I think it matters, Candace. Tell me. Did you hate her when she came back?

—*Yes...well, no, not exactly...(eyes drying)*

Do you remember her coming back?

—*(pause) Of course I do.*

So what do you remember?

—*Me jumping rope all day. Her white car crunching the gravel in the driveway.*

And Eileen? What do you remember of your mother?

—*Her hair, long black hair, and bare arms. Her white T-shirt, and tight jeans, and pointy black boots with heels, and dark glasses. Great big sunglasses that hid her eyes.*

How did you feel about your mother that day? Did you wish she was dead that day?

—*(sighing) No. I mean I was really excited. I don't know...I guess it started after...*

After? After what?

—*("Candy," her grandfather says. "Candy, come sit down here.") It was so long ago...and I...I don't remember everything. (sun goes away, shadows don't play on rug)*

I think you do. I think you can remember just fine.

—*No I tell you, I can't. (doctor's eyes behind glasses.)*

Try, please.

—*I can't. (frowning, just frowning)*

Try, come on Candace, just a little.

—*(squeezing eyes with fingers, wiping nose with sleeve of sweatshirt, head hurts, head hurts, throat thirsty) Can I have a glass of water?*

Sure...here. Now. Tell me more about the day Eileen came back.

—(black hair on bare arms, white shirt sleeves rolled) I was with her all that day…but….

But what?

—(gravel driveway, car tires, irises, blue sky, Eileen in aviator sunglasses, "I guess you know she's coming, Candy…") I wanted her there but…I…I was…scared too.

But why? Why were you scared?

—I (shrugging)…had to be careful. She ran away. When I was a baby, she left me.

She left you.

—(blue rectangles, eight, clouds drifting by, no sun, wind up, spring has officially begun, Moe said, Moe said spring…"Candy, you know that if she went away once, she could go away again, you know that, right, honey?")

Candace, I said she left you.

—I heard you.

And?

—(eyes blur, eyes fill with water) She left me. What else can I say?

And how do you feel?

—Now??

Now. Then. Whenever.

—Tired. (how tired, how slow, how long each day goes. Moe said spring, said spring, said warm weather coming) I wanted not to be scared that day…or ever.

So then why were you so scared?

—(Pressure in chest) Look, I'm very tired and I want to go now. We can do the rest tomorrow.

No. I know you are tired. And you want to go. And you can, shortly. But stay with me, stay with this a little while longer. You said you were scared but didn't want to be?

—I remember she drank coffee.

Coffee? (sitting at the table, watching Eileen's hair, her bare arms, her nose.)

—Yeah, with lots of milk.

Just that?

—She took me to school that September. To fifth grade. She'd never done it before.

Before, who took you?

—(first day, first day, blue and green plaid skirt, blue shoes, double straps, Lucy, Lucy, grey hair, kids staring.) My mother wasn't there when I went to school and my grandmother had to take me and all the kids…(shrugs)

What?

—*Oh you know...it was different. I was different. (Eyes, filling.)*

So you were angry your mother didn't take you to school?

—*Yeah, I was. She wasn't there. (Eyes, spilling.) She didn't care about me. (Spilling.)*

Oh, Candace are you sure about that?

—*(shrugs)*

She did come back.

—*Yeah...too late.*

Too late?

—*(nodding...looking at door...black coat on hook on door...still cold...Moe says spring, warm weather coming. Pink flowers.) I remember a picture.*

What picture?

—*I just remember it, from her prom.*

Who's prom?

—*My mom's. Grandma kept it buried in the dining room hutch. I used to open the musty book to that page, and touch the picture. She had pink flowers on her wrist and Daddy had his arm around her waist. In high school. I thought she was a princess...and they stood by the irises.*

So she came back, and you were happy, but scared too. Why Candace? Why were you scared? You still haven't told me.

—*I called it the princess picture, because...she had some shiny thing in her hair. A crown.*

Candace? Tell me what made you so scared when your mother came back?

—*I knew better...(bed, Lucy's white spread, Grandpa, weathered hands, Grandpa's black shoe, "Candy, I want to talk to you...")*

Candace?

—*What? ("to tell you, to make sure you know"...Can we go outside Grandpa? By the irises?)*

I want you to continue with that thought...you knew better...

—*(by the irises...such a smell....so sweet the smell of blue filmy petals "Like I said, Candy, you know you're mother is coming back but you know something, I want you to be careful because she isn't like other mothers...you better not go around thinking she is...")*

Candace?

—*("I don't want you expecting...I don't want you hurt, not by her"...eyes blinking, eyes in irises, irises in nose, so blue so filmy so purple) I knew better than to think...to trust her. I knew better than to let her...I just knew better, because Grandpa told me not to...*

Not to what?

—*(eyes off to blue sky, eyes flying to clouds)...Not to trust her...*

Why Candace? Why did he say that?

—*he (eyes on brown hair, eyes staring into eyes behind glasses) he said she wasn't....*

She wasn't what? Your grandfather told you what exactly?

—*(frowning, looking down, grey carpet, no sound, deep down, no sound) he said she...she couldn't be trusted to...*

She couldn't be trusted to what? To love you? Is that what he said?

—*(shake head, shake head)*

What else did he say?

—*(irises, irises, the smell of them, such a smell, "I want to tell you") His eyes were red...and...he said she might not...*

She might not what? What did he say?

—*I remember we were sitting by the irises the day Eileen came. We were inside on Lucy's bed and then I asked if we could go outside instead and so we did, we went out and we sat there and he said "Candy, honey, you never know, she could stay or she could just pick up and decide to go away again like before..."*

Why did he say that to you Candace?

—*(day bright, hot, iris smell, blue blue, yellow bermuda shorts.) He said she could (voice fading) never be...*

What?

—*(throat swollen, tongue thick, sunlight sticking in eyes) A real mother to me. He said a real mother wouldn't have run away...so she could never be...a real mother...*

Why did he say that?

—*Because...(shrugs)...she left me...and she couldn't be trusted... (voice a pinpoint)*

How did you feel when he said that Eileen couldn't be trusted? How did you feel?

—*Oh (sighing, crying again) scared. Happy she was there, but scared she'd leave. And then later I decided, much later...I knew I had to...*

What?

—*I had to be careful...I had to be careful and be...be good, I had to be a good....*

What? A good what?

—*A good girl and (sobbing) also...a...a good mother. Myself. Me. I started to...in high school or...even before, I can't remember anymore when* it started, but I wanted my own baby more than anything ... so I could show her. So I could show her how I would be a good mother, better than her, one who wouldn't...

Wouldn't what, Candace? What wouldn't that good mother do?

—(eyes stare, finger twisting hair, finger pointed upward, finger in woods, tree, tree, tree on fire, Audrey with pails? Where is Audrey with the pails?) She wouldn't...scare me, or...or...or leave me there, again...ever.

Right. Right, Candace, she wouldn't leave. She wouldn't scare you by leaving.

—But...But I...

Yes?

—I left her...I left her...that day (pails, fire, AUDREY AUDREY GOD WHERE IS AUDREY?) I laid Gretchen down...I didn't mean to...(nose blowing nose) I was sick, I was...

Yes?

—I was sick, I wasn't feeling well, my wrist, I didn't mean to...I just went to get help and...

You and your baby were both very sick and you were trying to be a good mother, trying to rescue her.

—I was. (tears, chest squeezed) I was trying to find help. Yes. (crying, crying more)

Go ahead Candace. Cry. Here. (pause, more kleenex, in a ball, tears all over) And there was no one to rescue you or her? Except at the very end, Eileen came.

—(head shakes up and down, hiccuping now) Y-y-yes. She did.

And how did that make you feel?

—(shadows shifting on carpet) Sc-c-c-ared. Ag-g-gain. Scared.

And?

—S-s-sad...s-s-so s-sad.. And m-m-mad...s-so mad

Mad at...?

—At me.

At yourself Candace? Why? Why were you so angry at yourself? And scared? And sad?

—B-b-because I wanted to...to show her...and I wanted to d-do it myself, but...

But?

—But I...

But what, Candace?

—I couldn't.

You couldn't. You needed help then didn't you, Candace?

— *(frowning, head nodding up and down.)*

And that's OK, Candace. To need help. And to get it from your mother. Because she wanted very much to help you. She wanted very much to be there for you.

—*(frowning, only frowning, only now the sound of hiccuping)*

In the end, then, she was a good mother, wasn't she? She was there for you that day in Vermont when you really really needed her, and when Gretchen needed her?

—*(nodding) She was. Only…(biting lip, hiccuping, whispering.) It… was sc-c-cary.*

That's right, Candace, it was and still is scary…you've been scared all your life, scared your mother would let you down, leave again. Not be there. And so you tried to be the best mother you could be, to make up for that. To be there for your own baby. To show her how well you could do. But then something terribly scary happened. You almost lost Gretchen. You were trying to show your mother how you could take care of your own baby, do a better job than she did with you and then you weren't able to, and that was awfully scary.

—*(Candace bawling, her face all covered by her hands)*

Only, Candace, think about it. You were doing OK at first with Gretchen, right? It was hard, and you were alone, but you were doing pretty well until that day in Vermont?

—*(Candace still bawling, all her salmon hair over her shoulders, shrugging)*

Candace? Weren't you being a good mother until that one very scary day up in Vermont? Because you yourself were sick?

—*(Candace looking up) Y-y-yes. I guess. I was sick. Tired and very sick.*

So do you think maybe, just maybe, you can forgive yourself this one mistake? Can you tell yourself that you were tired and very sick and that you made a mistake and that we all make mistakes, you, your mom, everybody? Can you do that and go on? Can you forgive yourself this mistake and learn to trust yourself again? And maybe not be so scared? What do you say to all that?

—*(Candace shrugging, rocking herself back and forth) I don't know, I don't know.*

Well, Candace, let me ask you something. Can you trust your mother now?

—*(sobbing less) I…I guess. (pause.) Yes, I mean I think so.*

OK. And can you forgive your Mom for not being there when you were little?

—(sighing) I...sometimes I think so, when I see what she went through...

OK. So maybe you can forgive your mother and maybe you can trust her. And are you happy about that? About maybe being able to trust her again?

—(nodding) I...I am...(crying more) awfully grateful for...for her saving Gretchen.

And so, do you think that in the same way you are beginning to trust and forgive your mother, you can also forgive yourself? Can you forgive both of you, and live with the mistakes both of you have made?

—(hair around finger, tight, finger whitening) I...I don't know. I hope so.

I hope so too, Candace. (long pause) Because you deserve that, Candace. You do.

—(Candace staring wide-eyed at the window.)

And one more thing (doctor glancing at wrist watch). Before you go, I want to make sure I understand why it is you didn't trust your mother before, when she came back. Do you understand why that was?

—(eyes stare, finger in hair, eyes stare, irises, irises, eyes stare, eyes stare, eyes stare, promise Candy, promise honey, sun, sunny day, "promise never to tell her what I said...better that way, not to say anything,") It was...because of him. A lot of why I was scared. He...m-m-y grandfather (whisper, no tears). He told me, he made me...he didn't want me to...to... to be close to her.

Yes, Candace. And how does that make you feel? How do you feel knowing that your grandfather tried to keep you from trusting her? Tried to keep you from being close to your own mother?

—(eyes drying, eyes drying, head nodding). Awful...awful angry and...oh God. So so...sad.

Why Candace? Why does that make you feel so angry and so sad?

...(Inhaling, rocking herself again.) Because he...he spoiled things. Way back then, when she came back, he had to go and spoil things. He tried to make them bad and he did. He did that to me. To...to us. And for that, I hate him. I just hate him..

CANDACE AND EILEEN

They are walking together, breathing cool air, inhaling the smell of raw spring earth, wet and warming after the melting of snow. Eileen is talking.

"So yes, Candace, I did think about coming back, all the time, but especially that first year after I left. For the first six months, though, I couldn't even bring myself to call. And then when I did call, once, it was in May, Mother's Day. I tried to talk to Grandma Lucy, but she wouldn't speak to me. Neither of them would. I guess I should have expected that."

"So were you thinking of coming back for me then? That May?"

Eileen stops, squints into the bright sunlight, puts both gloved hands into the small of her back. "I was always *thinking* about coming back for you, honey. But you have to understand. I was terrified and confused. When I left, I actually had three bruised ribs, from where your grandfather jabbed his boot into me. So I wasn't in much of a hurry to see him again. I was so traumatized by everything that had happened. I spent that first year, or most of it, just trying to recover. I had my ward clerk's job back at that hospital in Berkeley, and I was living with my friend Barbara Cicero and just trying to, you know...live."

Candace eyes a chickadee. She has been drawing birds lately. Eileen bought a feeder and hung it outside Candace's window at the hospital and now she draws every bird she sees.

"I never knew that side of Grandpa," she says finally, wrinkling up her face. "I mean, honestly, Mom, it's kind of hard to think of Papa Frank acting so...so violent."

"Well, he had a terrible temper, and I guess I just pushed him past his limit. He went kind of crazy with me at the end there, after I had you."

"I guess. So anyway, you said before you tried to come back. When was that?"

"You were two. Actually, it was just before you turned three. I had hired a lawyer in San Francisco and he said he saw no reason I couldn't just go home and take you back with me. You were my child and I had never relinquished custody." She sighs. "So I had the whole thing worked out. I had my ticket. And the lawyer had sent them the letter. I was all set to do just that. Or so I thought." Eileen sighs loudly.

"Yeah?"

"And so then I called. It was July, I remember, and I didn't even say hello, so they couldn't hang up. Lucy answered the phone. I said, 'I'm coming back for her.'"

"And?"

"She gave the phone to Grandpa and he threatened me. 'You come back here and we'll call the cops.' I mean it was silly, how could he call the cops? But that unnerved me. I think I would have come anyway, though, except then Grandpa unleashed his final weapon."

"What was that?"

"He had your dad call me. I mean, it made sense when I thought about it later. I ought to have expected it. Your father said to me, 'Look, Eileen, you know you can come back. Anytime. But you can't take Candace away. Not from me. And not from Lucy and Audrey. Because they are the only mothers she's ever known. She belongs here, near the people she's grown up knowing and loving.'" Eileen inhales, and her voice is small. "And of course he was right. It wouldn't have been fair to you or anybody else."

Candace stops. Frowns. Bends down and picks up a rock with a pretty white quartz streak. She doesn't speak for a long time. And when she does her voice warbles. "So this is where I'm confused Ma. I don't get it. Why didn't you just come back then? I mean…I was three…if you missed me so much…" She shakes her head. She wants to say, why the hell did you wait until I was ten? But then her throat begins thickening and her face muscles tighten as if she might cry and she gets that awful sensation in her stomach again…

Eileen stares at the ground, then looks up at Candace, but Candace won't look back at her. "I know this is hard for you. And in the end, I guess I have no reason to expect you ever to understand or…to forgive me." She inhales. "But the truth is I had to live something out in California. I know it's hard for you to understand this, but it took me all those years to get my act together. To find the courage to stand up to my father. I had to build some kind of life for myself, some kind of identity. I had to feel like I knew who I was."

Eileen stops talking, waits for Candace to reply. She doesn't. So Eileen goes on. "After a year or so, I went back to school, part-time, at Cal. It took me almost three years just to finish college. By that time, I was working in a lab at the hospital and also volunteering at the Berkeley Free Clinic. Everybody was telling me I really had to get an MPH to do what I wanted to do, the community health thing, so I applied to Berkeley and got an assistantship."

Candace's lower lip is sticking out, and she isn't listening that closely, because she isn't all that interested in how her mother became a public health expert. Feeling hurt now, she scuffs her running shoe back and forth through the soft wet mud on the road. A car passes and she follows it with her eyes. She clears her throat, doesn't like the sound of her voice when she speaks. "It's hard for me Ma…" she begins. "I mean, you were gone a long time…"

Eileen sets a hand on Candace's shoulder, but Candace jerks it away.

"Please, honey, don't. I know this is hard. But I'm trying to explain…time goes by so fast, especially when you're as busy as I was."

Candace sniffs, starts walking. Doesn't say what's on her mind: that time doesn't go by so fast at all if you're a broken-hearted little girl who is waiting for her mother to show up. No, time goes by very slowly in that case.

"Look, Candace, I wasn't going to mention this, but actually I've got these letters I wrote to you, every year on your birthday, they're a little like the journals but different too, I mean, if you want to read them I would be happy to…" Eileen is following Candace now, starring at her hair.

"No, Mom!" Candace screeches, tossing the rock with the quartz streak to one side. "No letters. No more journals." They've come up to a stop sign just before a parking lot. "I've had enough of that crap."

"OK, OK, I'm sorry." She pauses. "I just wanted you to know I've got them, I mean, if , you know, maybe someday you change your mind."

"Not likely," Candace says hotly. She turns around, starts walking away from her mother, so quickly that Eileen falls behind. "Not likely at all."

"OK, anything you say, honey. It's totally your call, your decision if and when."

"Yeah, well, it's totally my decision to go back inside," Candace says, feeling wounded again. "I'm tired, and I think after I take a nap I might want to paint."

❧

An hour later Candace is woken up by a bright shimmering peel of red light. When she opens her eyes, the light shifts like quicksilver to yellow and then just as fast to orange and blue. She sits up, confused, but then sees the reason for the lights: the large crystal Audrey brought to the hospital on her last visit, before she went up to Vermont to stay with Rusty, is spinning in the window reflecting the afternoon sun. Candace loved the crystal the moment she saw it. Audrey always kept one at the farm, and when Candace was little, she would refer to the dancing lights that the crystal cast on the wall as "rainbow fish." Now she thinks of the rainbow effect as "Audrey light."

Yawning, she lies down again, frowning, feeling bad about how mad she got at her mother at the end of their walk. She sits up. Has a notion to paint. Nurse Harrison's rule is that Candace can either paint in the common room, where others are gathered talking and watching T.V. Or she can paint in her own room, as long as Eileen, or some other adult, is there with her. So now Candace has to decide: join the crazies in the common room or wait for Eileen, who said she'd be back in a couple of hours.

She decides to wait, and while she does, she decides to sketch a Blue Jay. Eileen filled the feeder outside her window just this morning with more black oil sunflower seed and now there are more birds than ever. Candace has sketched chickadees and nuthatches, woodpeckers and finches and white-throated sparrows. The other day she tried a Blue Jay, to no avail, but now, the Jay is back, and she's going to try him again.

"If only he'd stay put," she murmurs, eyeing the big blue bird, trying to memorize its shape, and coloration. As she lays her charcoal pencil to paper, something jars her. She looks up to a three by five photo pinned to her wall. All of a sudden it hits her: the Jay's color mimics exactly the color of Gretchen's eyes. Bright blue with black streaks and flecks of white.

Four days ago, Mark visited and brought a new photo of the baby, and Candace has the picture tacked up right beside her bed. Within eyesight now. Maybe that's why she got it in her head to draw the Blue Jay today.

She sighs. Those eyes. Gretchen's blue and black-streaked eyes. Candace studies the eyes and the rest of the photo, the fluff of reddish blonde curls, the creamy white cheeks. A full baby face. Not what she expected at all. Until Mark brought the photo, Candace was scared to see the baby. Scared she would see a thin, sickly child. But no, this baby has the pink and white fullness of a healthy baby's face. Her mouth is pink like candy. And in the photo, she is smiling. *Smiling.*

Candace leans back against the wall. All it would take is her saying, *Yes.* Just that. Just *yes, bring her in.* Because Eileen announced last week that Gretchen is ready to leave the hospital. That all the doctors agree she can have the rest of her therapy at home. And then Mark came and handed her the photo and said that anytime Candace was ready, he would be happy to bring Gretchen in for a visit. His words to her were: "She's a beauty, Candace. She really is. When you feel up to it, I know you're going to…well, I just love holding her."

She bit into her lip then, told him she wasn't sure she was ready yet.

She bites into her lip again now. Her frown returns and she puts her charcoal pencil down. She's going to wait to do the Jay. He'll be back. The Jays are always there, ready to attack the feeder, greedy birds that they are.

There is a knock. "Hello?" Eileen calls through the door.

"Come in," Candace replies, wiping her eyes. Eileen comes in with a package, done up in a bow. And a large grocery bag too.

"Oh Ma," Candace says, blowing her nose. "You didn't have to buy me anything. You've gotten me enough things already."

"Well, so, here's one thing more. And when you see what it is, you're going to say, 'Gee whiz, Ma, I wish I'd had these before.'"

Candace drops to the bed. Shreds the wrapping. Inside the box is a pair of binoculars.

"I heard you tell nurse Harrison you wanted to see the birds up close." Eileen beams.

Candace looks up, smiles back. Shakes her head. "You're spoiling me," she whispers, her voice cracking. She turns back to the window, gazes into the binoculars, focuses on the feeder. She locks right onto the amazing tail feathers of the Jay. As if the blue and black and white tail is right up against her eyes. As if she can touch the colors.

"Thank you, Ma," Candace blurts out, her eyes filling.

"So OK, so here's one more thing. And you can throw this out the window if you want. And I promise I will never bring it back, ever ever again." She hands Candace the grocery bag. Candace takes it and reaches inside, and maybe because she's hungry, she is expecting something sweet, a treat, like chocolate cake.

But then, when her hand lands on the object, she can tell immediately this is no ordinary cake. It's the old yellow doll. Dollcake. DC2.

Candace pulls the doll to her lap and hugs it, and nodding, she starts to weep.

Eileen squeezes her shoulder with one arm. "Oh Candace, honey, I'm sorry, please don't cry. God, I don't care if you keep it or not. I just felt so bad before, when we were walking, and I suggested you read those stupid letters. That's all…"

"No Ma, no, it's OK," Candace is saying. "It's not the doll at all. It's just…I…" she pulls away from her mother and points to the baby's photo. "Just before you came I decided to draw a Blue Jay and as I started to draw, I saw that the bird is the very same color as Gretchen's eyes…and then, I felt so incredibly sad…I had to stop drawing." Candace shrugs, hangs her head and wipes her eyes with her sleeve. "I know it's silly."

"Oh honey." Eileen folds Candace into her arms. "It's not a bit silly. I told you, sweetheart, as soon as you're ready to see her, she'll be there ready to see you. You've got to make sure you give yourself enough time though." Eileen strokes Candace's hair, passes her hand along the tight French braid that runs like a crest down the back of her daughter's head.

Candace and Eileen stay like that, embracing, until Candace pulls away and says she wants to set up her easel. While Eileen sits with a book in the chair by the window, Candace sits cross-legged on the bed. Staring at the door. Waiting for something to come to mind. And of course the same blue comes to mind. The same Jay blue. Only then, thankfully, a second color comes to mind too: aquamarine. The two colors, aquamarine and blue, the colors of the ocean. Water shades. Closing her eyes, Candace envisions now the painting by Van Gogh, the one she liked so much in school: the famous vase of irises sitting on a table, the blue flowers, their long slender green fronds. Blue and aquamarine. Serene.

Standing, Candace faces the easel and begins painting. For who knows how long she paints. When she paints like this, she is always gone, somewhere, somewhere where there is blissfully no clock at all. At one point, Eileen leaves, goes down the hall, and returns with a newspaper. She returns to her chair and reads it cover to cover, occasionally looking up to see what Candace is painting.

In the space of no time, art time, time suspended, Candace has a copy of Van Gogh's "Irises" on her canvas. But as it is a copy out of memory, she has taken great liberties with the flowers, and after a short while, the flowers start to grow out of a different place, a different memory completely. They grow out of a yard, rooted beside a driveway, next to a short stretch of split rail fence. They grow ten years ago, and they unlock a store of memories surrounding her grandfather, standing in the driveway. Candace hadn't realized when she began that these were the irises that she would paint. But now, now that they are standing on the canvas, now that she has seen them, now that she has seen herself paint them, she stops. She steps away from the canvas, sits down on the edge of the bed. She eyes her mother reading and lets her gaze linger there.

"Is something wrong, honey?" Eileen asks.

"No. It's just..." Candace studies her mother carefully. "I need to tell you something."

"Sure. Go ahead," Eileen says. Candace remains silent.

"Is it about Mark? I mean, I couldn't help noticing the way you two were the other day, you seemed so close. I thought maybe he would be coming back to see you this..."

"No, Ma," Candace says, shaking her head. "He had to go out to L.A. for a few days. And then he'll be back. Next week. But it's not about him."

"Well, so...what is it? I hope not that business with the letters still. I am so sorry I offered them... I mean just forget I ever..."

"No, Ma. Look it isn't any of that. It's..." Sighing, she glances at the canvas, and a moment later, Eileen does too, wondering if there is something she is supposed to see there.

"That's very nice by the way. Very nice," Eileen says, standing, putting the newspaper aside. "I really like those colors, the cool blues especially."

"Mom." Candace slides back on the bed now, and rests against the wall.

"What?"

"Has Dr. Betz told you...has she said anything about my last couple sessions?"

"No. Of course not, Candace. I told you, when you talk to the doctor, you're talking just to her. Alone. She doesn't go telling me or anybody else what you said."

Candace nods. Closes her eyes. She believes that about Dr. Betz, that she doesn't reveal anything said in private. And yet, right now, oddly enough, Candace would almost prefer that Betz had saved her saying what she needs to say. She wishes, in one way, that Betz had told Eileen what Papa Frank said that day so many years ago.

Candace looks back at the canvas, and then out the window. The breeze blows in, catches at the curtains. The crystal spins and Audrey light flickers everywhere in the room.

"I....I told Dr. Betz something and...she thought I should tell you as soon as I felt I could," Candace begins. Silence. Candace sighs once, squints at the irises. Then at Eileen.

"What, Candace? What is it?" Eileen is speaking as quietly as she ever has. She has taken her seat at the edge of the chair again. Candace notices now how grey her mother's hair is. And how, now that she is greying, Eileen is looking more and more like Grandma Lucy every day.

"I...I told Dr. Betz about...about the day you...the day you came back." Candace licks her lips, folds them in on themselves. "About something that happened."

"Yes?"

"Well, I never told you this before. But that day, I remember it so clearly, and now again because of these irises. Somehow they remind me of that day. In June. I remember it was late morning and Grandpa had just cut the lawn. I can still almost smell that freshly cut grass. Anyway, he took me aside before you came, that morning, he told me he wanted to say something to me. And...then we sat by the irises and he did...he told me..." Candace's eyes narrow again now, as if she is seeing something within a slender space. "He...told me you would never ever be a real mother to me."

Eileen's eyes widen. Candace waits for her mother to speak. She doesn't, though, and so Candace goes on. "He said something else too. He told me I should never trust you, that I shouldn't expect you to stay, that any day, you could just...." Candace shrugs, looks down and then quickly looks up. "You could up and leave, run away again and never come back."

"My God." Eileen is nodding and her eyes are blank. Her voice sounds like it just sank through the floor. "My God he was cruel. But then, I knew he could be. I knew."

Candace's gaze drops. She is looking now at her hands, the ragged nails chewed to their lowest points, the skin in and around the nails ragged too. Outside, there is some sound. She looks up to see a red squirrel prancing along the branch that holds the feeder. Soon enough, the squirrel is swinging from the bottom of the feeder, his bushy tail flapping.

"You know he had no right to say that to you." Eileen has one fist, folded tightly, pressed against her mouth. She has her other hand gripping the wrist. The knuckles of both hands are white.

"I know, Ma. I know that now. But..." Candace takes a breath in, "but you can imagine how when I was only ten..." Candace shrugs, and now Eileen gets up from the chair.

"Of course, honey," she says. "I'm sure it was awful for you. I can't think of anything worse that he could have said to you that day."

Candace nods. "He really wrecked things, Mom. I feel...so angry."

Eileen drops beside Candace on the bed. She takes hold of Candace's hands. "I know you do. And sometimes I am still very very angry at him too. Even after he's dead, he is still making trouble. He has left all this terrible heartache behind." Eileen looks up to the ceiling. She concentrates because she doesn't want to give into the tears that are so near.

"I just want to say one thing. I want you to know that when I came back I made a conscious decision that I would never ever say anything negative to you about your grandparents, since they had been raising you." She clears her throat. And she waits to speak until she is sure her voice won't crack. "I thought I was doing right, Candace. I didn't ever want you to think that I was trying to pull you away, or sour you against them, especially Grandpa, especially after he had the stroke. But I tell you now, that was stupid of me. I realize now that I made a horrible mistake. I should have talked to you about him long before this."

Candace looks at her mother, and it is as if she is seeing another person, not Eileen, not her mother at all, at least not the mother she has always seen before. Eileen inhales and her shoulders curve in and suddenly she has the "old shoulder" look that Lucy always had. How can she look so much older than she looked just a few days before, Candace wonders.

"I wish I had done so many things differently," Eileen says. "So many things." She raises her face and Candace sees it swarming with sadness, as if the emotion had somehow become bees or gnats or flies. Candace looks away. She doesn't want to see any more weakness in her mother. "Look, Ma, it's OK. It's really OK. Whatever you did wrong, you realized it. You came back. The important thing is you always loved me and you came back." Candace begins patting her mother on the back. The motion jogs her memory: she remembers now how it was to comfort Gretchen. Instantly, she has in mind all the times she held the baby against her shoulder and circled her hand gently on the infant's back, exactly the same way she is now patting her mother. Something pulls at Candace's insides. She feels drawn to do something, or at least, to decide something about how she feels.

Just then, though, the phone rings, and Candace reaches for it, happy for the interruption. She has had enough talking and thinking and crying for one day. If the phone hadn't rung, she would have had to get off the bed anyway, would have had to make some excuse about why she needed to take a walk down the hall.

"Hello. Yes? Well, yes, that's fine. But who is it? I guess so. Yeah, that's OK." She replaces the receiver. "Somebody's here. But they wouldn't tell me who it was. I wonder why?"

Eileen reaches into her handbag for kleenex to blot her eyes and blow her nose. "I...I guess because the person wanted you to be surprised."

"They said them, though. They said it was them."

When "them" arrives, it is Rusty and Audrey. Audrey is balanced on her cane, and in her free hand, she carries a long slender roll of paper, tied with a blue bow. She takes a seat by the window and after some small talk with Eileen, Audrey hands the roll over to Candace.

"What is it, Grandma?" Candace asks, thinking it looks like an oversized diploma.

"Oh, now, just go ahead and unroll," Audrey says. Candace does, and discovers a blueprint. "For what, though?"

Audrey clears her throat. "Well, it's for a house. A new house."

"Actually, a new cottage," Rusty corrects her. "Let's not get carried away here."

"Oh yes, Rus, a cottage. A summer cottage for me and Marjory."

Candace nods, thinking how lovely, a cottage for the two of them in Florida. But what does this have to do with me? "Gee," she says pleasantly. "That's...swell."

"So aren't you going to ask where the cottage will be built?" Audrey asks.

"Oh, sure. Where?"

"At Maple Hill. On the five-acre parcel we kept when we decided to sell the farmhouse and the land. We need a place to spend the summers, don't we, I mean, we can't live down south through those awful steamy summer months."

"Great!" Candace says. "Oh Grandma, I'm *so* glad."

Audrey beams. "*And*, construction is underway, *and*, we should be done by the end of July, except for finish work inside, *and*, we have already moved the Hannah rock there."

"Yes," says Rusty, leaning against the windowsill, "and miraculously, we still have our backs and legs intact."

"You *moved* Hannah, Dad?" Candace asks, wide-eyed, seeing the gigantic sculpture balanced on her father's shoulders.

"Well, not with my bare hands, honey. We had help from a flatbed and a crane and a whole lot of straps and chains."

"Cool." Candace nods, smiling and gazing closer at the cottage drawing. She notices her father's name in the corner of the blueprint. "And you drew these too?"

"Yes, I'm afraid I must take responsibility," he says. "My first passive solar design in about eight years."

"Well, that's very, very cool," Candace says. A moment of silence passes, during which Candace studies the blueprints closer. She sees a massive stone fireplace labeled in the living room, a kidney-shaped hot tub in the downstairs bath. And then, just when she's about to hand the blueprints back, she notices something written in a note over the second floor: half of it is labeled, "Candace's suite, including studio and attached bath." Her jaw falls.

"Hey," she squeals, pointing at the drawing. "There's, there's...these rooms are for *me*!"

Audrey settles back in her chair. "Well I was wondering when you'd see. For heaven's sake, Candace, of course there's room for you. This is *your* house after all."

Candace's eyes pop. "My house? *My* house? For *me*?"

Audrey nods. "Yes, my dear. I will, with your permission, live there with Marj during the summer months. And you, you are free to come and go as you please. You can live there full-time, if you decide to, or you can rent it out, or rent out part of it, in the winter, as a ski house. But in the end, the house is yours."

Candace turns to Eileen, who nods back and smiles, her eyes red and her lips pressed together. "I'd say it's a pretty good deal," Eileen says quietly.

"But does that mean...I mean...do I have to pay...like...like a mortgage?" Candace asks, still unclear what she's been given.

"No, dear," Audrey says. "Marjory and I chipped in, and your Dad, and we had your share from the sale of the farm, and uh..." she turns to face Eileen, who shrugs, and calmly nods, "your Mom kicked in as well. We bought this cottage for you free and clear."

"Oh my God." For several seconds, Candace just looks from one to the other, her mouth open, one hand on her chin. She keeps shaking her head in wonderment. And then she claps both her hands over her mouth and jumps off the bed and runs around the room, squealing and hugging everybody, and jumping up and down. Finally, she goes to the window and opens it wide.

"I own it!" she yells out to no one in particular. "It has a studio and a hot tub and I fucking own it!"

Turning back to face Audrey, she squeezes her grandmother's shoulders and kisses her silver head, and Audrey grabs her hand and squeezes back and looks up at her and says, "Yes, Candace, you own it. And the nicest thing is, you can share it with anybody you want to."

GRACE

The window is wide open and spring air is filling up the room. Candace is painting and has been all day. First she does an oversized view of the Blue Jay standing at the feeder, his expression pointed and fierce. In the second painting, the bird looks smaller and further away. He has lifted off the feeder, is airborne, and in this position, his blue wings and tail are fanned, spread, the prominent black and white streaks forming wide crescents as the bird ascends. It is only because of these dark and light markings, and their resemblance to the streaks in Gretchen's eyes, that Candace does the paintings of the Jay at all.

When she finishes the second Jay, she takes a break. Walks to the common room, where Moe and the others are watching their favorite soap opera. Sitting there, staring at the screen, Candace comes to her decision easily. She turns to Moe. "I think I'm ready," she announces. "I think I'm finally ready to paint Gretchen's eyes."

Moe turns, distracted by her show. "Oh?" she says. "Is that right?"

"Yes," Candace says, nodding. "I've had her eyes in my head for days."

When they finally emerge, Gretchen's eyes fill the entire canvas. They are gigantic blue plates, glittering orbs with black and white streaks that snake through the bright blue color just the way the bird's markings radiated out of the tail and wings. Candace stands back, admiring. It is peculiar, she thinks, to be staring into these giant disembodied eyes, human eyes that are not human-looking at all. Eyes that are so large, so full of eerie detail and depth.

She moves across the room, sinks to the floor, stares up at the canvas. Squinting, it occurs to her that each of Gretchen's giant irises could be a painting in itself. Each iris, swirling blue and black and white, could be, at least abstractly, the earth. Each iris resembles the planet in those posters where the earth spins through the endless dark of the universe.

She leans against the door. Later she will say it was that cosmic view of Gretchen's eyes, that inspiring connection she made between her daughter's eyes and the planet, that gave her new inspiration. Or she will say that the inspiration came right through the window, floating on the spring air. Or she will say it was simply that wonderful color that did it, that blue of blueberries and Blue Jays and blue sky. Whatever it is, whatever it comes from, the inspiration is there. Candace stares at the photo of Gretchen beside her bed and suddenly the energy she has to paint that face is so strong that it squeezes her chest. Her heart pumping, she reaches under the bed, taking out the last of the canvases Eileen brought last week.

In no time at all, Candace is painting Gretchen. In no time at all, she has on the fresh canvas two new eyes, a pair of saucy blueberry irises, streaked in black. Soon these eyes are rising out of a small, perfectly round, perfectly luscious little face. Cheeks emerge, cheeks of creamy buttery white, cheeks like frosting, cheeks blushing pink at their rounded height. A face takes shape quickly: the small perfect curve of a nose, the tiny candy-colored mouth. Candace pauses, steps back from the painting. She giggles. She has painted Gretchen's face to look like an oversized cupcake. She laughs out loud. *A cup cake? A doll cake?*

Yes, she says, taking up the brush again. A *real* doll cake, and I am the one to make it: She dabs more creamy vanilla frosting against the face, fills out the forehead, adds white flecks to the eyes, sprinkles pink sugar all over the cheeks. Standing back again, Candace decides: Gretchen resembles that sweet portrait Renoir did, of the girl called *Margarite.*

She is delighted with the effect of the face, is about to go on, is adding a fluff of strawberry hair, a single curl, a blue ribbon tied to the fluff, just like in the photo Mark gave her, when something stops her. Something about the sugary cheeks, the blush of pink on the creamy vanilla flesh stops her. Something rushes through her. A feeling. Her mouth waters, and something else. She hasn't eaten all day and she is starving, and her stomach is starting to cramp, begging its need for food. She's hungry, but this hunger, this is something more. This goes deeper than ordinary hunger, the cry for food. She closes her eyes: she sees the delicate black streaks of the blueberry irises; clearly, so clearly. She sees the cheeks, has the sensation of them so real in her mind that she can feel them, pinch them. Kiss them. Taste them. She has the hold of them against her mouth. In her mouth. She has the feeling of what it would be like to let her lips and tongue linger against the frosting flesh, the cake beneath.

The thought of flesh like this, under her fingers, in her mouth, rubbing against her nose, her face, her hair, it's all there, buried in the painting, but inside her too, begging to be released. The longing is so strong that suddenly she cries out. For a moment, it stops her completely. It stabs at her with the force of all the hunger she has ever known. Suddenly she is weak, so weak that she has to sit down. She drops to the bed, and then, when that's not enough, she crosses her arms across her breasts and holds her shoulders, wraps herself within her own arms, and in that position, she goes to the floor, kneels there, sits back and just stares at the painting, shaking her head, wondering and dreading this feeling all at once, wondering where it came from, and dreading where it will go, where it will take her, this need, this desperate craving, a craving as powerful as any she has felt before. A craving for the touch of real flesh, the tender cake and frosting flesh of her precious little daughter. She has to have this feeling met, has to have this craving filled, now, today, soon, tomorrow, or the desire is going to drown her.

Candace stands. She knows how this need is filled — with something as simple as a phone call. All she has to do, Eileen said, was phone, all she has to say is, "Ma, I'm ready." Tears falling, Candace lifts the receiver. Her hand shakes as she dials. Already she imagines how it will be to relieve the hunger that is making her quake inside.

In the end, Mark carries the baby in. Mark, because ever since the beginning, when Gretchen went into the hospital, Mark was there, visiting, holding her, changing her, stroking her, talking to her, and often, singing for her, singing and playing the guitar. The first time he sang, one of the residents, a young physician who is herself a musician, praised Mark and told him she thought the music would help the baby. So he did it more, sometimes two, three, or even four times a week he would find time to come to the hospital, stay there, singing and playing beside the baby's crib for hours at a time. And when the baby finally came around, finally came out of the coma, Mark drowned the pediatric ward in songs, he played music so loud that a nurse came down the hall and told him he had to quiet down. And so he did, but he kept playing and that day, he wrote two songs, one for Gretchen, called "If Only You Knew," and the other for Candace, a melody without words, a haunting melody he still can't name.

It is ten o'clock and Candace is sitting on the bed waiting for Mark and Eileen and the baby to come. She is wearing a dress, actually a jumper and T-shirt, and the new running shoes Eileen bought, and her hair is in a tight French braid she made herself, and she looks rested. Her illness shows only in her slightly pale skin color, and in the fact that she is still quite painfully thin. She is so nervous now that her stomach hurts, and her chest has a vague achy feeling inside. For a few minutes, from nine to nine twenty, she sat in the common room, watching the "The Jenny Jones Show" with Moe, but it was so silly she couldn't stand it, so she came back to her room, straightened it up some more, and then sat down in the chair by the window, where she is now, holding Dollcake, squeezing her, and staring, staring, staring out the window to the parking lot.

At ten fifteen she jumps up. She hears a commotion, and throws open the door, sees a flash of dark curly hair down the hall and thinks to herself, all right, *all right*, this is Mark. But it is a false alarm, an aide is dragging a new patient, a Latina woman who has just arrived, by the arm and the woman is resisting because she doesn't want a shower.

Candace returns to her room wondering, what now? What can I do? She is too nervous to read, too excited to paint, or to write a letter, and anyway, who would she write to? Everybody she cares about is coming here today: Audrey and Rusty are scheduled to arrive just after lunch. Suddenly Candace is waiting so hard that she remembers waiting that other day, that day in June ten long years ago, that day suffused with irises, and for a second she wishes she had a jump rope, because it worked that day, jumping and waiting for Eileen. She needs it again today, desperately, she has more energy than a whole litter of puppies.

"Oh please come," she whispers, moving the curtain and watching out the window. But of course, the watching doesn't work, they don't come. And because Candace thinks she is going to jump out of her skin, because she is getting so anxious now she is starting to ache, to hurt, and because she is beginning to bite her nails again, and she promised Dr. Betz she would stop, she decides to take a short walk, just out to the side veranda and back.

She is half-way down the hall, all set to go out to the porch, when she catches a glimpse of Mark's black curls, and Eileen's tall slender frame. And then she hears Mark shout out her name: "Candace!" She stops in the middle of the hallway, covers her mouth. She turns. Down the hall she sees her: a very tiny girl, cradled in Mark's arms. Candace squeals, and breaks into a run, using the shoes for what they were intended, and in a second, she is there, staring at the back of Gretchen's head, lifting a little tuft, sifting silky curls the color of cantaloupe between her fingers. Biting her lip, she touches the baby's shoulder. "Oh please, Mark," she whispers in a hush, her legs and arms a rush of goosebumps. "Please let me hold her right away."

Mark turns the baby around, and Candace's mouth drops, because what she expected to see was a beautiful baby but what she actually sees is even more delicious. A more gorgeous creature she can't imagine. The baby drools over wet pink lips, and her cheeks are fair and soft and chunky, and yes, pink and white like frosting, and her eyes are even brighter and bluer than before, more like Audrey's, the black streaks even more distinct than when she was born. "Oh hello, sweetie," Candace breathes, putting her face in direct view of the child's. The baby's face lifts and then instantly, it splits into a big sloppy grin, cheeks spreading, eyes wide and round and content. A single tooth sticks up out of the bottom gum. Candace reaches for the child, takes her into her arms, and right away she notices that the baby's little stretch suit is blue, the same blue as her eyes. "I know you love that color," Eileen says shyly.

Candace sets her lips to the baby's forehead. "I do love that color," she says. "And I do love this baby, too." She holds the baby close, speaks into her skin. "This is a new baby," she whispers, feeling a wisp of hair against her lip. She kisses the baby again and again, relishing the delicious feeling of her lips on the tender flesh. And winding out of her heart at that moment is a decision: she knows then and there that she will care for this baby under a new name, that she will christen this child who was Gretchen anew, that she will call her by her middle name, Grace. "My baby," she says, whispering the words as if they are a prayer. "My baby. My little angel baby...Grace."

Eileen is standing off to one side, but when Candace turns to her mother, teary-eyed, and says, "Ma, look at this face. This is the face I painted. This is the face of an angel," Eileen nods, opens her arms and holds both of them in one tight embrace.

Eileen whispers her own prayer then, as she squeezes her daughter and her granddaughter all at once. To herself she pleads, "Dear God, please, please please," and she leaves it at that. And then she eases away. "I think I'll see the three of you later," she whispers, her voice a rasp. She pats the baby once on the back and kisses Candace's cheek and touches Mark on the arm, right above his new tattoo, a turtle with a heart, the tattoo he got the same day the baby came out of the hospital. "I'll be in the common room," Eileen calls, walking away abruptly. The other three, mother, father, and child, proceed down the hall, walking slowly; all the while, Candace is kissing the baby and Mark is supporting Candace's back with one hand.

❦

While Candace cuddles Gretchen on the bed, taking off her stretch suit, tickling the white folds of flesh in her thighs and beneath her chin, rubbing her finger on the saw-like edge of the single tooth, and caressing her sweet head over and over again, Mark examines Candace's new paintings. When he gets to the one that Candace calls the cupcake painting, the one of Gretchen's face, he asks why she didn't finish the rest of the painting, why there is only face and no body. Candace smiles and tries to explain why she stopped the painting there, how it happened, how the face reached out, touched her in a place she wasn't expecting it to, how the face made her, at least for that moment, set her vision aside, how it turned on what she calls her mother faucet, made her want the baby back, made her want nothing more than to pour herself fully into this helpless creature she loves more than herself.

"Wow," Mark says, replacing the painting on the floor, against the wall. "That's incredible...I mean...that's amazing."

"Yeah, it was kind of amazing," Candace says, rocking the baby, because now Grace is getting fussy, her face is wrinkled and Candace thinks maybe she's tired. "And uh...speaking of Amazing," Candace says, "I...I wondered if maybe we could start calling the baby...Grace?" She grips the baby under the rump, rocks her side to side, holding her head. Grace squeals and Candace decides. This is the sign. The sign that Grace is ready to christen herself.

"Grace?" Mark says, puzzled. "Grace? You really want to call the baby Grace?"

"Yes," Candace says. "You do remember, don't you, that we chose Grace as her middle name? Your *mother's* name?"

Mark looks at her blankly. Then he frowns. Looks down. "Oh…of course…of course I remember. What do you think I am?"

Candace laughs. "I think you're a total liar." The baby starts crying louder. Candace hands the child over to Mark. "But you are a liar I adore. So please stick around."

She leaves the room and returns a few minutes later with her paints. She picks up the painting of Grace. "I also think I just found the inspiration to finish this."

"Now?"

"Yup. Gracie here convinced me it's time."

The baby keeps fussing. Pumping her legs, knotting her forehead. Candace is not fazed. She sets the canvas on the easel. Turning to Grace, she takes the child's face in both her hands and gives the rubbery cheeks a gentle squeeze. Then she puts her nose to Grace's. "Shhhh," she says. "Look, little girl, I've got some work to do so if you don't mind I would kind of appreciate it if you would cooperate."

She makes a duck sound, the same squawking with her tongue her father used to make for her a long time ago. Something about the sound makes Grace let go of the crying. And then, the cupcake face splits into a one-toothed grin. "Oh yes," Candace whispers. "This is exactly what I need."

Mark puts the baby up to his shoulder and Candace sets to work. And while she paints, Mark feeds Grace a bottle and then he juggles her side to side, keeping her quiet. And all the while, he is thinking maybe he will try writing something. He starts humming, and soon he has the first line figured out, and as soon as he has the first line, he has already heard the first riff and then he's heard the second and the third too.

Before long, he is grinning, because he has it all spinning inside his head. The minute he gets home, he will put Grace down for a nap, or if need be, he will hold her on his lap. One way or the other, he will sit at the piano and write it. Jazz. But more. A new sound. Music that turns "Amazing Grace" upside down.

The End

ACKNOWLEDGEMENTS

All of this — the novel, the publishing company, the children's book — all of it is really Audrey's doing, Audrey being one of the three principal characters of *Dreaming Maples*. So it is Audrey X that I must acknowledge first. She appeared to me quite unexpectedly one day in February of 1991, as I sat drinking tea in my friend Michele Quigley Caldwell's living room (thank you Michele, for that cup of tea and for all the others we've shared!) I saw Audrey that day in a long wool coat the same grey color as the stark winter maples outside Michele's window. Audrey immediately intrigued me, in part because she was yoked, and carrying those shiny silver pails. Eventually, Audrey took me on a journey that profoundly changed my life, a journey that could itself fill a book.

But I didn't make the journey just with Audrey. It is often said that it takes a village to raise a child, and I agree. It also takes a kind of village to write a book. Thankfully, I have such a village behind me. Sure, it is the writer who bears most of the burden. Sitting there in front of the computer, day after day, month after month, year after year, staring into the screen (and the trees!), writing, rewriting, endlessly churning out words, it's a lonely affair. But if the writer is as fortunate as I have been, there is a community — family, friends, teachers, writing peers, and loyal readers — who offer their help and guidance and reassurance along the way. As I tell my fellow novel-writers, the only cure for the madness that comes with writing a book is the finishing of that book. More often than not, that first book seems like it will never ever end. But if the community of support is strong enough, and if the writer perseveres long and hard enough and with steady purpose, her book will find its conclusion.

To all of those who were there for me, I want to convey my deep appreciation; without you, I could not have finished this work, and I certainly could not have found the courage to take this final step, that is, putting the book into print myself.

I am most grateful to:

My parents, Ric and Dena Ricci. You have, all my life, believed in my ability to succeed at what I set my mind to do; you have never once failed to be there to help me, or your three grandchildren, Jocelyn, Lindsay, and Noah, who grew up over the years it took for this book to find the light of day; whenever the children needed looking after or picking up, you were always there. Thanks to my amazing in-laws, Robert and Abigail Kirsch; you have showed me by example that miracles are possible; that they are nearer than you think; you have always offered love, a helping hand, a willing ear, and now, you are supporting my new business, too. Thank you!

My amazing husband, Richard. You have believed in me so many times when I didn't believe in myself. You have read every one of the literally thousands of pages it took to produce this book of 400 plus pages. Thank you for a ferociously committed love, one that managed to conquer endless fear and despair. Thanks for being there, riding the roller coaster behind me, holding on tight, whether we were going uphill or down.

Thanks to my sister, Karen Ricci. I came across some handwritten notes on hypothermia the other day, and I realized that they were just a few of the many, many notes I scribbled while on the phone with you, picking your brain for medical information pertinent to my characters. Thanks for the countless details you provided, on everything from labor and delivery to the effects of drug addiction on newborns. And no, Kare, I still don't know how I understood post-partum depression so well, without ever having experienced it myself, and without researching the subject matter first. I guess that's just one of the miracles of writing a book, the "knowing" of things one has no logical reason to know. To my darling nieces, Sarah and Lauren Donohue, thanks to both of you — my younger readers — for endorsing this book; your approval mattered greatly, as I needed to know that Candace rang true with somebody who was about her age.

Thanks to my sister, Holly Ricci, for your wonderful reading of the novel, and for your constant love and support in dozens of phone conversations. So many times I called you, Holl, when I was tempted to give up. You said just the right thing each time to keep me going: that is, you reminded me how much I love to write. Thanks to my brother, Rick Ricci; very early on, you put me in touch with Harry and Kaye Burnham, maple sugaring experts near Craftsbury, Vermont, where you live and work every summer. Also, Rick, thanks for helping to promote the book even before it was in print among your friends and colleagues in the Northeast Kingdom. Thanks, too, to Fawn Walker, my sister-in-law and Rick's wife, for reading the novel and comparing it favorably to the other novels you have loved.

To my children, Jocelyn, Lindsay, and Noah, thank you for sharing your mother, time and again, with her characters; thank you for listening as I read chapters out loud more times (I'm sure) than you wanted me to; thank you for accompanying me on that crazy driving trip that year, a trip which took us through the back roads of southern Vermont into North Adams in a wild search for Candace's exact travel routes. I know you thought (think?) your Mom nuts, but we *did* find that bakery in North Adams, MA, where Candace's boyfriend lives, now didn't we? Thanks too, children, for being a constant source of love and inspiration to your mom; please know too that I never experienced any of Candace's or Eileen's difficulties or ambivalence when it came to you, my own infants. Being your mother has been a blessing since the very beginning.

To all my writer friends, for your patience, and for your careful reading and consideration of my prose: to Liza Frenette, one of the first to read the very early (delivery) scenes, in Gene Garber's fiction workshop way back in 1992, thank you Liza, for cheering me on ever since and for telling me time and again to keep the faith, and the vision, and the dream, alive; to Peggy Woods, I couldn't have done the Ph.D. without you talking (and emailing) me through it, Peg; thanks, too, for helping see this novel transformed into a doctoral dissertation and beyond; to Renee Geel, you not only read this book, twice, but you were so incredibly generous with your time and extraordinary talent, editing every single line of the novel. Without your precise questions and gentle suggestions, I could not have hoped to bring this book to its present form; to Jan Ramjerdi, who can now be told the truth, you, Jan, influenced my writing more in graduate school than any other single person, and it continues to this day! To Ron MacLean, your one-word reaction to the novel — "Wow" — made me think I actually had something that might be working; to Josh Powell, formerly my student, now, in so many ways, my teacher, thank you for your time and talent and advice as I have started up this publishing company; thank you especially for a web site that takes my breath away.

To Dr. Carson Carr, you, along with all my fabulous EOP colleagues and students, inspire me to be the best English teacher I can be. Thanks, Carson, for being so enthused when I told you about this novel, and thanks, too, for making EOP the miracle it is; you change lives day after day. Thanks also to my wonderful neighbors in the "hood" at EOP, Mr. Abdul Jarvis and Ms. Joan Foderingham, and to Ginny Rifenberick, who's read every word of the novels I've written.

To Karin Ludewig, who also has been a tireless reader of my work, and who, in writing her own novel, *The Animal God*, has made me realize just how much I enjoyed my years of toil writing *Dreaming Maples*. To Pam French, for your ever sweet smile and your splendid poetry and your kind way of saying, "Oh go on, Claudia, you can do it!" To Lori Lee Cullen, who writes like she was born to do it, you too are going to finish that novel of yours, I am willing to bet on it; to Bonny Curless, whose smile is infectious; gee, Bonny, while NOT an artist, you still manage to design some of the most beautiful artistry I've ever seen on paper; the inner space of this book, and the beauty of the typeface, and the spirit of the project, clearly speaks to your incredible artistry and to your "creative services."

To Kathleen Triem, the only person I know of who read this book going into labor (with twins!) And to her brave husband, Peter Franck, and the three kids, just be glad Kathleen didn't follow Candace's example!!!

To all my dear friends and loyal readers in Spencertown: to Leslie Gabosh, a painter and fiddle player and jewelry maker and an endlessly creative and generous person; you zipped through this novel in a matter of hours, and you have been reading everything ever since, thank you for your unfailing support and for being such a staunch advocate for this book's publication; Les, you remind me daily that I am an artist who needs to write as much as she needs to breathe; to Karl Gabosh, you put it so very succinctly when you said, "Hey, look, Claudia, writers write;" to Karen Jahn, who has the best barn in Columbia County, you helped convince me that the rejections I had from commercial publishers reflected not the quality of my work, but the sorry state of the publishing industry; Karen, thanks always for coffee in the afternoon, and for your humor and thorough sense of delight in life; please know, too, Karen, that you helped me see that I really could be my own publisher.

To a very special lady in Spencertown, Doreen McIntosh, who writes me cards that bring me near tears; you have given me and my family love since we first started living here; thanks to you and Jim, for all those years of Santa Claus, and for being so caring.

To my college roommates, the "Brown" women, Becky Burke, Cathie Murray, Cathy Shufro, and Kathleen Egan, with whom I have shared numerous weekend retreats while this book was brewing; thanks to all of you for all the enlightening conversation and the inspiring connections — through books, and movies, but most of all, through our long and loving histories together; thanks for sharing your lives in relationships that have grown over three decades.

To my teacher, Dr. Gene Garber, who has read this manuscript more times than any one human being should ever have to read a book; you always managed to see, and to convince me, what needed to be done: you wrote, among dozens of other brilliant comments, "I believe that if the structural problem is solved, the character problem will already be half-way solved." To my teacher, Dr. Dick Goldman, in whose marvelously inspiring class on "Literary Character" in 1993 I finally solved the "Eileen Problem," finding her voice in a set of diaries; thank you, Dick, for your extraordinary support to me as both a graduate student and a writer of fiction; thanks for suggesting that this novel had what you called a rare combination, both literary finesse and commercial promise. Thanks to Judy Johnson, for your astonishing mythic interpretation of the book, comparing Eileen and Candace to Demeter and Persephone, also, thanks for showing me that I had to take risks in my writing and in my artistic life; thanks to Gene Mirabelli, under whose direction I first started writing fiction at SUNY Albany; I can admit to you now, Gene, it's not exactly that I lied, but that short story I sent you in 1990, the one I needed in order to qualify for your wonderful workshop, that was actually the very first piece of fiction I had ever tried. Thanks, too, for all your words of advice on the publishing business.

Thanks to my incredibly talented and inspiring flamenco guitar teacher, Maria Zemantauski, whose virtuosity on the guitar is widely recognized. Maria, thanks, because without you, and that one sentence you spoke to me last summer, I would not be publishing myself and others; thank you for finally getting me to realize that we artists must stand up for ourselves, and get our work out in the world, no matter what it takes.

To my extraordinarily talented first cousin, artist Pat Rotondo, who painted the stunning cover image for the novel; your sublime winter scene gives a face to the book that I'm forever thrilled to have; Pat, thank you not only for the painting, but for the cover design that showcases the novel so well. My two words of advice: KEEP PAINTING! To my wonderful sister-in-law, JoEllen Kirsch, a third sister to me, and another early supporter of this work; a publisher herself, she kindly featured a story about *Dreaming Maples* in her wonderful Vermont newspaper, *The Cracker Barrel*. To another first cousin, Diane (Rotondo) Eberts, who bought more "Dreaming Maples" greeting cards than any other single person: your support and praise for my book has meant a lot to me, Di!

To Michael Ryan, of Digital Page, printer extraordinaire, thanks for your patience, help, and encouragement throughout the last six months, and thanks, too, to your mom, Nancy Ryan, up in Maine, who has been wisely telling you "to hurry up and get this novel into print."

To family and friends who spent money on this book before it was published: especially to that most wonderful pair, Joan and Lyn Wiener, who have been there all along; to Vicky Rollins, and Charlotte Rollins, to Sue and Ed Greenberg, and Jodi and Mitchell Efros, and Aunt Ruth Horowitz, I consider myself blessed to have such a wonderful extended family; to Alison Auerbach, a dear person and extraordinary culinary talent. All my thanks too to Sharon Flitterman-King, Ph.D., who shares a love of literature and a love of Saturday morning services at Hevreh of Southern Berkshire; Dear Sharon, there are some connections in the world that are made in heaven, and ours is one.

To all of those at Hevreh, and especially Rabbi Deborah Zecher and Assistant Rabbi Andy Klein, and to Shelley Rolf and Paula

Hellman and Andrea Patel and Rita Delgado and Robin Goldberg and Abby Chasky; thanks for making life as a Jewish woman so rich and special.

A special thank you to Ellie Sidel, who worked tirelessly on behalf of this book through the John Hawkins literary agency. Thank you for believing in me as a writer, and fighting against incredible odds for the publication of *Sugarbush*. It didn't work out the way we thought it would, but I couldn't be here doing this now if it weren't for the faith you demonstrated in me.

To the late Sumner Williams, formerly the director of the Proctor Maple Research Center at the University of Vermont, a scientist and extraordinary human being, who read an earlier version of this book in 1995, before his fatal accident. Sumner provided exceptionally helpful feedback and details about sugaring when I most needed them. This work is dedicated to his memory, and part of the proceeds from the sale of this book will be donated to Proctor in his name.

To those sculptors who gave me extensive help understanding the technical details and challenges involved in sculpture; I am particularly grateful to sculptor Elaine Warshaw, of Merrick, NY, who supplied much-needed information about sculpturing tools, techniques, and materials. To Roy Kanwit, of Spencertown, NY, who spoke to me at length about his work, and demonstrated the use of hammers and mallets and chisels, claws and rasps, and also kindly showed me how a stone is cut using power tools.

To painters Jim Coe, of Hannacroix, NY; Roger Mason, an itinerant painter who often appears in good weather on the streets of Chatham, NY; and to Jack Rosenhaft, formerly my next door neighbor in Spencertown, thanks to all of you for readily offering expertise as I shaped Candace into the painter she became.

To those friends who read the novel when it was still called *Sugarbush*: Dr. Dan Beauchamp, who has since become the Mayor of Bisbee, Arizona, to Larry Pruyne and Cortie Ervin and Joyce Hinnefeld and David Bookbinder, all of whom were so helpful with their workshop comments. To friends who have made the life of this writer so much more pleasant just by smiling and laughing in your own special way: Louise-Anne McNutt, Suzanne Wise, Greg Topakian, my "down the street" counselor/neighbors at EOP, Patrick Romain, Jim Thomas, Maritza Martinez, Monica Hope, and Chris Fernando, and my very special across-the-street neighbors in

Spencertown, Ken and Ginny Wilber, a sweet, sweet couple who themselves know the toil of boiling sap into sugar. Also my thanks to Lisa and Bob Schrenkeisen, for your help in making my household run so much more smoothly than it otherwise would.

To my oldest friend, Steve Bentley, of Littleton, Colorado, who has known me since third grade; Steve, I know you remember Miss Vreatt's 12th grade English class, and all those times I couldn't stop myself from writing and writing and writing; thanks for some mighty important details about chemical dependency, background information which helped me understand Candace better; also, thanks for clearing up some glaring deficiencies in my knowledge of motorcycles, in particular, thanks for "reminding" me that the accelerator throttle is not part of the foot pedal, but rather, it sits on the handlebars of a Harley. And thanks too, to both you and Nancy, for sending out a whopping 100 "Dreaming Maples" greeting cards to your reading friends!

Finally, I acknowledge Barbara Coles, of Wilmington, Vermont, for her patience and generosity in sharing with me information about the effects of pear thrips on the sugar maples at Maple Ridge Farm Camp, the Wilmington, Vermont, sugarbush she owns and operates with her husband, Bruce Coles.

I also acknowledge the following books and reading material which proved helpful to me in research: first and foremost, *The Maple Sugaring Book*, by Helen & Scott Nearing, an invaluable source of information not only on sugaring tools and techniques but also on the history of sugaring; *A Child is Born*, that photographic classic on birth, by Lennart Nilsson; *The Enchanted Garden*, by Claire O'Rush, a primer on the healing mythologies of trees and gardens (thank you particularly for the recipe that Audrey needed to work a fairy spell); the Vermont Natural Resources Council, for information on forest policies; the U.S. Department of Agriculture, Agriculture Research Service, Handbook #134, on the economics of sugar mapling; The University of Vermont, Department of Forests, Parks and Recreation, for annual surveys on sugar maples and the incidence of pear thrips, and the University of Vermont Extension Service's handout, "The Sugar Maple and Pear Thrips."

I am indebted, finally and forever, to maple trees everywhere. I would not have been able to write this book if the trees hadn't spoken to me via Audrey. Each word that came into my head is in some way a testimony to the deep and lasting beauty of the forest. Fortunately, I heard the trees whispering, and I heard Audrey saying, "go this way," and I let her take my hand and lead me steadily forward. So many, many, days, my eyes were closed, and I didn't have the least idea where I was going. Nor did I know, or have much confidence, that I would end up here. The only clear thing I have known all these years is that the trees were around me, and their majesty kept me going, and thanks to their shelter and protective inspiration, I found a voice for the sounds and visions inside my head.

Claudia Ricci
Spring, 2002

P.S. Dear Bear, how could I forget you, and all the tail-wagging you do to let me know that you adore my stories? Since I cannot express to you in words my gratitude for your undying loyalty, and for your willingness to lie there endlessly sleeping behind my chair, how about a cookie instead?

ABOUT THE AUTHOR

Claudia Ricci, PhD, lives in Spencertown, New York, with her husband and three children. A full-time faculty member at SUNY Albany, teaching English and writing, she has published fiction and poetry in several literary magazines, including *Another Chicago Magazine, Alaska Quarterly, Pacific Coast Review, The MacGuffin, Blueline, The Little Magazine, Reed, 13th Moon, Yemassee,* and *Barkeater.* Formerly a staff writer at *The Wall Street Journal* and the *Chicago Sun-Times,* Ricci is the author of three other novels: *Sister Mysteries, Eyes on Orion,* and *Pearly Everlasting.*